Expelled from Eden

Expelled from Eden

A William T. Vollmann Reader

Edited by Larry McCaffery and
Michael Hemmingson

THUNDER'S MOUTH PRESS
NEW YORK

EXPELLED FROM EDEN

A WILLIAM T. VOLLMANN READER

Published by
Thunder's Mouth Press
An Imprint of Avalon Publishing Group, Inc.
245 West 17th St., 11th Floor
New York, NY 10011

Library of Congress Cataloging-in-Publication Data:
Vollmann, William T.
Expelled from Eden: A William T. Vollmann Reader / edited by Larry McCaffery and Michael Hemmingson
p. cm.
ISBN 1-56025-441-6
I. McCaffery, Larry, 1946- II. Hemmingson, Michael A. III. Title.

PS3572.O295A6 2003
813'.54—dc21
2003040205

9 8 7 6 5 4 3 2 1

Book design by Paul Paddock and Maria E. Torres
Printed in the United States of America
Distributed by Publishers Group West

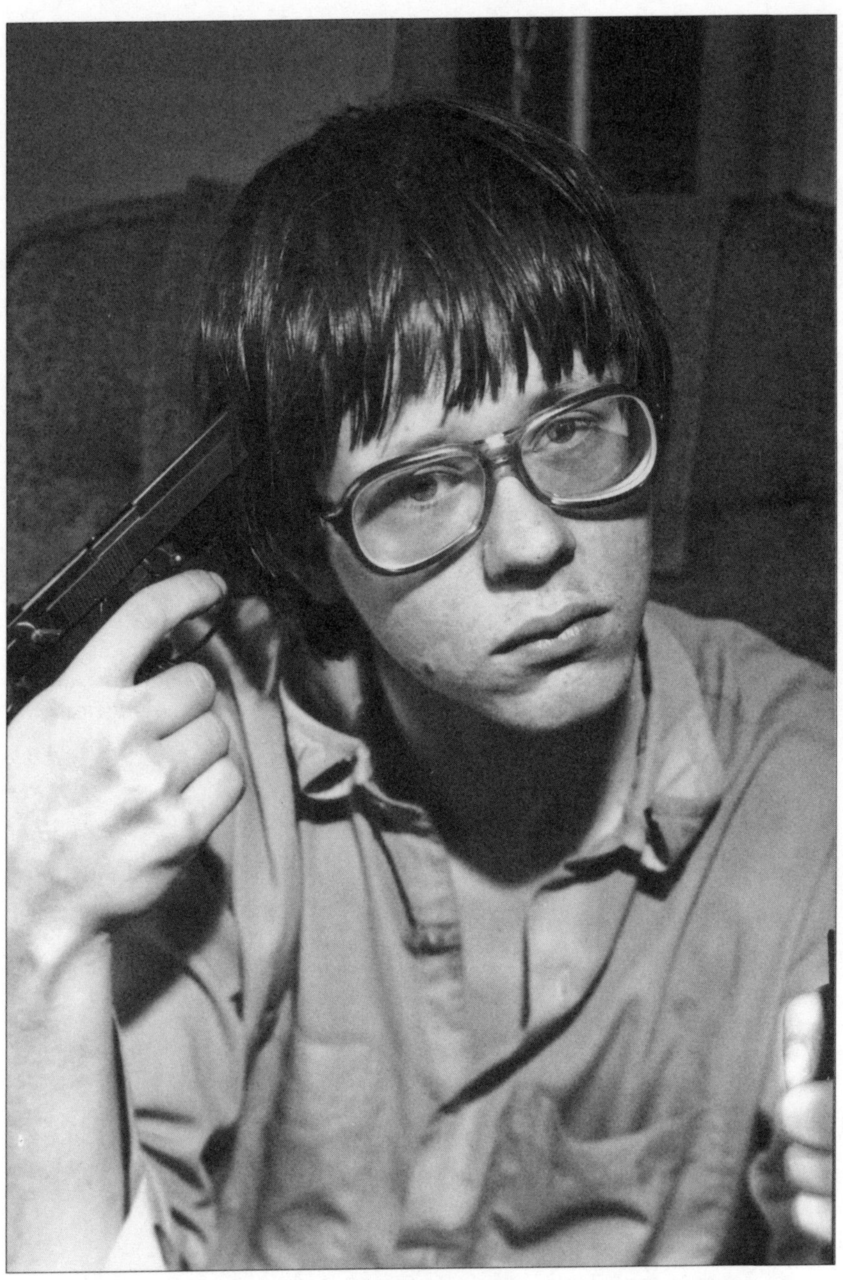

PORTRAIT OF THE ARTIST AS A YOUNG MAN WITH A BERETTA BDA-380 PISTOL;
WILLIAM T. VOLLMANN PHOTOGRAPHED BY HIS FRIEND KEN MILLER IN 1985.

For Sinda and Tara
and for Ronald Sukenick (1932–2004)

It is curious that so many people are becoming interested in Eden now that the end seems near.

—William T. Vollmann,
in a 1994 *Los Angeles Times* profile

And east of Eden he was cast.

—Bruce Springsteen,
"Adam Raised a Cain"

CONTENTS

Part III
On Love, Sex, Prostitutes, and Pornography

Part IV
On Travel

Part V
On Writing, Literature, and Culture

. . . the reason we love Eden is that we've been expelled from it.
—***William T. Vollmann, The Rifles***

I first heard William T. Vollmann's name at a party in mid-August 1991, from a professor at San Diego State University: Larry McCaffery. I had, the previous day, read McCaffery's re-processed essay on Donald Barthelme—where he'd handwritten, typed and cut/pasted various notes in the margins—published in the *Review of Contemporary Fiction*. The essay had plenty of "meta" qualities (for want of a better description) and it was fun to tackle on the page. I told the professor I liked it and he appeared surprised anyone had seen the inimitable and orphic piece. McCaffery—holding a beer in each hand and his glasses sliding down his nose—raved about this new young writer, Vollmann, and how I should go out and read the man's work immediately. "I mean, *really,*" McCaffery said, "this guy's important." That night, I returned home thinking I should look up Vollmann in the library. It would be my task for the next day.

I didn't.

At the time, I was renting a cheap room in a crack hotel, hanging out with prostitutes and drug dealers and waiting for my student loans to come in so I could move out of the den of iniquity (naturally, I later identified with such Vollmann novels as *Whores for Gloria, Butterfly Stories,* and his nifty tale, "The Best Way to Smoke Crack").

Vollmann's name didn't arise again, for me, until December 1992, when I was in the bookstore at Beyond Baroque in Venice, California; a paperback copy of *The Rainbow Stories* was there. The author's name was familiar; I remembered what McCaffery had told me. I perused the book with a posture of cool indifference the way all under-published young writers do at such literary centers. *Skinheads and whores, oh my.* I wanted it—to read and to keep—but I didn't have any money and it was too voluminous to steal. I went to the Beverly Hills branch library and found a copy of *The Ice-Shirt.* It was the only book of his they had on the shelf. I read it in two days.

I didn't read Vollmann again until I returned to San Diego in February

1993. I was, once again, down and out in San Diego and living in a hotel room; it was better than a crack hotel, but not by much. I spent many days in the library. This is when I simultaneously came across two novellas by Mr. V: "The Ghost of Magnetism" in *The Paris Review* and "De Sade's Last Stand" in *Esquire* (actually a condensed version of "More Benadryl, Whined the Journalist" from *Butterfly Stories*). These two works spoke to me in that magical way you can never explain to a commoner: you feel it in the gut and the heart and the brain. This must have been the same sense of recognition that Charles Bukowski felt when, sitting in a library to keep off the streets as a young man, he read John Fante's *Ask the Dusk* and everything changed for him; the same way Richard Brautigan felt when he first picked up Hemingway; and maybe the way Vollmann reacted when he discovered Danilo Kiš's *A Tomb for Boris Davidovich.*

Since that day in the library, I have been following Vollmann's career—as novelist, war correspondent, visual artist, traveler, essayist, and, yes, humanist.

There's also the "hero" factor—the literary (fantasy) hero on the page. The writer as a larger-than-life-editorial-man-of-action. Here we have a guy who goes out and does what many of his contemporaries—safe in their homes, offices, and academic settings—only daydream about: risking life and limb, courting misfortune in nations whose populaces hate Americans, exploring icy regions of the world not friendly to the human body, hanging out with whores, pimps, drug dealers, the dispossessed and delusional . . . and so on. As one reader on Amazon.com put it: "WTV is the revenge of the nerd." It's the Hemingway shtick, you know—Hemingway once claimed that going to a war was the best thing for a writer: the writer would amass several lifetimes of experience and the writing would be pure and honest. Hemingway created a hero myth around himself by going to various battlefields, crashing his plane in Africa, and emerging from the jungle with a bunch of bananas in one hand and a bottle of booze in the other—never mind that his body was in constant pain from all the hardship and his mental resolve was being chipped away at. It's the sort of stuff that looks great on paper and creates, for such a writer, many admirers and antagonists.

—Michael Hemmingson

Introduction

Adam Raised a Cain

Other echoes
Inhabit the Garden. Shall we follow?
—T.S. ELIOT, "BURNT NORTON" (NO. 1 OF "FOUR QUARTETS")

Giving It a Name
Or
Liner Notes for a Vollmann Boxed Set

In the fields of the Lord/Stood Abel and Cain
Cain slew Abel 'neath the black rain
At night he couldn't stand the guilt or the blame
So he gave it a name . . .
—BRUCE SPRINGSTEEN, "GAVE IT A NAME"

ALTHOUGH *EXPELLED FROM EDEN* is subtitled "A William T. Vollmann Reader," readers will discover that *Expelled* is quite unlike any other literary "reader" they've picked up before. That's to be expected, since from the moment Dan O'Connor, our editor at Thunder's Mouth Press, gave us the go-signal to assemble the first major anthology devoted to Vollmann, our real goal was to produce something more ambitious than the usual "best of" packages that comprise most literary readers. We wanted a collection that expanded the notion of what a literary reader might be—in much the way that Vollmann's mind- and genre-expanding approach had opened up the crime novel in *The Royal Family,* the historical novel in his *Seven Dreams,* and the essay format in *Rising Up and Rising Down.* There's really no term for what we wanted this project to be ("casebook" is probably the closest, but it sounds too dry), but it was something akin to what's involved when a curator at a big museum mounts the first major retrospective of a particularly significant new artist.

The best way to describe what we were shooting for is to say we wanted to assemble an anthological equivalent of a "Vollmann Boxed Set"—and not one of those pedestrian, irritating boxed sets, mind you, whose only raison d'être is to generate new sales by repackaging the same old singles —but one of those rare, really great boxed sets, like, say, *Charlie Parker, The Complete Savoy and Dial Studio Recordings, 1944-48* and *Frank Sinatra: The Complete Capitol Recordings.* Or, even more relevantly, Jon Landau's monumental twenty-CD Springsteen *Wreck on the Highway* boxed set (1985[1]). As was true of our Vollmann anthology, Landau's *Wreck* aimed at presenting a comprehensive overview of an artist at mid-career who'd already released a major body of work that was ecstatically praised by reviewers but was little appreciated outside of a devoted cult following. *Wreck* was also meant to be something more than just another compilation of greatest hits (though it featured plenty of those); rather, Landau wanted to resituate Springsteen's work in a fresh context offering new perspectives about it and establishing unexpected influences (not just Elvis, Van Morrison, and Dylan, for example, but Hank Williams, Muddy Waters, Flannery O'Conner, John Steinbeck, and William Carlos Williams). He wanted to foreground some of the key lines of thematic and formal preoccupations that critics and fans had missed (e.g., the spiritual, moral, and even philosophical dimensions of Springsteen's work, the ways the complex formal arrangements of his albums allow the individual songs to interact with one another, the way his use of allusion and reference—to other songs, films, and media sources in addition to his own earlier songs—create a kind of running dialogue with his own work that is, in Landau's phrase, "almost Nabokov-esque").

Landau's mega-set became a kind of working model for our own selection process in *Expelled from Eden.* Thus, in addition to featuring a wide and representative sampling of all of Springsteen's major label releases,[2] *Wreck* also includes lots of other materials of the sort that we wanted to include in our Vollmann boxed set—really cool stuff like:

—Early songs made before Bruce had signed with a major label. For the Vollmann equivalents here, see for instance, his first publication, the fabulous adventure tale, "The Conquest of Kianazor" (1978) and his early "Biographical Statement (c. 1989)."

—New material. See "Zoya" (from Vollmann's recently completed collection of World War II stories, *Europe Central*), "The Water of Life" (from his work-in-progress, *Imperial,* about the Imperial Valley), and "Some Thoughts on the Value of Writing during Wartime."

—Samples of lesser-known major label songs that mark important turning points in the artist's career. See our excerpts from *An Afghanistan Picture Show* and *Butterfly Stories.*

—Even lesser-known materials that never appeared on the radar screens of most fans because they represent significant departures from the styles and forms Bruce was best known for. See our selections of Vollmann's poetry, reviews and literary essays, screenplays, and book art.

—Alternate takes of works that not only put a fresh spin on familiar tunes but also reveal something about Springsteen's original intentions and aesthetic inclinations. Many of the inclusions here are original versions of stories and articles that were later edited and published in versions Vollmann didn't approve of. For an especially revealing example, see his auto-review of *Argall* ("The Stench of Corpses").

—Rarities that have never shown up even on the most obscure bootlegs. Among the Vollmann rarities included here: his afterword to Danilo Kiš's A *Tomb for Boris Davidovich,* a relatively obscure Eastern European novel that heavily influenced Vollmann's formal methods; his afterword to Mark A. Smith's book of photography, *The Students of Deep Springs College,* in which Vollmann summarizes the ways that his experiences at Deep Springs College became a touchstone for his life and work (see "Some Thoughts on Neglected Water Taps"); his foreword to *Open All Night,* a book of photographs by his close friend, Ken Miller, who first introduced Vollmann to the street life of San Francisco's Mission District; miscellaneous book reviews; copies of his correspondence with editors in which he summarizes some of his goals as a writer, defends and defines his works, and offers his own views about their central thematic preoccupations and formal methods; and—rarest of all—drafts of letters Vollmann wrote as a college student volunteering his services to be sent into outer space: See "The Advantages of Space (1978)" and "A Bizarre Proposition (1979)."

—Visuals: photos, album covers, and other sorts of visual documentation. Likewise, we have included author photos, as well as dozens of candid photos and other visual materials that provide a more personal glimpse into Vollmann's life and work. See, for example, the portfolio of Ken Miller's photographs of Vollmann and the visuals that accompany the Vollmann Chronology and the Book Object appendix, which includes reproductions of some of Vollmann's mixed-media work.

Expelled from Eden has therefore been assembled to showcase the full range of Vollmann's accomplishments—as storywriter, novelist, journalist, historian, photojournalist, reviewer, cultural commentator, poet, travel writer, literary essayist, and visual artist. We've made sure that *Expelled from Eden* offers enough "greatest hits" so that it can serve as an accessible introduction for readers unfamiliar with Vollmann, while also including enough new material to satisfy his devoted fans.

But irrespective of the terminology employed, some readers may be wondering whether, given the fact that most literary "readers" appear either posthumously or late in an author's career, the publication of *Expelled from Eden* is a little premature: what sort of justification is there for publishing an anthology devoted to the work of a writer who's still in his early forties, and hence presumably only in mid-career? There's a long answer to this question and a short one. As for the long answer, you're holding it. We feel confident that *Expelled* can speak for itself.

The short reply could be formulated in different ways, but the most obvious is simply the sheer, staggering, jaw-dropping *immensity* of what Vollmann has already accomplished. Certainly no other American author of his generation has emerged with the talent and the drive and crazed sense of self-assurance that propels one on a flat-out, all-cylinders-burning literary joy-ride, resulting in a series of masterpieces over several years—the kind of thing we saw, say, with Faulkner during the early thirties or with Pynchon during the sixties and early seventies. Nor has anyone else been willing to take on the range of social, philosophical, psychological, moral, and political issues as Vollmann, whose work, like that of early Pynchon's, seems able to unweave the fabric of modern history, then put it together again in a new garment showing off the features of this history in ways we've never seen before.

What the long and the short of it comes down to, then, is that the publication of *Expelled from Eden* is hardly premature—indeed, we're convinced it's overdue.

A Brief History of the Vollmann Literary Universe: Loomings

Just as the bespectacled ghost of James Joyce loomed large over the generation of modernist writers who followed in the wake of *Finnegan's Wake,* so too did Thomas Pynchon cast an enormous and intimidating shadow over the generation of American authors who emerged in the wake of his early megaworks *V.* in 1963 and *Gravity's Rainbow* in 1973. But literature's father figures can only loom, intimidate, and inspire for so long before they must be slain by their offspring. Perhaps sensing his vulnerability once *Gravity's Rainbow* had established him as the ur-postmodernist, Pynchon chose to exile himself for sixteen years before resurfacing with *Vineland.* With no means even to locate Pynchon, much less slay him, writers and critics began scanning the horizon for the arrival of someone possessing the right combination of ambition and formal originality to be able to cast his own shadow—and in the process suggest a way out of the quagmire in which American fiction had found itself mired since the mid-seventies, of scaled-back expectations ("minimalism"), self-distancing ironies and trendy nihilism (the "Brat Pack"), and illusionist game-playing (ghostly simulations of once-radical methods like metafiction and self-referentiality that had become appropriated by the mainstream as empty signs of counter-cultural radicalism). And although sightings were occasionally reported throughout the eighties—T. C. Boyle *(Water Music),* John Calvin Batchelor *(The Further Adventures of Halley's Comet),* Alexander Theroux *(Darconville's Cat),* Bret Easton Ellis *(American Psycho),* David Foster Wallace *(The Broom of the System)* were all hailed as The Next Big Thing—there was a general consensus that this new generation of post-postmodernist writers simply hadn't yet produced a book like *Gravity's Rainbow,* which blew you away with its vast scope and ambition, erudition, intellectual brilliance, and story-telling skills, while opening up new areas for the novel as an art form.[3]

Enter William T. Vollmann

The American literary scene that Vollmann entered in the late eighties with the publication of *You Bright and Risen Angels* (1987) and *The Rainbow Stories* (1989) was going through a down period. Wishing to distance itself from the first wave of postmodernist experimentalism but unsure of how to define itself once this separation was made, it seemed to be suffering the effects of an extended hangover.[4] Just as Springsteen in the mid-seventies was widely hailed as "the new Dylan" and savior figure who could lead American rock out of the desert of discomania and into the promised land, so too did the stir caused by his first two books result in Vollmann's being regularly greeted by critics and reviewers as "the new Pynchon."

Meanwhile, the extremity of vision and subject matter in these early books began to attract a cult following among members of the pop underground. This growing recognition, in turn, helped Vollmann (who was acting as his own agent) reach the attention of a sympathetic editor, Paul Slovak, at a prestigious publisher, Viking, which would subsequently publish most of his major books over the next dozen years.

By the early nineties Vollmann had hit his stride. During the next decade he published in rapid succession a prodigious amount of works, including novels, story collections, and books of journalism, as well as dozens of reviews and essays, journal publications (most notably in Bradford Morrow's prestigious *Conjunctions*), magazine articles (in *Esquire, Spin*[5], *Gear, The New Yorker,* and many others), literary essays, poetry, and other occasional pieces. Among these publications have been several huge, unclassifiable novels and two other even grander projects that are virtually unprecedented in terms of their range of styles and thematic ambition: his *Seven Dreams* series and his monumental study of violence, *Rising Up and Rising Down.*[6]

Vollmann 101

The following chronologically arranged account of Vollmann's major publications should give a clearer sense of the full scope of what he has accomplished.

You Bright and Risen Angels (1987). In the most startling debut since Pynchon's *V.*, Vollmann presents a dense, sprawling, cartoon-like portrait of the artist as a young bug who continuously falls onto the thorns of love, bleeds words, and leads a failed revolution. Inspired in part by Vollmann's experiences at Deep Springs College, *Angels* employs the motifs of bugs and electricity to develop an allegory about the failure of revolutionary impulses to counter the evils of racism, fascism, and industrialism. Unfolding as a series of interconnected narratives that move back and forth across vast areas of history and geography, overflowing with literary and historical references and other sources of arcane information, and full of surrealistic literalizations of sexual longings and violence, the book's wild flights of prose and its intensity of vision all served to proclaim that the post-Pynchon era of American fiction had finally arrived.

The Rainbow Stories (1989). The subject matter and symbolic implications of the title of Vollmann's second book are supplied in an epigraph from Poe's "Berenice":

> Misery is manifold: The wretchedness of the earth is uniform. Overreaching the wide horizon as the rainbow, its hues are various as the hues of that arch; as distinct too, yet as intimately blended.

This is the book where Vollmann first displays his great gifts as an investigative journalist to enter the mostly invisible lives of pimps, prostitutes, street alcoholics, skinheads, serial killers, and other social outcasts and misfits living in San Francisco's Tenderloin District. Like earlier masters of this form—Hemingway, Agee, Orwell, and Steinbeck—Vollmann carries the reader down with him into social depths never before explored with so artistic an eye; and like them, Vollmann combines art with personal testimony to explore messy details of these lives magnified through his own imagination. But there's also a lyrical side to Vollmann's literary descent: his descriptions of these dark crevasses are stunning in their power to attract and repel at once—so they're not only illuminated, but their terrible and beautiful integrity is allowed to shine forth.

The Ice-Shirt: First Dream[7] (1990). With this novel Vollmann embarked upon a seven-volume sequence of *Dreams* that will eventually form a symbolic history of North America from its discovery a thousand years ago by Norse Greenlanders until the present (when we will be taken inside a uranium mine on a Navajo reservation). Dealing with the labyrinth of history, blood, and personality that fueled the early

Vikings' violent intrusions into this continent, *The Ice-Shirt* centers around the discovery of "Vinland" by tenth-century Norsemen (and Norsewomen), their efforts over a period of three years to colonize this fertile but intractable wilderness, their squabbling amongst themselves, and their contact with the local Indians (or "Skrælings") that eventually results in their being attacked and driven out of North America. Unfolding through a kaleidoscopic mixture of saga, modern travelogue, obscure references and terminology, vivid sensory details drawn with hyper-accuracy, and personal vignettes, *The Ice-Shirt* requires readers to make connections between different eras and methods of learning, between literal fact and symbolic truth.[8] Moreover, as is true of all the other *Dreams,* Vollmann embeds his narrative within a broader framework that includes numerous illustrations and maps, glossaries, a chronology, and an elaborate series of source notes and footnotes. The latter includes not only the usual listing of references and sources for quotations, but discussions about his intentions in employing his sources and correspondence with experts in the field who comment upon (and occasionally disagree with) specific interpretations. In effect, then, *The Ice-Shirt* is not "merely" a novel, but a new sort of book entirely—a "textual assemblage" that consists of a novel *and* other documents providing a running dialogue about the novel with readers. All this makes *The Ice-Shirt* and the other *Dreams* perhaps the most unique reading experience since Nabokov's *Pale Fire.*

Whores for Gloria (1991). The brief, dark chapters of Vollmann's shortest novel to date are really prose poems describing the last, lonely days of Jimmy, an ex-Vietnam War veteran, as he wanders the streets of San Francisco's Tenderloin District searching for happy stories he can use to create the love of his life, the wondrous (and imaginary) prostitute, Gloria. What he finds instead are sad stories, loneliness, and, eventually, death.

Thirteen Stories and Thirteen Epitaphs (1993). A mosaic comprised of thirteen paired "stories and epitaphs" that reflect and illuminate each other. These paired texts are themselves constructed of bright, broken shards of autobiography, travel writing, reportage, and anecdotes told by a rogues' gallery of drifters and grifters, artists and con-artists, Thai prostitutes, crack addicts, witch doctors, gangsters, and Gen-X slackers. These mix together with other materials to establish unexpected connections among topics widely separated by time, distance, and literal context; in the process, Vollmann's intensely particularized sentences and soaring flights of lyricism manage to reinvent the world in startling ways.

An Afghanistan Picture Show (1992). A Failed Pilgrim's Progress, this novel presents a wry and (somewhat) fictionalized account of Vollmann's painfully naive efforts to join the mujahideen rebels during his 1982 trip to Afghanistan. The central narrative is punctuated by other materials, including anecdotes about his childhood that locate some of the sources of his original inspiration for this doomed adventure, lists, interviews, photocopies of correspondence and other documents relating to his trip, and incidents as seemingly irrelevant as a description of picking up beer cans along the roadway in Deep Springs Valley and a long sub-section about a hiking trip Vollmann once made in Alaska. In these queer juxtapositions, however, lies the real story—one that demonstrates Vollmann's great gift for vividly rendered travel writing and for braiding the abstract into the actual, as he dramatizes the innately human difficulty in empathizing with any culture other than one's own, and the limits of altruism and activism.

Butterfly Stories—A Novel (1992). A coming-of-age novel (note the genre-expanding implications of the title), *Butterfly* is set mainly in the same whorehouses, bars, and back streets of Southeast Asia that Vollmann visited in the early nineties, often accompanied by his friend and collaborator, photographer Ken Miller. Swerving unexpectedly between brutality and tenderness, the lush and the laconic, and the courtship of love and death, it tells of the abysmal lives of prostitutes and other characters in prose whose frequent eruptions into intense, often breathless expressions of lyricism have become Vollmann's trademarks.

Fathers and Crows: Second Dream (1992). This second installment of *Seven Dreams* is an account of the spiritually charged (and often extremely bloody) wars of conquest and belief between the French

Jesuits and Native Americans during the seventeenth century. Vollmann displays his debts to Tolstoy by presenting an epic panorama that recounts with powerful narrative drive and exhaustive particularity the French explorations of eastern Canada and the efforts of Jesuit missionaries to bring salvation to the North American native settlers.

The Rifle 5: Sixth Dream (1993). Vollmann here conflates two separate but parallel narratives. The first describes journeys taken by his narrator (Subzero) to the Arctic wilderness, where he witnesses first-hand the disastrous environmental and cultural consequences that the introduction of repeating rifles has had; these journeys also result in his tragic involvement with an Inuit woman who subsequently becomes pregnant, gives birth, and commits suicide. The second story describes the unsuccessful attempt to find the Northwest Passage by Sir John Franklin (England's most famous nineteenth-century Arctic explorer); faulty maps, bad luck, and several navigational errors eventually cause Franklin's two boats to become stuck in the ice. There in the dark and cold, Franklin and his men slowly starve and begin to exhibit symptoms of lead poisoning-induced madness (caused by their tinned food) and physical deterioration. Vollmann allows different aspects of these two parallel Northwest Passages—the idealism and egotism that motivates them; the inability of the explorers to understand the Arctic region, its inhabitants and environment; the consequences of a foolhardy reliance on technology—to slowly unfold, interact, and mirror one another. Readers are led on a nightmarish descent into madness, cannibalism, death, and self-confrontation—all depicted in excruciatingly vivid and emotionally honest detail. We also bear witness to one man's ability to test himself, as he confronts his personal weaknesses, and we see how some of humanity's noblest traits—our desire to seek the truth about ourselves and the world, to know and help others—can lead to unmitigated disaster.

The Atlas (1996). Inspired by Yasunari Kawabata's "palm-of-the-hand stories" and arranged as a gigantic thematic palindrome, the fifty-three interconnected episodes in this non-fiction book combine to form what Vollmann describes (in his "Compiler's Note") as "a piecemeal atlas of the world I think in." Based mostly on the far-flung travels he'd made during the previous decade to Mogadishu, the Arctic, Burma, Bosnia-Herzegovina, Cambodia, and other contemporary "hot spots" where simmering old hatreds mixed with new sources of conflict and estrangement, *The Atlas* movingly presents Vollmann as he seeks adventure, understanding, and personal connection with soldiers, gypsies, crack whores, children, Eskimos[9], salesmen, and even his dead sister Julie (see "Under the Grass"). Vollmann here brings the political and cultural realities of these places to life in miniature portraits, while also variously exploring the central obsessions of his life and work: death, loss, metamorphosis, and decay; the anguish and exquisite pleasures of love; the thrill of travel; loneliness; and the role of human memory and art in resurrecting and preserving the past.

The Royal Family (2000). A skewed postmodern crime novel—Dante's *Inferno* by way of Elmore Leonard and Melville—this unruly, unforgettable, politically incorrect eight-hundred-page epic takes readers on a journey into the lurid, luminous heart of San Francisco's Mission District. Like Joyce's Dublin or William Kennedy's Albany, this setting becomes at once a literal place meticulously grounded in actuality and a mythic setting in which the characters and actions represent timeless, universal patterns of human life. Drawing upon an eclectic array of influences (Ovid, Melville, the Bible, Buddha, Dostoyevsky, and Dante, among others), *The Royal Family* unfolds as a deliberately unsettling mixture of genres and narrative forms, including satire, heroic quest, allegory, first-person reportage, metafiction, cyberpunk, and family drama. In opening wide a window that allows us to see the dark truth of the Mission District, *The Royal Family* also reveals the district's lurid beauty, mystery, and, above all, its humanity.

Argall: Third Dream (2001). In the fourth novel of the *Seven Dreams* series, Vollmann retells the famous story of Pocahontas and John Smith. As might be expected, *Argall*'s version is considerably more complicated than the romantic myth taught in grade school; its vividly rendered historical backdrop and gritty realism also make it considerably bloodier and more tragic. *Argall* is arguably Vollmann's most formally daring literary experiment due to his decision to render the entire novel in the extravagances of . . . *Elizabethan-style prose!* Surely even Shakespeare would have had a difficult time sustaining the poetic intensity and inventiveness required of this form, not merely for an entire novel, but for a seven-hundred-plus-page novel. A word to the wise graduate student: the least appreciated of Vollmann's books to date, *Argall* is, hence, the ripest for reconsideration.

Rising Up and Rising Down (2003). When an author as grandly ambitious as William Vollmann is willing to indicate that he judges this extended, elaborately researched meditation on the nature of violence to be his "life's work," we should listen up (see "'My Life's Work' [2002]"). Synthesizing vast amounts of Western history and thinking about war and its rationale, *Rising Up and Rising Down* also offers a measured and very human perspective on the specter of human violence and brutality that haunts all of his work. In Vols. 1 through 4—"Categories and Justifications"—Vollmann develops a comparative and theoretical examination of violence from the age of the Greeks and Romans (Gibbon's *The Rise and Fall of the Roman Empire*'s being one of the models here), up through Robespierre, Napoleon, John Brown, Lincoln, Lenin, Trotsky, Hitler, Mao, Gandhi, Pol Pot, Saddam Hussein, and (by implication) Osama Bin Laden. In Vols. 5 and 6—"Studies in Consequences"—Vollmann adds to this material his own personal experiences as a witness to war. Anchoring the entire project is the stand-alone volume, "Moral Calculus," in which Vollmann invents a new means of identifying the different forms of violence and analyzing the excuses for their justifiability; he then leaves to us "the exercise of weighing those competing justifications according to our own predispositions." Not merely massive by Vollmann's standards, but one of the longest books ever published, *Rising Up and Rising Down* contains more pages (three thousand, three hundred, plus more than three hundred photographs) than many writers produce in entire careers. But as is true of his other major works, *Rising Up* impresses not due to its bulk but due to the insights and provocative speculations about human civilization that Vollmann manages to derive from twenty-three years' worth of reading great books, personal experience, and introspection.

***The Convict Bird, The Happy Girls,* and other "Book Objects"** (1986–2004). One aspect of Vollmann's career that most readers are probably unaware of is his work in mixed-media forms, which includes a number of limited-edition "book objects"—that extend his overall concern with integrating the design features of his books with their content. *The Convict Bird,* for example, is a work encased in a steel "cage" (designed by Vollmann and developed by industrial sculptor Matt Heckert of the Survival Research Laboratories) with padlock and key and a Vollmann etching of a woman's face. Inside this "cell" is a "Children's Poem" about a woman in prison, accompanied by Vollmann ink-drawings. Considerably more ambitious is *The Happy Girls*: a sixteen-by-twenty-inch text describing a Thai brothel (with photographs by Ken Miller), each page of which is illustrated and hand-painted by Vollmann. The text is encased in a large birch-wood box that contains a peephole, and a buzzer, which activates a red lamp allowing viewers to see the photograph of a naked woman inside.

Shape-Shifting: A Composite Portrait

As was true of Blake, Poe, Dostoyevsky, Lautréamont, and other writers Vollmann has expressed admiration for, his work emerges out of fundamental divisions lying at the very core of his mind and heart. These divisions—roughly analogous to the Apollonian/Dionysian oppositions that Nietzsche applied to Greek tragedy, or to the familiar left-brain/right-brain models used by psychologists—are at war with one another; and, like the enormous heat and friction released from the collision of tectonic plates, the effect of having these buried substructures rubbing against and riding over one another can be earth-shaking.

Vollmann is at once a deeply obsessive writer—someone whose work is fueled by undercurrents of psychosexual compulsions, guilt, and suicidal despair, and by other irrational, wildly contradictory combinations of insecurity and narcissism, vulnerability and egotism—and a highly rational, methodical, and disciplined artist who is capable of giving expression to these obsessions in work that is deeply intellectual and analytical and which is frequently rendered in sentences of delicate refinement and exquisite aesthetic control. Vollmann's work therefore offers us not only two bright, distinctive worlds for the price of one, but also the mad comedy and intensity of their conjunction.

Emerging out of these basic divisions are other contradictions. His attitude about women, for example, is at once protective, chivalric, spiritually motivated, *and* suffused with lust—a white knight with a perpetual hard-on. He's a recklessly daring, swashbuckling adventurer reporting back the news from exotic, dangerous places in the manner of H. Rider Haggard (think Hemingway/Orwell/Steinbeck/London pumped up on steroids), *and* a cautious, highly methodical individual who never ventures outside the safe confines of his home in Sacramento without having made absolutely certain he knows as much as he can about where he's heading, what risks he's likely to face there, and that he's done everything humanly possible to minimize these risks. A rigorously logical thinker (and disciple of Wittgenstein) who favors the syllogistic, let's-break-things-down-into-their-constituent-parts approach to problem solving, he's also someone whose rational impulses are constantly overrun by his incandescent reaction to life's beauty (which he finds everywhere) and its tragic ineffability. He's America's most crazed, suicidal, romantic visionary since Poe and Melville, *and* a scientifically oriented empiricist in the Naturalist lineage of Zola and Frank Norris. One of the most sophisticated thinkers around, he's *also* an unreconstructed adolescent drawn to doomed causes because he hasn't matured enough to realize the futility of the ideals he's based his life and work on. He's "hot" in the sense of passionate and very, very "cool" in the original sense of being "calmly audacious." Part sinner indelibly stained by the mark of Cain, Vollmann is also part saint who in Christ-like fashion embraces everyman and everywoman, lays his hands upon their scars, and forgives them their sins.

Rimbaud, then, but also . . . Rambo.

William T. Vollmann is, however, above all, a *man of letters.* A meticulous, even obsessive researcher and the most widely and deeply read person I've ever met, Vollmann is an old-fashioned humanist who sincerely believes that reading and writing profoundly matter not merely because they supply us with insights and information about the world, but because they can change it.

A Few Words about the Arrangement and Selection Process

Trying to devise a series of fixed headings that we could use to organize such diverse material often felt like holding out a sieve to catch rainwater.

Of course, this difficulty is to be expected, given Vollmann's enormous body of confoundable, genre-busting, category-defying work. In the end, rather than arranging our selections according to genre, we decided to place most of them under four categories that loosely correspond to the themes and topics recurring most often in Vollmann's work: Death, War, and Violence; Love, Sex, Prostitutes, and Pornography; Travel; and Writing, Literature, and Culture. We've also included an opening section on Background and Influences, and a concluding appendix that includes a Vollmann Chronology, a Book Objects Section, and miscellaneous other documents.

Note[10]

I feel it may be of some interest to the reader to know some of the factors that influenced my work as co-editor of *Expelled from Eden.* Here one walks the proverbial tightrope, on the one side which lies a slavish obligation to editorial objectivity, and on the other, purely personal taste, whimsy, and self-indulgence. Given these dangers, it seems wise to conclude my introduction with a brief account of my relationship with Vollmann.

As readers may infer from my Vollmann Chronology, I've mixed my editorial colors in *Expelled from Eden* not only from the palette of literary criticism, but also from that of personal friendship. The former was formed during the first phase of my relationship with Vollmann, which grew out of my "day job" as an academic critic, interviewer, and editor specializing in contemporary American fiction. My first involvement with Vollmann came about in early 1990 while I was completing work on a collection of literary interviews with "radically innovative American fiction writers." Sensing I needed a final interview that could sum up the features I was ascribing to contemporary innovation, I wrote my colleague Tom LeClair, a professor of English at the University of Cincinnati, for suggestions. Tom responded with a note suggesting several possibilities and concluded: "But if you really want radical, you should check out a new guy named William T. Vollmann." I borrowed *You Bright and Risen Angels* and *The Rainbow Stories* from the library and was only a few pages into *Angels* before I sat down and wrote Vollmann a letter asking if he would be willing to be interviewed for my book. He agreed, sent me a package of goodies including the galleys of *The Ice-Shirt* and a description of his *Seven Dream* series, and I interviewed him at his apartment in Manhattan in May 1990.

I came away from that first meeting convinced (as I would later put it to Mike Hemmingson), "I have seen the future of American fiction, and its name is William T. Vollmann." Over the next few years, I met with Bill a half-dozen or so times, eagerly read all his work, reviewed most of his books, published several interviews with him (including the initial one in my book, *Some Other Frequency*) and critical essays about his work, and guest-edited a "Younger Authors" issue of the *Review of Contemporary Fiction* featuring the first extended discussion of his writing. From 1990–95, I also edited several anthologies in which Bill's work figured prominently. There were different emphases in these projects whose details don't need to be mentioned here, but they all related to my growing conviction that the postmodernist paradigm that had emerged as a means of making sense of the first wave of literary innovation during the sixties and early seventies had become increasingly irrelevant when applied to the works of the second and third generations of American authors emerging in the eighties and nineties. In this regard, Vollmann—with his emphasis on sincerity and first-hand testimony, his wide range of pre-World War II influences (and general lack of interest in the work of his contemporaries), his disdain for television, the Internet, and most other contemporary media forms, and his many other decidedly un-postmodernist attributes—seemed to make him the perfect poster boy to illustrate my thesis about just how limiting and misleading this postmodern paradigm had become. My aim in developing these anthologies, then, was not to introduce a new paradigm (by that point I'd realized any "universal" paradigm only encouraged people to force messy complexities into pat categories), but to present representative works by contemporary authors within a narrower set of tropes, thematic preoccupations, and formal tendencies that would suggest more relevant ways of reading and interpreting them. Consequently, I situated Vollmann's work variously—as an avant-pornographer; as the leading figure of the "post-Pynchon" generation of American writers; as a mainstream equivalent of cyberpunk; as a "radically innovative" fiction writer; and as "Avant-Pop."[11]

Beginning in the mid-nineties when Bill moved from Manhattan to

California, our relationship changed from that of critic-author to one based on personal friendship. My motives in nurturing this friendship are surely self-evident—who *wouldn't* want to be able to hang out with someone who's not only the most dangerous man in America, but also (as I once put it in a review) "a rough-edged beast who has been slouching towards some Millennial Bethlehem with a kind of monstrous elegance, utter fearlessness, and voracious appetite that one associates with Melville, Whitman, and Pynchon"? At any rate, the regular visits I started making to see Bill at his home in Sacramento allowed me to peek into his bookshelves, look through his huge archive of photographs, watercolors, and ink drawings, watch him construct his book object assemblages, and gaze in amazement at the large map on his studio wall onto which he's carefully pinned innumerable colored markers indicating places he's visited while conducting research.

But the real change in our relationship began in July 1997 when Bill accepted my invitation to visit me at my home in Borrego Springs. Borrego Springs is a small, isolated desert community about eighty-five miles northeast of San Diego that is perched precariously in the midst of the awesome Anza-Borrego Desert, one of the most desolate, physically stunning, and geologically extreme places on the planet. On this first visit, we spent several days hiking and touring the area in my SUV, and made several extended side trips to the Salton Sea and the Imperial/Mexicali Valley to the southeast. Given his fascination with travel, danger, and extremity, I'd hoped Bill would find this region to be irresistible, and sure enough, he took the bait. Since that first visit he's revisited the area dozens of times to conduct research used in *The Royal Family,* various magazine articles, and for a non-fiction book about Valley that has, in typical Vollmann fashion, expanded and mutated in a manner comparable to *Moby-Dick*'s evolution during the latter part of its composition.[12] During this period, I've become Bill's part-time chauffeur, father confessor, tour guide, hiking buddy, literary confidant, and partner in crime.

This second phase of my relationship with Bill has brought with it all sorts of strange, hilarious, and scary consequences. It's not so much that Bill necessarily *wants* to put himself and his friends in unusual situations, but somehow that's what happens. In my own case, I've done a lot of things, met a lot of people, and wound up in a lot of places I wouldn't normally have. I've gone to strip joints and whorehouses, for example, slept in flophouses, discovered the best way to smoke crack (actually, they're all pretty good), and donned a flak jacket. I've fired off rounds from the world's largest handgun, been to cockfights, and descended into dark, watery Chinese tunnels beneath Mexicali. I've lugged a view-camera and tripod into the Anza Borrego badlands, glided along the most polluted river in North America in a rickety boat. I've met homeless people, drug dealers, migrant workers, pimps, prostitutes, and coyotes, sipped sake across the table from a Yakuza member, and followed the trail of illegal aliens' empty water bottles and discarded clothing to the top of Mt. Signal in Mexico.

I've also taught for a term at Bill's alma mater, Deep Springs College, an experience that was not only very rewarding as an educator, but one that provided me with the closest thing I've ever had to a "eureka" moment that could reconcile for me how the dreamy, shy youth who was forever being bullied at school somehow became the fearless adventurer and supremely confident literary artist who has almost casually embarked on physically dangerous projects; and not merely embarked on these, but possessed the discipline and the will to complete them.

Final Coda: The Ghost of Tom Joad[13]

These exotic incidents, however, hardly formed the entire basis of our new relationship. In fact, the most important aspect of our friendship isn't exotic at all—what we *mostly* do when we're together is talk about books. One of these conversations that particularly sticks in my mind occurred late one summer afternoon while we were hurtling eastwards over the mountains along I-8 into the magnificent desolation of Imperial Valley. Earlier that day, we'd followed the lead of Native Americans and the white settlers of the Imperial Valley by seeking refuge from the summer heat in the mountains on the western edge of Imperial, at a place called Jacumba; en route there we stopped at a tourist spot called the Tower which afforded sweeping views to the east and north, and Bill set up his view-camera and took a bunch of photographs while I talked with the Tower's new owner. Later on we drove off-road a couple of rugged miles to the Mexican-American border, and while Bill was setting up his view-camera again to get some shots of the area with the full moon that was rising, two Border Patrol agents drove up and politely inquired what a couple of gringos like us were doing. Bill smiled with that bottomless blue-eyed innocence he has, and patiently explained he was writing a book about Imperial. Afterwards, we hopped back in my SUV and as we began the long descent to Imperial we were talking and laughing, and I was sipping my drink and offering a running monologue about Springsteen's *The Ghost of Tom Joad* tape that was playing, and as we plunged down into one of the largest structural depressions on earth, our talk was zooming off in all directions at once, to the EAST, for example, where we could see eighty miles across the valley to the pinpricks of light just popping on around the Salton Sea and the Cargo Muchacho Mountains where I'd once foolishly driven Bill in a rental car and almost gotten us stuck, and I was trying to explain to Bill about the many connections I saw between his work and Springsteen's, their odd combination of ferocity and vulnerability, their efforts to give voices to the disadvantaged and social outcasts, the honesty and sincerity of their presentations, and Bill made me happy by saying his favorite Springsteen album was *Nebraska* and so I replayed *The Ghost of Tom Joad,* and while I was explaining why I felt they could both probably be best compared to Steinbeck I mentioned a *New York Times Magazine* cover article I'd once read about Springsteen called "Steinbeck in Leather" and I said that if they did a similar piece about Bill they should call it "Springsteen in Leather Flak-Jacket" and Bill laughed and said his favorite Steinbeck novel was *East of Eden;* and behind us to the WEST, where the last rays of the sun were shooting through the mountain passes and changing everything around us to Rothko hues, and I asked Bill about all the maps he supplied for *Seven Dreams* and whether he ever researched map-making, and of course he had, and after rattling off a half-dozen titles about cartography he told me a funny story about the map-making software he tried for a while before he decided it was too mechanical, and then we talked about Poe's science fiction and Bill mentioned that his sister Julie's death had been one of the inspirations for his treatment of Poe and Virginia Clemm in "The Grave of Lost Stories;" and off to the NORTH we could see Carrizo Gorge where de Anza had passed through in 1775 and where we tromped around once trying to find the tunnels and wooden trestles that the SD & AE Railroad used before everything got washed away by Hurricane Kathleen in 1977; and to the SOUTH we could see Mt. Signal looming up in the gathering darkness, and we agreed how different it looked from different perspectives, and we reminisced about the hike he and I and his friend Meagan Atiyeh had taken to its top, and off to our right we were passing the moonscaped Yuha Desert with its oyster shell reefs where we had once come upon a series of ancient geoglyphs, and Bill asked me if I'd ever read Heinlein's "The Moon is a Harsh Mistress," and I said yes, but I was really more of a Sturgeon fan, and then we zoomed off further to Ray Bradbury's and Philip K. Dick's and his own Phil Blaker's Mars, and then before you knew it, we were sitting in Calexico's traffic, waiting to cross over to Mexicali, when Bill said to me, "You know, I appreciate getting to talk with you about books—you're my only friend I really get to do this with," and even though I felt complimented I mainly felt saddened, because Bill really has been so isolated from other people for most of his life, and so I tried to lighten the moment by saying, "Well, talking with you about books is a helluva job, but, hey, somebody has to do it, right?"

What I didn't say to Bill then but will say now is just this: "That's okay, Bill—you don't really have to talk about books with anybody; you just need to keep *writing* them."

And write on he no doubt will. Let me conclude by saying to all readers who are about to venture forth into *Expelled from Eden* that I bring good tidings. After many years of wandering in the desert of late twentieth-century American culture, I have drunk deeply from the raging torrent that is Vollmann and found it good.

—Larry McCaffery

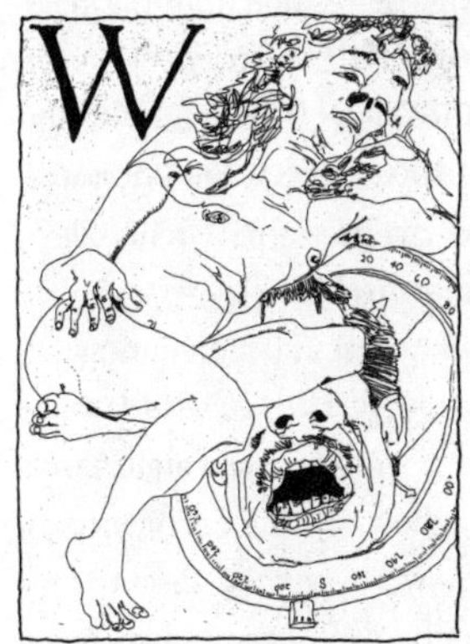

FOUR (UNUSED) INK DRAWINGS VOLLMANN CREATED FOR "THE GHOST OF MAGNETISM."

Endnotes from Intro:

1) This *would* have been the perfect date for *Wreck on the Highway* to appear, since it would have capitalized on the Boss's rise to superstardom following the release of his mega-hit *Born in the U.S.A.* in 1984 and the triumphant two-year tour that followed; but unfortunately Columbia Records never released it.
2) Some of the highlights of the equivalents of Vollmann's "major label work" appearing in *Expelled*: "Three Meditations on Death" (the opening section of *Rising Up and Rising Down*) and "Across the Divide" (Vollmann's impressions of Afghanistan on the eve of the U.S. invasion, published in *The New Yorker*); scenes from his childhood ("The Land of Counterpane" from *An Afghanistan Picture Show*, "The Butterfly Boy" from *Butterfly Stories*, and "Under the Grass" from *The Atlas*); sexual agonies, prostitution, and shape-shifting ("The Hermophrodite" from *The Ice-Shirt*, and "Nicole" from *Whores for Gloria*); "Subzero's Debt, 1991" (the harrowing description from *The Rifles* of Vollmann's near-fatal experiences conducting research near the magnetic North Pole); excerpts from "The Ghost of Magnetism" and "The Grave of Lost Stories" (from *Thirteen Stories and Thirteen Epitaphs*); "The Agony of Parker" (from *You Bright and Risen Angels*); "Sunflower" (from *The Royal Family*); "Debts and Debtors" (from *Fathers and Crows*); and "To the Right Honourable Reader" (from *Argall*).
3) For a less pessimistic account of what was occurring in American fiction during the mid-eighties, see my essay, "The Fictions of the Present" in *The Columbia Literary History of the United States* (1988), pp. 1161–1177. In that assessment I argued one of the most promising developments during the period was the emergence of cyberpunk, a form I later used to situate Vollmann's work—via the absent Mars subplot of *You Bright and Risen Angels* and his admiring riff, "The Indigo Engineers," about The Survival Research Lab in *The Rainbow Stories*—in my 1992 anthology, *Storming the Reality Studio: A Casebook of Cyberpunk and Postmodern Science Fiction*. It turned out that while my identification of Vollmann as cyberpunk was misleading (by the mid-eighties he wasn't reading much science fiction and hence had not been aware of the work of William Gibson and the other cyberpunks), it was accurate in suggesting that science fiction was an important influence on Vollmann's literary sensibility. Meanwhile, the fact that Vollmann's work in the eighties was so closely tied to the Bay Area began to attract the attention of San Francisco's vigorous quasi-punk and science fiction community, whose ranks by the early nineties had swelled to include Kathy Acker, John Shirley, Richard Kadrey, Mark Laidlaw, and the computer geeks associated with Silicon Valley and *Mondo 2000*. Thus, although Vollmann was never directly involved in this San Francisco scene (indeed, he's never been a part of *any* "scene" other than the Mission District street scene), the fact that his work began to be recognized and admired by Bay Area writers and artists did have several practical consequences. For instance, my own involvement in the Bay Area cyberpunk scene led to my

publication of an interview with Vollmann in *Mondo 2000* and to my soliciting Mark Laidlaw (who I had discovered was a huge fan of *Angels*) to contribute an essay on Vollmann for the *Review of Contemporary Fiction* "Younger Authors" issue (1993). Vollmann's proximity to this scene also encouraged him to read Kathy Acker's avant-punk fiction from this period, which shared with Vollmann's a number of commonalties, including their fascination with abjection, masochism, prostitution, and extremity, their analogous experiments in point of view and the shocking, brutally honest manner in which they depicted the vulnerabilities and sexual obsessions in fictionalized versions of themselves, and their mutual admiration for Lautréamont and Kawabata. Acker—who had become a fan of Vollmann's work even before moving to San Francisco (she had been asked to blurb *Angels* back in 1986 and later wrote a favorable review for *City Limits* [17-31 1987])—is one of the rare instances of a contemporary writer Vollmann felt a sense of kinship with; and although many reviewers and critics have assumed Pynchon had a major impact on Vollmann's work, certainly in terms of "influence," Acker was a far more important figure during this period than Pynchon, whose work Vollmann didn't read until after completing *You Bright and Risen Angels.*

4) David Foster Wallace develops a more extended version of this hangover analogy in his assessment of American writing during this period in "When the Party's Over: An Interview with David Foster Wallace," which appeared in the *Review of Contemporary Fiction* "Younger Authors" issue (McCaffery, 1993).

5) In particular, the assignments Vollmann did for Will Blythe at *Esquire* and Bob Guccione at *Spin* provided crucial financial support that allowed him to conduct research in Madagascar, Columbia, the magnetic North Pole, Southeast Asia, Afghanistan, and other far-flung places that would otherwise have been impractical to visit. See the Vollmann Chronology for a list of many of these assignments.

6) The only novel series I am aware of that may rival *Seven Dreams* in this regard are Durrell's Alexandria Quartet and Anthony Powell's *A Dance to Music of Time.* As for *Rising Up*, Gibbon's *The Rise and Fall of the Roman Empire* may rival it in page count but no other work surpasses it.

7) Vollmann's numbering of the *Seven Dreams* is based on their chronological sequence rather than publication dates; thus, the two books dealing with the earliest historical periods, *The Ice-Shirt* and *Fathers and Crows* appear as the "First Dream" and "Second Dream," while the third publication in the series, *The Rifles,* is listed as "Sixth Dream." For a more detailed description of this series, see Vollmann's "*Seven Dreams:* Description of Project" in the appendix.

8) See, for example, "The Hermophrodite," where Vollmann's heavily mythologized account of the transformation of Younger Brother into a woman is immediately followed by a description of two male transvestites in San Francisco undergoing their own man-to-woman transformations.

9) The doomed Inuk Reepah from *The Rifles* is one of several earlier characters appearing here in tales that are thematic reductions of his novels.
10) This note is loosely modeled on the notes Vollmann has included in *Seven Dreams* to preface source materials and endnotes, and on "The Ghost of Magnetism."
11) Interested readers may consult the following anthologies and special issues of literary journals: *Fiction International: Pornography, Obscenity and Censorship* (1991); Everything Is Permitted: The Post-Pynchon, Post-Modern Fiction of America—Special Issue of *Positive Magazine* [Tokyo] (1991); *Review of Contemporary Fiction—Younger American Authors: William T. Vollmann, Susan Daitch, and David Foster Wallace* (1993); *Some Other Frequency: Interviews with Innovative American Authors* (1996); *Avant-Pop: Fiction For a Daydream Nation* (1993); and *After Yesterday's Crash: The Avant-Pop Anthology* (1995).
12) See "The Water of Life" for a sample chapter from Vollmann's work-in-progress about Imperial Valley.
13) "The Ghost of Tom Joad" riff that serves as the "final coda" for my introduction was inspired by the concluding sections of Vollmann's "The Ghost of Magnetism," which similarly uses the four points of the compass as a structural device. Vollmann created the four illustrations that appear here for "The Ghost of Magnetism," but his publishers declined to include them. See also "The Ghost of Magnetism," an excerpt that concludes just before an exteded section entitled "The Compass Rose," where the voice of Vollmann's narrator zooms off into recollections that he associates with North, South, East, and West.

Part I

Background and Influences

Biographical Statement (c. 1989)

From
Wordcraft

I HAVE WANTED TO write (and I have been writing) ever since I was six or seven. While the other children played games, I sat indoors reading stories; and in those days it often seemed to me that I was inside the book, riding with the Caliph upon his magic carpet, and all I had to do was tap him on the shoulder for him to see me and greet me and accept me as his Vizier—but I knew that then I would have to be the Vizier forever and would never escape from the book; so I kept quiet. In the end the books won. I had simply spent too much time inside them. For the middle years of my childhood I was a prisoner on that magic carpet, flying above refugee camps and hot dusty cities whose inhabitants I could not see. I still don't know what happened to the Caliph over those years, but he lost both authority and corporeality, and by the end was only a figure woven into the carpet. I guess this happens to everyone. The tales we used to enjoy and be a part of are the ones we read to our children, and we watch our children's expressions as we read aloud, in order to remember how we used to feel. —But that happens when we're excluded from books; my loneliness was worse because I was trapped in books. Then I realized that if I could not get out of my books I could at least bring other people in to visit me. I could do this only by *writing books.* Once I understood this, my carpet set me down in the stock room of a carpet factory where I was janitor and sole proprietor. (You think I am exaggerating, but this is how it really happened.)

As a writer I tend to concern myself (possibly too much) with underdogs and doomed causes. I have written about retarded people, runaways, life-sentence prisoners, streetwalkers and anti-nuclear militants.

In 1982 I went to Pakistan on a tourist visa, made contacts in the refugee camps of the Northwest Frontier, and crossed over the mountains into Afghanistan with Islamic commandos. What we did not know about each other would fill a book, so I wrote one. I will never forget the morning we came to an apricot tree one hill away from a Soviet base. The tree was bowed beneath the weight of its golden fruit. In the sand by the tree was a human jaw.

By the time I finished writing the first version of *An Afghanistan Picture Show,* many more people in Afghanistan had been killed. I wanted to right the balance on paper (since I was impotent to do so anywhere else) by telling a story about a good extremist who triumphed over the bad guys. That was the genesis of my character Bug in *You Bright and Risen Angels.* I made the bad guys as bad as I possibly could, and I made them oppress Bug himself so that he would be unequivocally in the right. But as soon as Bug began to strike back he began to become evil, no matter what I did. What *You Bright and Risen Angels* turned out to be was a monograph on certain experiments conducted in my ethical laboratory—experiments involving the most powerful reagent: cruelty. Despite myself, it became my premise that cruelty corrupts its victims just as much as its perpetrators, that revolutionaries are or become as bad as their tyrants. This book is concerned with the consciousness of bugs and electricity, because a bug's life is one very practical way of surviving in a cruel world—survival by amoral, expedient scuttling, hiding and attacking; and because electricity can mythically exemplify the technological forces which impel people into a bug's life. Each of the characters in my book has been twisted by these forces. And just as Bug becomes bad through no desire of his own, so the original bad guys who made him what he is deserve pity as well as hatred. Once I understood this, I saw that my characters were suffering so much because they had misdirected their feelings of love. Instead of loving people who loved them and things they could have, they loved "ideals," or they loved their tyrants for guiding them, or they loved their ability to affect others (and of course destroying others is the most powerful ways of affecting them), or they forgot what love was and merely lusted.

To explore this further, I decided to write stories about prostitutes. I heard one man say to his whore, "Mary, do you love me?" And she smiled and said to him with real tenderness, "Listen, babe, I'll love you for a whole hour." These *Rainbow Stories,* as I call them, have gradually come to encompass other lowlifes as well, such as tramps, street alcoholics and Nazi skinheads. Love is what they all want. But they do not know how to get it, and so they become twisted.

Must life be like this for so many people? Does it come about from the way people are or the way people live? Was it always this way? I am an American, and at the moment my interest lies in writing about Americans, so now that I have finished my *Rainbow Stories,* I am writing a seven-volume novel about the last Americans that we know about—ourselves—and the first—the Indians.

From "The Land of Counterpane"

From
An Afghanistan Picture Show

IT IS PART OF the fragmentation of life that certain states of existence can barely be recalled in others, as to a storybook sailor long away the feel of walking in the street drains first from his mind, which can conceive of only present time; and then gradually from his hands, which once flashed in free arcs at his sides and now must always be grasping stanchions or rigging; and finally from his legs and feet, which, having through greatest proximity become most accustomed to the confidently repetitive action of striding over the unmoving pavement, are the slowest to forget; and at last the sensation of walking on land becomes an abstraction, like the mountains of some country beyond the horizon. This was especially true for me when as a child I was ill. —I would wake up feeling hot and nauseous; the breakfast which my mother had made me I was unable to eat, and there was no talk of my going to school. My father, who sometimes suspected me of malingering, would study me sharply, but in the end my pallor and forehead heat would convince even him, and I would be sent back to bed for the day. I would lie there, and watch the sun slowly ascend in the sky, the other children going off past my window with their schoolbooks slung under their arms if they were boys, or held tightly against their chests if they were girls; and then I lay still and watched the clock beside me change the position of its hands with all the monotonous slowness of the great geological epochs. At five of eight the hands began to move faster; eight o'clock was the fatal hour when school began, and I knew that if I jumped out of bed even now, and dressed and ran off to school breakfastless, then I might perhaps arrive before the teacher called my name, which, beginning as it did with "V," was at the bottom of the attendance list. And I knew that my father, too, if he had not already left for the office, was also looking at the clock, thinking that it might not be too late to force me out of bed and take me to school in the car; but he did his best to judge my case fairly, and reconsidered the evidence which he had seen me exhibit: Was my temperature genuinely high, and did I look all that pale? Eventually he decided that yes, I was sick; or that at any rate it would be difficult to establish that I was not well; and it would certainly be too late to take me to school; for achieving that would involve first confronting and then besting my mother, who stood with her back toward him, also looking at the clock, but only unobtrusively, between the breakfast dishes, so as not to give my father an excuse for reopening the subject; and then eight o'clock had come and the issue was decided. It was only then that the hands of the clock stopped once again, and I became completely absorbed in my state of sickness.

The world outside blurred in the sunlight, in the same way that a streetlamp, seen through tears, becomes a bright, vague star; and this lack of definition seemed to me a *force* with a self, swelling until it pushed against my windowpane, halted at first by the smooth, cold surface, but waiting there, growing stronger and more determined, until it was able to seep in through some edge-crack. My desk, my schoolbooks and the few toys which I had not yet given up slowly became enveloped in its luminous sparkle; the closet's black mouth filled with it; and then it flowed around me from three sides, and into me. Charged with it, I began to forget the cues and sensations of health, as in health I could not imagine myself as feeling sick, nor could I have much empathy for my sister Julie when she had the measles, nor keep from getting angry at my teacher when she did not come in that day and we had to have a substitute. The idea of a world beyond the window, which was now a translucent slab of light, or for that matter of any other possibility than that of lying in my bed immobile, became as dry and strange as some ontological argument of the Middle Ages, and by degrees ever less likely, until when at mid-morning, my mother came in to bring me a cup of tea or some soup, I refused politely, in the same way that I would have done if she'd come to ask whether I would be willing to study law at the university. This inability to grasp my own state of existence of the day before would have possessed me so much that by midafternoon, when my mother came in to read to me, I no longer shifted my position beneath the blankets at all, but lay absolutely still in the hot faintness of my malady as though I were one of those people one reads about in old books, who are always getting becalmed in the tropics.

As soon as I was old enough to read by myself I stopped having my mother read to me at night, because I always disagreed with my sister as to what should be read to us that evening; and it was so much better for me to read what I wished, while Julie sat on my mother's lap and listened to her reading from *Just So Stories* or a poem from *A Child's Garden of Verses* (both of which I now found childish) in her slow, soft voice; and when I was sick my mother would simply buy me a book, such as *Captains Courageous,* which I was too proud to ask her to read to me. But when I did still like having my mother read everything to me, and I was absorbed by poems like the one about the fight between the gingham dog and the calico cat, or the one that described a voyage to Africa, in which the traveler sees the knotty crocodile of the Nile (but I used to think that it was the NAUGHTY CROCODILE that had eaten people up and so must be spanked), and he finds the toys of the old Egyptian boys and all the other things which rhyme—there was still one poem which I dreaded. It was called "The Land of Counterpane," and it recounted the fantasy of a child who is sick and abed with his toy soldiers. This "Land of Counterpane" is simply the topography of the wrinkled and up-thrust blankets; and the child marches his soldiers up and down the quilt-patterned hills, skirmishes them on whatever rare plains there may be, and sets up ambushes and rescues at the mouths of little vales formed by pinching the sheets into contours of sufficient exactitude. My mother could never understand why it was that I so disliked this poem,* but, accepting my detestation as she would have accepted one of my father's pronouncements on some mechanical matter, she did not read the poem to me, and I felt grateful, dreading the sight of the very poem that preceded it as my mother slowly turned the pages, which were as colorful as butterflies' wings;

*The dislikes we have are such a mystery! My friend Seth was always terrified of whales, although he never met any, and I once met a little Afghan girl who screamed whenever she heard an airplane. Later I found out that an airplane had killed her parents and transformed her into a paraplegic.

and feeling the smug contentment of one who has arrived alive, most bones intact, after a session or two on the rack, when we were safely a couple of poems beyond. The truth of the matter, which I was always ashamed to explain, was that the image of the wrinkles terrified me, I having just become aware of the correlation between the wrinkles on the faces of my grandparents and the fact that they were going to die within the next several decades; and once I had been prevailed upon to accept the fact of my own death, I started feeling my face every day for wrinkles, knowing that one day they would come; and I watched my parents closely, noticing with horror the ever-lessening resemblance between my mother and her bridal picture in the family album, and the fact that my father's hair was slowly graying; and when I lay in bed all day, the eerie luminescence of my sickness in me and all about me, my inability to recall my healthy state in any real sense made the wrinkles of my own "Land of Counterpane" seem a menacing *memento mori*.

The Butterfly Boy

From
Butterfly Stories

Sometimes the best way for a writer to compose autobiographical fiction is to do it in the third person, to take that objective narrative a step back, which is what Vollmann does in *Butterfly Stories,* a collection of interrelated tales dubbed "a novel." *Butterfly Stories* follows an unnamed protagonist from childhood to middle-age—he's known only as the Butterfly Boy, the Journalist, and the Husband through his various stages of life. The following excerpt deals with those formidable and fragile times: the playground at school and coming to realize the differences between boys and girls. Here, the Butterfly Boy encounters his first love, a girl who will haunt him forever, whom he will match against every other woman to come into his life, from prostitute to spouse, at home and abroad (much of the novel takes place in Cambodia, as the hero of the book travels with the Photographer, a thinly veiled rendition of Ken Miller). —MH

The consequences beasts draw are just like those of simple empirics, who claim that what has happened will happen again in a case [that] strikes them [as] similar, without being able to determine whether the same reasons are at work. This is what makes it so easy to capture beasts . . .

G.W. Leibniz, *Preface to The New Essays* (1703–05)

1.

Under the leaning plant-tumuli were galleries of wet dirt in which the escapees hid, panting like animals, naked and trembling, gazing up at the flared leaves whose stalks, paler than beansprouts, wove each other's signatures. Not everybody was caught again. Their families had to be bulldozed into the American bomb craters without them. Wormy dirt pressed down on bloodstained dirt until everything stopped moving, and the slaves were forbidden to work there for a month, until the mound had settled. The slaves had no desire to go there anyway. Water buffaloes rooted and splashed slowly in the rice paddies. They were valuable. As for the slaves, there was a slogan: *Alive you are no gain; dead you are no loss.* So the slaves obeyed the rule of absolute silence. After a month, they were sent to plant the grave with cassava. Meanwhile, the ones who had gotten away lived hour by hour beneath the roof of maculed leaves swarming with darkness as they crept toward Thailand, ducking through green-fringed purple leaves, dodging golden berries as hard as copper. Sometimes a land mine got them, and sometimes a snake did. It did not matter whether the land mines were Russian or Chinese because they rended people with the same sudden clap of smokepetaled flame. But the snakes came in so many varieties as to guarantee an interesting death. One kind let you live a day after you were bitten. Another kind killed in an hour. There was a kind that let you walk two steps before you fell down dead. The people who survived the snakes fled on toward Thailand, where if they were lucky they might win admittance to a barbed wire cage. As they ran, they gasped in the strong wet smell of ferns. Fallen flower-bowls, red and yellow, lay in the knee-deep carpet of ferns. In the very humid places, moss grew out of the tree trunks and mounded itself upon itself in clusters like raspberries. From these places ferns burst out, and spider webs grew on the fern, and within the webs the spiders waited. Some were poisonous and some were not. Sometimes the people who survived the spiders became lost and came out into a clearing where their executioners were already conveniently waiting. Around the lip of the bomb crater, generous grass bowed under its own wet weight, the dark star leaved trees meeting it in a terrifying horizon. The people would begin to scream. The order was given to approach the grave in single file. Sometimes the executioners cut open their bellies or wombs with the razor-sharp leaf-edges of sugarplum trees. Sometimes they smashed their skulls in with pickaxes. The executioners who were especially skilled at this enjoyed practicing what they called "the top." When you stand behind someone and smash his skull in just the right way, he will whirl around as he falls and gaze up at you with his dying eyes. Sometimes they beat them to death with gun butts. Sometimes they pushed them off cliffs. Sometimes they crucified them in trees. Sometimes they injected them with poison. Sometimes they peeled back their skins and their livers while the victims were still screaming. Sometimes they wrapped up their heads in wet towels and slowly suffocated them. Sometimes they chopped them into pieces.

2.

The butterfly boy knew nothing about this, firstly because he was only seven years old and in another country, and secondly because it hadn't happened yet. It would be two more years before he even saw a dead person.

3.

The butterfly boy was not popular in second grade because he knew how to spell "bacteria" in the spelling bee, and so the other boys beat him up. Also, he liked girls. Boys are supposed to hate girls in second grade, but he never did, so the other boys despised him.

4.

There was a jungle, and there was murder by torture, but the butterfly boy did not know about it. But he knew the school bully, who beat him up everyday. Very quickly, the butterfly boy realized that there was nothing he could do to defend himself. The school bully was stronger and faster than he was. The butterfly boy did not know how to fight. When the school bully punched him, it never occurred to him to punch back. He used his arms to protect his face and belly as best he could, and he tried not to cry. If it had been just him and the school bully he probably would have cried, because he regarded the school bully as a titanic implacable force in comparison to which he was so helpless that he was a sacrifice to an evil god, so there was no shame crying before him. But since the other boys loved to gather in a circle and watch the butterfly boy being beaten up, he would not cry; they were his peers—not, of course, that they thought so. To every other boy in the school, the butterfly boy was so low and vile that he was not a human being.

5.

The school bully was retarded. He had failed fourth grade three times. He was therefore much bigger and stronger than any other boy in the elementary school. In the winter time the custodian shoveled all the snow in the playground into a great heap in one corner, and the pile froze into a mountain of ice that almost topped the fence by February or March. The school bully claimed this mountain as his kingdom. He stood on the summit of that dirty blue pile of frozen slush and picked out his victim, following a sporting algorithm that may have been similar to the butterfly boy's once he grew up and had to decide which whore to fall in love with. The bully, however, appeared to have studied at the school of eagles. He turned his hunched head in a series of alert jerks, his eyes rarely blinked, and when he spotted someone he could torture he shrieked like a bird and brought his arms up into wings. The way a boy walked, the color of his shoes, these and other unknown criteria were scanned by his hard little eyes, until he searched out a rodent worthy of his malice. It was always the butterfly boy first, but sometimes it was someone else, too. You might think that that someone else and the butterfly boy would become allies, but it never happened. Whomever the school bully hurt was so disgraced and humiliated that he was no good for anything. He had become so despicable by virtue of being hurt that not even other despicable people could stand him.

6.

So the only playmates that the butterfly boy ever had were girls. He loved girls. Sometimes he kissed them, and sometimes they kissed him. Occasionally the stronger girls would even defend him from the bully. But this only made the butterfly boy more miserable. He would have rather have gone home with another bloody nose than endure the additional odium of being defended by girls.

7.

So the butterfly boy's pleasures were of a solitary kind. One evening a huge monarch butterfly landed on the top step of his house and he watched it for an hour. It squatted on the welcome mat, moving its gorgeous wings slowly. It seemed very happy. Then it rose into the air and he never saw it again. He remembered that butterfly for the rest of his life.

8.

The last bell had rung. The children rushed into the wet and muddy hallway in a happy rage of shouts and clattering lunch-boxes. As the butterfly boy reached the halfway point with his galoshes buckles, a girl came to help him. Some of the buckles were crooked or a little rusty. Every day this girl did up the most difficult ones for him. The outer door kept banging open and closed as children ran into the snow. Through it the butterfly boy caught stroboscopic glimpses of the waiting steaming school buses, not as yellow as they would be in the spring rains when their gorgeous new yellowness shouted itself even more brightly than the No. 2 pencils given out for penmanship; the sticky snowflakes paled and frosted the buses into something coy and lemon-gold, more fit now to swim through blizzards illuminated by their pale yellow eyes.

Want to come to my house? the girl said.

When? said the butterfly boy, startled.

Now.

The butterfly boy smiled down shyly as the girl fastened the last buckle for him. —Yeah, he said.

When he got into her bus with her, he had a sense of doing something deliciously wrong. Her bus had a different black number on it, and a different driver. The black vinyl seats smelled different. There was chewing gum stuck in different places. The children who got on the bus were different. They seemed quieter and happier and more perfect to him. They left him alone.

The bus that he usually rode drove away first, and when he saw it go he felt nervous for a moment. His parents might be angry.

The girl was taking him somewhere he'd never been. They sat warmly together with their lunchboxes on their laps, passing white winter hills and farmhouses and horses shaking snow off themselves. Some of the trees were only dusted with snow, as a cake might be with sugar, while others below, onto which they had discharged their loads, resembled snowmen or plump downy birds. They passed a little evergreen heavily lobed with it like a brain stood on its end, and by its agency the light passing into the bus window was whitened, so that when the girl turned suddenly toward him her face resembled a marble angel, and then the tree was past, and her features obeyed the vibrations of a rosier light. Without knowing what he as doing or why, he suddenly plunged his face into her warm hair. The girl looked at him with great seriousness. The snow was getting deeper the farther they rode into this unknown land, and it had begun to get dark. He was entirely happy by the girl's side. The bus stopped more frequently now to let the pupils off. It was almost empty. Then they traveled for another long interval along the edges of snowy fields. The butterfly boy saw a low pond in the direction of the setting sun. A wavy black channel had formed between its plates of ice. —Our dogs like to play there, the girl said. —A great rolling hill caught the sunset in the distance. Below it was another wide field of steep-roofed farm sheds and half-frozen ponds and trees becoming successively more frosted in the distance. They drew closer to the base of the hill, and the girl pointed to a white house. —That's where I live, she said.

It was late twilight, and getting cold when the bus let them off. —Now we have to walk a minute, the girl said. —She took him up a wide road that swiveled through the bare and spacious forest. The road was irresistibly blank and creamy with snow like the notebook-paper that they used at school. The butterfly boy drew loops and circles with his mittened hand. —Come on, the girl said. I want to show you my things. —The road had steepened as they curved up through snowy shade. Whitened limbs hung over their heads, and they turned one more bend, and came to the field again and they saw the girl's house. —I'm sad, the girl said. 'Cause I wanted to show you the footprints I made in the morning. But the snow's covered them up.

The butterfly boy realized that the girl liked him very much. Without looking at her, he followed her inside, glowing with a soft warm joy.

Who's this? said the girl's mother in surprise.

He's coming for dinner, the girl explained.

She took him up to her room, and giggling, opened her chest of drawers to show him her folded white underpants. He had never seen girls' underpants before. He was as happy as when he'd seen the butterfly: the special secret had now been revealed to him.

After that, he and the girl read storybooks together until dinnertime. There was one book about five Chinese brothers who couldn't be killed. One was condemned to be drowned, but he drank up all the sea. The page showed a night scene, glowing with the rich pigments of children's books like some lantern-lit stand of fruits in bowls. People were diving in the stagnant pond. Their ploughs parked under the trees. They were bringing up armloads of skulls. Across the brown river's bridge, a white monument rose like a Khmer tombstone. Here the executioners, skinny serious men in black pajamas, were trying to drown the Chinese brother. They had tied his hands behind his back with wire and forced his head down into the water, but he was drinking it all up with bulging cheeks; they couldn't hurt him even there at the foot of the lion's gape where white teeth blared. Making a festivity of the event, little kids were beating a drum and leaping barefoot down the dirty street lit by a single orange-shaped lamp held to a power pole. They didn't see the man in black pajamas who was coming with an iron bar to smash the lamp. The Chinese brother was still drinking; the water got lower and lower. On the bridge, a one-legged boy leaned on his crutch in astonishment. There was a golden temple in the background, with snarling stone figures carved on the pillars; other winged figures were about to swoop. Skinny boys in black pajamas were smashing it down with pickaxes. There were dark gratings in front of which people sat under lightless awnings and the girls laughed. They were eating at a table crowded by bowls of string beans, limes, yellow flowers, peppers, a bowl of red chili powder, chopsticks, the people putting everything into their soup, sitting down on little square stools with other big bowls of soup steaming at their back. Their backs were turned, so they didn't see the men in black pajamas coming towards them with machine guns. The butterfly boy had never seen anyone who wasn't white. He wondered if all Chinese people possessed these supernatural capabilities.

This is my favorite picture, said the girl, turning to a page, which showed another unkillable Chinese brother being pushed off a precipice. The cliff was walled with dark green palms that glistened as if dipped in wax, and there was glossy darkness between them down which children scrambled barefoot, their shirts fluttering bright and clean in the hot breeze; palm-heads swung like pendulums. Men in black pajamas were waiting for them. Banana leaves made green awnings; then other multirayed green stars and bushes with dewy leaves that sparkled like constellations held the middle place; below them, rust-red compound blooms topped lacy mazes of dark grayish-green leaves, everything slanting down to the dark water, white foamed, that came from the wide white waterfall towards which the Chinese brother screamed smiling down.

The butterfly boy looked as this picture with her for a long time. Then he hung his head. —Can I see your underpants again?

9.

The next year the school districts changed, so he didn't see the girl anymore. Another girl invited him over to make creepy crawlers. He only had the Plastic Goop, but she had the other kind that you could bake into rubbery candy. They made candy ants and beetles and spiders and ate them and he was very happy. But he was afraid to invite her over because he didn't know what his parents would think about his playing with girls, so she never invited him again.

10.

The school bully roared, ran down from his mountain of snow and ice, and charged the butterfly boy with outstretched arms. The bully's parka was the same every year. His parents never seemed to wash it, so it was very grimy, and it had become too small for him. The bully had thick hairy arms like a monster and a reddish-purple face full of yellow teeth. He knocked the butterfly boy down and sat on his stomach. Then he began to spit into his face. He spat and spat, while the other boys cheered. Then he took the butterfly boy's glasses off and broke them. He punched the butterfly boy in the nose until blood came out. Then he stood up. He jumped on the butterfly boy's stomach and the butterfly boy puked. Everybody laughed. He let the butterfly boy go. The butterfly boy staggered into the far corner of the chain-link fence and tried to clean the blood and vomit off himself.

11.

You fell down *again*?   said the butterfly boy's mother in amazement.

Yes.

What happened this time?

I don't know. I just fell.

Maybe he needs his glasses changed,   she said to his father.

12.

I don't want to go outside for recess anymore,   the butterfly boy said.

You have to go out,   the teacher said.

Why?

Because if you stay in here with me you'll never learn how to take care of yourself.

What can I do? Every time I go out there I get beaten up. He's waiting for me right now.

The teacher sipped her coffee, trying to think of some miracle strategy that would make the butterfly boy grow out of his subhumanhood. But she couldn't think of anything.

You can stay in with me today,   she said.   But only today.

Thank you,   the butterfly boy said gratefully.

She let him look through the schoolbook that the grade above him was reading, *People from Foreign Lands*, so he got to peer down a page of partly shaded bystreet, drivers resting in their cyclos under the trees, sun hot on their toes, stacks of hollow-cored building bricks on the street corners, and he was contented, but then the second hand of the big clock made a ticking sound and he found himself already beginning to dread tomorrow's recess.

13.

High up upon his filthy crag, the school bully crouched, flapping his arms like an eagle muttering to himself. His head jerked back and forth as he scanned the playground, searching for victims. The substance that his soul was composed of was pain. Since the most basic pleasure of substance is to see or dream or replicate itself, the bully fulfilled himself by causing pain in others. This proves that he could perceive and interpret, since otherwise how could the agonies of others enchant him? However, if we allow what certain philosophers do, namely, that memory is a necessary component of consciousness, then we cannot say for certain that he was conscious. He always attacked in the same way, and seemed to derive exactly the same joy from the butterfly boy's anguish. Conscious pleasure, on the contrary, seems to require a steady and continual augmentation of the stimulus, since comparison of the pleasing sensation with the ingrained memory of that sensation will gradually devalue it. This explains why the higher order connoisseurs must inevitably shuck their rubbers after beginning years, and hence contract sexual diseases.

The butterfly boy took as long as he could in buckling his galoshes. (He could do all the buckles now.) The other boys were shouting: Come on out! Don't be a sissypants! —When he came out, they started to clap and shout. Their heads swiveled expectantly toward the pile of ice where the bully lived. The bully began to gnaw very rapidly on his lower lip. His eyes rolled. The he screeched, raised his arms, and rushed down upon the butterfly boy like death.

Don't you dare hurt him!   a big girl shouted. She ran up to the bully and punched him as hard as she could. The bully cowered away. He began to sob hoarsely. Instantly the other boys forgot about the butterfly boy. They threw delighted snowballs at the bully and called him a nasty stupid retard. The bully sat down. A steaming yellow stain began to form in the snow around him. The boys laughed and the girls whispered.

The butterfly boy did not join in the attack upon his enemy.

He went to the part of the playground where the girls played, and stood timidly beside the big girl.

You can't play here, the big girl said. But I wish you were a girl, so I could play with you. You're so cute.

The butterfly boy was silent. He went slowly back to the other boys.

14.

The boys had declared war against the girls. Girls were ugly. Girls were sissies. Girls polluted the playground just by being there. It was an outrage that the boys would have to breath the same air the girls did. They ran them down, shouting and knocking them to the icy asphalt and pulling their hair. Yowling, the girls scratched back. It was not a precisely coordinated campaign of gun butts and pickaxes because these were boys who soon would be upstanding Eagle Scouts, lighting fires, prancing about in jungle-green uniforms, holding lighted torches aloft to conduct smoke-signaled conversations with one another about the sizes of various girls' boobs, stealing each other's neckerchief rings, farting into each other's faces, striding through the woods without ever getting lost; thus to the teacher who sat sipping her coffee indoors and very occasionally glancing out the window, it seemed as if her pupils were playing exactly as usual, a bit more boisterously, perhaps; the girls were not jumping rope, which was odd or maybe not so odd since they had been doing that every day; they appeared to be mingling with the boys most energetically, which was all to the good, the teacher thought, and maybe she was right because when the bell did ring and the pupils came in they bore no wounds more serious than bruises, from which it follows that it had all been in fun. So they captured the big girl and tried to figure out what to do with her. Then they remembered the butterfly boy. —Make him kiss her! a boy shouted.

What they wanted was to degrade and brutalize. The girl would be tortured by being kissed, because it was a universal truth that kissing was disgusting, and because everyone would be watching. The butterfly boy would be likewise raped by the procedure, although it was unfortunately possible that he might rise a little in their esteem by becoming their instrument. All in all, the scheme was as elegant as it was practical. One must admire such cleverness.

For precisely the same reason that they did not subject one of their own to this humiliation, they did not lay hands on the butterfly boy. He was not one of them. His closest kinship was with the bully. He was untouchable, a prostitute, an eater of dirt. There was thus no need to force him. Because what they demanded of him was disgusting, he would do it of his own accord. That way there could certainly be no trouble, for if any crime were about to be committed, it was not theirs, but his. —Another point for cleverness.

And weren't they right? No free will, bravery, or self-confidence could be attributed to this creature. He came when they called him.

It was always possible that the end-of-recess bell might strike if he stalled them, but he could not walk too slowly or something worse would be done, so he watched the glossy black tips of his galoshes crunch down upon the white snow with spurious deliberation. With every step, the playground contracted, tightening the ritual bond between himself and the other victim. The crowd of boys had pulled in close. They had been shouting and then they had been quiet and the girl had screamed and then they had shouted again. Now they parted silently to let him through. He did not look into their eyes. He gazed only at the crouching girl, who no longer screamed or struggled. One of the big boys yanked her hair hard.

He was almost upon her now, and he had no knowledge of what he was going to do. But it was not up to him to know what he was going to do. His act would rise up red like a pepper, a penis, a pistil of a tropical orchid. Of course he did not think in those terms. He did not think. The world was now no larger than the slanting plane between the toe of galoshes and her straining face, teeth clenched in fear and hate, neck corded like a tree trunk down to the collar of her sweater; she was jerking and gasping like an animal in the boys' unescapable hands, her nostrils drawn almost flat as she sucked in breath to face him and the butterfly boy took one more step and now there were no more steps left to take. The boys' hands fell away from her as the circle tightened about them both like an anus. They wanted to see her go mad, no doubt, running about, kicking and scratching and clawing at the butterfly boy (no danger of her escape). Her eyes slammed themselves down to slits. She didn't recognize or remember him. He reached slowly toward her and she stood stock still as he pulled the hood of her parka back up over her head because he knew only that she was shivering, and she glared at him for a moment and shook the hood back down just as a dog shakes itself dry and he embraced her.

He kissed her the only way he knew how, as he would have kissed his mother's cheek or his aunt's cheek or the cheek of any of the nice ladies who came to visit. (The other boys made loud noises of revulsion.) He felt something happening to her but he did not understand what it was. He said: I love you.

Then she was squeezing him back in tight defiance. —I love you, too, she said.

The boys made barely feigned vomiting sounds. They raised their fists in horror.

Teacher's looking! a boy shouted.

Get the bully! Get the bully!

The bully stormed bellowing down from his hillock, and they dropped back to form a line that would protect them from implication but insure that the girl and the butterfly boy could not escape punishment. What a horrible spectacle it had been to see them enjoying themselves! —Beat 'em up, retard! a boy shrieked, and the bully snorted like an ox and was just about to fall upon them with feet and fists when he recognized the girl who had beaten him, stopped, and slunk away.

Teacher's coming, teacher's coming!

The boys exploded into individual atoms, fleeing everywhere, circling the other girls like maddened sharks (what the girls had been doing the butterfly boy would never know), and the girl and the butterfly boy were by themselves.

Are we going to get married? she said.

This eventuality had not occurred to then butterfly boy before, but now that she had said it, it became the only conceivable choice. He nodded.

For the rest of the school year he considered them engaged, but in the fall he learned that her family also had moved away.

Hanover, New Hampshire, U.S.A. (1968)

From
"Under the Grass" in *The Atlas*

This is the most extended literary account of perhaps the single most significant event in Vollmann's life: the death of his sister Julie in a pond where he and she were swimming. For other descriptions of this primal scene, see "Three Meditations on Death" and "The Grave of Lost Stories." —LM

YOUR LITTLE SKULL'S A light-globe to help my shadow lead me as you did when I was your brother, older than you but small like you, afraid of the toilet's cool skull-gape at night. You always held my hand. Now please take me down the slippery dark path, down between the crowds of palms to the lava-walled, frond-curtained river of broad and rapid waterfalls. Until now I've scrubbed at the stain of your face on my brain's floor, your sky, your headstone—I never wanted you to come back! But whenever you did (your ghost some ignored dog to raise itself hopefully at every word), I convinced myself that you loved me most, because when I thought of you I thought of you alone. Can't you understand that I'm afraid of you? (You're only *caput mortuum*.) Now take me to you.

(Thus my briefless brevet, blotted, illegally disquisitive, which must be sealed with a crimson spider.)

Under your moldy stone, you radicate where the lava's tapestried with mossy crotches, ferns, leaves dark and pale so subdivided into heart-leaflets as to baffle my eyes. Within all this fineness, almost as fine as the humid air, I find something finer still, a spiderweb on whose lattices hang a huge yellowbodied spider, vertical, legs wide and strong, waiting. Closing my screams with phosphorite consolations of words that hiss out like hollow jets of flame, I uncrumble your chamber's riddled copper to reach you lying in the black dirt's guts. I sweep back your hair, breach your skullhelm in the muggish air. From behind your hinges and bismite-yellow pivots the crimson spider scuttles out. He rushes on his sister with a bravery as bitter as camphor, determined to gnaw her as I once effaced you with my exclusionary conceit. But the golden one snaps him up. His legs fibrillate. A single crimson droplet tumbles from strand to strand, is drunk by my warrant now validated:

They told me to take care because you were littler, but I forgot. Brawny ropes of water captured you. The fishes asked to drink your gurgling breaths. The mud asked to kiss your eyes. The sand asked to fill your mouth. The weeds asked to sprout inside your ears. Outside the night skull, a tunnel of blue light led you to India. Inside the night skull, your blood became cold brown water.

They said: Where's your sister?

They said: Where's your sister?

When the sea draws away from lava-islands, a thousand rills of white run down, like Grandfather's hair-roots. When the water dribbled out of you as the desperate divers breathed into your mouth, each drop was whitish-blue with the lymph of your death.

That night I had not yet drunk the ginger of sunlight that made my soul walk widdershins: My little sister was dead! No one had liked me, but now everyone would be nice to me because you were dead. I had not yet drunk the perfervid ginger of sunlight because our mother and father came to my bed with the minister to say to my night skull: *Julie is dead*. Choking, I turned to the wall until they left. Fat white tears rolled like pure light behind bamboo. In the morning my tears became a waterfall partially and temporarily catching itself on ledges. —I heard your sister died, they said. —I nodded with tinsel rectitude. I had the passkey to peachworms. Your death was a great gift you gave me.

Your coffin, that closed vacuole, went bitch-hunting for the blackest dog of all, the black and rotting bitch called earth, whose nipples feed leeches, rats, worms and moles, her ill-assorted blind sucking whelps. —Suck the blackest opium-tinctured drop, said the minister as they lowered you down the ropes.

Immensely long skinny leaves of fear (spider lily, *crinum asiaticum*) grew around my throat every night like thick sad trees over a lava hole where the sea comes sadly in. You rushed as a yellow skeleton into every dream. If I screamed myself awake, you waited until the long skinny leaves of sleep choked me back to you again. You came clacking and scuttling like a yellow spider until I screamed crimson tears. A package arrived from the post office of dreams and you skittered out to punish me. Something smelled bad in my closet and everyone knew that you were rotting there. I walked a hotly endless course of graves that suddenly whirled like marble trap doors beneath my feet to pitch me down to black liquescent corpses whose stench screamed through my dreams.

Our parents gave me a toy of yours to totemize you by and told me to keep it forever because you were never coming back. When they were gone, I buried it in the garbage so that it couldn't hurt me with its horrifying screams.

Outside the night skull, you looked for me to hold your hand, but I only screamed.

Sometimes we used to visit your headstone, under which your bones lunged muffled in black dirt. Our mother would cry but I tried not to cry because then you would hear me and get me.

I made your birthday gutter out like wax-light and stumbled the slime-slaked anniversary of your death. I forgot every word you ever said and the sound of your voice and how we played like salamanders, but Mother mothballed your dresses in a cedarwood chest where every year they went smaller and yellower (although I never looked) as your face grew along with mine. Now you're my white witch.

Suppose I'd never done what they never said I did, my execution-eering I mean, would I still have been brazed to ferocity year by year by the memory of your blue face? My blood-writing has quarried you, but I wish that you were still my sister, dancing above the grass.

Some Thoughts on Neglected Water Taps

In this afterword to Michael A. Smith's book of photographs, *The Students of Deep Springs College,* Vollmann offers a series of amusing, self-deprecating anecdotes about some of his memorable experiences at Deep Springs and his recognition about how these formed a touchstone for living.

NO ONE CAN UNDERSTAND Deep Springs without reference to the "Grey Book" of the founder, Lucien Lucius Nunn. Deep Springs is a (usually) all-male junior college through which good, bad and mediocre students and faculty have passed. So what? Deep Springs is a cattle ranch. As a cattle ranch, Deep Springs is not especially efficient. How could it be? The wise, grizzled ranch manager often has one professional farmer to help him, but most of his other irrigators, ditch-diggers, feed men and roundup cattle-branders are novices who learn on the job—or not.

I myself have no idea as to whether on balance I was a good or bad feed man. I never overslept or broke anything. But I remember quite well the winter morning when the ranch manager, Mr. Holloway, whom I idolized, said to me with a grim little laugh, "Are you making a skating rink, Bill?" and I realized I'd forgotten to shut off the water in one of the cattle troughs. I'm only grateful that no calf slipped on the ice and broke a leg.

I also remember the first time when as irrigator I noticed that one of the rainbirds wasn't spinning. If I didn't fix it, that patch of alfalfa would stay thirsty. So I shut down the wheel line, opened the rainbird in question, and discovered inside the incredibly compacted corpse of a mouse which had evidently gotten sucked into the intake valve, drowned, and crushed into a furry, cylindrical occlusion. What to do? Removing the plastic toothpick of my Swiss army knife, I pried the dead thing out. Then I pressured up the line again. Every rainbird whirled happily; every water-jet made a rainbow. I felt proud. I wiped the toothpick on my shirt and picked my teeth with it. Here was I, a pimply teenager unloved by girls, a clumsy, four-eyed sort with no previous experience of manual labor (my father and grandfather were both machine shop whizzes, and I'd never even been able to hammer a nail straight), and in spite of all this I'd actually been able to fix something. Probably Mr. Holloway could have done it in five seconds without even turning off the water; and he wouldn't have been impelled into any rituals of triumphant adolescent savagery. I must have wasted fifteen minutes on this operation. That's why I say that the ranch would undoubtedly turn a more consistent profit without students like me.

I remember the physical work I did in the valley with joy. It was all for a purpose, and we ourselves often got to decide how to perform it. We were responsible; we succeeded or failed, and the results directly affected our community. And everywhere around us, the land was lovely beyond description, a beauty that grew on me with the seasons. Sinking my left hand-hook into hay bales as I crouched on the bed of "my" 1953 Chevy feed truck, which I'd left in gear so that it bumbled across the desert by itself (a method of driving no doubt highly approved by the California Department of Motor Vehicles), I slashed twine, then kicked the alfalfa off into the snow. Black cows loomed beautifully in the fog, waiting to eat. In the spring everything would be olive-green; in the summer, grey and bright, with arrowheads twinkling at dusk. I remember petroglyphs and pictographs, snowy mountains and lizards in the heat; it was all heaven.

As for my academic experiences, well, I was the only student in Dr. Mawby's biology class. And when he'd say, "Does anyone know the phylum of the polychaete flatworm?" I'd look around to make sure, but "anyone" was always me. I was only a B student, but I loved Dr. Mawby for his immense knowledge, patience, and corny deadpan jokes. He was the perfect teacher. How could he not have been? I had every opportunity to learn, and no excuses. Sometimes we'd go to places in the valley or the mountains that Dr. Mawby knew (the land was his; he'd written the article on Death Valley for the *Britannica*); and he'd show me the living or fossilized truth of the words he'd just uttered in the classroom. Everything was whole and logical. That too was perfect.

At the request of another student from my home town, my philosophy teacher, Alan Paskow, hosted a series of sessions in "applied philosophy" in which we first defined the meaning of life, then built upon that definition to suggest specific improvements which we could make at Deep Springs itself. And we *were* Deep Springs; we were the minds and also the ditch-diggers. The place was ours. Within L. L. Nunn's gentle limits, we were free to make of it what we would.

I remember my solar energy teacher, Peter Lehmann. We spent the first semester studying thermodynamics. For the second semester we used thermodynamics to conceptualize a practical project which would be useful and also save the college energy. We decided to build a solar hot water system for the dairy barn. And we built it. Every now and then my nails went in straight. My friend Jake, who later became a mechanical engineer, deserves principal credit for the magnificent truss which still adorns the dairy barn roof. The solar collectors, alas, have long since become useless relics. Thus the typical doom of most Deep Springs projects, for each new student body reinvents the wheel. But they worked splendidly for a few years; it used to make me proud to see them.

About the female faculty I can only say that (as were many of my classmates) I was hopelessly in love with all of them. Peter's wife Carolyn Polese used to critique my short stories for me. Alan's wife Jackie was my French teacher, and I still remember the excitement of reading Gide, Malraux and Proust in the original—looking up every third word in the dictionary, to be sure, for I've never been good at languages. Sharon Schuman, who with her husband David taught English composition and public speaking, was fearsomely logical and hard to please. It was hard to get a sloppy composition past her. I was crazy about her.

I remember listening to David read his short stories aloud at night, and longing to write short stories just like him. (Jake wrote short stories, too, some of them quite beautiful and all of them sincere. At Deep Springs it was pretty ordinary to write prose in the morning and weld a truss in the afternoon.) I remember sitting down to dinner in the boarding house next to Dr. Mawby and his shy wife Diane, with some new question about why butterflies were related to shrimp; probably I was wearing the castoff coveralls I'd found in the "bonepile" downstairs, for I would have just come back from the feed run at that hour; the coveralls reeked of gasoline, dirt, blood and grease. Since I got up early for the morning run, I often slept in those coveralls. Come to think of it, I really must have smelled bad. But Dr. Mawby never said an unkind thing.

None of this would have any relevance without the Grey Book. The dream of L. L. Nunn was that his graduates would serve the world somehow. A good blacksmith served as well as a good President, Nunn said. What if that was true? What if my remembering or forgetting to turn off the water on the feed trough actually made a difference? (It obviously did.) What if philosophy could be applied right down to making suggestions about the curriculum? (It could.) What if Dr. Mawby really cared about helping me learn? (He liked me; he always helped me; he was my friend.) What if I could go out and do good? Of course I'd fail most of the time, just as I usually failed at Deep Springs. One student, a sullen gifted painter whom I admired mainly at a distance, because he detested me, even said that the point of Deep Springs was *learning how to fail*. And there's much truth in that. Often the rainbird will get stuck and we can't figure out how to remove the dead mouse. But we can also learn *from* our failures, and try in our small way to do good.

A few years ago in south Thailand I met a twelve-year-old girl whose father had sold her into prostitution in order to pay for a new roof. I asked this child if she liked her job, and she told me she didn't, because the men often hit her, and sometimes she got diseases. So I kidnapped her and put her in a girls' school in Bangkok. It was scary, and I might have failed; I might have left the water tap on and gotten her and me hurt. But I didn't. I helped that girl. I didn't solve all her problems, but I got her to a place where she could choose what to do next. And we tested her; she didn't have AIDS. One of my guiding principles in that kidnapping was the maxim we'd derived in the applied philosophy class at Deep Springs: We ought to identify and empathize with the physical and moral order of the universe, whatever that may be, and we should help others do the same. It was that second clause which operated here. I just did my best to take her someplace where the universe might be easier for her to empathize with. Sometimes doing my best has brought about disasters, but (as Alan Paskow convinced me in his Heidegger-Wittgenstein class) it's almost always better to do your best, and do *something,* than to do nothing out of fear of making mistakes or causing evil. I'm not talking about mindless, self-righteous activism. I'm talking about doing the best job you can to fix a problem you really *know* about. The blacksmith shouldn't walk right into the Oval Office and be President. He's got to do a little reading and flesh-pressing first. For that matter, the President is unlikely to make a horseshoe on his first attempt. People who want to ban female circumcision without ever having seen it, or people who just know that the Serbs are bad because the television says so, may well be correct about both issues. But if in the background some water trough unmentioned by the television has begun to overflow, those do-gooders might not see it; and their neglect might cause harm. Deep Springs taught me to go and see things for myself, to get the best information about problems I could, to worry a lot and plan a lot, until the unfamiliar became comprehensible, and only then (crossing my fingers and hoping for the best) to *do* my best. For what does a Deep Springs education ask of us, if not to do our best? Since we've been given every opportunity, we now have no excuses.

List of "Contemporary" Books Most Admired by Vollmann (1990)

When I first interviewed him in 1990, Vollmann immediately caught me off guard after I posed the usual question about which contemporary authors he most admired, by remarking dryly, "By 'contemporary' I'll assume you mean from the last two hundred years." Then, before I had time to protest or fully digest the implications of what he'd just said, he began rattling off the names of writers and books included in this list. As his list grew, I found myself reacting first with surprise (these were not the citations I'd expected) and embarrassment (I'd never even heard of at least a third of the references), mixed in with the sneaking suspicion that he was putting me on.

But in fact Bill was being dead serious here: his perspective on literature is broad enough that he actually does consider nineteenth-century authors to be his contemporaries. And in retrospect, the list he supplies here turns out to be extremely revealing—just not in the way I had anticipated. For example, given his own predilection for constructing elaborate encyclopedic narratives, one would assume he'd cite Pynchon, Burroughs, Coover, Gaddis, and other contemporaries who'd produced analogous, grandly ambitious "mega-works" early in their careers. But, other than the names of several science fiction authors, the list of authors and works he supplied were almost completely devoid of just about anything that could be described as "contemporary." As it turns out, contemporary fiction is one of the few areas of literature Bill has consciously avoided; this "gap" is relative, of course—thus, I later learned he had read *Gravity's Rainbow* (though only after completing *You Bright and Risen Angels*—"I never really saw the connection [with Pynchon]," he added; he was also an admirer of Burroughs's work, although he was quick to note that it was "Lautréamont, not Burroughs" who had most influenced *You Bright and Risen Angels*).

And although I hardly recognized it at the time, from today's perspective it's obvious that this list—with its casual intermingling of European, American, and Japanese authors, and its quirky mixture of multi-volume Scandinavian epics, pulp science fiction (by Blish, Dick, and Miller), political satires by Eastern Europeans, American documentary works (Evans and Agee's classic study of life in the Dust Bowl era), Gnostic fantasies (Lindsay), and the like—actually does offer a fascinating glimpse into the eclectic array of sources that helped shape his literary sensibility. —LM

1./2./3. Right now it seems like I've learned a lot from Mishima, Kawabata, and Tolstoy;

4. Hawthorne may be the best;

5. Then Faulkner;

6. Hemingway is usually a wonderful read, especially *Islands in the Stream* and *For Whom the Bell Tolls*—that is to say, the grandly suicidal narratives;

7. Tadeusz Konwicki's *A Dreambook for Our Time* is beautiful;

8. I also love everything I've read by Pär Lagerkvist;

9. Sigrid Undset's trilogy, *Kristin Lavransdatter;*

10. Multatuli's *Max Havelaar, or the Coffee Auctions of the Dutch Trading Company;*

11. Kundera's *Laughable Loves;*

12. Andrea Freud Lowenstein's *This Place* (which deserves more recognition than it has received);

13. Jane Smiley's *The Greenlanders* (which I had the wonderful experience of finding and reading a few months after completing my own book about Greenlanders, *The Ice-Shirt*);

14. Evans and Agee's *Let Us Now Praise Famous Men;*

15. Farley Mowat's *The People of the Deer;*

16. The first three books of Mishima's *Sea of Fertility* tetralogy (how could I have forgotten that?);

17. Random bits of Proust, Zola's *L'Assommoir;*

18. Shusaku Endo's *The Samurai;*
19. The first two books of Mervyn Peake's *Gormenghast* trilogy;
20. William Hope Hodgson's *The Night Land;*
21. Poe's stories about love;
22. Everything by Malraux (especially his *Anti-Memoirs*);
23. Nabokov's *Glory* and *Transparent Things* and *Ada;*
24. Melville's *Pierre;*
25. Thomas Bernhard's *Correction;*
26. David Lindsay's *Voyage to Arcturus;*
27. Philip K. Dick's *A Scanner Darkly;*
28. A few of Böll's short novels *Wo warst du, Adam?* and *The Train Was on Time;*
29. Walter M. Miller's *A Canticle for Leibowitz;*
30. James Blish's *Cities in Flight* tetralogy (which is just plain fun);
31. The first three volumes of Lawrence Durrell's Alexandria Quartet;
32. Elsa Morante's *History: A Novel.*

Bill concluded by saying "There's lots more," adding that he was "sorry not to be able to put down less contemporary things such as *The Tale of Genji,* which is one of my all-time favorites. But you did say 'contemporary,' didn't you?" —LM

From "The Ghost of Magnetism"

From *Thirteen Stories and Thirteen Epitaphs*

SPEAK MEMORY. This excerpt—taken from the opening of the novella that launches Vollmann's 1993 collection, *Thirteen Stories and Thirteen Epitaphs*—describes a farewell party Vollmann's friends threw for him in the late eighties, just as he was about to leave San Francisco with his girlfriend Janice to live in Manhattan. Vollmann uses the occasion of this extended farewell to create a loving portrait of the friends and experiences that comprised the Edenic world that had nurtured his growth as a writer and as a man during the previous decade. Vollmann opens the story by immediately establishing its central device—the use of San Francisco as a kind of crystal ball whose curved surface enables him to gaze on images of his past that have been distorted by the effects of memory and nostalgia. He then introduces the phrase "I remember" as a Proustian device—the sights and sounds of the present moment serving as departure points connecting him to fragments of his cherished past via the process of memory and imagination. Moving backward and forward in time, the remainder of the story thus unfolds as a rush of vividly drawn character portraits of friends and lovers, and of hallucinatory vignettes that collide unexpectedly as they are spontaneously conjured up by Vollmann in sharply etched, sensuous prose that recalls Kerouac at his most incandescent. One of the most startling displays in all of Vollmann's work of his remarkable powers of memory, "Ghost" simultaneously evokes his tragic awareness of the limits of memory and art. Thus even as we witness Vollmann's furious effort to give expression (and hence preserve) these precious shards of "memory flesh" before he forgets them, we recognize he already senses that even his own remarkable powers as an artist are helpless to counter the forces of change and loss—that everything is already rushing away from him and slipping into the dark emptiness of the undifferentiated past. —LM

> *After running full speed through the green segment of your route, you reach a point where you realize that more care is needed. An imaginary yellow light is flashing and demands that you make more exact use of the Orienteering skills you have learned. It is a matter of locating and passing all the checkpoints you have on your map that lead you in the right direction.*
>
> —**Bjorn Kjellstrom,**
> ***Be Expert with Map and Compass (1976)***

Tremblings of the Needle

Before I had even gone away, I started polishing San Francisco as if it were a pair of glasses to look through and every *new* thing dust and dandruff; so the day of the farewell party gleamed and curved the world to the degree required by my nearsightedness: I remember the breeze as we stood on the deck of the ferry; hot sun on faces, shoulders and railings; my friends with their coolers and picnic baskets; and the Bay all around and everything perfect (which is to say ready-polished), Margaret smiling (she had arranged this ocean occasion as a surprise), and the greenness of Angel Island just ahead with people playing frisbee and the good smells of barbecue coming over the water; while I stood so happy to be with my friends, wondering who else might already be waiting on Angel Island as part of the surprise. As I looked into their faces, they seemed to me so dearly lovable—in part, I think, on account of the effort and expense they had gone to for me, which proved that they cared about me; but I like to think that had I provided the party for them it would have been the same; I was already burnishing them so delicately that their very failings had become endearing. —Beside me stood Martin in the sunlight, squinting and holding onto the railing with both hands. Too often I had considered him spineless, insipid, unintelligent. When he spoke it was difficult to pay attention to him, for he stuttered and rambled. But today he seemed to me submissive like Christ, with a gentle, timid childishness that needed to be loved and protected. How could I forget the journeys that he and I had taken together, the midnights when we had driven home through the Central Valley, when it was warm and the sky was greenish-grey, the fields greyish-black; and through the open window of the truck came the smell of alfalfa? We saw cars (very few, very late), and white road-dots gleamed in our headlights, and we played good old songs over and over in the cassette player and for hours our neighbor was the humid presence of fields. Now on the ferry he was quiet, for large groups intimidated him. I remembered ascending the steep gorges of dry mountains ten years before and being desperately thirsty, my lips grainy with blood and salt, and finding Martin at last and asking for water, Martin taking off his pack so patiently and handing his canteen to me, and the goodness and sweetness of that water. —Chubby Monique sat behind us, letting the wind flutter her sweatshirt, laughing and hugging her lover, Vera, whose narrow little face had sometimes been for me a banner of boredom, but which today suggested serenity. How limited I had been, that I had not always seen her that way! As for Monique, her laughter opened up her face in an unaffected way, and I suddenly understood that what I had sometimes mistaken in her for rudeness or selfishness was nothing less than honesty. I had never known Monique and Vera well, it occurred to me now, but I recalled the time when we had gone out to dinner together at some vegetarian Chinese place or other in the Richmond and I took a liking to them both because from appetizer to dessert they behaved as purely as butter virgins, feeding each other with the same spoon, nourishing each other with Calistoga water; then I felt a sharp pang as though I were excluded from something, and I longed to see them at home, where among the plump hard pillows of their futon, or condensing on the dark-lobed underleaves of their many houseplants, their innermost tendernesses must live, freshened by a thousand kisses, guarded and protected by the horned ram-skulls that hung on the walls; and although I could never see this it made me inexpressibly grateful that I might at least know of it; and the pang I felt, of loneliness or jealousy, was not unpleasing, because I imagined that these two and their love would at least dwell *near* me forever, increasing luxuriously like every other good thing. But presently Monique began complaining of not feeling well, and at dessert she scarcely opened her mouth when Vera lifted the spoon to her, but sat there drooping. —Baby, did you forget your pills again? said Vera. The other woman nodded miserably. Then she groaned, and pitched forward into her plate. —Vera cried out and half rose in her chair and said goddamn oh why did this have to happen again? She was wringing her hands, and her face was shiny with tears. I looked around me for the waiter, and saw that everyone in the restaurant had gathered around us staring with big spooky eyes like the cows in the south field would do when Martin and I had butchered a steer and the blood ran across the concrete floor of the slaughterhouse and through the corner drainpipe, sinking into the soft alfalfa of the south field, sinking, sinking underground to swell that dark black river of blood that must run beneath the Sierras and through the sewers of Sacramento and probably all the way to San Francisco but first the other cows smelled it and gathered around the slaughterhouse, staring with black-masked eyes from whitish faces in the hot twilight, staring at the trickling blood, at Martin and me—and Vera and I wiped the milky sticky dessert rice out of Monique's face with a wet napkin; we left some money on the table, and then Vera slung her friend over her shoulder and carried her out to the car; she did not want me to help. The willless arms and legs swung hideously; the Volkswagen shuddered home, stalling at almost every intersection. I sat with the unconscious girl in the back seat. Neither Vera nor I said a word. When we turned down the hill onto Mars Street, with the lights of San Francisco below us and then the soothing darkness of the Bay and the dense low ridge of lights that was Berkeley, Monique's eyes snapped open and then she closed them again, sighing and shaking her head and grinding her face in my lap, and I said how bad do you feel Monique? and Vera had turned off the ignition and was saying take it easy honey we're home now I'll put you to bed, and I lifted Monique's head as slowly as I could, but she had become still paler and her face and hands were sweaty and she said I'm going to be sick, so Vera rushed to open the door for her and carried her out and said I'm with you darling I'm holding you, and she laid her gently down where the grass was softest and knelt beside her and raised her head up into her lap, stroking her temples with such love and gentleness, and

Monique began to retch and Vera was kissing her head all over and saying that's a good doll that's right I'm here with you I won't let anything bad happen to you so go ahead and let it come out you'll feel better, but Monique started moaning no no and she pulled away from Vera and sat up trembling with her eyes starting from her head and I heard a gulping noise deep in her throat and she was struggling feebly with her little hands to push Vera away and Vera said to me or herself shit here she goes again this is the part I hate the worst and Monique whispered *don't touch me I'm the Ghost of Magnetism!* and I thought what the *hell* and I heard her teeth chattering and she said no don't spin me but Vera only said come on honey you can't feel better till you throw up and Monique wailed what have I *done* to you that you're trying to make me—oh! and she slumped in Vera's arms and Vera explained to me you see she *hates* to throw up and I said ah and I said but what does she mean exactly by the Ghost of Magnetism? and Vera said distractedly it's not *her* it's Elaine Suicide and I said what about her? and Vera ran her hands through her hair and said oh God that girl cracks me up she just *slays* me I wonder if she learned to talk like that at her rebirthing class . . . but I knew that Vera was not telling me the truth, that this was some secret between her and Monique which their skulls and houseplants guarded like a rain forest's mystery; as for Elaine Suicide, whom I knew well, she had never to my knowledge taken a rebirthing class; nor had she confessed to any kinship with the eighteenth-century French physicists who played the compass false for the greater good; anyhow, Monique finally threw up and felt better. Now she and her lover were happy and laughing on the ferry, and I did not want to leave them and never see their Volkswagen again, whose windows were precariously held on with duct tape; I wanted to keep knowing them whether they laughed or cried, but even if I had been the Grand Demon of Magnetism at the center of the compass dial I would *still* have to vomit them up, along with the sweet water that Martin gave me, because I was leaving. —It was the same with all the others, who were spending the day with me for the last time, making a constellation of remembrance for me that I could not keep in my sky, no matter how much I wanted to, and they did not have and never had had any faults: —neither Margaret, who had never complained when I turned the stereo up loud, nor earnest Paul and

Nancy who sat together as quiet as Quakers and left early, nor Elaine Suicide who lay sulking prettily in the sun as she had done at the beach when I drew sketches of her naked; nor old Laddie the hobo, who was more lovingly patient than Santa Claus (when he was not drunk); once when he and Elaine and I were coming back from the beach and Elaine had to drive round and round the block looking for parking until she was close to tears, Laddie simply beamed and said well, how *nice* that we get to look at the view! Elaine, I sure hope you don't run out of gas! —yessir, Laddie was as perfect a being as Sharie the pathologist who let me eat all her ice cream or Painter Ben who had invited me to Thanksgiving dinner every year, because he was once lonely himself and so at holidays he had all the losers like me over for Thanksgiving, but I never went, preferring to get depressed alone over cheap and watery food in my chilly flat (although of course I was *never* as depressed as Elaine Suicide) and I wished now as I stood behind Ben on the ferry that I had come over more often to watch football on Sundays, that I had been at all his grand dinners (Vera and Monique always came)—as if I could *collect* them somehow in an album of imperishability, in which I could always see Ben's kitchen table where I used to sit down with him over spaghetti piled with the bright red meat sauce that he made by the quart and stored in the freezer along with packages of frozen spinach and squash puree, and the phone rang for Ben and the phone rang for Ben and I ate spaghetti to my heart's content; even Elaine, who seldom agreed with people, did not hesitate to say that when you ate at Painter Ben's house there was always more than enough to eat, which was both good and necessary as I had learned since Ben had once gone camping for six weeks with me and lost fifteen pounds on my food, which is why he now had another helping; and the phone rang for Ben and Ben said *that* one wanted me to take her climbing with me! and I said what did you tell her? and Ben grinned and said I told her no and I said she bores you? and Ben said *sex* bores me more and more and I said Ben you can jerk off to my girlfriend's picture anytime you want and Ben said I only jerk off to hundred dollar bills and the phone rang for Ben; after dinner he'd lead me down into his basement where everything smelled of paint and Ben said these paint-fume chemicals must sure be fucking me up but you know what? I don't care, because I don't *want* to be normal!

and upstairs the phone rang for Ben and we played around at marbleizing and stippling his paints on practice squares of masonite because there was *money* to be made in such projects, as evinced by the subtly marbled walls of the beauty parlor on Polk Street where the Handcuff Queen served you wine as she permed you; so Painter Ben, who made money because he bid high with calm conviction and worked very fast, had learned to make masonite look like agate or jasper or tiger's eye; he could turn a piece of cardboard into a vanilla tombstone; he could marbleize any rich bitch's fireplace into translucent mauve and porphyry and he was so handsome with his moustache, his iridescent blue-green eyes, his outdoor face whose cheeks creased widely whenever he smiled, that women were always calling his answering machine; yes indeed, in his way Painter Ben was perfect, like weather-beaten blonde Megan, who had once been the beauty queen of Georgia, whom I had a crush on, so one very cold New Year's Eve in Berkeley I was doing everything I could to get Megan to go to bed with me like a magnetic flux line desiring to encircle the sweetest electric current and my friend Seth wished me luck and Megan spent hours cleaning her room and primping herself for her great date with me and my heart pounded *ba*-BOOM! *ba*-BOOM! with excitement at the thought that I would most certainly screw Megan, who had just graduated with honors from her safe sex seminar; and like all generals on the eve of victory I reflected on my long and cunning campaign of love-notes to Megan hidden in the closets, in the bathroom behind the toilet roll, in the kitchen under the nutmeg jar, to say nothing of love-notes boldly written summer and winter on the bulletin board or even on the back of Megan's junk mail—but always, it must be said, plotted and thrillingly accomplished when I was visiting Seth and Megan was out so that Megan would be surprised; and Megan had laughed and kissed me and her hair smelled like all the flowers of Georgia; therefore, as Seth and I strolled across the Berkeley campus that night passing the time by singing "Helplessly Hoping" and inspecting leaves and trees while Megan made herself perfect for me, I slammed my fist into my palm and said   Seth I've *got* her I *know* I do!   and Seth said sincerely that would be *so wonderful!*   and Seth said   look at this pinnate leaf structure   and Seth said   Megan must really be smitten she's working so hard to fix herself up   and I said   I can hardly wait!   and the globe-lights shone hopefully through all the pinnate leaves even as we went jogging valiantly home where we heard the hair dryer purring Megan's promise and Megan called from the bathroom almost ready guys and Seth nudged me with his bony elbow and winked, right as Megan came out, and she was so beautiful and Seth grinned and said see you later pal and I said oh Megan and hugged her and buttoned up her coat for her and took her hand and we went running, running, with the New Year's Eve darkness stinging and refreshing our foreheads, and Megan was laughing and I thought soon I will be kissing this lovely face (a privilege which in fact she was to refuse me over white wine in the Thai restaurant as I sat looking into her eyes thinking well *that's* a fine how-d'you-do which translates into *now* what do we do? —even though we did have fun just the same, skipping hand in hand down Shattuck Avenue at midnight singing "What Did the Deep Sea Say?" at the top of our voices so that everyone stared at us) and when we got back to Megan's house she turned on the space heater; sitting beside her close enough to touch her cheek if that had been granted me I said well if you won't let me *sleep* with you can I at least *kiss* you? and Megan said no and I said well if you won't let me *kiss* you can I *hold your hand*? and Megan smiling said you know I don't believe you can! and I said well all right and went upstairs to Seth's absent sister's hard cold bed on which I sat all night, the better to stare sulkily down at the floor immediately beneath which my former beauty queen was even at that moment (I presumed) sleeping happily alone with her face glowing pink in the light of her space heater and her hair radiating away from her to instruct her lucky pillows in all the directions; I felt so heartsore and anguished and sorry for myself that I never even lay down although I certainly longed for morphines and semi-morphines to close my swollen eyes but the next day was next year and it was bright and sunny and cold and I felt deliciously debauched with grief as Seth and I drove up the coast singing "Chalk Up Another One, Another Broken Heart" and walked in the woods chewing tree-sap and we astounded Seth's father with the vampire-blood capsules that Megan had given me last night for a present and I was as happy as could be; Megan was perfect, even if I never saw her again (for you must not imagine that all these friends of mine came to Margaret's surprise party or were even invited; Margaret did not know them all and even if she had known them I don't think she'd have asked them because they would have hated each other); —speaking of which, I must not omit to praise the perfection of Mark Dagger, who once said to me if there's one thing I love in this world—no, *two* things . . . *three* things!—it's **DRUGS, PUSSY** and **GUNS!** *I* said it first: FUCK apple pie, baseball, a-a-and hot dogs! It's all about *drugs, pussy, guns!* —while beside him Dickie swivelled his pale shaven head left and right, left and right, as if it were on greased bearings, and he clasped and unclasped his hands and said now Dagger don't forget beer! And beer! and beer!— Beer! shouted Dagger. —WHISKEEEEEEY! screamed Dickie. —One ice cube, sighed Dagger lovingly, make it a triple shot! —Alcohol! said Dickie. *—Codeine!* said Dagger. More alcohol! said Dickie. —But I *do* love acid, Dagger brooded, and Dickie said yeah I remember you on acid, all right; you was yelling *General Lee! General Lee!* and then you was kicking soccer balls down the hall! The next thing I heard, you'd jumped through your window, CRASH! and Dagger said hey Massah suck my grits! —and he was perfect, like Dickie, like Sheet-Rock Fred who sighed and had a beer and said Hitler used to say the will is all; now I say the will is ill; feeling ill, he wrote poems sitting in his truck at lunch and then it was back to the mysteries of the mudding tray, the ladder and the bazooka; he was always sailing out past the Golden Gate into storms and talking about weighing anchor for India never to return; he was going to be a pirate, a Buddha, a samurai; he would commit *seppuku;* he broke his arm when a ladder caved in on him but he wouldn't stop working so they had to reset the bone twice, and Fred had a beer and said I'm the plaster man with the master plan! and he would say you know all about Dr. Johnson don't you? you know about Mishima? and sometimes Fred would just laugh, and you felt very sad looking at his long beard and his jacket that was white-smeared with mud from a thousand ceilings as if all the seagulls of life had crapped on him. He was my friend, and so was his sometime employee Sheet-Rock Seth who as I have intimated was skinny and tense and stopped the car every ten minutes to jump out into the dew because he'd seen some lovely plant that had to be picked and keyed and admired while Fred sat laughing to himself very quietly; likewise Seth shinnied up pine trees from sea to shining sea and vanished among the shaking branches as Fred sat reading again about the twenty-three hundred Japanese warriors who rode silently across the moonlit snow to avenge some humiliation or other of their lord's which had happened a generation ago and most of them would get slaughtered by the castle's defenders and the ones that didn't would have to slit their bellies open anyway to show their sincerity but the important thing was HONOR as Fred agreed, sighing and sighing to think that his beautiful samurai sword had gotten stolen so how could *he* die like a warrior? . . . while meanwhile among the thrashing bowing branches whose needles raked his face and smeared his knees with sap, Seth was collecting and keying the biggest cone, which he dipped in Varithane to make it last forever and when he had a bunch of specimens rattling around in Megan's tampax box he mailed them to the lab in Gatlinburg, Tennessee which was not far from where Seth's friend Patricia lived, Patricia who slept all her nights with a stuffed dolphin and loved Seth (hopelessly, because at that time Seth preferred to walk the Berkeley campus looking the coeds up and down and then go home to jerk off—he was not even interested in Megan!); Patricia loved him because while there were many naturalists in Tennessee none compared to Seth in thinness as she well knew and so did the scientists at the lab when they put down the leaves they'd been holding to the light and brushed the bark-chips off each other's shoulders and sighed oh look here's *another* bunch of Seth's cones and they said that *rascal* and they opened up the box like it was Christmas and juggled the cones and called hey *Elmer* look at this one yessir I've never seen anything like it and they said is this a new *species* or a whole new *genus*? and they said now *look* at the work that boy Seth's just given us 'cause the darn pine tree textbooks will have to be *revised*! —although had the Tennessee scientists never said any of this but simply thrown his pine cones into the wastebasket, Seth would not have cared because what he enjoyed, you see, was climbing trees and finding things, —but you must not believe Seth to be a mere harum-scarum conifer-thief who was UNENLIGHTENED; no indeed, he went to see a shaman who groaned *ohh* I feel so sorry for the ocean; the ocean is very angry with us because we never give it anything good to eat; we only feed *garbage* to the ocean! and everyone else stared at the shaman as blankly as subway tokens but Seth went to the store and bought a dozen of his favorite candybars and then he rode the streetcar all the way out to Ocean Beach, standing very straight and stern so that all the old ladies thought what a nice boy, and the driver said Ocean Beach *last* stop! and Seth got out and walked slowly through the fog toward the ocean and the beach was littered with thousands of dead little jellyfish that the ocean had vomited up for an awful warning (what would poor weak-stomached Monique have thought?); thus Seth stood all by himself in his falling-apart old sneakers, right at the tide line, and the waves rolled foamily white around his ankles as he endured, throwing the candybars as far out to sea as he could, and the ocean swallowed them and gurgled happily, at which Seth was happy, too, because he always wanted to give things to people and spirits; once he found a run-over snake for me to boil so that I could make things out of its beautiful bones. Indeed Seth was my friend, and so was Bootwoman Marisa and so was Catherine and so too Ken the street photographer who went out with Elaine Suicide for years until he got sick of her for being so difficult (not that he didn't *used* to admire her for her extreme moods, as when the three of us would go down to the Mission some winter evening with Elaine weeping and bitter for no reason the whole black time, walking three discrete paces behind us, bundled up in her thick wool coat, her arms fiercely crossed while beside me Ken said proudly isn't she *something?* isn't she *great?*); well, to make a long story longer, after Elaine moved away, sobbing it's not my fault you can't love me; it's only my fault that I found out, why, Ken rose into a whole new career: he screwed white girls and black girls and never changed the sheets so that his van reeked of pussy and Ken pissed in a juice jar and saved it until it was full (a practice he had in common with Seth, except that Seth dumped his out the window every morning, whereas Ken was certain that his was some golden California wine that increased in value with age) and Ken walked down the street with a denim cap pulled very low over his eyes because he said if you don't wear a hat then God *sees* you and *spits* on you! but though his life was almost perfect the sad truth was that he had never yet *SCREWED AN ASIAN GIRL*, while *I* had my own Jenny Park who cooked me pork kat-su-don and was sweet to me and yelled at me and made me buy nice clothes and did my laundry, at which Ken said with true reverence, *wow* you better *marry* this one! so once upon a time Ken happened to be driving slowly down a Tenderloin street looking for Brownie, his favorite black whore who wanted to be his girlfriend and had even offered to fuck him in the North Star Laundromat, but on this most momentous afternoon Ken saw, instead of Brownie, a young Japanese woman standing very mournfully on the corner and I wish I could describe the beauty of her smooth face whose eyes conveyed nothing and her black glory of hair, which fell down to her breasts as she leaned a little forward with her lips pursed, looking at Ken in a way that he had never seen before, so he assumed that she must be a hooker wafted to him by the spicy winds of chance and commerce, and pulling over he stuck his head out the passenger window with his faded cap very low above his eyes like a cloud-bar, and he rubbed his unshaven chin and said get in and the woman got in and he said hi and she smiled very shyly and said hi and Ken said you are so *beautiful!* and she leaned her round cheek on her palm staring at him as she caressed her elbow and her skin was so soft and fine that Ken could hardly believe it so he said how much? and the woman just sat there because she didn't understand for as it turned out she wasn't a whore at all but something yet more still and secret who for some reason never to be known to Ken had just signed an eight-month lease on a Tenderloin apartment that smelled of insecticide while downstairs the old manageress kissed her pet bird over and over as it sat on one finger watching you with its little round eyes just as the manageress was to watch Ken and Satoko with such polite suspicion that the wrinkles radiating from her lips were like a zipper's teeth; and the manageress disconnected the front door buzzer at eight-thirty every night so that no visitors could announce themselves, which in the end was why Ken asked Satoko to give him a key, but I am now anticipating myself like a bad storyteller, for it is even possible that Ken had not yet learned these details when he banged Satoko that first day in his van and her pale shoulders trembled as she made small sounds and the next thing you knew he was buying her groceries and showing her how to cook because she knew hardly any English and was unfamiliar with American foods; Ken therefore became her mentor, pointing to a cat and saying *dog!*, pointing to a dog and saying *cat!* and at first Satoko believed everything that Ken said so he kept teasing her more and more until she laughed and hit him and Ken would say aw *that's* my girl Tokyo! and Satoko's father was in the Japanese Mafia and Satoko's upper teeth were false teeth because some medicine she'd had to take as a child had stained her real teeth brown, but for reasons of economy she had kept her lower teeth, which were brown, too, and Satoko lay in bed all day listening to heavy metal music very softly through her headphones while Ken was working and when Ken bought her a chicken she never bothered to put it in her refrigerator, so it rotted on the kitchen counter, at which Ken said *wow! she's amazing!* and Satoko, who sometimes lay on the bed looking at Ken like an animal with her hands dangling down from the edge of the bed like paws and her lips parted and her pale face shining in the darkness and her black eyes glowing and glowing at Ken, was very melancholy and cried a lot and hardly ever said anything and Ken would come in tired from working for Sheet-Rock Fred and take his dusty jacket off saying aw *Tokyo* aw *girl* until Satoko laughed and hit him and I said when was the war of 1812 Satoko? and Satoko just looked at me; and my friend Bob said how long have you been in this country Satoko? and Satoko just looked at him (so Bob said to me later in private indignation why she's a moral pincushion!); and Ken said aw *Tokyo* aw *girl* and an enigmatic tear crawled down Satoko's cheek and she hung her head and Ken and I took her to stripshow bars and Satoko just sat there and the three of us rode around in Ken's van very slowly and Ken rolled down his window to yell whenever he saw a whore *hey* don't you remember me it's *me* it's *Ken Photographer!* and Satoko just sat there and I made funny faces for Satoko until she smiled. —Satoko, I said, are you happy or sad? but Satoko just sat there. Later Ken said she told him *I don't like these kind of question!* —Ken gave her his denim cap to wear so that she would be protected even though that meant that God could see *him* now and spit on him. But Satoko rarely put it on. Ken gave her a sketchpad for Christmas and then she realized that she should give him something, too, and went out to buy him a shirt. Ken put the shirt on and wore it for five weeks straight. Sometimes when Ken was working I bought Satoko a beer in some bar and every washed-up Vietnam vet would say to me you got yourself a *honey* she's from Saigon isn't she I can tell a V.C. a mile off and I said that's right and the vet would say lemme buy you both a drink and Satoko would stare down at the counter very peacefully as the vet called out hey Suzy a round apiece for Beauty and the Beast! and I said thanks and he said I'm telling you she's a *honey* by which time I would be explaining all the jokes on the cocktail napkin to Satoko who laughed politely and then our two brown-bottled pledges of allegiance would arrive, thump, thump, and Satoko would say very softly to the vet *thank you* and she'd drink very delicately beside me until four o' clock had come and Ken came bursting in with a big smile and hugged Satoko and said aw *Tokyo girl!* and Satoko nodded very seriously and cradled her head against his shoulder. —These outings gradually became infrequent as Satoko developed a somewhat cryptic coloration and withdrew more and more from everybody except Ken. She lived on Oreo cookies and steadily lost weight. If I came to see her (she could not be expected to respond to her buzzer but the manageress knew me by now and let me in if each time I promised never *ever* to do it again), if I went up the stinking stairs and knocked, I might hear Satoko stirring in bed, but she would not answer the door. Whenever Ken went to see his friends she waited in the van, weeping. Ken never knew why. —Neither of them used birth control once Satoko's weird Japanese contraceptives had been successfully used up, so Satoko became pregnant because as Ken said to me Satoko just *loves* to fuck! and he said Satoko marry me and have our baby I'll support you I'll get you U.S. citizenship I'll get us a place to live because he loved her so much—but Satoko just sat there and raised her chin at him with her heart-locket gleaming against her black dress and then she got an abortion, for which Ken paid half, *then* Ken took her to see his parents and said *hey* Mom and Dad guess what this is my wife Satoko she's going to have my kid can you give us some money for a wedding present how about it huh? but Ken's parents would not believe him, and Satoko just sat there staring expressionlessly at Ken's parents until her visa expired and she went back to Japan at which I said to Ken why did she come here? and Ken said laughing I never *did* figure that one out! and he loved her and missed her so much that he could scarcely bear to screw other women—although he managed once in awhile, it is true, because that way he didn't have to sleep eternally in his van which he drove down to his post box twice a week or more hoping for mail from Satoko who at least would come back in the fall to fly to Bangkok with him, a plan to which she never alluded in the letters that she wrote, saying instead *I thought I hate fuckin America but I hate more Japan cuz*

Japan's fuck'n small country. Fuck'n expensive. Fuck'n SAFETY *country. I like New York. I love skyscraper. That was so beautiful. Especially night view* and Ken cried aw Tokyo what a girl! and Satoko wrote him saying *I'm really interested in Occultism, Eroticism, Cruelty, Violent and of cause Insanity. I think I'm mental masochist. Not physical! I don't like to think about happiness. I like dark side of human. I want to go to Greece someday. But I have a problem. Because I don't like Greek food!* at which Ken laughed and laughed reading her words aloud to me over and over in his van and I was so happy for him and said Ken don't let her get away I can see you really care about her at which Ken laughed again because he was embarrassed to be caught caring for someone and Ken showed me a photo he'd taken of Satoko staring so dreamily at a poster of her favorite heavy metal band with skulls and skulls all over and Ken said I hope she's saving up enough money to come back here and Satoko wrote Ken *I'm not alone anymore now. So long* (Ken did not tell me this for quite a long time; I heard it first from Painter Ben) and I told Ken I would go to Japan with him and help him kidnap Satoko if he wanted, but Ken only laughed. Once he called my answering machine in the middle of the night to say *well* I'm photographin' the whores [he meant lawyers] in the financial district! My agent is raisin' two thousand dollars for printing an' it's only gonna cost me two hundred! I got my first closeup encounter of a transsexual's pussy, an' I took a picture for you. It kinda caves in, an' she says its always stays tight an' she can't get any diseases 'cause it doesn't go anywhere—that was *so* beautiful! and I called the next day to say Ken have you heard from Satoko? and he said I wrote her twice but she didn't answer and I said that's a shame and he said Satoko's *still* my girl and I *respect* her; I'm stopping in Tokyo on my way to Bangkok and I sent her the flight time but she never answered and if she doesn't come to the airport I'll respect her more than ever! —Ken was a friend of mine, and so was stern and tousleheaded Lance in his greasy black leather jacket who loved to build machines of attack and destruction and spidery evasion and sat at the keyboard of his computer smoking and drinking beer and the keyboard was black with grime and he said now this here is a horse-skull robot that can only shake its head no at all the *tortures* that this other machine will *judiciously* administer! and I said well I'll be jig-jagged and he made me a knife out of horse-bone and I hired him to make me a book with a twenty-pound steel cover and it was the most beautiful book that I had ever seen and Lance would always come with me to the transvestite bars and we'd fall in love with the transvestites together until they would squeeze us and go *oh* such muscles, at which we'd oblige ourselves to buy them drinks and I'd try to buy Lance a drink and he'd say to the bar-girl better take mine because *his* money's no good! then we'd swig and Lance would say time to get back to work and he'd hop on his motorcycle and I'd wave goodbye and stand on the corner where Ken first saw Satoko and I'd lean against the liquor store wall until a pimp would say you got any questions? and I'd say yeah when was the war of 1812? and Lance always called me Commander and gave me good recipes for napalm. So the day went through all of them, stringing them like pearls onto a necklace of memories. This is why funerals have their place. My friends were more beautiful to me than they had always been, simply because I was going away. —But as yet I did not believe the fact. I could not believe that this wide throat of sunlight that had swallowed us and the ferry so that we could sail to the island of light ahead must soon be strangled, that something would put black fingers on it and squeeze and squeeze until the sunlight choked and died and then the place that I found myself in would be a black place, which was where Elaine Suicide lived. As long as I had known her she had been crying, because although she was loving and wanted to be glamorous (unknowing that she already was) she could not help lashing out carelessly and childishly and selfishly, so she drove away the men she adored and then was miserable and dreamed about them and cried herself to sleep or sat in bed at night smoking cigarettes and watching the moon. I did not want to go to this Crying Place, but because I was leaving my home I knew that I had to; it was black in every direction.

Preface to Ken Miller's *Open All Night*

This is really a prose poem, a love letter, to a man who became a significant influence on the direction of Vollmann's writing and the subjects he became interested in, as we can clearly see in *The Rainbow Stories, Whores for Gloria, Butterfly Stories*, and *The Royal Family.* A more personal account of their friendship can be found in "The Ghost of Magnetism." —MH

I SOMETIMES THINK THAT Ken Miller would prefer to treat the world with the honeyed blandness of a high-priced psychiatrist, accepting of all, pleasantly inscrutable, wise and tired. He avoids defining his photographic project; he avoids it in an insistent, aggressive, irritating way. If pressed to explain what he is doing, he will, if he is feeling extremely good-humored, put on a smile of deliberately crafted stupidity, and say something like, "I'm taking these pictures just to document." Yet the truth is that Ken is no camera eye, tumbling in magisterial orbit from pole to pole, clicking every three point four seconds on whatever has shown itself to be documented in that interval; for he has strong dislikes. What most people call beauty annoys him; what they call riches disgusts him, and the manners of his own class, the middle class, incite him to grinning personal taunts. This genuinely ugly side of his character frames his work, because it is what is called the *ugly* that attracts him. He will forgive you your theories if you limp or have a cast in one eye. A thug hideously tattooed, a street witch whose rat-familiar peers out from between her breasts, a stinking bum who pisses in Ken's sink—these are the people who will open the shutters of his heart to maximum aperture, like a high school girl who was just given a rose. But it is not that he is a mere pornographer of the abnormal. There are too many of those; we see their productions every week in the magazines—sometimes a starving African child with a bloated belly, or other times the clutching fingers of a dying earthquake victim. These images soothe people's passivity because they do not teach them anything. What makes Ken's work so remarkable is the sense that these squashed lives are not just isolated bugs on the windshield, but *parallel worlds* of hermetic secrets, like the nine cities of Troy stacked one upon the next inside the earth. This comes across in part because Ken takes many different pictures of his subjects and gets them to trust him. You can see it in the way they look at the camera. Imagine the excitement of the fellow who discovered Pluto through his calculations, realizing gradually from the color temperature of his integrals that there is something cold and black and unknown far out there, following our sun its own way, and it had been there forever but we had never known that it was there. That is how I felt one afternoon when Ken took me to Golden Gate Park, five minutes away from the playground, five minutes away from the bus stop, into a little thicket of wet stinking trees, and he introduced me to the Wrecking Crew on their mattresses, with their sad alcoholic lore about Smackwater Jack and the wild blue yonder. It was not that he had shown me a group of tramps who had been living in the Park for years that impressed me. It was that he knew them by name and they knew him, and that was the open sesame for me to understand that they had an identity and a place; that this was their kingdom with its own rules and stories and lice; and that in fact the whole world was like that, and if somebody had enough time he could map it out into these kingdoms (how many millions of them must there be in San Francisco alone?) and *document* them, as Ken would say, before they burst like rainbow-colored soap bubbles. Thanks to Ken I was able to meet the S.F. Skinz in the turning year of their decline, to meet the secret clan of old electroshock patients who lived in fly-infested hotels whose floors were rubbery with their puke, to draw in rough outlines the world-frame of streetwalkers and trainhoppers, and, most importantly, to understand that every person is like an exotic book, and if you go to the trouble of reading it you will learn about things that you had never imagined. I hope someday that Ken will crack the private worlds of the secretaries and the grocery store proprietors. I do not think that would weaken his focus. It would be wonderful if he did begin to *document* everybody.

But at the moment his interest is in "lost souls" (his words). It is a fine sight to see him walking down the streets with his heavy view camera slung over his shoulder, and his watchdog padding alongside, ready to bite any enemy. He has a very young face, and bright eyes. He wears a faded denim jacket. His hands are callused and cracked. Every few steps, he will see somebody that he recognizes. He stops, yells: "Hey, Smiley! *Kirby!* How ya doin'? *Laddie!* When did you get into town?" He has pictures for all of them. They come running, hopping or hobbling. They love him because he gives them pictures. When they clutch the new images in their hands, so happy and proud, anyone can see that they are not as lost as you or I might think, or want to think. And if they are lost, it may be because they want to be one of those undiscovered black planets spinning so quietly and secretly that most people never find it, never meet its kings and warriors, never run their fingers through its cold black treasure.

Photos by Ken Miller

From

Open All Night

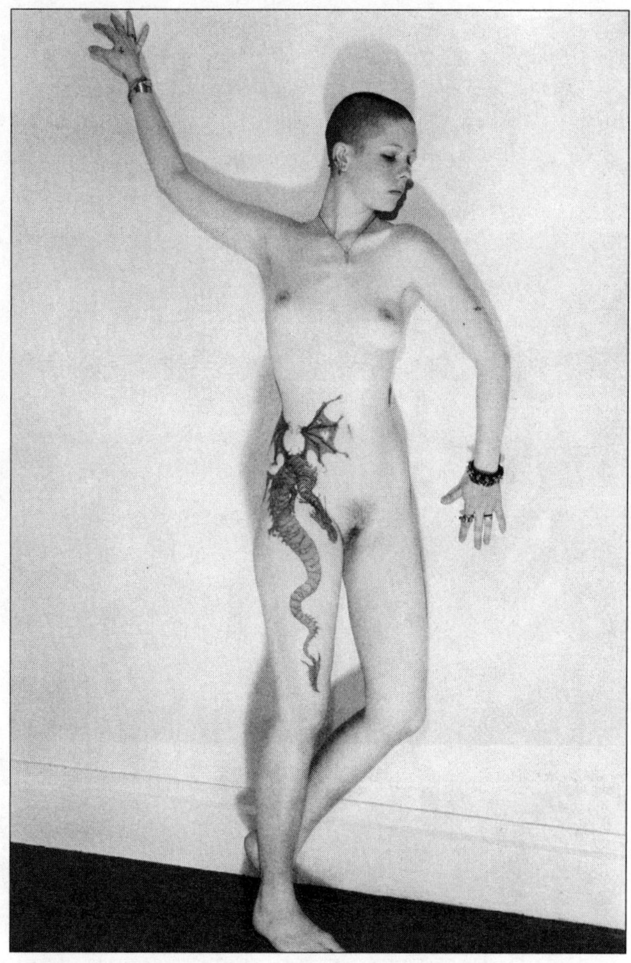

TRUSTINGLY SHE PULLED DOWN HER PANTS TO SHOW OFF BRONSON'S NEW WORK ON HER TATTOO WHENEVER I ASKED.

—"THE WHITE KNIGHTS" *THE RAINBOW STORIES.*

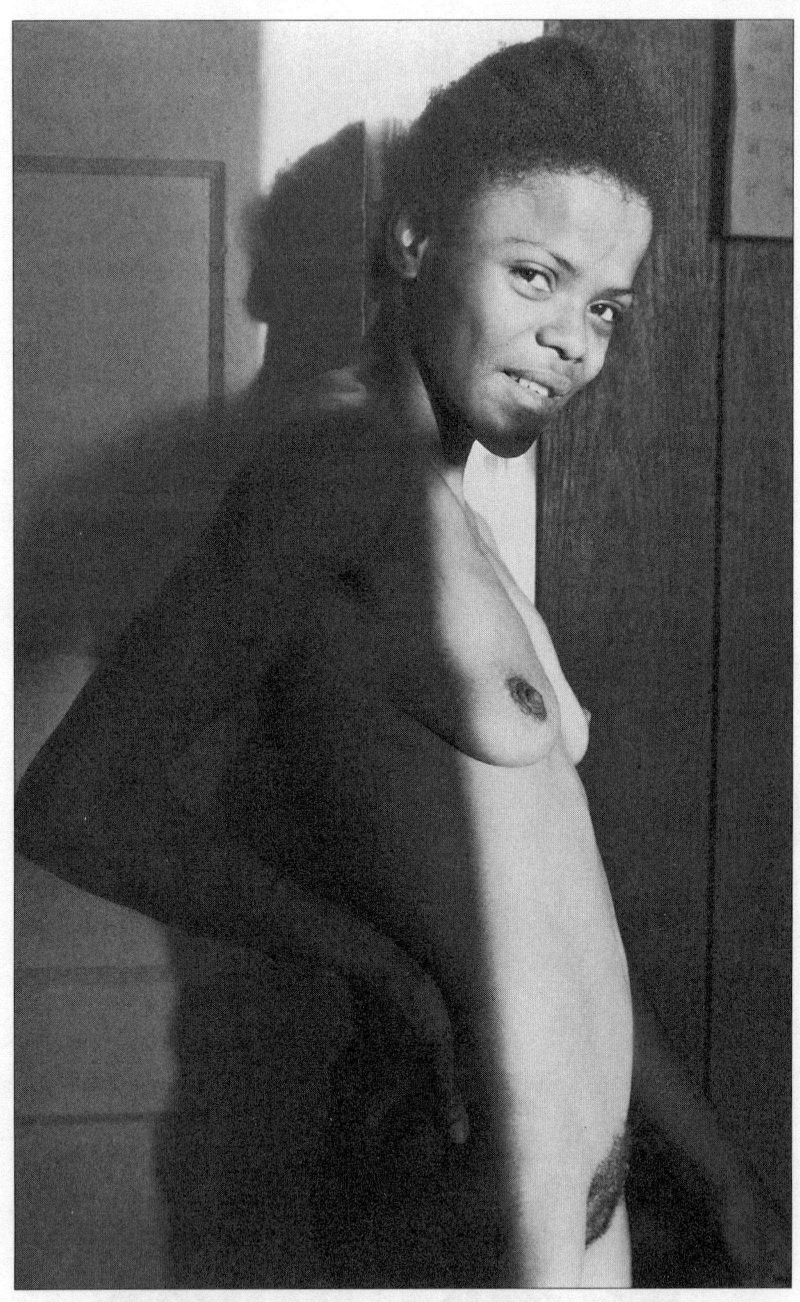

"I HAD A LOT OF MEN IN LOVE WITH ME." SHE CHUCKLED. "AND I TAKEN *ADVANTAGE* OF IT." —"LADIES AND RED LIGHTS" *THE RAINBOW STORIES.*

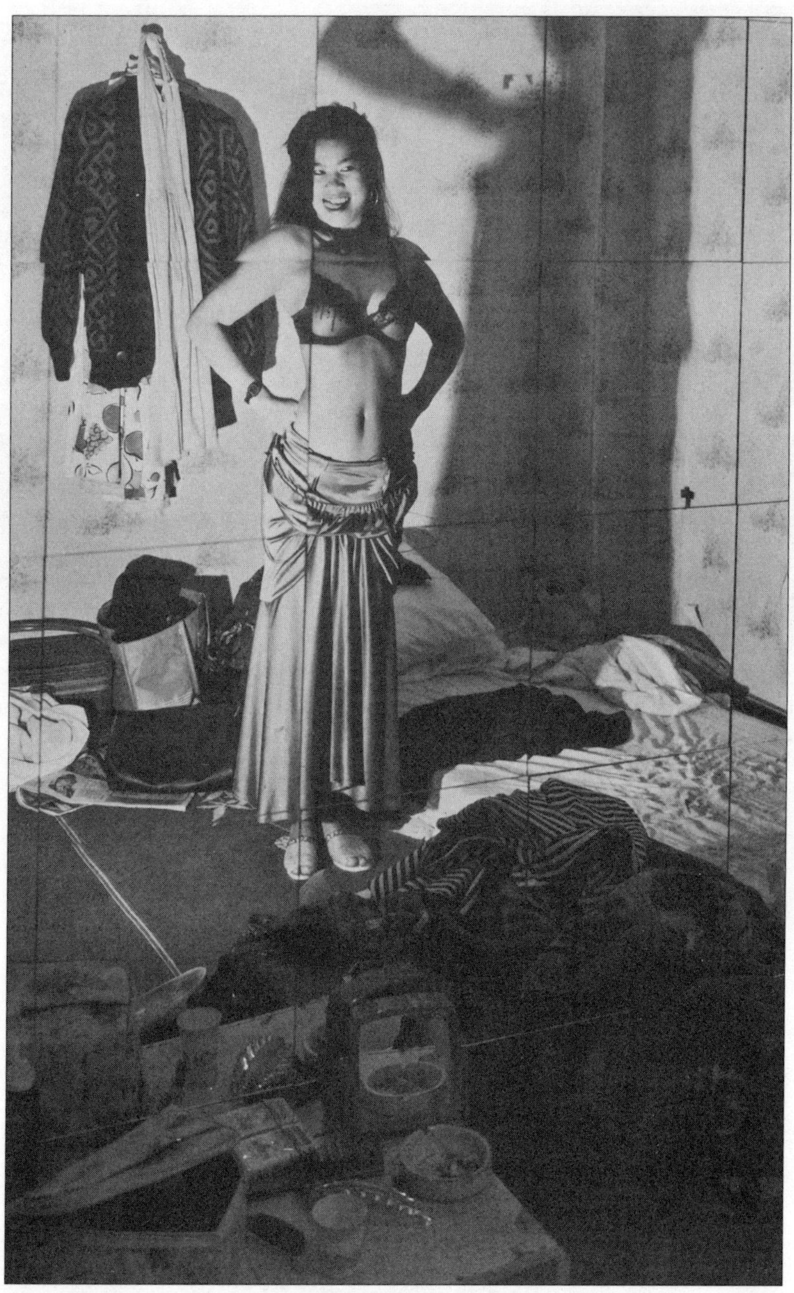

OY SAT BY THE WATER JUG AND WAGGLED HER TONGUE AT IMAGINARY CUSTOMERS AGAIN. —"THE HAPPY GIRLS" *THIRTEEN STORIES AND THIRTEEN EPIGRAPHS.*

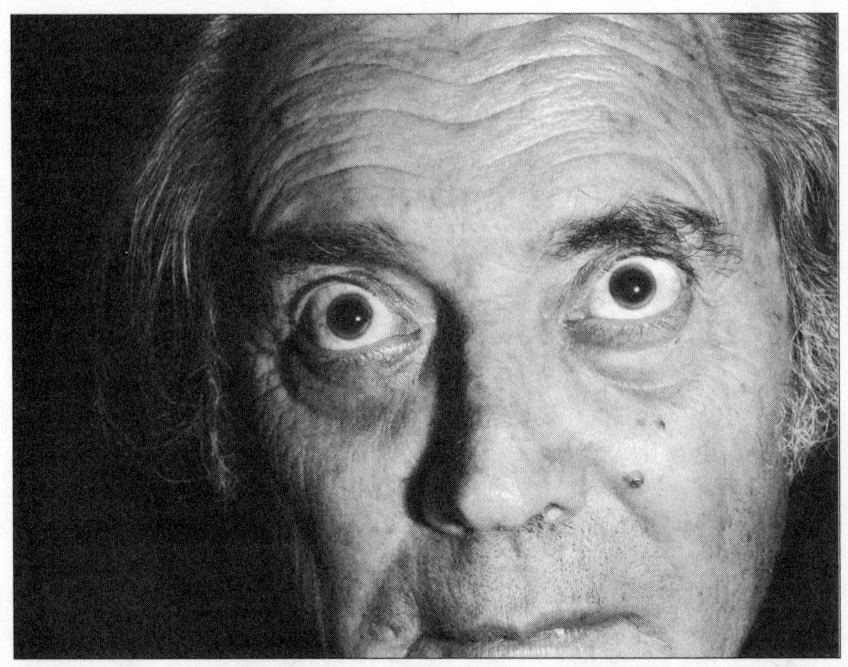

YOU MAY ON OCCASION LIKE JIMMY FIND YOURSELF LOOKING DOWN A LONG BLACK BLOCK, DOWN THE TUNNELS OF INFINITY TO A STREETLAMP, A CORNER AND A WOMAN'S WAITING SILHOUETTE. —*WHORES FOR GLORIA.*

Honesty

From *Four Essays*

This essay touches on a subject that Vollmann values tremendously from a personal standpoint; it's central to his art as well. "Honesty" first appeared in *Esquire* in 1993, in a slightly different form. "Writing"—another section of *Four Essays*—appears here separately in the "On Writing, Literature, and Culture" section.

I speak truth, not so much as I would, but as much as I dare; and I dare a little more as I grow older.

—***Montaigne,*** Essays

It is not so hard to be honest, merely a little embarrassing. When we employ the word "honesty" we rarely connote somebody's happiness. I would argue that this is because life is a series of failures punctuated by a few mild successes which better wisdom would probably teach us are failures, too. So why should I be honest? One honest answer is: Because *Esquire* pays me. With that out of the way, allow me to be honest about why I like to be around prostitutes.

I think I have always been ashamed of my body. I was born with as many moles on my back as a leopard has spots. These are not flat circles of pigment, but actual protrusions. When I was in second grade one of them had to be cut off. A boy who didn't like me ripped open the stitches, which left a scar about as big as a fifty-cent piece. So I was embarrassed to go swimming with the other children. Later on I got acne. In the past two or three years I've begun to get fat—nothing yet more grotesque than the jellyroll thighs of self-indulgence (which actually help keep me warm when I'm in the Arctic), but still something I try to hide. So I never wear shorts, and because of the moles and the acne scars I never take my shirt off, either. I guess that covers most of me.

The inner person, I fear, is equally disappointed in himself. Until I was in high school I had very few friends. No matter what I did, it seemed, others saw through me to the wretched hollowness, the failure that constituted me. Nowadays I get plenty of fan mail. Boys at least as intelligent as I ship off copies of my books to be autographed; girls regularly send naked photos. While this is gratifying, I cannot rid myself of the superstition that they love the fact that I am for sale, not the fact that I am me.

The first time I was with a prostitute (over a decade ago now), I was feeling worse about myself than usual. My fiancée had just told me that she didn't love me anymore. For two years I waited for someone else to come along. Finally I dialed a call girl.

This woman did not care about me as a person. She did not want to know anything about me. She certainly was not interested in me sexually. All she wanted was to get her job over with as quickly as she could, get paid and leave. Being ignorant, I felt hurt. Then I began to consider the business more fairly, and saw the good: There was no need to feel ashamed of myself in front of her because my self was irrelevant to her. I could be happy and she could be happy. We were both getting what we wanted.

A year or two later I began to study the world of San Francisco streetwalkers—this time with my notebook and tape recorder as well as with my penis. There were many things that saddened and appalled me: the dirt, the disease, the hard carapace over the fearful soul, the hatred, the danger, the addiction, the premature death. Any stereotype is partially true. Yet I also remembered the work I'd done in offices, and what I'd witnessed there seemed at least as terrible: the lying, the scheming, the same fear, really: —how could I forget the morning when most of my division got fired? We were ordered to leave the building by noon. Our health insurance terminated at midnight. One of my co-workers began crying. She said she didn't know how she'd feed her children now. The few who'd been kept on avoided us, guilty, afraid of being next. In that office, and in all the others, my constant sensation was of being constricted. I worked for others, not for myself, giving my best to "managers" who used us as prostitutes are used. We lived sealed away in glass buildings, with a mere television understanding of the world! We truly were the pallid subterranean half-humans in E. M. Forster's "The Machine Stops."

Compared to us, the prostitutes were Renaissance women. They dealt with all comers, sizing them up instantly and usually accurately (after all, their lives depended on it). They worked on the street corners, standing in the world, not out of it. They owned themselves. It was their choice to go with the man or not. What they sold was comfort, relief, joy, pleasure, friendship, love of a sort, happiness. They were patient and wise, their wisdom that of a mother who cleans her baby's filth so many times that filth can no longer touch her. They had the knowledge of the woman who gives birth, the pathologist who opens chest and skull, the policeman who's seen every kind of cruelty, selfishness, trickery. What didn't they know?

So many times I've seen a whore take off her clothes, and her body is so burned and scarred and slashed and shriveled and starved and drugged and bloated and bled, and yet she is not ashamed; she stands honest; she says: "This is me." And when I saw that I said: "I'm going to try to be me, too."

I remember how proud I was the first time I became friends with a prostitute. This person actually allowed me to talk with her and walk with her without charging me money! That was when I knew I was making progress. The next step was when they'd drop in on me at dawn to tell me how their night went: "Oh, it was pretty slow for six hours, but then I got a fifty dollar blow job." And now I've truly arrived. Now they give me crack and do my laundry.

I became a connoisseur of the ballet of a dancing street-whore sending out her fishhooks of glamour and grace to attract the prey. I grew to admire the true pro's accomplishment of giving as little as possible and getting as much as possible (my former managers would have called this "capitalism"). And, above all, I slowly began to understand that there is no such thing as a prostitute, since we're all prostitutes; there are only human beings. When I see a woman's body covered with abscesses, needle tracks, motorcycle scars, bruises and bullet wounds, I experience awe at the endurance of this person in the teeth of the forces to which her flesh bears witness. When I see a younger girl just beginning the trade, reeking so richly of sex, I glimpse her as an icon of what makes and renews us, a literal fertility goddess, the perpetuation of life. But the person stands beyond and above the body, as I know now in my own case. And I am proud to have come to know some of these streetwalkers as ladies, as people. I write their names in every book I make; I think about them often and steadily. From them I continue to learn how to be free.

So what's the truth, the real truth? That shame and nakedness are the beginning, and nakedness without shame the end? How about if we always or never wore clothes? All I know is that what I get from being around these women who have helped me so much is something very pure and uncomplicated, something so good that I cannot be much hurt when somebody says that I or the prostitutes are bad. Nor am I surprised by such judgments, for there's another proverb about truth, a Turkish one, which runs: "Whoever tells the truth is chased out of nine villages."

Part II

On Death, War, and Violence

Part II
On Death, War, and Violence

Three Meditations on Death

From
Rising Up and Rising Down

These meditations serve as front matter to Vollmann's *Rising Up and Rising Down* and were first published in Dave Eggers's *McSweeney's Quarterly Concern.*

I. CATACOMB THOUGHTS

DEATH IS ORDINARY. BEHOLD it, subtract its patterns and lessons from those of the death that weapons bring, and maybe the residue will show what violence is. With this in mind, I walked the long tunnels of the Paris catacombs. Walls of earth and stone encompassed walls of mortality a femur's-length thick: long yellow and brown bones all stacked in parallels, their sockets pointing outward like melted bricks whose ends dragged down, like downturned bony smiles, like stale yellow snails of macaroni-joints of bones, heads of bones, promiscuously touching, darkness in the center of each, between those twin knucklespurs which had once helped another bone to pivot, thereby guiding and supporting flesh in its passionate and sometimes intelligent motion toward the death it inevitably found—femurs in rows, then, and humerii, bones upon bones, and every few rows there'd be a shelf of bone to shore death up, a line of humerii and femurs laid down laterally to achieve an almost pleasing masonry effect, indeed, done by masonry's maxims, as interpreted by Napoleon's engineers and brickmen of death, who at the nouveau-royal command had elaborated and organized death's jetsam according to a sanitary aesthetic. (Did the Emperor ever visit that place? He was not afraid of death—not even of causing it.) Then there were side-chambers walled with bones likewise crossed upon bonebeams; from these the occasional skull looked uselessly out; and every now and then some spiritual types had ornamented the facade with a cross made of femurs. There had been laid down in that place, I was told, the remains of about six million persons—our conventional total for the number of Jews who died in the Holocaust. The crime which the Nazis accomplished with immense effort in half a dozen years, nature had done here without effort or recourse, and was doing.

I had paid my money aboveground; I had come to look upon my future. But when after walking the long arid angles of prior underground alleys I first encountered my brothers and sisters, calcified appurtenances of human beings now otherwise gone to be dirt, and rat-flesh, and rootflesh, and green leaves soon to die again, I felt nothing but a mildly melancholy curiosity. One expects to die; one has seen skeletons and death's heads on Halloween masks, in anatomy halls, cartoons, warning signs, forensic photographs, photographs of old SS insignia, and meanwhile the skulls bulged and gleamed from walls like wet river-boulders, until curiosity became, as usual, numbness. But one did not come out of the ground then. Bone-walls curled around wells, drainage sockets in those tunnels; sometimes water dripped from the ceiling and struck the tourists' foreheads—water which had probably leached out of corpses. A choking, sickening dust irritated our eyes and throats, for in no way except in the abstract, and perhaps not even then, is the presence of the dead salutary to the living. Some skulls dated to 1792. Darkened, but still not decayed, they oppressed me with their continued existence. The engineers would have done better to let them transubstantiate. They might have been part of majestic trees by now, or delicious vegetables made over into young children's blood and growing bones. Instead they were as stale and stubborn as old arguments, molds for long dissolved souls, churlish hoardings of useless matter. Thus, I believed, the reason for my resentment. The real sore point was that, in Eliot's phrase, "I had not thought death had undone so many;" numbness was giving way to qualmishness, to a nauseated, claustrophobic realization of my biological entrapment. Yes, of course I'd known that I must die, and a number of times had had my nose rubbed in the fact; this was one of them, and in between those episodes my tongue glibly admitted what my heart secretly denied; for why should life ought to bear in its flesh the dissolving, poisonous faith of its own inescapable defeat? Atop bony driftwood, skulls slept, eyeholes downwards, like the shells of dead hermit crabs amidst those wracked corpse-timbers. This was the necrophile's beach, but there was no ocean except the ocean of earth overhead from which those clammy drops oozed and dripped. Another cross of bone, and then the inscription—

SILENCE, MORTAL BEINGS—VAIN GRANDEURS, SILENCE—

words even more imperious in French than I have given them here, but no more necessary, for the calcified myriads said that better than all poets or commanders. In superstition the carcass is something to be feared, dreaded and hated; in fact it deserves no emotion whatsoever in and of itself, unless it happens to comprise a souvenir of somebody other than a stranger; but time spent in the company of death is time wasted. Life trickles away, like the water falling down into the catacombs, and in the end we will be silent as our ancestors are silent, so better to indulge our vain grandeurs while we can. Moment by moment, our time bleeds away. Shout, scream, or run, it makes no difference, so why not forget what can't be avoided? On and on twisted death's alleys. Sometimes there was a smell, a cheesy, vinegary smell which I knew from having visited a field-morgue or two; there was no getting away from it, and the dust of death dried out my throat. I came to a sort of cavern piled up to my neck with heaps of bones not used in construction: pelvic bones and ribs (the vertebrae and other small bones must have all gone to discard or decay). These relics were almost translucent, like seashells, so thin had death nibbled them. That smell, that vinegar-vomit smell, burned my throat, but perhaps I was more sensitive to it than I should have been, for the other tourists did not appear to be disgusted; indeed, some were laughing, either out of bravado or because to them it was as unreal as a horror movie; they didn't believe that they'd feature in the next act, which must have been why one nasty fellow seemed to be considering whether or not to steal a bone—didn't he have bones enough inside his living meat? He must not have been the only one, for when we came to the end and ascended to street level we met a gainfully employed man behind a table which already had two skulls on it, seized from thieves that day; he checked our backpacks. I was happy when I got past him and saw sunlight—almost overjoyed, in fact, for since becoming a part-time journalist of armed politics I am not titillated by death. I try to understand it, to make friends with it, and I never learn anything except the lesson of my own powerlessness. Death stinks in my nostrils as it did that chilly sunny autumn afternoon in Paris when I wanted to be happy.

In the bakeries, the baguettes and pale, starchy *mini-ficelles,* the croissants and *pains-aux-chocolats* all reminded me of bones. Bone-colored cheese stank from other shops. All around me, the steel worms of the Metro bored through other catacombs, rushing still living bones from hole to hole. In one of the bookshops on the Rue de Seine I found a demonically bound volume of Poe whose endpapers were marbled like flames; the plates, of course, hand-colored by the artist, depicted gruesomely menacing skeletons whose finger-bones snatched and clawed. I spied a wedding at the Place Saint-Germain, whose church was tanned and smoked by time to the color of cheesy bones; I saw the white-clad bride—soon to become yellow bones. The pale narrow concrete sleepers of railroads, metallic or wooden fence-rails, the model of the spinal column in the window of an anatomical bookshop, then even sticks, tree trunks, all lines inscribed or implied, the world itself in all its segments, rays, and dismembered categories became hideously cadaverous. I saw and inhaled death. I tasted death on my teeth. I exhaled, and the feeble puffs of breath could not push my nausea away. Only time did that—a night and a day, to be exact—after which I forgot again until I was writing these very words that I must die. I believed but for a moment. Thus I became one with those skulls which no longer knew their death. Even writing this, picking my letters from the alphabet's boneyard, my o's like death's-heads, my *i's* and *l's* like ribs, my *b's, q's, p's* and *d's* like ball-ended humerii broken in half, I believed only by fits. The smell came back into my nose, but I was in Vienna by then—whose catacombs, by the way, I decided not to visit—so I went out and smelled espresso heaped with fresh cream. The writing became, as writing ought to be, informed by choreographies and paradigms which mediated that smell into something more than its revolting emptiness. I take my meaning where I can find it; when I can't find it, I invent it. And when I do that, I deny meaninglessness, and when I do that I am lying to myself. Experience does not necessarily lie, but that smell is not an experience to the matter which emits it. Death cannot be experienced either by the dead or the living. The project of the Parisian workmen, to aestheticize, to arrange, and thus somehow to transform the objects of which they themselves were composed, was a bizarre success, but it could have been done with stale loaves of bread. It affected bones; it could not affect death. It meant as little, it said as little, as this little story of mine. It spoke of them as I must speak of me. I can read their meaning. Death's meaning I cannot read. To me death is above all things a smell, a very bad smell, and that, like the skeletons which terrify children, is not death at all. If I had to smell it more often, if I had to work in the catacombs, I would think nothing of it. And a few years or decades from now, I will think nothing about everything.

II. AUTOPSY THOUGHTS

It shall be the duty of the coroner to inquire into and determine the circumstances, manner, and cause of all violent, sudden or unusual deaths . . .

California State Code, Sec. 27491

Aldous Huxley once wrote that "if most of us remain ignorant of ourselves, it is because self-knowledge is painful and we prefer the pleasures of illusion." That is why one brushes off the unpleasantly personal lesson of the catacombs. But we can extend the principle: Not only self-knowledge hurts. Consider the black girl whom an investigator pulled from a dumpster one night. Her mouth was bloody, which wasn't so strange; she could have been a homeless alcoholic with variceal bleeding. But, shining the flashlight into that buccal darkness, the investigator caught sight of a glint—neither blood nor spittle sparkling like metal, but metal itself—a broken-off blade. In her mouth, which could no longer speak, lay the truth of her death. The investigator couldn't give her her life back, but by this double unearthing—the knife from the corpse, the corpse from the stinking bin—he'd resurrected something else, an imperishable quantity which the murderer in his fear or fury or cold selfishness meant to entomb—namely, the fact of murder, the reality which would have been no less real had it never become known, but which, until it was known and proved, remained powerless to do good. —What good? Quite simply, determining the cause of death is the prerequisite for some kind of justice, although justice, like other sonorous concepts, can produce anything from healing to acceptance to compensation to revenge to hypocritical clichés. At the chief medical examiner's office they knew this good—knowing also that the job of turning evidence into justice lay not with them but with the twelve citizens in the jury box: —what coroners and medical examiners do is necessary but not sufficient. Probably the black woman's family had figured that out, if there *was* any family, if they cared, if they weren't too stupefied with grief. The morgue would be but the first of their Stations of the Cross. (Afterward: the funeral parlor, the graveyard, perhaps the courtroom, and always the empty house.) Dealing with them was both the saddest and the most important part of the truth-seeker's job: as I said, knowledge hurts. Dr. Boyd Stephens, the Chief Medical Examiner of San Francisco, would later say to me: "One of the things I hoped you'd see was a family coming in here grieving. And when it is a crime of violence, when someone has her son shot during a holdup, that makes it very hard; that's a tremendous emotional blow." I myself am very glad that I didn't see this. I have seen it enough. In the catacombs death felt senseless, and for the investigator who found the black woman, the moral of death remained equally empty, as it must whether the case is suicide, homicide, accident, or what we resignedly call "natural causes." Twenty-six years after the event, a kind woman who had been there wrote me about the death of my little sister. I was nine years old, and my sister was six. The woman wrote: "I remember you, very thin, very pale, your shoulders hunched together, your hair all wet and streaming sideways. You said, 'I can't find Julie.' " She wrote to me many other things that she remembered. When I read her letter, I cried. Then she went on: "I am tempted to say that Julie's drowning was a 'senseless death' but that's not true. I learned the day she died that there are realms of life in which the measure of sense and nonsense don't apply. Julie's death exists on a plane where there is no crime and no punishment, no cause and effect, no action and reaction. It just happened." Fair enough. Call it morally or ethically senseless, at least. (I don't think I ever wrote back; I felt too sad.) Only when *justice itself* condemns someone to death, as when a murderer gets hanged or we bombard Hitler's Berlin or an attacker meets his victim's lethal self-defense, can we even admit the possibility that the perishing had a point. Principled suicides also mean something: Cato's self-disembowelment indicts the conquering Caesar who would have granted clemency, and whose patronizing power now falls helpless before a mere corpse. But most people (including many suicides, and most who die the deaths of malicious judicial injustice) die the death of accident, meaninglessly and ultimately anonymously discorporating like unknown skulls in catacombs—and likewise the black woman in the dumpster.

No matter that her murderer had a reason—she died for nothing; and all the toxicology and blood spatter analyses in the world, even if they lead to his conviction, cannot change that. The murderer's execution might mean something; his victim's killing almost certainly will not.

From the White Hearse to the Viewing Room

In fiscal year 1994–95, slightly more than eight thousand people died in San Francisco County. Half of these deaths could be considered in some sense questionable, and reports on them accordingly traveled to Dr. Stephens's office, but in three thousand cases the doubts, being merely pro forma, were eventually cleared, signed off by physicians—that is, explained circumstantially if not ontologically. The remaining 1,549 deaths became Dr. Stephens's problem. His findings for that year were: 919 natural deaths, 296 non-vehicular accidents, 124 suicides, ninety-four homicides, thirty mysterious cases, six sudden infant death syndromes, and eighty vehicular fatalities, most of which involved pedestrians, and most of which were accidents (there were six homicides and one suicide).* And now I'm going to tell you what his people did to reach those findings. In San Francisco they had a white ambulance, or hearse as I might better say, which was partitioned between the driver's seat and the cargo hold, and the cargo hold could quickly be loaded or unloaded by means of the white double doors, the inside

*Medical Examiner's Office, City and County of San Francisco, annual report, July 1, 1994 June 30, 1995, pp. 9, 36.

of which bore an inevitable reddish-brown stain: anything that touches flesh for years must get corrupted. It smelled like death in there, of course, which in my experience is sometimes similar to the smell of sour milk, or vomit and vinegar, or of garbage, which is to say of the dumpster in which the murdered girl had been clumsily secreted. A horizontal partition subdivided battered old stainless steel stretchers into two and two. Because San Francisco is hilly, the stretchers, custom-welded years before by a shop just down the street, were made to be stood upright, the bodies strapped in, and rolled along on two wheels. "Kind of like a wheelbarrow in a way," one stretcher man said. This might be the last time that the dead would ever again be vertical, as they serenely travelled, strapped and sheeted, down steep stairs and sidewalks. The ambulance pulled up behind Dr. Stephens's office, in a parking lot that said AMBULANCES ONLY. Out came each stretcher. Each stretcher went through the door marked NO ADMITTANCE, the door which for those of us whose hearts still beat might better read NO ADMITTANCE YET. Inside, the body was weighed upon a freight-size scale, then wheeled into the center of that bleak back room for a preliminary examination, and fingerprinted three times (if it still had fingers and skin), with special black ink almost as thick as taffy. Finally it was zipped into a white plastic bag to go into the fridge overnight.* If the death might be homicide, the investigators waited longer—at least twenty-four hours, in case any new bruises showed up like last-minute images on a pale sheet of photographic paper floating in the developer, as might happen when deep blood vessels had been ruptured. Bruises were very important. If the body of a man who seemed to have hanged himself showed contusions on the face or hands, the investigators would have to consider homicide.**

By now perhaps the family had been told. In the big front room that said ABSOLUTELY NO ADMITTANCE I heard a man say, "Yes, we have

*Stylists frown upon the passive construction. But I fail to see what could be more appropriate for dead bodies.

**For this information on ante- and postmortem contusions I have, as so often, relied on Lester Adelson, *The Pathology of Homicide: A Vade Mecum for Pathologist, Prosecutor, and Defense Counsel*, Springfield, Illinois: Charles C. Thomas, 1974.

Dave. I'm so sorry about what happened to Dave." If the family came, they would be led down a narrow corridor to a door that said VIEWING ROOM. The viewing room was private and secret, like the projectionist's booth in a movie theater. It had a long window that looked out onto another very bright and narrow room where the movie would take place, the real movie whose story had already ended before the attendant wheeled in the former actor. The movie was over; Dr. Stephens needed the family to verify the screen credits. They only saw the face. There was a door between the viewing room and the bright and narrow room, but someone made sure to lock it before the family came, because they might have tried to embrace this thing which had once been someone they loved, and because the thing might not be fresh anymore or because it might have been slammed out of personhood in some hideous way whose sight or smell or touch would have made the family scream, it was better to respect the love they probably still felt for this thing which could no longer love them, to respect that love by respecting its clothes of ignorance. The people who worked in Dr. Stephens's office had lost their ignorance a long time ago. They blunted themselves with habit, science and grim jokes—above all, with necessity: if the death had been strange or suspicious, they had to cut the thing open and look inside, no matter how much it stank.

A Solomonic parable: Dr. Stephens told me that once three different mothers were led into the viewing room one by one to identify a dead girl, and each mother claimed the girl as hers, with a desperate relief, as I would suppose. I know someone whose sister was kidnapped. It's been years now and they've never found her. They found her car at the side of the road. My friend used to live with her sister. Now she lives with her sister's clothes. From time to time the family's private detective will show her photographs of still another female body partially skeletonized or not, raped or not, and she'll say, "That's not my sister." I know it would give her peace to be able to go into a viewing room and say (and believe), "Yes, that's Shirley." Those three mothers must all have given up hoping that their daughters would ever speak to them or smile at them again. They wanted to stop dreading and start grieving. They didn't want to go into viewing rooms any more. And maybe the glass window was dirty, and maybe their eyes were old or full of tears. It was a natural mistake. But one mother was lucky. The dead girl was really her daughter.

The Innocent Metermaid

To confirm that identification, someone at Dr. Stephens's office had already looked inside the dead woman's mouth, incidentally discovering or not discovering the gleam of a knife-blade, observed her dental work, and matched it to a dentist's files. Somebody had fingerprinted her and found a match; somebody had sorted through her death-stained clothes and come up with a match. Starting with flesh and cloth, they had to learn what the mothers didn't know. The meter maid didn't know, either, and I am sure she didn't want to know. A young man eased some heroin into his arm—maybe too much, or maybe it was too pure (heroin just keeps getting better and better these days). He died and fell forward, his face swelling and purpling with lividity. The meter maid didn't know, I said. Even after he began to decompose, she kept putting parking tickets on his windshield.

"I'm a Happy Customer"

A stinking corpse, pink and green and yellow, lay naked on one of many parallel downsloping porcelain tables each of which drained into a porcelain sink. The man's back had hurt. Surgery didn't help, so he took painkillers until he became addicted. The painkillers proving insufficiently kind, he started mixing them with alcohol. When the white ambulance came, there were bottles of other people's pills beside his head. He was not quite forty.

"Everything's possible," said one morgue attendant to another leaning against a gurney, while the doctor in mask and scrubs began to cut the dead man open. "You're limited only by your imagination." I think he was talking about special effects photography. He had loaned his colleague a mail-order camera catalog.

Meanwhile the dagger tattooed on the dead man's bicep trembled and shimmered as the doctor's scalpel made the standard Y-shaped incision, left shoulder to chest, right shoulder to chest, then straight down the belly to the pubis. The doctor was very good at what he did, like an old Eskimo who I once saw cutting up a dying walrus. The scalpel made crisp sucking sounds. He peeled back the chest-flesh like a shirt, then crackled the racks of ribs, which could almost have been pork. His yellow-gloved hands grubbed in the scarlet hole, hauling out fistfuls of sausage-links—that is, loops of intestine. Then he stuck a hose in and left it there until the outflow faded to pinkish clear. Beset by brilliant lavender, scarlet, and yellow, the twin red walls of rib-meat stood high and fragile, now protecting nothing, neatly split into halves.

The dead man still had a face.

The doctor syringed out a blood sample from the cavity, sponged blood off the table, and then it was time to weigh the dead man's organs on a hanging balance, the doctor calling out the numbers and the pretty young pathology resident chalking them onto the blackboard. The lungs, already somewhat decomposed, were indistinct masses which kept oozing away from the doctor's scalpel. "Just like jello," he said sourly.

The right lung was larger than the left, as is often the case with righthanded people. Another possible cause: the dead man had been found lying on his right side, a position which could have increased congestion in that lung. Either way, his death was meaningless.

His heart weighed 290 grams. The doctor began to cut it into slices.

"This vessel was almost entirely occluded with atherosclerosis," explained the resident. "He used a lot of drugs. Cocaine hastens the onset of atherosclerosis. We get lots of young people with old people's diseases."

That was interesting to know and it meant something, I thought. In a sense, the investigators understood the dead man. I wondered how well he'd been understood before he died.

"God, his pancreas!" exclaimed the doctor suddenly. "That's why he died." He lifted out a purple pudding which spattered blood onto the table.

"What happened?" I asked.

"Basically, all these enzymes there digest blood. This guy was hemorrhagic. The chemicals washed into his blood vessels and he bled. Very common with alcoholics."

Out came the liver now, yellow with fatty infiltrations from too much alcohol. "See the blood inside?" said the doctor. "But the pancreas is a sweetbread. The pancreas is a bloody pulp. Blood in his belly. Sudden death. We got lucky with him—he's an easy one. This is a sure winner."

Quickly he diced sections of the man's organs and let them ooze off his bloody yellow-gloved fingers into amber jars. The pathology and toxicology people would freeze them, slice them thinner, stain them and drop them onto microscope slides, just to make sure that he hadn't overdosed on something while he bled. Meanwhile the doctor's knowledge-seeking scalpel dissected the neck, to rule out any possibility of secret strangulation. Many subtle homicides are misdiagnosed as accidents by untrained people, and some accidents look like murders. The doctor didn't want that to happen. Even though he'd seen the pancreas, he wanted to be as thorough as he could to verify that there was no knifeblade in the mouth, that all the meaning had come out. "Okay, very good," he grunted. Then the attendant, who I should really call a forensic technician, sewed the dead man up, with the garbage bag of guts already stuck back inside his belly. His brain, putrefying, liquescent, had already been removed; his face had hidden beneath its crimson blanket of scalp. The attendant sewed that up, too, and the man had a face again.

"I'm a happy customer," said the doctor.

Of Jokes and Other Shields

If the doctor's wisecracks seem callous to you, ask yourself whether you wouldn't want to be armored against year after year of such sights and smells. Early the next morning I watched another doctor open up an old Filipino man who, sick and despondent, had hanged himself with an electric cord. I have seen a few autopsies and battlefields before, but the man's stern, stubborn stare, his eyes glistening like black glass while the doctor, puffing, dictated case notes and slashed his guts (the yellow twist of strangle-cord lying on an adjacent table) gave me a nightmare that evening. This doctor, like his colleague, the happy customer, was doing a good thing. Both were proving that neither one of these dead men had been murdered, and that neither one had carried some contagious disease. Like soldiers, they worked amidst death. Green-stained buttocks and swollen faces comprised their routine. They had every right to joke, to dull themselves. Those who can't do that don't last.

Strangely enough, even their job could be for some souls a shelter from sadder things. Dr. Stephens himself used to be a pediatric oncologist before he became coroner in 1968. "At that time, we lost seventy-five percent of the children," he said. "Emotionally, that was an extremely hard thing to do. I'd be dead if I stayed in that profession."

The thought of Dr. Stephens ending up on one of his own steel tables bemused me. As it happens, I am married to an oncologist. She goes to the funerals of her child patients. Meanwhile she rushes about her life. Embracing her, I cherish her body's softness which I know comprises crimson guts.

Evidence

The little cubes of meat in the amber jars went across the hall to pathology and to toxicology: underbudgeted realms making do with old instruments and machines which printed out cocaine-spikes or heroin-spikes on the slowly moving graph paper which had been state of the art in the sixties. But after all, how much does death change? Ladies in blue gowns tested the urine samples of motorists suspected of driving while intoxicated, and with equal equanimity checked the urine of the dead. Had they, or had they not died drunk? The drunken motorist who died in a crash, the drunken suicide who'd finally overcome his fear of guns (in seventeenth-century Germany, the authorities encouraged condemned criminals to drink beer or wine before the execution), the drunken homicide victim who'd felt sufficiently invincible to provoke his murder—such descriptors helped attach reason to the death. Meanwhile, the blue-gowned ladies inspected the tissue samples that the doctors across the hall had sent them. I saw a woman bent over a cutting board, probing a granular mass of somebody's tumor, remarking casually on the stench. If the stomach was cancerous, if the liver was full of Tylenol or secobarb, that comprised a story, and Dr. Stephens's people were all the closer to signing off that particular death certificate.

In her gloved hands, a lady twirled a long, black-bulbed tube of somebody's crimson blood. On a table stood a stack of floppy disks marked POLICE CASES. Here was evidence, information, which might someday give birth to meaning. Kidneys floated in large translucent white plastic jars. They too had their secret knives-in-the-mouth—or not. They might explain a sudden collapse—or rationalize the toxic white concentration of barbiturates in the duodenum, if the decedent's last words did not. In San Francisco one out of four suicides left a note. Some of the laconic ones might leave unwitting messages in their vital organs. "I would say that about twenty-five percent of the suicides we have here are justified by real physical illness," Dr. Stephens wrote me. "We had one gentleman recently who flew in from another state, took a taxi to the Golden Gate Bridge, and jumped off. Well, he had inoperable liver cancer. Those are *logical* decisions. As for the others, they have emotional causes. A girl tells a boy she doesn't want to see him anymore, so he goes and hangs himself. No one talked to him and got him over to the realization that there are other women in the world."

Look in the liver then. Find the cancer—or not. That tells us something.

"And homicide?" I asked. "Does that ever show good reason?"

"Well, I've seen only a few justified homicides," Dr. Stephens replied. "We handle a hundred homicides a year, and very few are justified. They're saving their family or their own lives. But the vast majority of homicides are just a waste, just senseless violent crimes to effect punishment."

And accident? And heart attack, and renal failure? No reason even to ask. From the perspective of the viewing room, it is all senseless.

Death Can Never Hurt You Until You Die

On the Saturday morning while the doctor was running the hanged man's intestines through his fingers like a fisherman unkinking line, and the forensic tech, a Ukrainian blonde who told me about her native Odessa, was busily taking the top of his head off with a power saw, I asked: "When bodies decompose, are you at more or less of a risk of infection?"

"Oh, the T.B. bacillus and the AIDS virus degrade pretty quickly," said the doctor. "They have a hard time in dead bodies. Not enough oxygen. But staph and fungus grow . . . The dead you have nothing to fear from. It's the living. It's when you ask a dead man's roommate what happened, and the dead man wakes up and coughs on you."

He finished his job and went out. After thanking the tech and changing out of my scrubs, so did I. I went back into the bright hot world where my death awaited me. If I died in San Francisco, there was one chance in five that they would wheel me into Dr. Stephens's office. Although my surroundings did not seem to loom and reek with death as they had when I came out of the catacombs—I think because the deaths I saw on the autopsy slabs were so grotesquely singular that I could refuse to see myself in them,* whereas the sheer mass and *multiplicity* of the catacomb skulls had worn down my unbelief—still I wondered who would cough on me, or what car would hit me, or which cancer might already be subdividing and stinking inside my belly. The doctor was right: I would not be able to hurt him then, because he'd be ready for me. Nor would his scalpel cause me pain. And I walked down Bryant Street wondering at the strange absurdity of my soul, which had felt most menaced by death when I was probably safest—how could those corpses rise up against me?—and which gloried in removing my disposable mask and inhaling the fresh air, letting myself dissolve into the city with its deadly automobiles and pathogen-breathers, its sailboats and bookstores; above all, its remorseless *futurity.*

III. SIEGE THOUGHTS

And now, closing my eyes, I re-glimpse tangents of atrocities and of wars. I see a wall of skulls in the Paris catacombs. Likewise I see the skulls on the glass shelves at Choeung Ek Killing Field.** In place of the tight wall of catacomb skulls gazing straight on at me, sometimes

*Fresh death or old death, it was not my death, and I shrugged it off. In the catacombs they were so anonymous, with such clean carapaces, that it seemed they'd all died "naturally." At the medical examiner's office, some had died accidentally or strangely, a few had ended themselves, like that old man who'd hanged himself with the electric cord, and every now and then the odd murder case was wheeled in. Looking into the hanged man's stare, I'd felt a little creepy. But to protect me from it, Dr. Stephens had established the doors marked NO ADMITTANCE and POSITIVELY NO ADMITTANCE. As I sit here now, trying to refine these sentences, the only dead thing I can see is a spider glued to my windowpane by its withered web. For the most part I see cars in motion on the wide road, glorious trees, people walking down the sidewalk. The doughnut stand where a juvenile homicide occurred a couple of years ago now glows with sugar and life. I remain as yet in the land of the living, and will not believe in my death.

**I went there twice, and the second was more horrifying than the first. Here those technical-political details don't matter.

arranged in beautiful arches, I see skulls stacked loosely, laid out on the glass display shelves in heaps, not patterns—although it would give a deficient impression to omit the famous "genocide map" a few kilometers away in Phnom Penh; this is a cartographic representation of all Cambodia, comprised of murdered skulls. At Choeung Ek, they lie canted upon each other, peering and grinning, gaping and screaming, categorized by age, sex and even by race (for a few Europeans also died at the hands of the Khmer Rouge). Some bear cracks where the Khmer Rouge smashed those once-living heads with iron bars. But to my uneducated eye there is nothing else to differentiate them from the skulls of Paris. The Angel of Death flies overhead, descends and kills, and then he goes. The relics of his work become indistinguishable, except to specialists such as Dr. Stephens, and to those who were there. (I remember once seeing a movie on the Holocaust. When the lights came on, I felt bitter and depressed. It seemed that the movie had "reached" me. And then I saw a man I knew, and his face was very pale and he was sweating. He was a Jew. He was really there. The Nazis had killed most of his family.) Before the Angel strikes, of course, the doomed remain equally indistinguishable from the lucky or unlucky ones who will survive a little longer. Death becomes apprehensible, perhaps, only at the moment of dying.

To apprehend it, then, let's approach the present moment, the fearful time when they're shooting at you and, forgetting that your life is not perfect, you crave only to live, sweat and thirst a little longer; you promise that you'll cherish your life always, if you can only keep it. Thus near-death, whose violence or not makes no difference. A woman I loved who died of cancer once wrote me: "You will not be aware of this but it is the anniversary of my mastectomy and I am supposed to be happy that I survived and all that. Actually it has been a terrible day." She'd forgotten, like me; she'd shrugged death off again, not being godlike enough to treasure every minute after all. The first time I survived being shot at (maybe they weren't shooting at me; maybe they didn't even see me), I pledged to be happier, to be grateful for my life, and in this I have succeeded, but I still have days when the catacombs and Dr. Stephens's autopsy slabs sink too far below my memory, and I despise and despair at life. Another fright, another horror, and I return to gratitude. The slabs rise up and stink to remind me of my happiness. A year before her terrible day, the one I'd loved had written: "They had to use four needles, four veins last time. I cried as they put the fourth needle in. My veins are not holding up. I vomited even before leaving the doctor's office and then spent four days semi-conscious, vomiting. I thought very seriously about immediate death. Could I overdose on the sleeping pills, I wondered . . . My choices aren't that many and I would like to be there to hate my daughter's boyfriends." I remember the letter before that on pink paper that began, "I know I said I wouldn't write. I lied. I've just been told this weekend that I have invasive breast cancer and will have a mastectomy and removal of the lymph nodes within the week. I am scared to death. I have three small kids . . . I am not vain. I do not care about my chest but I do want to live . . . So, tell me. This fear—I can smell it—is it like being in a war?" —Yes, darling. I have never been terminally ill, but I am sure that it is the same.

In one of her last letters she wrote me: "There was definitely a time when I thought I might die sooner rather than later—it took me awhile to believe that I would probably be okay. It still doesn't feel truly believable but more and more I want it to be the case—mostly because I want to raise my interesting and beautiful children and because I want to enjoy myself . . . My hair grew back to the point that I no longer use the wig."

In another letter she wrote me: "Here are the recent events in my life. I am not unhappy with them but they do not compare with being shot at and losing a friend and perhaps they will amuse you. I set up a fish tank in my study . . . I got the kids four fish. They named only one. I told them once they had learned to clean and change the tank and feed the fish and explain how gills work, then they could get a guinea pig. I am not into pets, preferring children. The one catfish in the tank is in great distress and swims around madly looking for a way to die."

When I close my eyes, I can see her as she looked at seventeen, and I can see her the way she was when she was thirty-four, much older, thanks in part to the cancer—bonier-faced, with sparse hair, perhaps a wig, sitting on the steps beside her children. I never had to see her in Dr. Stephens's viewing room. I never saw her body rotting. I'll never see her depersonalized skull mortared into a catacomb's wall. Does that mean I cannot envision death, her death? The six million death's heads under Paris weigh on me much less than her face, which you might call too gaunt to be beautiful, but which was still beautiful to me, which only in a photograph will I ever see again.

But—again I return to this—her death was meaningless, an accident of genetics or environment. No evil soul murdered her. I am sad when I think about her. I am not bitter.

I am sad when I think about my two colleagues in Bosnia who drove into a land-mine trap. Their names were Will and Francis. I will write about them later. At the time, because there were two distinct reports and holes appeared in the windshield and in the two dying men, I believed that they were shot, and when armed men approached I believed that I was looking at their killers. Will I had known only for two days, but I liked what I knew of him. Francis was my friend, off and on, for nineteen years. I loved Francis. But I was never angry, even when the supposed snipers came, for their actions could not have been personally intended. We were crossing from the Croatian to the Muslim side; the Muslims were sorry, and such incidents are common enough in war.

But now I open a letter from my Serbian friend Vineta, who often had expressed to me her dislike of Francis (whom she never met) on the grounds of his Croatian blood, and who after commenting in considerable helpful and businesslike detail on my journalistic objectives in Serbia, then responded to my plans for the Muslim and Croatian sides of the story (my items seven and eight) as follows: "You see, dear Billy, it's very nice of you to let me know about your plans. But, I DON'T GIVE A SHIT FOR BOTH CROATS AND MUSLIMS!" At the end of her long note she added this postscript: "The last 'personal letter' I got was two years ago, from my late boy-friend. The Croats cut his body into pieces in the town of B_____ near Vukovar. His name was M______." Then she wrote one more postscript: "No one has a chance to open my heart ever again."

This is what violence does. This is what violence is. It is not enough that death reeks and stinks in the world, but now it takes on inimical human forms, prompting the self-defending survivors to strike and to hate, rightly or wrongly. Too simple to argue that nonviolent death is always preferable from the survivors' point of view! I've heard plenty of doctors' stories about the families of dying cancer patients who rage against "fate." Like Hitler, they'd rather have someone to blame. "Everybody's angry when a loved one dies," one doctor insisted. "The only distinction is between directed and undirected anger." Maybe so. But it is a distinction. Leaving behind Dr. Stephens's tables, on which, for the most part, lie only the "naturally" dead with their bleeding pancreases, the accidentally dead, and the occasional suicide, let us fly to besieged Sarajevo and look in on the morgue at Kosevo Hospital, a place I'll never forget, whose stench stayed on my clothes for two days afterwards. Here lay the homicides. I saw children with their bellies blown open, women shot in the head while they crossed the street, men hit by some well-heeled sniper's anti-tank round.* Death joked and drank and vulgarly farted in the mountains all around us, aiming its weapons out of hateful fun, making the besieged counter-hateful. Every morning I woke up to chittering bullets and crashing mortar rounds. I hated the snipers I couldn't see because they might kill me and because they were killing the people of this city, ruining the city in every terrible physical and psychic way that it could be ruined, smashing it, murdering wantonly, frightening and crushing. But their wickedness too had become normal: this was Sarajevo in the fourteenth month of the siege. Needs lived on; people did business amidst their terror, a terror which could not be sustained, rising up only when it was needed, when one had to run. As for the forensic doctor at Kosevo Hospital, he went home stinking of death, and, like me, sometimes slept in his clothes; he was used to the smell, and his wife must have gotten used to it, too, when she embraced him. (Meanwhile, of course, some people had insomnia, got ulcers or menstrual disturbances, went prematurely grey.** Here, too, undirected anger might surface.*** Political death, cancer death, it's all the same.

The night after Will and Francis were killed, a U.N. interpreter from Sarajevo told me how she lost friends almost every week. "You become

*For a description of this place, see "The Back of My Head," in *The Atlas* (p. 5).

**Fanon found these psychosomatic symptoms in Algeria, and mentions that they were very common "in the Soviet Union among the besieged populations of towns, notably in Stalingrad" (*The Wretched of the Earth*, pp. 290-93).

***For one of Fanon's patients, an Algerian who survived a mass execution conducted by the French because "there's been too much talk about this village; destroy it," the Angel of Death wore everyone's face: "You all want to kill me but you should set about it differently. I'll kill you all as soon as look at you, big ones and little ones, women, children, dogs, donkeys . . ." (op. cit., pp. 259-61).

a little cold," she said very quietly. "You have to." This woman was sympathetic, immensely kind; in saying this she meant neither to dismiss my grief nor to tell me how I ought to be. She merely did the best thing that can be done for any bereaved person, which was to show me her own sadness, so that my sadness would feel less lonely; but hers had wearied and congealed; thus she told me what she had become. Like Dr. Stephens and his crew, or the backpack inspector at the catacombs, like my friend Thion who ferries tourists to Choeung Ek on his motorcycle, I had already begun to become that way. Sarajevo wasn't the first war zone I'd been to, nor the first where I'd seen death, but I'll never forget it. The morgue at Kosevo Hospital, like the rest of Sarajevo, had had to make do without electricity, which was why, as I keep saying, it stank. I remember the cheesy smell of the Paris catacombs, the sour-milk smell of Dr. Stephens's white hearse; after that visit to Kosevo Hospital my clothes smelled like vomit, vinegar, and rotting bowels. I returned to the place where I was staying, which got its share of machine gun and missile attacks, and gathered together my concerns, which did not consist of sadness for the dead, but only of being scared and wondering if I would eat anymore that day because they'd shot down the U.N. flight and so the airport was closed and I'd already given my food away. Death was on my skin and on the other side of the wall—maybe my death, maybe not; trying to live wisely and carefully, I granted no time to my death, although it sometimes snarled at me. Ascending from the catacombs I'd had all day, so I'd given death all day; no one wanted to hurt me. But in Sarajevo I simply ran; it was all death, death and death, so meaningless and accidental to me.

I wore a bulletproof vest in Mostar, which did get struck with a splinter of something which rang on its ceramic trauma plate, so to an extent I had made my own luck, but Will, who was driving, discovered that his allotted death was one which entered the face now, diagonally from the chin. His dying took forever (I think about five minutes). Vineta said that I had been cowardly or stupid not to end his misery. I told her that journalists don't carry guns. Anyhow, had I been in his seat, my bulletproof vest would have done me no good.

The woman I loved simply had the wrong cells in her breast; Vineta's boyfriend had fought in the wrong place at the wrong time, and perhaps he'd fought against the Croats too ferociously or even just too well.* For the woman I loved, and for me in Sarajevo, the Angel of Death was faceless, but Vineta's tormenting Angel of Death had a Croatian face; she hated "those Croatian bastards." Vineta, if I could send the Angel of Death away from you, I would. Maybe someone who knows you and loves you better than I can at least persuade your Angel to veil his face again so that he becomes mere darkness like the Faceless One of Iroquois legends, mere evil chance, "an act of war," like my drowned sister's Angel; and then your anger can die down to sadness. Vineta, if you ever see this book of mine, don't think me presumptuous; don't think I would ever stand between you and your right to mourn and rage against the Angel. But he is not Francis. Francis was good. I don't like to see him stealing Francis's face when he comes to hurt you.

The Angel is in the white hearse. Can't we please proceed like Dr. Stephens's employees, weighing, fingerprinting, cutting open all this sad and stinking dross of violence, trying to learn what causes what? And when the malignity or the sadness or the unpleasantness of the thing on the table threatens to craze us, can't we tell a callous joke or two? If I can contribute to understanding how and why the Angel kills, then I'll be, in the words of that doctor who swilled coffee out of one bloody-gloved hand while he sliced a dead body with the other, "a happy customer." Hence this essay, and the larger work from which this is extracted. For its many failures I ask forgiveness from all.

*Martin Luther King insisted in his funeral for victims of the Birmingham bombing that "history has proven over and over again that unmerited suffering is redemptive. The innocent blood of these little girls may well serve as the redemptive force that will bring new light to this dark city" (King, *Testament of Hope,* p. 221; "Eulogy for the Martyred Children," September 1963). As for me, I don't believe that such redemption occurs very often.

Across the Divide

From
The New Yorker (May 15, 2000)

This abridgement of a chapter that appears in *Rising Up and Rising Down* went through approximately forty separate edits by *The New Yorker,* which also substantially rearranged the sequence of materials.

DESCENDING THE KHYBER PASS from Pakistan one enters a tan-colored desert that resembles the tough interior membrane of a pomegranate—a wearying, lifeless place. Emerald wheat fields, trees shining with figs and oranges, and armies of snowy hills present themselves from time to time, but the region is mostly sand, pebble heaps, and drum-hard earth, tramped down by glaciers and soldiers. I remember gazing into that desert from Pakistan, back in 1982. The Afghan insurgents I was traveling with had shown me a Soviet sentry box and the road behind it that went on into infinity. It was a reasonably good road then. By the time I returned, last January, hardly a scrap of asphalt remained on its bomb-cratered, potholed track.

I had never driven down it before. In 1982, my companions had led me over the mountains from the Pakistani town of Parachinar in order to avoid the Soviet garrison. Now this border crossing was open. After eighteen years, I was going back to a country that had been my symbol of heroism—a place where poor peasants had risen up against arrogant and cruel invaders and washed them away with their own blood. Those invaders had been gone for a decade. The new government, run by members of the fundamentalist Islamic movement known as the Taliban, was literal-minded and stern, like the freedom fighters who'd inspired me years before. It was despised by much of the Western world, but I wanted to know what the Afghans, who had to live with it, thought.

My translator and I changed money in the border town of Torkham, got a taxi, and rattled down into Afghanistan. For scenic attractions, we had the stumps of a razed orange grove, wrecked Soviet tanks, and refugee mud villages, abandoned now and crumbling into dust. There were warnings of land mines, and once in a great while a listless-looking man could be seen far off on the dreary plain, dragging a golf-club-shaped mine detector through the rocks. I saw virtually no usable habitation, not even a tent. Nevertheless, every few hundred yards there'd be a dirty boy or girl waiting by the side of the road. As our taxi approached, the child would sink a shovel just far enough into the dirt to collect a few clods, then dribble them into the nearest pothole, pretending to improve the road for our journey, hoping for payment. A burning stare, a shout, and then we were on our way to the next beggar.

If I stopped and gave money to a child, others came running. I slipped one boy five thousand afghanis—about ten cents—and when I looked back in the rearview mirror it seemed that the other boys were practically tearing him to pieces. On a road bend where no other beggar could see, I gave a twenty-dollar bill to a boy who stood beside the carapace of a Soviet armored personnel carrier, and he took it and held it as if he were dreaming. I wanted him to hide it before anybody else came or the wind took it from him, but the last I saw of him he was still standing there with the banknote dangling from his hand.

It was like this most of the way to Kabul, some hundred and twenty miles from the border. Inside the capital's war-pocked walls, beggar women and children would wait outside the windows of restaurants, crowding against the glass and drumming on it desperately. If I sent a plateful of food out to them, they'd fall on it in the same way that skates and manta rays occlude their scavenged prey—guarding it with their own flesh while they eat. When I left the restaurant and got into a taxi, the children would try to climb in, too. I couldn't bring myself to slam the door on their hands, so the taxi would roll down the street with the door open, gradually increasing speed until they had to let go. Once I went out alone at dusk, and an army of children fell upon me, clawing at me for money, shouting obscenities, and laughing that the Taliban would kill me because I wore bluejeans instead of the stipulated shalwar kameez—a long shirt and baggy pantaloons. They were the children first of war and then of poverty, growing up hungry and ignorant (although some of the boys claimed to go to school), with not much either to amuse them or to make them hopeful.

But I must have been missing the point: in Pakistan, where I'd spent almost three weeks waiting for an Afghan visa, people had rhapsodized about the quality of life in Afghanistan. Several Afghan women teachers I met in a refugee camp expressed admiration for the Taliban—even though under Taliban rule they wouldn't be allowed to teach. A Pakistani government official in Islamabad said that he adored the Talibs. And in the border city of Peshawar, where I stayed in a six-dollar hotel, the clerk, a gentle, bad-complexioned boy, who came to my room every evening to answer questions about the Koran, told me, "Afghanistan is now the most perfect country in the world." Times had changed. In 1982, every Pakistani male I met had wanted to be photographed. But although this boy trusted me, he refused to let me take his picture, because the Taliban had decreed that doing so broke the rules of Islam.

The Volunteers

In Afghanistan's deserts, plains, and valleys live many ethnic groups—the Pashtuns, the Tajiks, the Hazaras, and others—who greet strangers with a welcoming hand on their hearts and devote themselves with equal zeal to blood feuds. The mountains stand sentinel between them, and each group tends to keep to itself. Thanks to Islam, each sex likewise keeps itself apart from the other. So Afghans live both separately and inwardly, whether they sleep in tents or wall themselves away in fortresses of baked mud. They are watchful, hospitable, yet withdrawn, magnificent and vindictive, kind and lethally factional, untiringly violent. In the fierce stewardship of their honor, Afghans sometimes remind me, despite their religious differences, of the Serbs. But, unlike the Serbs, they are repelled by the concept of nationality. Each group tells its own stories—the Caucasian-looking Pashtuns badmouthing the Asiatic-looking Hazaras, and vice versa—and "government" operates in a distant dreamland where houses have electricity, women can read, and officials flaunt the money they've extorted from the people. What unites the Afghans, if anything, is the monitory, glorious religion of Islam.

It follows, then, that those who do not pray, or who pray to other gods, must stay forever beyond the pale, while those who believe as the Muslim does, no matter what their color, language, or nationality, are his brothers and sisters. This is why Muslim zealots call for a worldwide Islamic state, and why the Iran-Iraq War was infinitely more distressing to Muslims than any conflict between two Christian nations would be to us in our easy secularity. (So ingrained is this notion of Muslim kinship that the very few secret Christians of Afghanistan, who risk imprisonment to hold clandestine Bible readings at home, unfailingly embraced me and called me "brother.") Therefore, when the Soviet Union invaded Afghanistan, in December 1979, fighters came at once from Saudi Arabia, and, to varying degrees, from Pakistan, Yemen, Libya, Tajikistan, and other Muslim regions. There may have been some thirty-five thousand of these nominally foreign volunteers.

Afghanistan had been far from stable before the invasion. The longstanding Afghan monarchy had been overthrown in 1973, in a military coup led by a cousin of the king, Muhammad Daoud. Then, after five years in power, Daoud and seventeen members of his family were killed by pro-Soviet Afghan leftists, who planned to achieve their own form of utopia by forcibly de-Islamicizing the countryside. By the time the first Russian troops arrived, a year later, those Communist Afghans had been largely discredited among the masses, who resented their atheism and cruel vanguardism.

Ironically, the Soviet invasion did much to unite Afghanistan. The country's many tribes and factions banded together to proclaim a jihad, or religious war, against the Soviet infidels. And the United States helped to arm these insurgents. In those days, they were "freedom fighters" to us, not "terrorists." They called themselves mujahideen, or holy warriors, but to the C.I.A. the religious aspect of the jihad was irrelevant—the war was "strategic," a good way to get back at the opposing chess team in Moscow.

When I went to Afghanistan in 1982, I supported the struggle in every way that I could, because it seemed one of the clearest cases I had witnessed of good versus evil. The mujahideen were certainly not guiltless then, but the deeds of the Soviets were unspeakable. They raped women in the name of emancipating them. In the defense of national security, they machine-gunned illiterate peasants who couldn't have found Moscow on a map. They burned people alive and drowned them in excrement. They razed villages, slaughtered livestock, and destroyed harvests. They even scattered mines disguised as toys, to lure people to their own maiming. In 1982, I saw several of these mines lying, unexploded, on the ground. Between a million and two million Afghans were killed in that war, ninety per cent of them civilians. (Of the more than six hundred thousand Soviet soldiers sent to Afghanistan, fewer than fifteen thousand were killed.) The Afghans I met at that time were bright-eyed with fervor. Sick refugees said, "Tell America not to send medicine. Send guns." In the secret insurgent base where I stayed, not far from the Pakistani border, a commander told me, "I am not fighting for myself or even for Afghanistan. I am fighting only for God."

On February 15, 1989, to the world's amazement, the Soviets marched out of Afghanistan. The Afghans had won the war! Within a few years, they had ousted the Russians' last show ruler, President Muhammad Najibullah, and installed in his place a white-bearded Islamic scholar named Burhannudin Rabbani. But, instead of putting war behind them, the mujahideen—who had now organized themselves into seven factions, constituted, in customary Afghan style, along geographical, tribal, and sectarian lines—trained their weapons on one another. Each camp struggled for supreme power in Kabul, some supported by puppetmasters in other countries—Iran, Pakistan, Saudi Arabia, and, perhaps, the United States—transforming the war for liberation into a bloody and protracted civil war.

With the factions locked in battle like fighting beetles in a jar, five years went by and, according to one estimate, twenty thousand people died. Then, in 1994, the residents of Kabul heard a rumor from the south. It seemed that a group of young men—Islamic students, or *taliban*—had risen up in Kandahar, Afghanistan's second-largest city, which was then proverbial for its lawlessness. In the name of Allah the Beneficent, these Taliban, as members of the movement came to be known, had slain, captured, or driven off every criminal. Then they had confiscated all weapons, promising that they themselves would provide protection for the citizens. The streets secured, they applied Islamic law as they saw fit: they banned photographs, education for girls, and music. They demanded that women cover their faces in the street and leave home only in the company of a close male relative. All men found themselves required to grow beards and could be sent to prison for ten days if they shaved. In keeping with the Koran, the Taliban amputated the right hands of thieves. Kandahar was now so safe, it was said, that anyone could leave a bar of gold in the street and it would be there three days later.

The origins of the movement are murky. It reportedly began with forty Talibs, but no one could tell me how quickly other Afghans decided to join them. Their leader, Mullah Muhammad Omar, who'd lost an eye in the jihad, was reputed to be a quiet, simple man, although it was also said that he enjoyed a legal complement of three wives, one of whom was rumored to be as beautiful as any princess in the Arabian Nights. The fact that almost nobody was allowed to meet him enhanced his mythic stature. Some claimed that Mullah Omar and his followers were soldiers of the old king, Zahir Shah, who'd been deposed more than two decades before and was now in exile in Italy. Others suspected that they might be fanatics who meant to take away what scant freedoms remained in Afghanistan. But they were not rapists or wanton murderers like the other fighters, and most Afghans, paralyzed by decades of war, withheld judgment, as the Taliban spread to other cities and provinces, calling upon each man in their path to lay down his weapons in the name of Allah. For the most part, they were received with respect, even love: they brought peace. "I was proud to give up my arms," a tea-shop proprietor I met told me. "I started my jihad for an Islamic Afghanistan, and so we succeeded." Every time the Taliban disarmed others, their own arsenal grew.

In a few places, however, they encountered significant opposition. It took the Taliban cadres several attempts to conquer the northern city of Mazar-i-Sharif, which was then occupied by a former mujahideen general. The first time, the Taliban were invited in and then betrayed, thousands of them killed in cold blood. Their second attempt to take the city was repulsed. The third succeeded, at which point the Taliban are said to have murdered a thousand civilians. (I heard this figure go as high as five thousand. In central Asia, as in every other part of the world, atrocity statistics are always suspect.) A Hazara former civil servant told me that after the massacre he had seen stray dogs eating human flesh in the streets, and stacks of corpses, "like piles of firewood."

The Taliban also encountered resistance in Kabul, which, when they arrived in 1995, was still under the control of President Rabbani and his most famous general, Ahmed Shah Masoud, a brave and brutal Tajik fighter. The resistance that Masoud mounted against the Talibs in Kabul, together with the city's perceived decadent cosmopolitanism, made the Taliban especially harsh on the people there, once they had won control.

Still, by 1998, the Taliban had conquered about ninety per cent of Afghanistan. Despite their frequent attempts to complete the takeover—which are said to have caused as many as forty thousand casualties—the other ten per cent, a swath of land in the northeast of the country, remains under the control of Masoud, Rabbani, and their supporters, who call themselves the National Islamic United Front for the Salvation of Afghanistan, and are also known as the Northern Alliance.

Who are the Talibs who are running Afghanistan now? They are Muslims, only a little more so. At five-thirty every morning, they don black, white, or green turbans and go to the mosque like other Afghans. (The muezzin, whose beautifully quavering song calls everyone to prayer, is now most often a Talib.) They come home and read the Koran or the hadiths—the recorded sayings and doings of the Prophet Muhammad—until sunrise. Afterward, they take tea. They go to work. Some Taliban are shopkeepers. Some work at the Ministry for the Propagation of Virtue and the Prevention of Vice.

Fifteen minutes after I arrived in Kabul, I met one of these worthies (my translator, awed and anxious, warned me how powerful he was). He was walking down a snowy street, across from a park in which children were playing. Kabul is high and cold—a ruin surrounded by mountains—so poverty is more lethal there. Men struggle to support their families, selling their belongings for a little food. They lurk on corners, looking for buyers. When I greeted the Talib, he instantly invited me home for tea. His responsibility at the Ministry was to police the front lines for anti-Taliban sentiment and to insure that all the soldiers wore beards and refrained from smoking opium. He also investigated cases of Talibs who misused the signature turban in order to extort money. He and three colleagues who shared his house—two young men, one shy older man—sat with me on the floor of a bleak concrete room. They treated me with the usual Afghan politeness—handshakes, the most comfortable cushion, hands on their hearts. Even when they learned my nationality, their courtesy did not flag.

Diplomatic relations between our countries were suspended in 1998, when the United States bombed bases in Afghanistan that it claimed were run by Osama bin Laden, a Saudi-born former mujahid, who United States officials believe was responsible for the 1998 bombings of American embassies in Tanzania and Kenya. Later, when the Taliban refused to hand bin Laden over to American justice, the United Nations imposed sanctions. Now most of the Afghans I met hated the United States, and they withdrew from me a little in dignified sadness, but they still, like these four Talibs, spoke with me and invited me into their homes.

The concrete walls of the Talibs' room displayed nothing but cracks; all emblems were prohibited. Even their Korans were wrapped lovingly out of sight. When I unclothed mine, in order to ask them some textual questions, tears started in one man's eyes. They wanted to help me learn. A space heater waxed and waned, according to the vagaries of that day's electricity. As we sat and chatted, they scrupulously filled my tea glass. We passed the time. I asked how I might go about interviewing a woman, and they said that they could arrange a conversation through a black curtain, but once I pressed them they retreated, and after some discussion they concluded that to speak with any female I would first need to get permission from the Ministry of Foreign Affairs. I told them not to trouble themselves further in this matter, and their spirits lifted.

We talked about the jihad. All four had been mujahideen. The three younger men had spent their childhoods wandering in and out of Pakistan, as their families changed refugee camps according to the latest military reverse or factional split. When they were about ten years old, their fathers had enrolled them in madrasahs, or religious schools, the only remaining institutions of learning in the country. (This was, and is, the way to become a member of the Taliban.) There they were taught Islamic law without ambiguities: Cut off the thief's hand. The woman must cover herself. How much of herself must she cover? The Koran doesn't tell us exactly, so make her cover everything! Such an edict is easy to enforce. This is army life, and these boys were soldiers. Every summer, they would take up their Kalashnikovs and shoot at Soviet tanks or gunship helicopters. They were taught that if they fell in battle they'd go to Heaven. After the war, they returned to their religious studies, and, when they heard about the corruption of the former mujahideen and the emergence of the Taliban movement, they travelled to Kandahar to enlist.

"Were you feeling happy, or did you simply feel compelled to do your duty?" I asked the man who'd invited me to tea.

"So happy! We volunteered," he replied.

"What was the first thing you did in Kandahar?"

"We instituted Islamic law."

"And were the people pleased?"

"They gave us flowers and money."

Later, a little awkwardly, he pulled up the baggy cotton legs of his shalwar kameez and showed me the scars on his legs from fighting for the Taliban. He had spent a month in the hospital. Smiling, half proud, half ashamed, he gazed down at his wasted purple flesh.

On my innumerable trips between Peshawar and Islamabad to obtain an Afghan visa, I had travelled through the little Pakistani town of Akora Khattak, the site of the most famous madrasah, Darul Uloom Haqqania, where the three younger Talibs had studied. The madrasah stands right on the main road, and an armed guard lazes outside its high white walls. About thirty per cent of the current Taliban leadership, including the Ambassador to Pakistan and the Foreign Minister, have passed through the school's spiked iron gate. The rank and file study there by the thousand.

The head of the school was in Libya on the day of my visit, so I met with his son, Rashid ul Haq, the editor-in-chief of the militant Islamic monthly *Al-Haq*. If anyone could help me understand the Taliban's interpretation of Islamic law, or Shariah, I thought, it was he. We sat on the carpet of an inner room, attended by bearded, shining-eyed men in prayer caps or turbans.

"What makes the Taliban government different from that of other Islamic states?" I asked.

"You have seen the other countries," ul Haq replied, "but the others are living not according to the Koran but according to their own choice."

"Why have the Taliban made beards compulsory for men?"

"All prophets have beards," he said. "So we want to have beards. Some of the people, you know, live their lives according to the hadiths."

I wondered if he knew how unpopular this edict had become. As slang for "I left Afghanistan," some Afghan men had begun to say "I shaved the beard." Surgeons especially hated the rule, because in their own compulsory beards dwelled their patients' worst enemies: microbes.

"And why is music forbidden?" I asked.

"Islam does not permit it. People who sing create the thing that causes cowardice. And when a person spends his time in singing he loses his time."

"And what about the prohibition on images of people and animals?"

"In the hadiths, the picture is forbidden for the man," ul Haq said, and later added, "But Islam allows it when there is a need, as for visa photographs and pictures on currency."

I had just interviewed two Afghan brothers in a nearby refugee camp who loved the Taliban, except for one thing. Their father had been martyred in the jihad, and all they had to remember him by was a small photograph. They told me that if the Taliban ever found it they might tear the picture into pieces.

"And exactly why does Islam say that such pictures are forbidden?"

"We do not want to see the logic of this talk," one of the other Taliban interjected. "What the Koran says is right. The logic is present."

The Western notion that the Taliban imposed themselves by force on an unwilling population is less than half true. Six years after that first unexpected uprising against the bandits of Kandahar, when one might well expect the Afghans to be heartily sick of any regime in whose name their misery continued, many people I spoke with expressed contentment with the Taliban. Why? Quite simply, because they could not forget how bad it had been before.

Afghanistan was never rich. During the war with the Soviet Union, men used to fight over the scrap iron of Russian bomb casings even as other bombs fell upon them; one entrepreneur actually posted mujahideen slogans in the desert so that the Soviets would bomb them and he could collect the metal. And, by the time the Taliban marched onstage, the civil war had made matters worse.

In a long, thick-walled teahouse in the Abrishini Gorge, on the main road between Jalalabad and Kabul, I sat cross-legged on a concrete platform and ate oiled chicken and bread while a middle-aged former taxi-driver told me how it had been in that vacuum of years between the Soviets and the Taliban. Pointing down at the gray-green river, he said, "That was where they took my two passengers."

Back then, in this part of the country, ex-mujahideen gunmen had established roadblocks every kilometer or two, where they would extort money from the taxi-driver's passengers. One night, when the taxi-driver reached one of these roadblocks, the men gestured with their rifle butts and summoned two men from the back of his car. The driver watched them being frog-marched into the gorge, and then the gunmen told him that he could go. His remaining passengers urged him to resist, but he was terrified. Fortunately, the two kidnapped men were released, although, of course, they'd been stripped of their possessions. The driver never forgot his helpless fear and shame. That was why he revered the Taliban. Not a single one of those checkpoints remained in the Abrishini Gorge: now Talibs sat tranquilly beside machine guns, gazing down at the road from their stone forts.

"You know how hard it is to take the weapon from Pashtun people," one Talib had said to me proudly. "Ninety per cent of the Afghan people now live in weapon-free areas."

"If things keep getting safer," the former taxi-driver said, "I don't care about not being allowed to listen to the radio."

"My two sons were both martyred by Masoud," an old beggar woman in Kabul had told me—illegally, since it was against the law for her to talk to me. "One lay for forty-seven days in a well. My husband was also martyred when the Masoud people stole his car. Now I'm looking for food in the streets. At least the Taliban won't kill me."

"They are better than everyone," another beggar woman said.

* * *

How many Afghans truly felt as those women did? Predictably, when the happiness over the restoration of peace wore off and the poverty and hardship remained, some of the gratitude soured. On the street in Kabul, late one cold evening, I met an old night watchman with a long snowy beard. All five of his sons had died in the jihad, he told me. To lose five children—I can hardly even understand the grief, and one must understand it, or at least try, if one wants to come close to experiencing the terrible reality of Afghanistan's misfortunes. One must also consider the plight of the homeless orphans—there are so many of them—and of the hungry widows and the brideless boys. "I have given my children and my brothers for this country," the night watchman added. "Now look at me. I am doing this job for my food only, and it is very cold. What kind of life is this?"

His words were not quite an indictment of the Taliban. I've met many human-rights advocates who, exasperated with the regime's judicial and extrajudicial abuses, rushed to lay blame on Mullah Omar's cadres for everything else—the short life expectancy in Afghanistan, the extraordinarily high infant-mortality rate, and so on. The fact is that the Afghan countryside was always unclean and unhealthy; people have always died young. To me, it is indicative of the regime's popularity (or, in some cases, of the fear that it inspires) that more Afghans do not denounce its turbaned agents of perfection.

But some do. Whereas the jihad and the civil war had harmed the population almost indiscriminately, Taliban policy has created a smaller, more specific class of victims. More than two-thirds of Mullah Omar's cadres are Pashtuns, who make up about fifty-five per cent of the general population, and several of the other ethnic groups feel a certain chill in the air. Some were victimized during the Taliban takeover. Many of the civilians killed by the Taliban in Mazar-i-Sharif, for instance, were Turkmen, Uzbeks, and Hazaras. Some are discriminated against by the Taliban for religious reasons; the Hazaras, who comprise about eight per cent of the population, tend to belong to the minority Shia sect of Islam, whereas most Pashtuns are Sunnis.

Women, particularly urban, educated women, have suffered some of the most painful consequences of the Taliban's interpretation of Islamic law. Many who had lost family members in the jihad or civil war then lost their jobs under the Taliban—along with their freedom of movement and dress—and now have no means of supporting themselves; most are forced to beg.

In the opinion of a Kabuli boy, who resented this strictness—he could not get enough work and was the sole source of money and food for the women in his family—forty per cent of the people support the Taliban now, but only five per cent are true members.

"How can they keep control?" I asked.

"They have Kalashnikovs," he said.

The Women

Jalalabad, a city forty miles west of the Khyber Pass, has a rural feel, with long strings of laden camels on the main streets and packed-earth dikes curving crazily through the wheat fields just outside town. Amid the city's wide, slow streets of rickshaws, bicycles, and very occasional cars, I saw boys bearing metal trays of eggs on their prayer-capped heads. The ringing of bicycle bells, the tapping of hammers, the splash as a man emptied a pot of water in the street, the clip-clopping of horses—all these sounds enriched the air, as did the scent of the fresh oranges and the fat, nearly scarlet carrots that lay everywhere on venders' tables. Here came a woman in a green burka—the head-to-toe veil required by the Taliban—holding a dirty little boy by the hand. A woman in a blue burka, whose pleated wake streamed behind her as she walked, carried a baby girl wrapped in a blue blanket. Nothing seemed wrong; it could have been Peshawar, except that the air was less sulfurous and the rickshaws were not adorned with the faces of Indian movie actresses.

To be sure, the scene was overwhelmingly male; after the two women had passed, I saw only men on bicycles, with white prayer caps and brown or gray blankets. But maybe in this, too, Jalalabad was not so different from Peshawar. The wife of my driver in that city never went out except to visit her close relatives; her husband and sons did all the shopping in the bazaar, because (her husband explained) once or twice nothing would happen, but if she went a thousand times alone, why, sooner or later she might cross glances with some bright-eyed young boy and wonder how his kisses would taste.

One Tajik Afghan woman I met in Peshawar spoke for herself. She had fled the capital for Pakistan the year before. "The first day the Taliban entered Kabul, all the people were in a state of panic, especially us women," she told me. "The first announcement was that all women must cover their faces with a black cloth. Later, they decided that we should use the national burka. The teachers went to school just to sign their attendance sheets, then went straight home. I was formerly in charge of the literary programs of Radio Kabul. For about six months, I stayed at home."

On the subject of female employment, the Koran clearly states, "For men is the benefit of what they earn. And for women is the benefit of what they earn." The Taliban got around this by continuing to pay male and female schoolteachers the same munificent three or four dollars a month they got before but prohibiting the women from working in exchange for their salaries. With the exception of doctors and nurses, professional women in Afghanistan were no longer allowed to exercise their vocations.

"And after six months what did you do?" I asked.

"As the Taliban didn't have qualified workers, they had to use some of the former employees, even some women, to help them." She gave me a bitter flash of teeth. "They had to, because they were not fully literate."

"What's the worst thing they did?"

"My worst memory is of when they beat a poetess, a friend of mine. I was not the eyewitness. My friend went shopping one day and wanted to buy some fruit. When she needed to pay the fruit seller, she lifted the burka to see the money in her purse, and suddenly a Talib began beating her with a whip. For about one week, she was in very critical condition."

"What did the fruit seller do?"

"Nothing. He could do nothing. No one defended her."

"And what incidents of this kind did you personally see?"

"Well, I went together with another lady to get our salary from Radio Kabul, and one of my female friends, when she got the salary, thought no one would hurt her, and she opened her burka to count the money in the yard. Then suddenly a Talib whipped her." She cleared her throat and added, "The person distributing the salary was an old man. So they took him into the street and beat him also, two or three times. He kept silent. They asked him, 'Why do you let the ladies show themselves like that?' "

In the most orthodox galaxies of the Muslim universe, the admiration of women's faces is thought to distract men from their duty, to tempt them to fornication, adultery, and rape, and, in cases of obsessive love, to cause them to ascribe, blasphemously, divine qualities to their beloved. "Say to the believing men that they lower their gaze and restrain their sexual passions," the Koran warns. "And say to the believing women that they lower their gaze and restrain their sexual passions and do not display their adornment except what appears thereof. And let them wear their head-coverings over their bosoms.

In Malaysia, a head scarf is often considered sufficient to obey this edict. In Pakistan, however, as you move north and west the weight of seclusion falls more heavily on overt femininity, until by the time you reach the Northwest Frontier Province, where the Khyber Pass leads to Afghanistan and the Pashtuns live in mazelike compounds of plaster and baked mud, almost every woman one sees on the street is a generic ghost in a burka or a shroud. In Afghanistan, a man may speak with a strange woman under almost no circumstances. If a beggar woman on the sidewalk stretches out her hand, he may put money in it, but looking directly at her or communicating with her for more than a second or two is indecent. Should any friend invite him home—and Pashtuns are the most hospitable people I've met—then sweets and tea will be presented by the host himself, who brings them from behind a closed door.

Travelling in this area, I often thought of the words of an old major general, a kindly, respected, and powerful Pashtun, who took me into his household in 1982. After I had stayed with him for some weeks, he brought me from the guesthouse into the sanctum, where I met and even conversed a little with his wife and daughters. He was still alive when I returned to Peshawar this year. Since I'd seen him last, he had endowed a hospital with separate entrances for men and women, a boys' high school, and a girls' high school. He said to me, "A woman is a housewife. She raises your children, she gives you food, she keeps everything in order. Can you do as much? Of course not. That is why you must respect her." On another occasion, when we were talking about the Western custom of dating, he said, "How can a boy be so cruel? He takes a girl and he uses her like a football. Then he kicks her away to the next boy. Poor girl!"

Fatana Ishaq Gailani, a politician and the wife of a famous mujahideen leader, detested the Taliban, but when I asked her how she felt about the sura, or Koranic verse, regarding head-covering she replied, her voice rising, "It is for the safety of the woman. It is *kindly* for the woman. We are so happy we are a Muslim woman."

"The Taliban are giving rights to the woman," Rashid ul Haq had insisted. "That right is to live safely in their homes." He added, "Right now, if a single woman wants to go anywhere in a village without fear, she is free to do so."

That was true, I suppose, if we discounted the fact that doing so alone was illegal. But ul Haq did not see this as a contradiction, perhaps because in the countryside the Taliban's edicts are almost unenforced. Just outside Jalalabad, one sees raised paths subdividing wheat fields into arcs and polygons in which men and women work together and the women rarely wear the burka; indeed, since they are sweating and stooping so much, their heads often remain uncovered. The Taliban has scarcely altered the lives of uneducated women, except to make them almost entirely safe from rape.

A baffled and angry Talib asked me why the American media worry so much about the tiny number of Afghan women who had actually belonged to the educated labor force. And from a practical point of view he had reason to be mystified. But the aspirations of those Afghan city women he dismissed had been utterly dashed.

According to a 1997 United Nations report, less than a quarter of the women in Pakistan can read, whereas almost half the male population is literate. Women receive twenty-one per cent of the national income. We can assume that in Afghanistan the figures are even more skewed. In Kabul, I looked through the shattered windows of a girls' school that had closed long ago, during the civil war.

"Why don't they open it now?" I asked a Talib.

"Because the war is not yet over," he explained. "We need to protect the ladies."

* * *

"If a Talib sees a woman wearing a head scarf but no burka, what will happen to her?" I asked a man in Kabul.

"She will be whipped. If they see girl and boy talking together, they will take them to the stadium and lash them."

"How many times have you seen that happen?"

"One. She was speaking with boyfriend. And they punish her in the stadium. They lash the woman. Make her sitting down, and lash her through the burka."

"How many days afterward was she likely to remain injured?"

"For two, three months. Some die from this action."

"Do they punish boys or girls most often?"

"Mainly girls. Boys can run—boys can escape from them," he said, adding shyly, "I have heard that in America the girls can walk uncovered even above the knee. It is true?"

It was strange to think that in the seventies, before the Soviets and the Afghan factionalists destroyed it, there had been a Kabul University, that some of the students there were female, and that some of them even wore miniskirts.

In Peshawar, I met one of those former cosmopolitan girls from Kabul. She had been a member of what the Soviets would call the "possessing classes"—she had a baccalaureate in electrical engineering and had been an employee of the Ministry of Civil Aviation. One might imagine that a person with such advantages would enjoy some protection from war. But by the time I met her she was a beggar and a prostitute. She was twenty-three and looked forty. She told me that, six years before, she had been walking home when troops commanded by a former mujahideen general, Rashid Dostam, entered Kabul. By that time, more than half the city had been destroyed by bombs, and the ruined houses resembled the jagged undulations of the mountain peaks around the city. As the girl was crossing a bridge, four armed men rose up. To save her honor, she pounded on the door of the nearest house and was sheltered by the man who lived there, at great risk to him. After some hours, she assumed that the soldiers had found somebody else to rape, but the moment she appeared on the street they fired a rocket-propelled grenade that wounded her in both feet. Luckily, the man took her back in, and she later returned home. I said that her family must have been relieved to see her. Staring at me wide-eyed, she replied that her father had been killed a year or two before that. Her mother died later, in the fighting between Masoud and the Taliban. The girl had hung on until the edict against female employment ended her government job, and she was forced to beg and prostitute herself to survive.

It was a sharp-edged and pointless story no matter how it ended. A silence ensued, and then the woman remarked that at one time she had known how to speak a little English and Russian. Exhaustion and hunger had injured her memory. She was half broken. She was one of thousands.

In the ruined parts of Kabul, I spoke with a number of other beggar women. For the most part, these interviews were quick and almost sordid, like acts of prostitution. The taxi waited with the motor running; if any Taliban came, I could always speed away. "What if I were to bring one of those women back for tea?" I asked my translator once. "You cannot," he said. "First of all, look at these Taliban behind us." (I looked and suddenly saw a whole squad of them, long-bearded and dark-eyed, in their green turbans.) "And, second of all, it's illegal." Every single time (except in the case of one Hazara woman), the woman would say that she supported the Taliban regime because it was better than any other in recent memory. Then I'd give her money, and we'd flee our separate ways, for fear of the Taliban.

In Jalalabad, a man told me that a beggar woman had come up to him and wept, "Don't you recognize me?" She turned out to be his elementary-school teacher. Then he, too, had burst into tears and given her all the money he had. She was almost inexpressibly sad and furious at the Taliban. The beggar women I met in Kabul, though, either were not educated or had suffered terrible things at the hands of previous factions. Or perhaps they just feared to tell me the truth. I will never know how they really felt. But they spoke to me without shame and let me photograph them through their burkas as much as I liked, and even see their faces if I asked to.

On the sidewalk beside a destroyed department store in Kabul, a blue burka stood looking at me, and I heard a young girl's laughter inside it.

Next to the blue burka, a yellow burka was begging, its inhabitant also young, or so I guessed by the speed and mobility of the movements within it. Side by side they stood chatting, their faces shining vaguely through the mesh. It was a chilly day, and a steam of pure-white breath came from them. What were they saying? They gestured within their shrouds, then sat down on the sidewalk, and suddenly their burkas flowed together, forming a tent beneath which the girls could meet face to face. To the girls, no doubt, what they were doing was quite ordinary. To me, it was nearly a revelation. Now the one in blue separated herself, then raised her burka over another girl, maybe her little sister, who was so young that she could go about with her face uncovered. I could see, within the warm and secret tent, the two heads moving together, maybe whispering—no, they were sharing food! Remembering the story of the Tajik woman's friend who'd been beaten for raising her burka to count money, I realized that this must be the only way for women to eat in public. There was something mysteriously amoebalike in the way the blue tent rippled as the two heads touched beneath it, the mouths tearing at bread or a scrap of chicken.

This transitory zone of female privacy struck me as ingenious. Perhaps, under the best of circumstances, it might become an actual shelter, like the red-carpeted rooms into which Afghan men retreat to sit on soft cushions, unwrapping themselves from their tawny blankets. In those rooms, the men hatch business schemes and tell tall tales about their deeds as mujahideen, while outside the plastic-sheeted windows prayer songs emanate from loudspeakers. If the men are not Taliban, they boast about the women they've spoken to on the telephone—human nature being what it is, men and women court as they can. A young man in Kabul gleefully pointed out to me how a woman in a blue burka showed her ankles; she was wearing fancy socks. He said, "When you are living in a society with the burka, when you see even her hand, you think maybe she is beautiful." Another young man said, "Some of my friends have girlfriends, if the girls' parents are democratic. They talk to them by telephone. Taliban cannot listen, because our phone system is primitive. So it goes like this: She will come to the corner at such and such a time. That way, she will see the boy, although of course the boy cannot see the girl. But if she likes his face, then maybe some go-between can bring him her photo." And a taxi-driver proudly confided that he was carrying on an affair with a beautiful beggar woman; he'd pick her up in his car as if she were a passenger, and no one suspected.

So much of Afghan life occurs in secret. A young woman I met in Jalalabad had, in defiance of the edict against female education, taught herself English by book and radio. Now she was thinking of organizing an illegal home school. I'm told that women often smuggle heroin and other contraband because they feel immune from search—no women are still employed by customs to search them. What other dreams, successes, and business dealings take place in that world beneath the burka?

I have promised not to say where I met the brave girl, or who she was, but I can tell you that she lived in Kabul and that her family was cosmopolitan and affluent. They had chairs in their apartment, and they seated me at a table laden with pastries, apples, and oranges.

The brave girl's father had given me permission to meet her, and I asked her how she had felt when the Taliban came. She said, "At that time, I thought they were mujahideen. Then when I learned that they hated people, especially women, I knew that they understood nothing about civil rights, especially human rights. When a person hits a woman on the street, what must that person be thinking? It is against humanity."

"And have they improved at all?"

"I never used to go out even to the bazaar," she said. "But now I think their behavior has been affected by humans. Really, I don't have any clear idea about them. Of course, they started a hospital for us, but what about the other women who stay at home without anything to eat?"

She and I were, of course, not alone together. Her father sat on the sofa beside her, listening with increasing disapproval. Her husband sat across the room; he was angry at me for seeing his wife, whose dark hair and eyes were not covered. There were also two male cousins, my translator, and me. By now, they were all shouting furious interjections at her, and the thought crossed my mind that perhaps they had never really put themselves in their own women's shoes. She bit her lip and lowered her head whenever she contradicted her father.

"Do you believe that the Koran requires you to wear a burka?" I asked her.

"No, I think there is no need to wear the burka," she said bitterly. "I myself don't like it, because I think I'm a human. Because I have my human rights. And it's difficult to see, especially for the girls who wear glasses—all my friends agree."

"Do you have anything else to say about the Taliban?"

Twisting her hands in her lap, she said, "Peace is the most important thing in our country."

"Can you tell me about something you have experienced that might—"

"But she cannot go anywhere!" her father interrupted testily. "She has seen nothing until now."

"May I take your photo?"

"No!" they shouted—all of them except her. She smiled sadly. When I thanked her, she covered her face and went back behind the closed door.

Punishments and Other Stringencies

Again and again, I was faced with contradictions, with the question of how to balance the feelings of the people for whom the new regime was a welcome kind of peace against the rights of those for whom it was a form of oppression.

I remember a sallow boy who hated the Taliban and whispered hideous details of punishments he'd witnessed in the stadium at Mazar-i-Sharif: a thief's right hand severed with a scalpel (by a doctor; it took ten minutes); the shooting of murderers. He claimed to have seen about thirty executions over the last two years—not because he had to but only "to see something new." Without music or movies or magazines, one might as well go to watch the punishments. Once he had seen a couple stoned for adultery. "They were in one bed, and Taliban see them. First, judge begin with one stone, then all of the people hit them with stone. They cry—they cry! Very high cry."

"How long did it take?"

"I think for one hour or one and a half hours, maybe two hours." He went on, "It's too bad, in my opinion. I feel the Taliban are wild. Please, I never tell any other foreigner these things. You are my brother.

Please, dear brother, you will not tell them what I say? Because they will cut off my head!"

He went to the door of his room to see if anybody might be listening. No one was.

"What do you think?" he asked me.

"I don't know what to think," I said. "I'm only a Christian. Those punishments you speak of, they're all here in the Koran. What do you think?"

He took my Koran in his hands and began kissing it, agonized, whispering, "Koran is a very, very good book."

Afghans insist upon the Koran's absolute legitimacy in all walks of life—as an ethical guide, a primer on hygiene and food preparation, a marriage manual, a tax code, a dress code, a body of criminal law. In that last capacity, it clearly conflicts with several articles of the Universal Declaration of Human Rights, which Afghanistan signed in 1948. The stoning of adulterers presumably falls under the category of "cruel, inhuman, degrading treatment or punishment"; the constraints on relations between the sexes violate the declaration's "right to freedom of peaceful assembly and association"; and so on. But if a believing judge sentences a believing thief to lose his right hand it is none of my business.

There are times, however, when the Taliban rulers winnow from the hadiths the most punitive interpretations of Islam. In the Koran, we read over and over that the compassion of Allah forgives transgressions in emergencies. A man in Kabul, who had just served a prison sentence for having defied the prohibition on images, told me about a scene he had witnessed: a thief whose right hand had already been cut off had stolen again, and so the Taliban cut off his left foot. Afterward, when they were beating him in prison, he shouted, "If you cut everything off I will continue stealing with my teeth! *Because I have nothing to eat!*" Yet the punishment was still carried out. And why was it that the boy who told me those tales of public penalties enforced on legally convicted criminals found it necessary to scutter to the door every minute or two, terrified that someone might be listening?

"They misuse the Koran," the woman who had worked for Radio Kabul insisted. "In the Koran, it is not written that even for pilfering you must cut off the hand. No, the real meaning of that verse is metaphorically cutting the hand from robbery, for instance through imprisonment." Her argument is somewhat plausible; the Koran explicitly warns against literal interpretations. But I assume that the allegorical suras are not the laws. Otherwise, why not say that the requirement to pray five times a day or to keep Ramadan can be satisfied metaphorically?

I am not a Muslim; I have read the Koran only twice. I needed to question a Talib whose authority allowed him to take some responsibility for legal questions of right and wrong. The Minister of the Interior, Mullah Abdul Razzaq, was kind enough to see me without advance notice.

After being searched by Kalashnikov-adorned young cadres at the entrance to the Ministry building, I was conducted upstairs and through halls where Talibs flurried around my foreignness. When the interview was over, I gave a chocolate bar to the dirtiest, hungriest-looking one of them. He was wearing a T-shirt that said "Oakland Raiders." When I told him that the Oakland Raiders were American, he was crestfallen, and the others all laughed at him. He did not seem to know what the chocolate bar was, although I had bought it in Kabul, at one of the few fancy stores still in existence. He peeled off the foil wrapper with a filthy thumbnail, then stared at the chocolate in amazement, while the other Talibs gathered around, crowding so tightly against me that I could hardly breathe.

In the inner offices, however, a glacial decorum reigned. Ten farmers involved in a land dispute sat silently around a stove, wrapped in blankets, while the official to whom they'd referred their case was seated at a low coffee table, his great desk swept clean behind him. Beyond them lay an unheated conference room, and then a sanctum with carpets, cushions, and a little bed, where perhaps the Minister of the Interior took catnaps when he had to work all night. I took off my shoes and sat down on the floor to wait for him.

Mullah Abdul Razzaq is said to have been one of the founders of the Taliban movement. Of course, he'd fought bravely in the jihad and attended the madrasah. He'd been captured by Dostam during one of the battles for Mazar-i-Sharif. I had heard that he could be very emotional, but he and his colleagues entered the room calmly. His turban was white, and his black beard was very long. The other Talibs in the room bowed and nodded when he spoke, and his hands gestured slowly, serenely, in his lap.

"Why did you decide to become a Talib?" I asked him.

"It is said in the Holy Koran that when there is crying and corruption the people should fight against that," he said.

"As Minister of the Interior, you are in charge of security. Who controls crime in the streets, the police or the Taliban?"

"We control the crime," he said. "We control every department."

"What is the most frequent crime against the Shariah?" I asked.

"The Taliban have full control," he replied. "Right now, there is no crime."

A police officer I met in Kabul, a twenty-seven-year veteran, had written a letter for me to smuggle to distant relatives in California, and he whispered that the Taliban had robbed the police of their power. Possibly he and his colleagues had been corrupt before, as is frequently the case in Third World countries where the salaries of officials are so low that their only hope for survival is graft. If so, then Taliban rule might have been a change for the better. On the other hand, one can easily imagine the impatiently righteous graduates of the madrasahs preferring lampposts to courtrooms. There had been highly publicized instances of this already: on the night that the Taliban entered Kabul, Afghanistan's former President, the pro-Soviet Najibullah, was plucked from the United Nations compound, in which he had been cowering, and was tortured, castrated, shot, then hanged outside the palace. A similar fate befell his brother. (I was told by a reliable source—the same person had informed me that Osama bin Laden had a kidney complaint a day before the international media picked up the story—that Razzaq had personally ordered these executions.) No Afghan I've met has ever lamented these two men, but the speed of their killing, which was carried out within a couple of hours of the Taliban's arrival, not to mention the absence of judge, jury, and other formalities, occasioned some brief international embarrassment.

"Is it true that the penalty for beardlessness is ten days in jail?" I asked Razzaq.

"Yes, that is true."

"And why not nine or seven days?"

"That is the job of the Department of Religion. Only security is our job."

"Why is a burka better than a chador?" I asked.

"A burka covers all, so it is the real thing for women."

Razzaq became glum at this mention of the Taliban's treatment of women, much as he did when I later raised the question of Osama bin Laden, and we moved briefly to other subjects. "Sir, do you have any special message for the Americans?"

"We fought against Russia for years, and the Americans helped us," Razzaq said. "And we ask them and their government to help us again. As Afghanistan is destroyed, we expect help in reconstruction, and facilities for widows and orphans."

The matter of widows and orphans had particularly weighed on me. I felt that the Taliban government had no Islamic justification in its treatment of them. Since Razzaq had brought the subject back around to women again, I asked him, "Who is helping those widows now?"

"The Minister of Religion has promised some programs. And also the NGOs"—nongovernmental organizations, or charities—"have done something."

"Does Islam permit widows with no other resources to go out and beg?"

"We are trying our best to prohibit them from this, and we are trying to give them facilities."

"But if they have no such facilities, if they are hungry, is it permitted?"

"It is still prohibited."

A Glance From Across the Divide

The Minister's answer gave the Taliban a pitiless public face indeed, scorning the needs of the literally faceless. In truth, though, this regulation did not seem to be enforced. The beggar women plied their trade quite openly, even when Taliban passed by.

Afghans are no less pragmatic than other people, and continued exposure over the years to the realities of government and society seemed to be helping these Taliban children of war to mature. Year by year, even in Kabul, the theocracy was growing more moderate. As the brave girl had told me, the behavior of the Taliban has been "affected by humans."

When the Taliban first came to Jalalabad, in September 1996, they searched house to house, for televisions, videocassettes, and other irreligious items. They used the confiscated televisions for target practice. They required stores to remove labels from shampoo bottles wherever a human face was shown. But this February a retired professor there told me that the searchers had quickly tired of their unpopular investigations. Originally, he said, they'd believed that all urban dwellers were corrupt, but now they'd begun to realize that most citizens were not so bad; or perhaps some of the Taliban were growing corrupt themselves. (The Talib who worked the reception desk of my guesthouse in Jalalabad kept hitting me up for film in a most un-Islamic manner.) The professor watched television every day now—an activity that, in 1996, would have meant a fifteen-day jail sentence. Now the Taliban would not bother to come to his home unless someone proffered eyewitness testimony against him, and even in such a case they would merely confiscate his television—and possibly keep it for themselves, he said, laughing. He felt safe, and pleased to have the Taliban in power. They didn't care anymore if women went out alone, he told me. (I myself had verified this: when I visited the Talib dignitary from the Ministry for the Propagation of Virtue and the Prevention of Vice, he had tried to persuade me that women didn't have it so bad in Afghanistan. At one point, he and his three friends had called out excitedly for me to come and look at the street. "Look, look! Do you see? A lady, and her face is not covered, and no one is caring!")

In Kabul, I discovered in store windows one or two soap labels that bore the likenesses of women. And there was even a photograph of people (with no faces showing) mounted on the door of a taxi. Outside the cities, my taxi-drivers always listened to music, lowering the volume when they approached Taliban checkpoints, but not troubling to turn the radio off. In Pakistan, I'd met a doctor who had emigrated when the Taliban banned the possession of anatomical diagrams. But a doctor who'd stayed told me that things were not so bad now. "Before, we saw them beating women in the street. Now for a long time I don't see these beatings anymore. And now we have a camera in my operating room, and even projectors. I'll tell you a story. One Talib brought his wife to me. I refused to treat her without a letter of authorization, because that is what they make everybody else do. So he brought his wife to Pakistan. And I think he started to wonder about this policy."

One United Nations official, speaking of the Afghans, told me, "What they need is more outsiders, more exchange of ideas." Thanks to the United Nations, that is precisely what they aren't getting. The sanctions have begun their strangling work. Gasoline and wheat are smuggled in from Pakistan (and duty-free appliances and cars are smuggled from Dubai through Afghanistan and out to Pakistan), but the price of bread is rising in Kabul, and hungry families blame the Americans. An Afghan rug merchant told me, "First you created one Osama. Now you are creating many, many Osamas."

Americans worry that Afghanistan has become a petri dish in which the germs of Islamic fanaticism are replicating—soon Afghans will be hijacking American planes and bombing embassies everywhere. And their fears are not necessarily unfounded. The Taliban are unemployed war veterans, ready and even eager to return to the battlefield. "In the nineteenth century, we beat the British more than once," Afghans often told me. "In the twentieth century, we beat the Russians. In the twenty-first, if we have to, we'll beat the Americans!" Sarwar Hussaini, the director of a Peshawar-based human-rights organization called the Coöperation Centre for Afghanistan, told me that Afghanistan was full of terrorist-training camps, that Pakistanis, Chechens, Uzbeks, and Arabs were there, learning to fight for Islamic supremacy in their own countries.

But is Afghanistan the puppet-master or the puppet? Masoud is said to receive money from Russia and Iran. Pakistan, a patron of all seven factions during the jihad, is now closely allied with the Taliban. The Iranians have financed some Hazara groups in Afghanistan. China is also dabbling, for fear of Muslim power invading its own territory. And Saudi Arabia has broken off diplomatic relations with the Taliban, and therefore is suspected of aiding either Masoud or Gulbuddin Hekmatyar, another former mujahid. The Afghans themselves blame neighbors and superpowers for everything that has befallen them.

The Taliban could have come to power in any war-torn Islamic country. They gained supremacy in Afghanistan because all other leaders and movements there had discredited themselves through selfishness, vanguardism, gangsterism, and, above all, factionalism. Barring further mischief on the part of the superpowers, the Taliban may defeat Masoud and win their civil war. And it's entirely possible that as rulers they are preferable to any of the competition.

"I think Afghan people should choose neither Taliban nor Masoud," Hussaini told me. "Masoud is not a good alternative—he's proved that by his corruption. And the Taliban are not the kind of people one should like." But whom should the Afghans choose instead? A few old-timers long for the King to come back, but most people just say flatly that no good leader exists. Should the Taliban fall apart, it seems likely that the political and educational vacuum in Afghanistan will remain.

In Kabul, I stood in a grimy, unheated bookstore, some of whose books had been Islamicized, the faces on the jackets blacked out with splotches of Magic Marker. The bookstore seemed to have been subjected to this process randomly, though, as if the morality police had got tired or wandered off to look for something to eat. In the corner stood a rack of postcards from before the war, the faces depicted on them untouched. Dusty travel posters of "exotic" tribesmen remained on the wall.

As I talked to the bookseller, three Talibs entered the store, with black turbans wrapped around their faces like coiled cobras. Slowly, with wide eyes, whispering each word, they began to sound out the titles of the books. Soon, another joined them, whether searching for vice or merely passing the time I didn't know, and neither did the bookseller, who hung his head in breathless silence. They were looking for something—they seemed suspicious and disapproving—but perhaps they doubted their ability to find what they sought. Or maybe they were just cold. We could all see our breath condensing.

With the frightened bookseller translating, I asked one of them to tell me his happiest and saddest memories, and he said, "In my twenty-eight years of life, there's been nothing but war. Of course I have never been happy."

"Not even when you took Kabul?"

"That one day," he conceded without interest.

The Taliban asked me where I was from, and when I told them they fixed me with looks of rage.

"Tell the Americans that we believe their government is responsible for all our problems, and that they must stop this terrorism against us," the leader said curtly.

But they meant well. What they really wanted to do was to invite me into Islam. I showed them my Koran, and, as all their comrades had, they took it eagerly into their hands, kissed it, and slowly and silently began reading from it, their lips moving in a rapture. They promised me that if I became a Muslim they would take care of me forever. They'd feed and shelter me for the rest of my life. They'd find a special teacher for me. I'd become their brother. They gazed at me from across the divide, waiting.

Regrets of a Schoolteacher

(Smiyoshi, 5th rank)

This is the concluding scene from an article about the Japanese Yakuza that originally appeared in *Gear* as "Goodfellas" (a more complete version is in *Rising Up and Rising Down*). By a happy coincidence, I was in Tokyo in September 1998 while Vollmann was finishing up his research for the article, and when he invited me to join him on the last of his interviews I naturally agreed. We met beforehand in his hotel room, and I asked him to explain how he had managed to arrange to meet so many figures of this notoriously reclusive organization. He laughed and said, "THE YELLOW PAGES!" Letting his fingers do the walking, he had contacted a Japanese private investigator, made him a financial offer he couldn't refuse, and then one thing led to another. Later that night in a quiet Japanese restaurant, we met the Japanese man whose sad story is related here. For me, anyway, it was an absolutely mesmerizing evening. —LM

ON HIS BACK, THE man who'd wasted his life wore a tattoo (of which he was now ashamed) of a carp swimming up a waterfall. The carp symbolizes good fortune, happiness; and he told me a legend that the carp which attains the top of the fall becomes a dragon. Skinny and wrinkled, he was fifty-six years old, and had been a Yakuza member for four decades. Like Mr. Suzuki, whom he revered, he had joined right after Japan lost World War II. He too had never completed high school. —My family was poor, he said. Everybody was poor. It was easier to live this way, and it matched my character.

You were in many fights?

Of course.

And you won many?

Some, he said modestly. In the Yakuza, if you're too strong, you are no good. You tend to get killed.

So what was your first job in the organization?

I was a bookie for the horse races. The orders to do that didn't really come from the top. We all did it to live. And then I did some things which were real estate–related, some things I prefer not to talk about.

In the bubble economy period, the street agent put in (for this interview he was my go-between), what happened was you intimidated people and got rid of them and then sold their land for high prices.

What's been the greatest difficulty you ever had to face?

The Sumiyoshi man replied: The hardest thing was whenever I had some personal problem. I couldn't rely on the organization and yet I couldn't damage the organization's face. For example, if you start fighting with other members, that's the most difficult.

How many times have you been in prison?

Four times, he said with his sad little smile.

Some Yakuza told me that the longer you're in prison, the more you're respected.

Is that true?

Depends on your personality. Some people stay a long time in jail and nobody respects them.

Did you go to jail mainly for yourself or for the organization?

For myself.

Do you have any stories about that you wish to tell?

I was involved in a murder. —His eyes wrinkled up miserably, and he began drawing invisible lines on the tablecloth. —But I don't want to tell about it.

What was it for?

It was territorial.

Were you the killer or were you just there?

Let's say I was just present, he replied, licking his lips anxiously.

How did you feel when your target died?

Well, nobody likes it.

Was it necessary?

Yeah, it was necessary, because otherwise you get killed, he said, so quiet and ruthless and weary.

That sounds the same as being a soldier in a war.

It's actually different. In the war your boss is the Emperor, and he's so far away; you can't see him. So it's not real to me. But in this case I knew the head. I did it for him.

If the target person comes to beg your organization's pardon, can you spare him?

Of course.

What's the most efficient way to kill a person?

Nowadays, it's just to shoot, he said with a quiet smile. But with a Japanese sword it's more scary. Cut him in the neck, down the side of the head. He bleeds to death. Blood splashes out, so there's almost no possibility of survival. That's also the best place to kill yourself.

If you had your life to live over again, would you be a Yakuza?

No, he said, staring at his skinny old fingers. I'd be a schoolteacher.

And what would you teach your students?

That the Yakuza is bad.

Then why have you stayed in the organization?

One reason is that I like the leader. Also, it's more easy for me to be here.

He could have meant that reply in either of two senses. Perhaps the Yakuza was his business now; it was his living; without that, he'd have to begin all over in his old age. Perhaps also it was that only the Yakuza accepted him. More than one Japanese has told me that if a child becomes a delinquent, he'll be ostracized forever. —In many cases, said my private detective, if you want to go out and lead a normal life, once your past is revealed they make you go away, because they are not as nice to you as before.

—Where else could that would-be schoolteacher go now but to the Yakuza?

His cell phone rang just then. It was his "parent." He spoke anxiously, getting retroactive permission for the interview. I waited until he had finished. Then I asked: Do you believe that the purpose of your organization is for the strong to help the weak?

No, he said without a smile. That's an old story. The reality is different.

If you got ten million yen, what would you do with it?

I'd gamble it away.

Zoya

From
Europe Central

"Zoya" is from Vollmann's collection of World War II stories, *Europe Central*, which is scheduled to be published by Viking Penguin in 2005.

The essential thing about anti-guerrilla warfare—one must hammer this home to everybody—is that whatever succeeds is right.

—*Adolf Hitler (1942)*

1

Zoya's story has no beginning. Defined only by its end, which takes place not far westward of Moscow, in a village called Petrischevo, the tale projects itself backwards through predictable and possibly fallible contrasts into the sunny prewar collectivity for which Zoya chose to give her life. But what if she didn't choose? The crime for which the Fascists condemned her—setting fire to a stables, in obedience to Comrade Stalin's scorched earth policy—would surely have been followed up by grander salvoes had luck permitted. In brief, Zoya didn't mean to die—at least, not then, not for a stables! But then, to how many has it been given to reckon at all, let alone to conclude: *My death is a fair price to pay for this objective?* The July Twentieth conspirators might have been thus satisfied, had they succeeded in their intention of assassinating Hitler. They didn't, and got hanged with piano wire. General Vlasov, who fought first against Hitler, then against Stalin, met a kindred death. Was that "worth it"? What about the Berliners and Leningraders who died in air raids, or the soldiers on both sides who perished merely because their respective Supreme Commands, from fear, vanity or incompetence, forbade retreat? Or, to take the case still further, what about the random deaths that we die in peacetime? Looked at in this light, Zoya's fate becomes supremely ordinary.

2

In those days, neutrality meant friendlessness at best, while allegiance to either side invited a capital sentence from the other. Moreover, these punishments usually visited themselves upon the innocent. For every German soldier killed by the Partisans, between fifty and a hundred civilian hostages got stood against the wall. Accordingly, it was no "traitor," but a reasonable conclave of the villagers themselves, who went to report Zoya Kosmodemyanskaya, member in good standing of the Moscow Komsomol, to the Field Police. If somebody had to go to the gallows for what appeared to have been a rash, even absurd action, then why not the perpetrator, who'd endangered them all without their consent? Indeed, they were just in time. The S.D. lieutenant sat looking out the window of what had once been the school. (He'd had the teacher hanged in the very first batch of hostages. One of her high heels fell off at the very end; he remembered that.) Making a vague gesture at the huts across the street, he said: Arrest all that scum. —Just then the delegation of villagers came in.

In a photograph which a peasant soldier, hopeful of sausage or a wristwatch, found on the body of a battle-slain Fascist, we see Zoya (whose *nom de guerre* was Tanya) with downcast head as she limps through the snow to her execution, wearing already the self-accusing sign around her neck. It is 29 November 1941. Her eighteenth birthday was in September. A crowd of young Germans escort her, gazing on her with the sort of lustful appraisal which is common currency in a dancehall.

Now she has arrived. The snow is hard underfoot. A dark oval wall of spectators—Fascists whose double columns of buttons gleam dully on their greatcoats; kerchiefed village women, whose faces express the same pale seriousness their grandmothers would have worn for any camera or stranger; small, dark, hooded children in the front row—encloses the scene. Beside the sturdy, three-legged gallows, which rises out of sight, a pyramidal platform of snow-covered crates allows one party, the hangman, to ascend, while a tall stool awaits the other. Zoya stands there between two tall soldiers. Clenching her pale fists, shaking her dark hair out of her eyes, she swings her head toward one of the soldiers, who draws himself up stiff and straight to accept her gaze. She says: You can't hang all hundred and ninety million of us.

Some say that it was General Vlasov's soldiers who found her at the beginning of the Moscow counteroffensive the following month. I myself can hardly credit that, for Vlasov, who commands my sympathy, if not my imitation, would surely have hesitated to collaborate with the Fascists had he found such early and striking proof of their cruelty. No doubt he saw the final photograph (taken, so I've read, by the *Pravda* journalist Lidin), the one which presents to us her naked corpse in the snow, her head arched back as if in sexual ecstasy, her long-lashed eyes frozen tightly shut, her lips clenched, as if to protect her broken teeth, and that noose, now hard as a braid of wire cable, still biting into her neck, her face swollen with blood into a Greek mask. Perhaps Vlasov convinced himself that this image was a propaganda fake, or even that she could by some sufficiently draconian interpretation of military law have been construed to be a fifth columnist worthy of death.

It was the night before they retook Solnechnogorsk. Vlasov was pacing a riverbank like the frozen, snow-crusted defile between Zoya's breasts. Beside him strode a scout who'd just returned from the Fascist lines. The two men had finished discussing the enemy dispositions. Now they were talking about Zoya.

What they did to her will make us all fight more fiercely tomorrow, I guarantee it, Comrade General.

So would you say that she distinguished herself?

Why, she's a national heroine!

And that's what's strange. Why on earth would the Fascists want to give us a national heroine?

They returned to camp in silence. Vlasov was still considering how best to deploy his three hundred and eleven mortars and heavy guns. Back in '36 he'd attended a lecture given by the late Marshal Tukhachevsky, who'd aphorized that *the next war will be won by tanks and aviation.* He was correct, and Vlasov possessed neither. What could he do, but expend men like bullets?

His Siberians were waxing their skis with plunder taken from a half-burnt beehive. They'd already masticated every trace of honey from the comb. The antitank riflemen in the breakthrough echelon were lubricating their rifles one last time, and two beardless boys were singing in a loud pretense of bravery: *Into battle for our nation, into battle for our Stalin.* On the radio, Beria and Zhukov were threatening all defeated generals with death. At the edge of the sunken, snow-rimmed fire, the commissar was scribbling out a speech of which Zoya would be the subject, reminding everyone that the goal of partisan activity was to do *anything,* however much or little, which might hinder the movement of enemy reserves toward the front line. By this rather lenient criterion the girl had succeeded; and the restive troops, who longed to believe in something, would be, he hoped, inspired into emulation. *He* knew that every Soviet battle-death was worth it! Who am I to call him stupid, cynical, incurable? Most of Vlasov's men would end up killed or in the German prison camps, where they could look forward to being the subjects of experiments involving poisoned bullets, Zyklon B, decompression or freezing. (When Russian inmates died, no death certificates were required.) Well, if murdering them delayed a few thousand Fascists from manning the front line, then one had to keep calm and—

General Vlasov stood gazing down at the frozen river. The pincers of despairing, hopeless responsibility gripped his heart until he almost groaned. But suddenly peace came to him, and he muttered, not quite knowing what he was saying: Between the breasts of Zoya.

3

Here is what I imagine he meant by these words.

Because he was an outstandingly charismatic commander who never failed to make his men feel that they were brothers, and because he did everything honestly, we can assume that Vlasov already possessed the sense, which for the past quarter-century Communism had done everything possible to destroy, that the Soviet Union really was a union, that it comprised a single desperately embattled organism whose long chance for survival could be improved only through a selfless coordination *(Gleichschaltung,* his Fascist counterparts called it) of every cell, tentacle, cilium and internal organism, that the overstimulated endocrine secretions of hatred which had half poisoned and half crazed the organism for so long could now finally be usefully concentrated in fangs and stingers to be discharged against Germany, whose defeat, because Germany had struck first, could even be called a noble purpose.

As for the masses, they needed Zoya's dead breasts to drink from. They drank. Then they became likewise poisoned with resolve.

Zoya's fate stained and hardened the women night bomber pilots who laughed and smoked cigarettes, the peasant boys who shot rifles at the Fascist tanks, and even Comrade Stalin himself, whose speeches now invariably ended: *Death to the Fascist invaders*. Zoya's frozen blood, darker than steel, strengthened the upraised sabers of Cossacks galloping into the heavy grey photographic plates of myth. Her death became a movie (Soyuzdetfilm, 1944), with a score composed by Shostakovich. Decades after the war, memories of Zoya reincarnated themselves in the witch Loreley, who sings an irresistible song of suicide in the same composer's "Death: Symphony." By then, Zoya's corpse had become the Russian landscape itself, and I don't just mean that streets and tanks were named after her, which they were; Russia actually became Zoya, and when General Vlasov studied the map, preparing to thrust his breakthrough echelon against the Fascist Army Group Center, he seemed to see the body of a young giantess lying there beneath the snow, her arms and legs the ridges whose loved and familiar contours would help him, her thousand lips the antitank ditches which were delaying and exhausting the Fascists, her womb, silvergold with the sparkling sheen of snowy trenches, a bunker from which unending new divisions, airplanes and T-34 tanks would be born—yes, she'd died a virgin, but she was now literally the Motherland!—her hair the frozen thickets from which the partisans could ambush the enemy forever and ever, her breasts the points of strategic concentration whose investiture would save the Red Army—and between the breasts, between the breasts of Zoya, there lay the valley of perfect whiteness and smoothness; it was here, when Vlasov's striving finally ended, that he could lay his head.

From "The Grave of Lost Stories"*

From
Thirteen Stories and Thirteen Epitaphs

One would expect Vollmann to be a fan of Poe's brand of dark, emotionally wrenching horror, and of the rational, empirically-oriented Poe, inventor of the classical detective story and frequent speculator about cosmology and the limits (if any) of rationalist investigations of the mysteries of life. This conclusion to his masterful metagothic reinvention of Poe becomes a means for Vollmann to explore the meaning of death and to express his lifelong urge to save the doomed of all the lost stories and people (note the way his appropriation of the Poe/Virginia Clemm narrative must surely suggest his own relationship with his lost sister, Julie). The extended footnote Vollmann supplies at the beginning of this story offers a good indication of just how thorough his research methods are—and of how he integrates research into his fiction. Vollmann has also created a book object version of this story. —LM

*Poe's "final poem" is, of course, *Eureka* (1848). While I have breathed deeply of its dreamily logical atmosphere, I have also felt free to distort or ignore its arguments. Poe himself would not agree with the hypotheses that I attribute to him. The conversation between Poe and Mrs. Osgood is excerpted from an entry in the diary of Elizabeth Oakes Smith for 1845. Poe's hopeless cries to the first of the dying stories are partly based on a letter of his (I believe the last) to Mrs. Shew. The sentence in italics about the planet Neptune comes from *Eureka,* in an astronomical context. The conversation between Mrs. Clemm and Mrs. Phelps is reconstructed from a brief mention by Mrs. Phelps's daughter. The anecdote about Poe's biographer keeping Virginia's remains under his bed is given in Hervey Allen's *Israfel: The Life and Times of Edgar Allen Poe* (NY: Farrar and Rinehart, 1934, p. 581n). The marginal note on Livy is given in Poe's "Marginalia" (November 1844). The lines in italics attributed to "Berenice" do in fact come from that story (1835). Ditto for "Hans Pfaal" (1835). Ditto for "Ulalume" ("Our talk had been serious and sober . . ."). (I have slightly abridged some of the excerpts.) "Sepuleth," however, being one of the Lost Stories, is of course imaginary. For some of the Psyche's views on dead stories I am indebted to Miss Moira Brown, who lost her life-work of paintings in a fire.

He followed the Auber River past the red cliffs of Circassy, and sunset came, and he descended into the Valley of Unrest where the lilies bowed over a grave—he did not know whose; he refused to know; and now it was dark at last, and he was in the ghoul-haunted woodland of Weir; and the water of the Auber was a mottled silver that showed him his own reflection. Psyche met him at the bank and he was glad to see her, but as he wrote *Our talk had been serious and sober, but our thoughts they were palsied and sere* and truthfully her unfocused eyes with the glittering whites and the pupils like green marbles disturbed him far more than the barkings of the ghoul-packs who ravaged the churchyards in the misty darkness behind them; and suddenly a star-ball of glowing gases descended through the trees and Psyche said I fear the pallor of that Star but he showed his teeth in a laugh and said don't be afraid Sis I assure you that a star as bright as that can only light our way but she said no Eddie I don't want it to. —*Then* certainly he pacified his sweet Psyche; he had to; I am entitled as a reader to say that he kissed her, still thinking of the crystalline light of that Star that maddened and exalted him; but Psyche still sniveled and trailed her little wings in the dust, so to distract her from her scruples and gloom he asked her what do you think happens to the dead Stories? and she said oh Eddie they're not as unhappy as you think because I see them all around me so brittle and sparkling, blowing everywhere like dandelion seeds, so many of them, even here in this horrid dark place, that they're around me in constellations of stars! but saying this, she remembered the evil Star that drew them both on, and her happy face fell again, so to keep her from dwelling on her fear he said but aren't these dead Stories restless? and she said yes, but they try to be patient because someday someone will write them again and they'll be reborn as new living girls and brides so healthy and happy and she also said Eddie you should not destroy the paper of the dead Stories because that hurts them as they walked deeper down the cypress ways in the direction that the Star was pulling them, and the ghouls had fallen silent, and Psyche said please Eddie don't make me go on with you anymore and her plumes were dragging in the dust again, but he put his arm around her and said what makes your dead Stories happiest? and she said when a child thinks of them! have you ever heard children tell each other Stories? and he said no and she said poor Eddie and he said but you do grant that they remain bound to their bodies? and she said yes and he said triumphantly well then that's why we go to the graves of our dead women, because their skeletons are lying there for us to love and treasure beneath the marble slabs! Don't you admit that a grave and a corpse are more real than a memory and a lock of hair? and she said I never thought you such a materialist, Eddie and he laughed and they went on into the suffocating gloom and the Star set slowly over the black valley which his reasoning powers in combination with his accurate knowledge had enabled him to predict in bold relief, and as the Star set it cast a last beam down through the night-trees that occluded the gulf, and tenderly brushed the pure darkness below, like the hem of a skirt brushing his lips; and Psyche said let's go home now Eddie please! but he kissed her so many times and fell on his knees and entreated her and made her laugh by telling her how her cat Catarina had chased her tail and how Muddie had been so astounded, until again he quenched her tears; and so hand in hand they walked among the sad-scented night-trees and descended into that gorge of coagulated darkness, and on the opposite wall he saw that a face had been carved—a titanic face, whose mouth could have swallowed armies; and he stiffened like a galvanized corpse to see that it was the face of the *Vulpine Presence!* Its jaws champed and it ground its black stone teeth together. Its eyeballs were the size of millstones, and they rolled to and fro with a sullen thundering sound. But he would not let poor little Sissy see it. So he talked and talked to her ever more rapidly and gaily like his pen speeding so desperately across the paper to save the dying Stories; and Psyche was smiling again through her tears and saying oh you're so funny Eddie and so they descended hand in hand into that sweet-sulphur stench of concentrated mortality. They were in a narrow valley of bones and smoldering fumes, made still narrower by the ledges that projected overhead, comprised of a pinkish mineral such as chalcedony, into which were set white nodules of a cuspid shape; from these little drops of moisture unpleasantly dripped. She continued to grasp his hand, and he was so happy to be with her even though her face was so ghastly pale and there was black mold around her eyes and lips; and the yellowish greenish smoke that swirled around her made her hair smell singed and he felt the mold growing cold and clammy on his eyebrows and the taste of death was in his mouth and so they came to a gigantic door of tarnished iron. He said Sissy what does it say on the door? And she leaned forward to spell out the letters with her fingers (for in truth the dark air was so thick that despite the globules of light that writhed in the atmosphere like maggots it was very difficult to see); and she said U and she said L and a sudden agony of terror made his heart beat so loudly that he could not hear what she said and he cried yes? yes? with his haunted face uplifted . . . and she said ULALUME! and his heart became as ashen and brittle and brown as a dead leaf. —I *killed* her, he said in a kind of choked wonder. He remembered now how the suffocation had been consummated. —Psyche had begun to walk away. A chilly and rigid magnificence issued from her. She called back over her shoulder: —

Yes, she is dead, but *she is waiting for you inside!*

Please don't leave me, he said in a very small voice, as if to himself.

Remember, laughed Psyche from far away (she was almost out of sight), they're all waiting for you!

A key was in the lock, high above that name carved in weeping letters. The lock was thickly overgrown with fungi, and condensation from the reeking mists all about him had scored the iron with a thousand little channels like tear-trails, now choked with rusts and lichens. From the crack where that massive block of iron had been fitted into the doorway of the tomb, a sickening exhalation issued, and he thought to himself it was *thus* in the place where we buried Madeline Usher! —Immediately there came to him a vision of those thousands of wives and daughters of his who waited within, their white bodies puffing outward with the gases of decomposition; which convinced him, by right of the Grave's position as universal vortex, that these horrible vapors might indeed become the *vaporous rings* of the outer planets. —He rose from his desk and rushed outside to look for Saturn. It was a clear night; Mrs. Shew had very kindly lent him her pocket telescope. —Yes, yes! —Indeed, since all the planets were no more than globular condensations of these ring forms, the conclusion was inescapable (despite the laughable ignorance of the astronomers), that the universe was composed of nothing other than this miasma. And in consequence, since the law of gravitation was nothing but the fact of inexorable collapse, one could expect, after untold millions of epochs, all matter to congeal into that jet-black, obsidian-like form of which the Valley of the Grave was comprised! Some might call this rash speculation; as for him, he could not but smile at the numbskulls who thought to confute him.

Standing on tiptoe, he was just barely able to get the tips of his fingers around the key. It would not move. He leaped up and hung from the key with all his weight; he raised his body halfway above it and locked his elbows; he braced his feet against the door; his face glowed with the fiercely radiant joy of self-destruction. He strained and strained to turn the key in the lock, but it would not move. In his anxiety and frustration he began kicking the door, which resounded with sullen hollow boomings like an immense drum; at last he placed one hand over the other, and then, squeezing until the veins stood out on his forehead, he wrenched the key clockwise with all his strength. There came a great squeaking and grinding. Flakes of rust showered him like bloody sparks. Now the key turned with ease. He let himself down to the ground and took hold of it again; the revolution of the circle was completed, and he heard a click. The massive door swung slowly inward. A foul wind rushed out from that dark place. Now he would discover the corpses. Now the tomb would open for him like a vagina. With a cry of joy, he ran inside. Too late, he saw that the interior was a wedge-shaped *cul-de-sac* lined with spikes. In horror and dismay, he wheeled around to escape, but long before he reached it, the door had slammed shut with a malignant boom; an instant later, the wall-jaws closed upon him.

Review of *Reporting Vietnam*

From
Sacramento News and Review (March, 1999)

Written before September 11th, this review's final line eerily anticipates what would occur later, when the U.S.–led coalition launched its war on Iraq..

I WAS BORN IN July 1959, which is when the very first American "advisers" in Vietnam were assassinated, and it is with a brief account of their deaths (which occurred between the reels of a banal movie) that *Reporting Vietnam* begins. Befitting that steadfast beacon of mediocrity, *Time* magazine, where it originally appeared, the article does not attempt to conclude or predict. "The presence of the Americans," it ingenuously mourns, "symbolized one of the main reasons why South Viet Nam, five years ago a new nation with little life expectancy, is still independent and free and getting stronger all the time." With this sinister and retrospectively ironic prelude, the curtain rises on death and pain—for Americans, that is. The stage is already slippery with other people's blood. Vietnam has risen against the Japanese during World War II, against the French before and since, against the Cambodians and the Chinese for centuries before that. North Vietnamese propaganda never hesitates to invoke the names of patriots whose bones were dust long before Communism had a name. In other words, the danger of impressive compilations such as *Reporting Vietnam* is that talent and a certain comprehensiveness might mislead American readers into thinking: Read this, and you'll know everything you ought to know about Vietnam. Two or three years ago, I remember seeing the title of an article in *Newsweek,* I think it was: "What Vietnam Did to Us." This would have infuriated me less, had there been a follow-up article entitled "What We Did to Vietnam," with ample footnotes on the French at the very least; and then a third piece called "What Vietnam Did to Itself."

But, like a good American, let me ignore all that, rushing instead to harp on my own individuality. The Vietnam War haunts me. That birthday of mine fell one year too late for compulsory draft registration. I remember checking the Selective Service posters every time I went to the post office, wondering what would be the right thing to do if they did call me. My friends were discussing the same question—to be sure, not as anxiously as they might have done five years earlier, because the war was pretty obviously being abandoned. None of us had any desire to volunteer. Our televisions had shown us too many joints of human meat, served punctually at dinnertime along with the rest of the six-o'clock news. Probably I would have gone to Vietnam had I been inducted. Probably I would have gotten injured or killed. Granted, my luck as an international journalist and occasional war correspondent has been pretty good so far. In a couple of weeks I will be in Kosovo, and I do not feel especially worried because I trust my strengths and acknowledge my limitations. Had I fought in Vietnam, however, my commanding officer might not have had time to draw up an order of battle based on my bad eyesight.

The war ended before I voted for the first time (Republican like my father, then later Democrat like my mother), but its consequences will remain as long as steel plates remain in the skulls of veterans. I find its traces everywhere, in the hordes of one-legged children I meet whenever I go to Cambodia, in gloomy and terrifying stories from the mouths of Vietnamese refugees in Paris, Bangkok, and Sacramento. In my opinion, the "defining event" of the first half of the twentieth century was the career of Stalin; of the second, the Vietnam War.

The Vietnam War showed that America, supposedly the strongest, and in her own mind the most perfect nation on earth, could throw any number of corporations, napalm-scientists, politicians and machine-gun-wielding men against a few jungle peasants, and still lose. The First World could not utterly dominate the Third anymore, nor could money and technology beat out ideology and self-defense.

I am among those who believe that our involvement in the Vietnam War was wrong. Perhaps in the beginning it was excusable. To the extent that our century has been Stalin's century, it has been monstrous. We did not want Stalin's system to spread anymore than it already had. And so, rightly accusing the Communists of installing themselves under the guise of national sovereignty, we ourselves ignored Vietnam's right to self-determination. We fought evil first with "advice," then with outright force ourselves, and finally with despairing, on-again-off-again brutality. Once we had made up our minds to fight, could we have done it any differently? I doubt it. Toward the middle of the first volume of *Reporting Vietnam*, Tom Wolfe in his wryly brilliant piece on a carrier pilot and a gunner who overflew North Vietnam in 1967 describes how President Johnson's efforts to create a more "humane" war endangered aviators, whose lives were already dangerous enough already. Johnson said don't bomb churches, so the North Vietnamese turned churches into arsenals. What was the right thing to do? Whatever it was, perhaps we didn't do it. Our policymakers killed a lot of Vietnamese and Americans without accomplishing anything—and I don't just mean that we lost the war; it seems to me that we left America and southeast Asia worse than we found it. ("Well, I hope to think he died for a purpose," says the father of an Appalachian boy to a reporter in 1969. "Do you have any feelings about what the purpose was?" asks the reporter, whose name is Jeffrey Blankfort, and whose almost deadpan article achieves its effect by quoting one Vietnam-bereaved family after another in a single small town. The bodybagged boy's father replies simply: "No.")

Whether you agree or disagree with my views, the two volumes of *Reporting Vietnam* are well worth your study. Hamburger Hill, self-immolating monks, Viet Cong diaries, leftwing and rightwing answers to double-winged questions, the Tet Offensive, POW stories—they're all here.

A good reporter investigates his story without undue regard for personal risk. He tells that story, whether it will get him promoted or whether it will get him arrested. He tells what he believes to be the truth. This is one of the most honorable callings possible for a human being. Most of the one hundred and sixteen pieces in this anthology offer, with varying degrees of ideological engagement and stylistic skill, the Vietnam War as it was refracted through the multifaceted crystal of *professional eyewitnesses*. In eloquent paragraphs or in dry, staccato sentences which were probably homogenized still further by editors and the exigencies of dispatch offices, these observers describe what they saw. Sometimes, as in the case of Wolfe's article, they go beyond their own experiences a little. Wolfe evidently interviewed his two aviators and spent time on their air craft carrier, because his descriptions of large details and small (he likens the flight deck, for instance, to an immense, black, greasy, dangerous frying pan) ring so vividly true. When he tells how his men, their plane shot in the hydraulics, have to bail out and are rescued, I assume that he wasn't present for that but that he listened to them describe what happened and that he flew on at least one aerial mission himself. He writes about fear in a way which reminds me of the fear I have felt, say, in Sarajevo when I was getting shot at. I don't know what research Wolfe actually did, but I believe that he experienced that fear, too. He convinces me.

At the beginning of volume two, it is 1969 and we find Seymour Hersh breaking the My Lai massacre in his careful, understated way. As a writer of sentences and paragraphs, Hersh remains far inferior to Wolfe. As a bearer of truth, however, he is just as stellar. He was not at My Lai, but he interviews people who were. How many civilians did Lieutenant Calley's men kill? The numbers are not quite in yet, and Hirsch presents them tentatively, admitting their discrepancies. (This is one hallmark of a decent journalist. Anybody who never says, "I don't know," is not to be trusted.) Then Hersh raises the larger question: In Vietnam, who is a civilian? If he acts friendly by day and shoots at you by night, what is he? And how do you know what he does? Your answers to this question will have some bearing on whether or not you think Calley was justified in gunning down old men, women and babies. Hersh's article, like so many others in this anthology, raises one of the most important issues human beings can ask themselves and each other: *When is violence justified?* I recently completed a book on this question, and one of my case studies was My Lai. Read Hersh's contribution to *Reporting Vietnam,* and you will get some sense of how *sickeningly confusing* war is.

In 1975, at some danger to himself, Sydney Schanberg witnesses the fall of Phnom Penh to the Khmer Rouge. Holed up in the French embassy, then convoyed out to Thailand with the other foreigners, he sees almost none of what Pol Pot's black-pajamed cadres are doing, but he suspects a little of it. They separate families forever and drive everybody out of the cities to grow rice. "We could hear shooting," he writes, "sometimes nearby but mostly in other parts of the city. Often it sounded like shooting in the air, but at other times it seemed like small battles. As on the day of the city's fall we were never able to piece together a satisfactory explanation of the shooting, which died down after about a week." Once again, there is honor in Schanberg's confession of ignorance. He describes what he sees and what he infers, not putting himself and his own peril forward except where the story requires it. Several years later, a Communist film crew from East Germany will be allowed to enter Cambodia, and their record of what they saw will contain images of scenes that Schanberg and other American journalists never got to see firsthand during the entire period of Khmer Rouge rule. (I have not viewed this film but I have read about it.) The East Germans, of course, will edit themselves and their footage. And they'll let themselves be edited by the Khmer Rouge. Schanberg, like a creditable many of the journalists in *Reporting Vietnam,* tells what he says, as he himself sees it. He doesn't say that the Khmer Rouge are utterly bad; he describes how after looting shops they pass out the plunder to their comrades. Nor does he omit to describe the selfish arrogance of his fellow foreigners, who steal cigarettes from each other and feed their pets more than many Cambodians eat. His account is *balanced.* What will happen next in Cambodia? Schanberg can't know, but we do, and the gloom and dread in his account will prove all too well founded.

I have given you the merest sampling of these two generous volumes, which offer so much in the way of history, gore, and eternal questions. Read this anthology, and learn about our unhappy world, about this country of ours, and about yourself—for no matter who you are or when you were born, if you are American then the Vietnam War remains in part your war. Let me give you one more reason why this is so. In what may be the most gripping account of all, Navy Lieutenant James S. McCain III, hawk and hero, with whose views on the war I do not agree, tells how he survived POWdom in North Vietnam from October 1967 until March 1973. McCain refused to compromise with his captors in any way, and *especially* refused to let them make propaganda out of him. Toward the end of his memoir, he reveals part of his code of conduct, with which I very much agree: "I want to say this to anybody in the military: If you don't know what your country is doing, find out. And if you find you don't like what your country is doing, get out before the chips are down. Once you become a prisoner of war, then you do not have the right to dissent, because what you do will be harming your country." McCain's warning applies, I think, not only to every American soldier, but also to every American citizen. Find out what your country is doing. Find out what your country has done. Someday the chips will fall again.

Some Thoughts on the Value of Writing During Wartime

Partly recycled from his Iraq chapter in *Rising Up and Rising Down* and originally delivered as a speech in Sacramento in November 2002 while the U.S. was preparing for war against Iraq, Vollmann's remarks here were interrupted by his audience on several occasions with cheers and boos.

NABOKOV ONCE SAID THAT whenever he came across a novel which tried to teach him something or even just convey a point of view, he banned it from his bedside table, because literature should not be anything but beautiful. Of course his own books, beautifully written though they mostly were, express many a message, from the anti-totalitarianism of *Bend Sinister* to the skewering of psychoanalysis and American parochialism in *Lolita*. Whether or not you believe, as I do, that art is inherently and inescapably political is up to you.

But we live in political times. We always have and we always will. Unfortunately, American writers tend to neglect politics, while American politics tends to neglect writers. Last spring I was one of two American authors in a European city at the behest of the State Department. The audience asked us quite a number of questions about September 11th and subsequent U.S. policy. In Europe a writer is still supposed to be a leader. His opinions about life and history and politics matter. I regret to say that the other writer, who was good at public speaking and had published many books, seemed blindsided when these political questions began. Perhaps none of his readers had ever expected him to come to conclusions about, say, the Middle East, much less articulate them. He was uncomfortable, and I felt sorry for him.

Later on I began to wonder why, after all, anybody should care about anything we writers have to say beyond rules of comma placement. Here are two thoughts I came up with.

First of all, a writer ought to be able to make everything interesting. I know so many Americans who say, "You know, I'm not really interested in politics." Unfortunately, as September 11th showed, politics is interested in us. If we writers can do our job well enough, perhaps we can further the cause of collective self-preservation.

Secondly, a writer can promote empathy. Many or most of you, I'm sure, know the distinction between flat and rounded characters. A flat character is at worst a cardboard villain, a stereotype, at best a predictable sort. Flat characters certainly have their place. Someone who buys pornography expects the characters to get down to business as rapidly and frequently as possible, with each succeeding act one-upping the one before, which is why this genre actually sports a kind of plot development. And where would murder mysteries such as September 11th be without their flat characters? Even the novels of Raymond Chandler, although they are much greater literature than mass media accounts of atrocities, always arrive at a predetermined end, namely the solution of the crimes. To that extent, and this is not a negative criticism, Chandler's detective protagonist Philip Marlowe is or becomes a flat character in a world of very subtly conceived round characters. We know that at the end of the book, or slightly before, but not too much before, there will be a surprise, at which point Marlowe will pull everything together for us. We wouldn't have it any other way. We wouldn't want, say, Osama bin Laden to disappear just when Marlowe thought he'd caught him.

A round character is somebody who, like you and me, is complex enough to be unpredictable. The tormented schizophrenics of Dostoyevsky, who lurch from one emotional extreme to the next, the inhabitants of George Eliot's universe, with their myriad flaws and silent virtues, the elusively vast people in Faulkner, who are more than human because they're language itself; the lost souls that Philip Marlowe encounters, they surprise us more surprisingly than does Marlowe himself, and because their authors know exactly what they are doing, upon surprising us these characters allow us to see that their behavior was appropriate, *in character.*

What we can take from this, if we read enough and think enough, is that life is less simple than it seems, which means that a government which tells its citizens that the world is black and white is not lying, necessarily, but at best it's a Raymond Chandler government, whose characters will use their skills, if they possess any, to move the story toward a predetermined result.

Great literature is as capable of making judgments as Philip Marlowe, believe me. Shakespeare's Iago remains a very wicked man, and we easily see him as such. At the same time, he's round enough to make us wonder what makes him the way he is, and even pity him. Some of you may believe that holding such an attitude about real-life evildoers comprises weakness. I am sure that it is not. Understanding is the opposite of weakness.

I will try to show you what I mean by saying a few words about Iraq. As a journalist I've been fortunate enough to visit a number of the so-called rogue nations, including Yemen just last month, Afghanistan under the Taliban, Serbia during the Yugoslavian civil war, Somalia during its civil war, and of course Iraq. What the media tells you about those places is not necessarily untrue, but it's mostly less than the truth. It makes their people into flat characters.

Most of us would agree that Iraq committed an act of unjustified aggression in invading Kuwait. The Iraq-Iran war involved atrocities on both sides. There is evidence, although I haven't myself verified it, that Saddam Hussein stands guilty of genocide against the Kurds, and that torture, mutilation and extrajudicial killing is common in his system. So far, he is a flat character. He is also, and I can personally assure you of this, quite popular in Iraq, Jordan, Yemen, Algeria, and no doubt other countries. I can only speculate on our President's real motives in determining to remove him. It can't be his murderousness, because the United States, like most powerful countries, has allied itself with butchers many times before and is doing so now. The reason may be Saddam's dangerousness to American citizens or interests, but so far our President has given us, and the rest of the world, no hard facts about that. It is as if we read a Raymond Chandler novel which simply asserted, rather than proved, that a certain person were the killer. I think we'd feel a little disappointed. I myself am not necessarily against invading Iraq, if our government can do us the courtesy of making a decent explanation. Until then, the best service I can perform for all of you today is to get across how the Iraqis feel about us—in other words, to treat them as round characters.

When a foreign journalist arrives in Baghdad, he must register in one particular hotel. Upon the granite threshold of this cavernous palace crawling with police spies has been engraved a demonic caricature of a well-known American face, the face of President George Bush, Sr., who was commander-in-chief during the Gulf War. The caption reads: BUSH IS CRIMINAL. In other words, Bush is a flat character to the Iraqis, but since we Americans don't often see this other flat side of him, this glimpse of his backside may make him a little bit rounder. To enter the hotel you walk on our former President's face, and if you are an Iraqi, you may well spit on it. Why would Iraqis want to do that? The flat characters in our newspapers might not tell you, so I will.

Let's give ourselves the benefit of the doubt and assume that in principle the Gulf War was entirely justified. Let's even imagine that the Iraqis believe that. Now we'll round out history a little. On February 13, 1991, the United States dropped two smart bombs or cruise missiles, depending on whom you ask, on the Amiriya air raid shelter near Baghdad. Inside, according to the Iraqi government, were civilians only. The first missile penetrated the concrete shell of the structure. The second missile was then able to do its work. Almost all of the inhabitants burned to death. The total number of victims was 403, of which 261 were women and 52 were children. An official pamphlet at my hotel called this event "the most horrifying U.S. crime ever committed against the people of Iraq . . . professional killers are always killers no matter when or where . . . U.S. excuses are merely [a] desperate attempt to cover up the impudence and enormity of the crime." I gazed up through the hole through which American death had entered, and perceived flying and singing birds. It was cool and dank inside. My driver prayed for the victims, as he always did, and sternly motioned for me to cross myself. The blackened, blistered concrete walls were hung with photographs and wreaths. There were also photographs of the corpse retrieval crews, some with masks over their mouths, I suppose for protection against the stench. I saw photographs of them lifting corpses on planks, a photograph of a row of charred corpses on the sidewalk. A black-clothed woman who'd lost her sister and her children came to me and silently pointed out the sheets of scorched human skin and clothing stuck to the walls. She took me downstairs, needing to show me more skin, lavender and tan patches of it, in places not washed off by the flood of water when the warhead's detonation had shattered the pipes and drowned the people it didn't roast. The woman's sandals click-clicked in the dark. Pointing to the ceiling, she pantomimed for me burning people being flung against the ceiling, trying to protect themselves with outstretched hands, and I saw the blackened skin of those hands sticking like squashed burned gloves up there. Since children are especially little and light, it was the forms of their tiny little hands that I frequently saw, and this memory has become especially agonizing to me now that I'm the father of a four-year-old girl. Meanwhile the woman in black showed me the solarized shadows of incinerated human beings on the wall.

When an Iraqi asked me what I thought about Amiriya, I replied that it sickened me. I also said that I believed it to be an accident. I said that in war the innocent always suffered and probably always would. He smiled angrily.

To ordinary Iraqis, the long quiet cruelty of sanctions has been a series of Amiriyas. My country's permanent representative to the U.N. crowed that our embargo, which was meant to be in effect for six months or so, would create "clear incentives for rapid implementation and trade-offs which will in stages produce a return to normalcy and non-belligerency in the Gulf." Were this a work of fiction we'd have to call him an unreliable narrator, because the sanctions are in their twelfth year now. For comparison, consider that a mere three years after we defeated Nazi Germany, the Marshall Plan began to rebuild the economies of our former enemies. My American friends and neighbors speak of punishing Saddam Hussein, of keeping the pressure on until he divulges the location of every last crypt or cache of poison, of driving him out, of rendering him so odious that the Iraqis will cry uncle and install a pro-American government. This approach is our habit; this is what we have done in Afghanistan, too, and I am sure that five or ten years from now you will see that it has not worked there, either. Meanwhile the Iraqi men, women and children who have little to do with weapons or government fail to see why they must suffer. That is why on so many walls one sees the slogan DOWN WITH AMERICA.

Let's visualize the sanctions on Iraq, and as we do, let's ask ourselves how we would feel about any country which did these things to us. We are round characters in the Book of Life, and Iraqis are, too.

A man walks down the street in a nice shirt. You get closer and see the tiny holes.

Three brothers share a shirt. Each day another brother wears it.

A woman stands begging beside her pale, sweating child. She doesn't have enough money for a taxi to the hospital.

Visit the old Christian who runs a delicatessen in the center of Baghdad. His son in California recently died of a stroke. He wants to know how the grandchildren are. He's written his daughter-in-law, but received no answer. Was she indifferent, or does the embargo prevent communication between them? Not knowing breaks his heart. I mailed a letter for him in California, but I wonder whether he'll ever receive a reply.

In a dirty-pale two-room house, a husband and wife live with their five children (two more children have already died from leukemia). "We eat some food bad for animal, for *animal,*" the husband says, showing me a large plate inside the refrigerator, to which still cling a few patches of feculent yellow mush, because while in Jordan you can get half a roast chicken for a dinar and a half, which is less than the price of a medium-length taxi ride, in Iraq it will be several thousand dinars, which might be a month's wage. Certainly this householder has little hope of eating chicken. Every now and then, he supplements his income by buying and selling gasoline. The mush costs a hundred dinars per meal. The man says to me, "You tell them, it very hard life and our best wishes to United States."

If you don't care to dine with his family, then take lunch at the fast food place, with its marble, its burgers, and its student couples from the technical college across the street, the girls usually not veiled. The couple next to me can't afford to get married, for which they rightly or wrongly blame the embargo. The boy used his Brazilian-made car as a taxi, but it broke down too frequently now, and he spent more dinars fixing it than he took in from his fares. Let's call him Ali. The girl's name is Maryam. "My love," Ali repeatedly says of her, clasping her hands. Whenever he looks at her, his eyes shine. They touch their heads together and whisper. Maryam offers to prostitute herself to me, in order to pay for her wedding ring. And we wonder why they hate us.

In a fancy secondary school for girls, wires dangle from a socket in the wall of the principal's office. They don't have enough pencils. Pencils have been embargoed, you see, just in case some cunning Iraqi pulls the graphite out for use in nuclear weapons. Why not? Flat characters can do anything. —The teachers' hands flutter. They all want to ask me whether the sanctions will be lifted soon or not. I say I don't think so, and that I am sorry. —A teacher says: "I have four children and I can get no milk. What can I do?" Unlike Philip Marlowe, I have no answer, no solution.

In the pediatric hospital—named, of course, after Saddam Hussein—the doctor insists: "Most of Iraq's children have been affected by sanctions." He says that there is no more serum for vaccinations, no media for blood tests. A wrinkled infant weeps in its black-robed mother's lap as she slowly rocks it on her knee. The doctor says he'd already given the child two bottles of blood obtained from relatives. What's wrong? An undiagnosed case, he says with a shrug. Maybe it will die. "Now we treat according to the availability of resources, not according to the prognosis," he says.

Which misery should I caption "embargo," and which "preexisting class exploitation"? Well, we do know for a fact that during the Gulf War our bombers targeted "Iraqi infrastructure," which included water pumping and filtration plants. The sanctions made it impossible and illegal to repair most of them. The logical result: even from bottled water one can get amoebic dysentery, as I did. This was simply not the case before the Gulf War. One of my guides who worked at the Ministry of Information's press center, a relatively well-off man to whom I paid ten dollars for a morning's translation, mourned a little son who'd just now died of diarrhea. Rehydration salts and antibiotics would have saved him. In my opinion, that boy's death was a war crime.

According to Mr. Eric Falt, the spokesman for the U.N. Office of the Humanitarian Coordinator for Iraq, "We monitor the access, and we can report that 99.5% of the population is provided with equal access to our food basket."

"Are you saying they're eating well enough?" I asked.

"No. I'm not saying that. Let's not forget the goal of the operation. We have not been asked to launch a Marshall Plan for Iraq. We have been asked only to prevent *further deterioration.*"

My flesh began to crawl.

"We quickly realized that the $1.3 billion is not enough to prevent further deterioration. It gives them two thousand calories per person per day, and an ideal minimum level would be two thousand five hundred. We calculate that our food baskets, delivered monthly, last approximately three weeks, which goes down to two weeks for the poorest families."

"And medicine?"

"Prior to 1991, Iraq was making available—I don't say spending—about thirty dollars on drugs and medicine per person per year. By 1995–96, that figure had decreased to two or three dollars per person per year. The World Health Organization target for this region is thirty to thirty-five dollars per person per year."

A child with leukemia lay weakly, her eyes half closed.

"She has beautiful eyes," I said to the mother.

"If you praise her on her beauty, don't praise her. Help her," the mother replied.

"What would you have me do?"

"End the sanctions," said the mother.

I had nothing to offer but money and candy.

One figure I heard cited in Iraq is that our sanctions have killed a million children since 1991. Let's suppose that this number is grossly exaggerated, which it may not be. Let's suppose that the true figure is a mere hundred thousand, or, if you like, only thirty thousand—ten times the number of people murdered in our country on September 11th. How much have thirty thousand dead children hurt our archenemy who was once our ally? "Saddam Hussein could care less if one million or two million babies die in Iraq," an Amnesty International spokesman told me. "This serves as very strong propaganda in his favor. And to a certain extent it suits his interest because the biggest victims are the babies from the Kurdish areas from the north. They are the offspring of people who have opposed Saddam Hussein."

As Talleyrand said about some French atrocity, "it was worse than a crime; it was a mistake."

"And what do you think of Saddam Hussein now?" I asked a man who'd lost his leg in the Gulf War and whose wife was sick without medicine, thanks to our sanctions.

"He is hero of the Middle East. To thirty-three countries President Saddam Hussein say no and is fighting."

"Believe it or not, we are challenging the U.S.," another man said proudly.

"And the U.N.?" I inquired.

"U.N. lying. And America is father of the United Nations," he said. "China, Britain, France, Russia follow only America. America is big problem for the world."

His grey-faced wife brought us tea. I thanked her and asked him: "If the embargo is lifted, what's the first thing you'll do?"

"Make some lamb, a gift for my God."

Later, when I went to the U.N. Special Committee's office in Baghdad—the embargo was their department—I asked their press liaison what she had to say about the relation between sanctions and the lack of medicine. "Oh, we don't talk about that," she said.

To you and me, the sanctions mean nothing because we are Americans and every country outside America is a faraway, insignificant country. To Iraqis, as you've seen, they mean considerably more than nothing. So, as you might imagine, they spend a considerable amount of time trying to determine why we are doing this to them. Here are some of their explanations:

An art gallery owner: "The reason for the embargo is Israel, and Israel make from Zionists. 'Braham Lincóln, first President of America, he say in his first speech, make careful with Jewish or they make you servant. It's true. Israel is ten times more powerful than America."

A distinguished old lawyer: "America is afraid that these weapons should not be put in the hands of totalitarians, retarded people, Orientals, because there will be no deterrent," he said to me while his secretary served us more Turkish coffee in tiny glasses and his partner nodded agreement beneath a giant portrait of Saddam Hussein. "But in the Iraq-Iran war, and in the Gulf War, we proved that we respected the deterrent. Because we didn't use chemical weapons. You Americans have the full right to be proud of the strong economy you have and the very high-tech life you lead. But you do not have the right to become arrogant. You should not feel that you are different from others, some superman, something like that."

In 1998, returning from Iraq, I wrote: *The notion that stern domination of a country can prevent its evil resurgence did not work against Germany after World War I. It will not work here. It will succeed only in creating and hardening new enemies for America and her sister powers. Sooner or later, some Iraqi clever enough to build a destructive device will try again, and his hatred will not be restrained by memories of our kindness.*

Unfortunately, the events of September 11th have borne me out, although they might have been planned in Afghanistan or Saudi Arabia instead of Iraq. I am not a diplomat or a strategist. I am a writer, which means that I possess the ability to see and state the obvious. If you went to a Muslim country and observed the things which I have just described, how could you not anticipate September 11th? Americans like to say, "they're just jealous of us." That's not it. They hate us. Until we reach out to them, they will continue to hate us. Every new country we terrorize will make them hate us more. After we attack Iraq we must expect another September 11th.

My advice to the writers among you would be as follows:

> 1) Never forget the other point of view. No matter how you judge it, try to see it fairly and try to describe it accurately. Failing this, you will remain unable to evaluate the ideological claims to which you will be subjected for the rest of your life. Whatever you write about, let your subjects teach you in their own way, and show them that you have learned it and respect it. Let them be round characters always. The most anti-American Taliban officials were kind to me when I showed them my own copy of the Koran.
>
> 2) Never forget your own point of view. If extremists convince their neighbors in the Muslim world that we are all pawns of Israel, maybe you can unconvince them. If our government presents our next archenemy as a flat character, learn enough to present him as a round character. If you become a reporter, you will have to live with the dumbing down of your message, but please never, ever allow the fundamental essence of that message to be distorted. Remember, we writers are among the few who enjoy the privilege of presenting and standing by our own independent position to the world. We are beholden to no one.

> 3) In these times, any one of you who feels inclined to risk a little and learn a lot should travel to an Islamic country to make friends and to learn, not to teach. I can promise you that the mere fact of your interest will make a difference in a world where most Americans are seen as ignorant bullies. You should consider it an honor and a duty to keep those friends for life. You should get to know them well enough to understand why what they believe is plausible to them, and you should explain their views to other Americans as sympathetically and as accurately as you can.

On a more general note, I'd like to end by relaying to you the advice given to me when I first went to Afghanistan in 1982. The giver was a decent, intelligent, experienced, and very powerful old Pakistani general who adopted me as his son. I will never forget him. At that time I wanted to do something to help the Afghans in their fight against the Soviet invaders, but General N. helped me to understand how ill-prepared I was to help anybody but myself. He said to me that in order to carry out any project, one needs a brain, a heart, and hands. The average brain is perfectly good enough for most worthwhile things. Many of us also have the heart, the desire to do something good. The hands are another matter. By "hands" the General meant "capability." What are you good at? More practically, what are you good at that you have the resources to accomplish? Can you paint a mural of goodness and truth before you find the right wall? The issues of September 11th and the coming war will not resolve themselves in our lifetimes. It is up to each of us to do whatever he or she can to understand the grievances of others and, to the extent that we can lovingly and legitimately do so, to satisfy them. This defines not only our obligation as decent human beings, but our self-interest as terrorist targets.

Thank you.

From "Moral Calculus"

From
Rising Up and Rising Down

"Moral Calculus" is a 282-page compendium to Vollmann's seven-volume, 3,300-plus page essay, *Rising Up and Rising Down,* a treatise and meditation on the history and nature of mankind's tendency towards violence. It is Vollmann's intention for the reader to use the "Moral Calculus" volume as a guide and point of reference to the case studies presented in the essay. Vollmann posits the questions: when is violence justified, and are the justifications moral, right, wrong, or barbaric? The small excerpt here is meant to give the reader of this *Reader* a taste of the style and direction of "Moral Calculus" because neither a long nor short selection would do the work justice: to absorb its complete intent requires reading all 282 pages. —MH

5.2 JUSTIFICATIONS: SELF-DEFENSE

5.2.A WHEN IS VIOLENT DEFENSE OF HONOR JUSTIFIED?

FOR OUR PURPOSES, HONOR is *the extent to which the self approaches its own particular moral standard of replying to or initiating violence.* Honor is neither good nor bad without a context. It has four categories. Every type of honor falls into one of the first two and one of the last two:

- Inner honor: the degree of harmony between (a) an individual's aspirations, deeds and experiences, and (b) his conscience. As such, it remains unknowable to others.

or

- Outer honor: the degree of esteem in which someone is held. It derives either from his status [5.2.B def], or from the amount of consonance between (a) his professed aspirations and known deeds and (b) the values of his judges.

EXAMPLE: Cortes, in a pro forma reference to Montezuma, whom he has not yet met, speaks of "the honor and authority of such a great prince."

and

- Individual honor: one's honor as a person.

or

- Collective honor: one's honor as a citizen or member of a group.

EXAMPLE: Jung Haegu: "Korea's modern history is stained with dishonor and disgrace, and the people have been forced to accept frustration and shame" because of President Park's abuse of power.

Outer collective honor comprises the group's official face; inner collective honor is its esprit de corps as well as its degree of actual adherence to the ideals it professes.

VIOLENT DEFENSE OF HONOR IS JUSTIFIED

1. When honor is altruistic—that is, when honor demands the deliverance of a third party from imminent violence.
2. When defense of honor perfectly corresponds with other justified defense.

NOTE: This rule is weak almost to uselessness because defense of honor is so often unjustified. Best to limit this excuse for violence as much as possible!

COROLLARY: When defense of honor is in accordance with the fundamental right of the self.

EXAMPLE: During the Cultural Revolution, Nien Cheng refused to bow to Mao's portrait or to confess to imaginary crimes. Imminent self-defense would have justified her had she taken the course of acknowledging authority's outer honor. This is Dwight Edgar Abbot's course. Instead, she defends her own inner honor, a course which is allowed by the fundamental rights of the self to defend itself or not.

3. When the defender's peers would agree that dishonor is equivalent to, or worse than, physical harm, and when the dishonorer willfully disregards that standard.

EXAMPLES:

1. A raped woman in Afghanistan may very possibly be killed by her male relatives. The rapist becomes therefore her proximate murderer, and can be treated as such. Killing him before he dishonors her, or killing him later to keep the dishonor secret, may save her life.
2. Julius Caesar: "Prestige has always been of prime importance to me, even outweighing life itself." In fact, his prestige, his outer honor, is his power, without which he'd become anyone's prey. Regardless of the injustice of his war aims, to this simple extent Caesar's defense of honor is justified as imminent self-defense.
3. Dwight Edgar Abbot in juvenile hall: "There was never a doubt I had to retaliate. I had to save face. "My honor and ability had been questioned. A punk had made an unusual attempt to hurt a straight. No mild retaliation would save face for me or my clique. I had to cut Blinky." Otherwise Abbot will be despised and treated with violence indefinitely after.

Part III

On Love, Sex, Prostitutes, and Pornography

The Agony of Parker

From *You Bright and Risen Angels*

There's undoubtedly a sadomasochistic undercurrent in my work, just as there is in almost anyone who chooses violent subjects.

—William T. Vollmann,
in the 1992 interview appearing in
the *Review of Contemporary Fiction*.

There have been many depictions of the act of love in Vollmann's work that seem to illustrate the phrase "HURT IN LOVE" tattooed across the ass of the prostitute photographed by Ken Miller for Vollmann's *The Happy Girls* book object, but perhaps none of these depictions is more memorable, or shocking, than this hallucinatory passage from *You Bright and Risen Angles* describing Parker's nightmarish coupling with the Caterpillar Heart. This episode is the culmination of the revenge wreaked by Bug on Parker for the many torments and humiliations he had earlier inflicted on him. The Caterpillar Heart used to ensnare Parker had been grown by Bug's insect cohorts and was described in an earlier scene as "covered with rich soft fur and baiting with the cool green juices of love; this would be veiled by human skin. If Parker hugged it to him tight with his long arms, it would hurt him badly. . . . the reader is invited to imagine how effective a weapon the Caterpillar heart could be, when insect goals dictate its every beat and it is not bound by even the deficient rudiments of human pity. This, then, was what Parker was about to be faced with." —LM

Way down yonder in the meadow,
There's a poor little lambie;
The bees and butterflies pickin' out his eyes,
The poor thing cries, "Mammy" . . .

—Slave lullaby (1950s)

PARKER WAS NOW COMPLETELY hypnotized by the Caterpillar Heart, even though people still called him up all the time, he being an essential person and all, and said, "Say, Parker, baby, do you have any time this afternoon? What I can do is send you the pair of EXEC files to your graphics terminal. And you send me the DOD files through the load-macro register. Now, what is your user I.D.?" —and there would be an expectant silence, but Parker wouldn't say anything; and this did not unduly perturb the customer, because Parker never said anything, but what did perturb the customer was that his or her modem didn't light up and start chirring the way it used to when Parker was asked for something and sent the requested information over directly in a hexadecimal dump. —No, Parker just sat there and gangled his toes in the dark. At rare intervals he still went outdoors, and you might see him if Security was sloppy, a tall, greenish fellow leaning against an alley wall, with tufts of dirty-blond hair sprouting out around the rim of his camouflage cap; but there was no cunning cautious hostility in his eyes the way there would have been in the old days; he was too busy watching himself. There was a bulge under his jacket; it was the Caterpillar Heart, who sometimes applied her suckers to his armpits and the spaces between his toes, making him thrash and gulp dreadfully (if Parker had not been mute he would have screamed), and then Parker would try to pull her off, but, as Hitler remarked, "On the whole, we only laughed in those days at all these efforts."

Sometimes she was black and brown like a woolly bear caterpillar that Parker could hug tightly in his skinny arms like the teddy bear that he had never had as a child because in Omarville there was nothing to play with except nut casings, so because Parker had nothing soft to hug he grew up shy and often gangled his arms 'way 'way out at great distances to bring things close to him or to insinuate his arms into things; he never would have done that if he had been given a pillow which he could have thrown his green arms around when a boy, but maybe I am being sentimental, for what good would a pillow have done him after all? —The truth is that Parker, like the blue globes, was born evil. —But he did not want to be evil when the Caterpillar Heart came to see him, and he lay down in the space under the chemical basins so she could inch herself across his stomach and tickle his chin with her bristles. Later his skin would be inflamed by a gigantic pinprick rash. —Other times she was the hue of a Gulf fritillary caterpillar, which is to say glossy tacky black, like asphalt, with narrow red stripes and six rows of branching spines that stung Parker very gently, so that he writhed in startlement but let her sting him again in her advance across his body; she gradually grew longer and fatter and stronger with his special lymph in her, and would never have thought of leaving him for anyone else; and since she was stronger she could put on new colors for him, like the silver-spotted skipper caterpillar, whose body, aside from the nutlike head with the lost-looking stare of its orange eye-spots, seems to be wrapped round and round with one long strand of yellow yarn; then Parker coiled himself into a comfortable ball to watch the succeeding displays of his glutinous lover; and as he winked and blinked with his yellow eyes she took on a complex white shape, extruding double parallel rows of bristles, white on top and honey-orange underneath; and her body fissured into gummy white cylindrical segments, each having two white dots in a row, then three stepped ones, equivalent to the arrangement on dominoes, then one more; and a succulent butterscotch head on each end of her body; she was a French vanilla truffle that Parker wanted to eat, but he didn't eat her because then he would have nobody left to be in love with; that was the phase of the cynthia moth caterpillar; then she became pink and furry again, losing one of her heads and watching him lovingly with the remaining one, which now resembled a strawberry; but all the time Parker was not eating her; she was eating him. —Eventually she turned lime-green, like an Eastern tiger swallowtail caterpillar. For Parker she was always as sleek as a leggy brunette in the Alps posed beside a touring car.

Of course she loved Parker only as any other caterpillar would have loved a green leaf, but to Parker she seemed to be far more conscious of his self than she was; and when she homed her eyes upon him, resuming her true form of bristle-hooked artichoke heart, he felt that she was showing her nakedness to him because she understood how much he wanted her to trust him; in fact she never understood him or cared to understand him; though as far as Parker was concerned, when he extruded his knees up to the ceiling to make a mountain for her to hook herself up and over, confronting him from the peaks of his kneecaps as she dug into his patella and her ocelli focused vaguely upon him, then he was confident that she was his own Heart who would never leave him, who as she inched down the long skinny pipes of his inclined thighs would never slip; who was to be relied upon even in preference to Wayne; who as her urticating hairs and hooklets bored into him to inflame the flesh just like Clara Bee's study lamp warming the snakes' cage so that the snakes could bask, made Parker go slack and forget his political aims; who as she stung her way across his lower abdomen proved herself to him by the steadiness of her merciless progress, staring at him with every one of her round white eyes that faced his direction; who as her suckers penetrated his navel to drink the lymph beneath it gave Parker the first sexual spasm that he had experienced since being hung by the older boys at summer camp, so that Parker climaxed in a terrible thrashing of limbs that shattered the red safelight on the ceiling and rocked the Great Enlarger, and then Parker was punished by her in parallel to the way that his stern-stemmed plant parents used to punish him in Omarville by wafting agonizing cocklebur-seeds down onto his bed as he slept; for the Caterpillar Heart had just drilled entirely through his belly for the first time (there is always a first time), in order to suck down slow droplets of his spinal fluid, for it was her instinct to do this when her victim convulsed helplessly; but to Parker it seemed that she was being severe with him because he had had his dirty orgasm; and Parker basked in being punished for his snakelike behavior, which he had always been ashamed of, having grown up in the Age of Electricity when even the reactionaries considered snakes to be feudal elements which should have been extirpated by the tenth anniversary of the founding of the Society of Daniel at the very latest, so that it felt so good for Parker to be punished by someone whom he could love, as he had never been able to love the older boys, that Parker came again, spraying her with veined greenish threads of mucus, which she gobbled *before* stabbing her hooklets into his stomach, much more painfully than before, triumphantly scraping the moisture from the surface of his liver and absorbing it to allow her to grow larger and heavier, weighing down on his ribs like a ton of avocados to keep him still as she cracked another of his vertebrae like a hazelnut, making Parker arch himself and vomit bile, in his agony, rolling over and cutting himself upon the shards of safelight glass; and she clamped her suckers to his shoulders and throat, injecting an acidic fluid that made him bleed in black funereal clots; and then she sucked the venom out and stung the wounds so that once more they got blissfully inflamed and Parker lost himself ecstatically, like a water-snake in a bottle to which alcohol and formaldehyde are slowly added so that the water turns milky and the snake swims more and more wildly and lashes the sides of the bottle and suddenly goes rigid, braced against the glass in a spiral coil resembling a heat exchanger, and snaps its head back, and then very very slowly riffles down dead to the bottom of the whitish fluid, crystals falling gently upon its open eyes as softly as snowflakes; so Parker blacked out; and his ecstasy remained to some degree when he once again became a purposeful tenant of his shrunken scaly bulk, for the pleasurable swelling of his limbs seemed to him a token that after having punished him she had forgiven him.

These sessions lasted almost continually, interrupted only by Dr. Dodger's shrill coaxing and admonitions to Parker (Dr. Dodger did not dare to discipline Parker in any way because he needed Parker and couldn't tell whether Parker's horrid marriage to the Caterpillar Heart was or was not the custom in Omarville) and by Wayne's visits, upon each of which Parker would have to leave the honeymoon, shambling weakly into his quarters at the Society of Daniel where Wayne sat waiting upon Parker's cot, which was so neat and tight that Wayne liked bouncing a quarter on the bedspread aw-*RIGHT!* when he came by, but Parker merely lifted his shaggy head and moved his yellow eyes into alignment with Wayne's anxious reverent gaze, and stretched out a limp frog-green arm which shook Wayne's hand in a fishy kind of way.

Wayne wondered if Parker were testing him because Parker had tested him before; when Wayne and Parker were boys Parker summoned Wayne out to Omarville one August night to test him and subject him to a most comprehensive renewal. Wayne did not really want to go because no one except Parker liked to go near Omarville where they murdered people and the Plant Clan held its rallies at high noon and there was nothing that the justice Department could do because the local sheriff was one of them. But off he went because Parker had told him to. Parker and Wayne were each armed with firecrackers. They stood in the center of the road walled in by sumac trees with fuzzy berries ripening in the night; and it was a very hot night so that if you were a boy and were out in it you felt that some adventure such as running away was about to happen to you; you would run away to sea and sail into warm blue oceans and find islands full of jungles and cannibals and weird fruits and beautiful princesses who wanted you to marry them; and if you were older and had to work in an office you saw the night outside and maybe opened your window and felt funny and wished that you could be out in it but realized that you could not, for fiscal reasons, and that anyhow because you had been doing what you had been doing for so long you would not know how to conduct yourself even if you could be out in it, so you went back to your ledgers and on-line data entries with a *pleasurable* feeling of regret; and if you were older still you weren't even up to thoughts like that; you just grunted, well, my stomach's hurting me; I wonder if it's cancer yet; guess I may as well sit here and keep working until a blood vessel bursts in my brain. —Meanwhile the night went about its business. Wayne and Parker shook hands. Then they turned back to back, and each boy took twenty-five paces forward; and then when Parker gave the signal by making a dry cracking sound inside his cheek they both stopped and turned around to face each other. Wayne, out of tradition, was allowed to throw the first cracker. It landed on the road and burst at Parker's feet, throwing out a great green Catherine wheel around Parker like one of those screamin' Russki Katyusha rockets so that Parker glowed in the dark and was showered with sparks, and little holes were burned in his clothes from head to toe, but he was unhurt. It was now Parker's turn, O Things That Go Bump In The Night! Slipping a hand into his pocket, Parker slyly removed a big bundle of M-80s, red and cheery-papered, all tied to one fuse; Parker struck a match on his fly and lit the fuse, BSZZZZZZZ! and hurled the firecrackers straight at Wayne, who stood invisible in the darkness like black against black, but the white and yellow glare of the firecrackers found Wayne and enveloped him as the firecrackers blew up right in Wayne's face! Wayne was badly burned, but recovered, being a youth; and the important thing was that as the crackers came hurtling towards him he had stood straight and tense and ready to take it; glorying in Parker's scrutiny, he had not flinched; thereby he had lived up to Parker.

The Shame of It All: Some Thoughts on Prostitution in America (1999)

The theme and subject of prostitution is, by now, a signatory aspect of Vollmann's work—even to the extent that critics have become negative in their assessment: "enough already!" Still, any writer must remain true to his obsessions and those things that call him to put pen to paper. Prostitutes appear in just about every book Vollmann has written—from appearances by the familiar Brandi in *You Bright and Risen Angels* and *Rainbow Stories* to some of the case studies in *Rising Up and Rising Down* (all over the world). Note how Vollmann explains the importance of prostitutes in his work as a whole. —MH

1

I HAVE WORSHIPED THEM and drunk from their mouths; I've studied at their feet. Many have saved me; one or two I've raised up. They've cost me money and made me money. People might say that we've "exploited" each other. Some have trusted me; a few have loved me—or at least said so. They've healed my loneliness, infected me with diseases and despair. Some I pity; some I envy; most equal me in their fortunes. One robbed me at knifepoint in a hotel room in Montréal; dozens ran off with my cash over the years; the greatest number honorably remained after getting paid. (If I write so much of payment, that's because it's one core of this double-cored subject.) All too many feel stained by their profession; they're the ones to weep for. As for the new-met desperate companions who snatched my proffered dollars, then waited, stiff with stoical terror; I never made them do anything. There were others who slept in my arms, then shook me awake in the middle of the night, sobbing with sexual need. Three or four refused money, and one even gave me money. —"You gotta remember every girl's different," a call girl sighed not long ago. —They're coldly proud—no, tender, passionate, vacant, malignant. Can I truly claim to "understand" them? When he neared his eightieth birthday, the great Japanese printmaker Hokusai wistfully complained that he was only just now beginning to learn to draw. And I, myself not as accomplished or experienced as I would like to be, gaze at a waterfall of dark hair upon a soft white pillow; I see a naked shoulder pulse in sleep; I see an earring on the sheet, and confess that my desire to know the soul within this woman's flesh is several orders of infinity greater than my actual knowledge. Yet we feel at ease together, she and I. She's a prostitute; she's a woman; she's a human being. Isn't that enough? —Not for ideologues, who long to categorize her as *exploited, free* or *corrupt,* nor for body-renters, who yearn to define her according to one of the motifs in the yellow pages: *blondes, exotic Orientals, bored housewives, secretaries* or *nursing students* (the last with a photograph of steel gurneys), *dominatrices, cowgirls, big girls, old women* . . . What is she? What is she?

2

We usually explain prostitution as *the exchange of sexual services for compensation.* In that case, the monkey who picks a banana for his mate, the nervously exalted fellow who buys his bride's wedding ring, and the truck driver who after unpeeling a $20 bill ejaculates into a consenting woman's mouth, all employ prostitutes.

Matrimony's defenders might express offense—indeed, in many a formulation of whoredom, the word *non-marital* gets inserted like a diaphragm slick with the most arbitrary of all spermicides. What do such people think prostitution is? They know nothing of it, or else resort to it in secret, hating the hired bodies as they hate themselves. —Most, I truly believe, are merely ignorant. But they *think* they know. Like the Muslims I've met who refuse to read Rushdie's *Satanic Verses* but would kill Rushdie if they could, because the book is evil—authority told them so!—like witch-burners through the ages, like good Stalinists, like my little girl's fundamentalist babysitter who just gave two weeks' notice because I interview prostitutes, our prudes know what a sinner is. Ask them, "What is a woman? What is a human being?" and they'll fall silent in confusion—or more likely they'll say, "You know what a woman is! Look, there's one!" and thus they've proven that they know all women. A woman—well, she's a human being with breasts and a womb. (A transsexual—never mind about transsexuals.) —"But what is a woman *emotionally and spiritually?*" —Who's wise enough to answer that?

Enough. Call a prostitute someone who exchanges non-marital sexual services for compensation. And, to be sure, that's what she is—maybe not *all* she is; maybe the definition rings a little cold, but that's to the prude's advantage, because he wants to present prostitution as cold—yes, cold and sad like frozen tears. And isn't it? Listen to a very polished, lethally beautiful Las Vegas call girl named Collette spewing out her bitterness in a chirpy, lisping voice: "I hate the work. It's disgusting and it makes you feel like a real piece of shit. Recently this old man, he's a local, I'm alone with him in his house, right? And he says, I got a gun, I'm mad, I been looking for somebody to use it on. I had to call the agency and they had no idea. But of course they have no idea how we have to act, what we have to do. They're *phone girls*. They're too good for us." —Collette's voice rang with the merciless hatred of the scorned for their scorners. When this feeling gets widespread enough, revolutions happen, but in this case the only widespread thing is Collette herself, biting her lip with pain and rage while the old man hurts her.

"So what did you do with the old man?" I asked.

"I calmed him down," she said with a smile of fury. "I deliberately stayed. And I—*made him happy*. But that's why I don't go with locals. I usually say hello to locals and they say hello to me, but that's all. I like out-of-towners. I like one-on-one and a $100 bill and let's get this over with."

3

Collette speaks for many of her sisters when she says, "Let's get this over with." If you are very rich or very spendthrift in America, you can find a call girl just as beautiful as any Asian "flower," but it is almost certain that she will ruthlessly extract as much money as she can, then leave as quickly as she can. I remember one beautiful blonde who took

$300, told me I could do whatever I wanted, but I couldn't touch her and I had to use my own hand, then departed. (Fortunately, it was *Esquire's* money.)

Then there was the strung out Las Vegas call girl who said: "I'm not bein' rude, but when we go in a room, we do business first. Excuse me, but you kinda remind me of a psycho person. Okay, so are we gonna talk about tips? Well, I told you I don't come into a room for nothing. On top of the agency's $250, I get $500 to $1,000 an' up. I'm makin' the big bucks. I don't begrudge them their $250 'cause they're paying for all the advertising."

She was supposed to be named Nikki—well, actually, the glamorous-voiced woman who'd answered the agency's phone had said that *she* was Nikki and was coming right over to dance nude for me for a whole hour, but then somehow in the next call her voice changed to the anxious, whiny, gravelly scraggly voice of this old crackhead whore who insisted she was the same Nikki but later forgot that and asked my companion Lizzy whether *she* were Nikki.

"Do you shave down there?" she asked Lizzy, smoking a cigarette.

"No, because it itches."

"Then you're not shavin' right. Then you get those little bumps an' you . . . You should do it the right way. Just 'cause your skin's nice. Hey, are you Lizzy or Lezzy?"

"Lizzy."

"Okay, that's it," she said, hunched, clenching her wrists nervously, smoothing down her hair. "When I hit rock top, you'll remember who I am. There's more to you two than . . . You're not just here. You're fucked up. I'm not sayin' this in a bad sense, Nikki, I . . . Hey, let's talk about tips."

4

Bleakness, sadness, people using people as if they were machines from which any joy issues only in commodity form, like the vacation-hours purchased in casinos between brass palm trees and brass pillars, the dull, hollow coughing of quarters in the jackpot-pans of slot machines, while tropical night-flowers glow on all the carpets—that's Collette's picture; and we'll find it reliably replicated. Just as

Las Vegas Boulevard remains itself even though its grandeur dwindles westward from the Luxor's pyramid and the Bellagio's expensive collection of paintings all viewable for hire, dwindles down to gas station casinos, then pawn shops and nude revues, so Collette's dismal picture retains its integrity no matter what the pigments. We can paint it in the brassy golds and nickel-silvers of the high roller hotels where she spreads her legs for pay; or we can paint it in piss and shit and blood, using for our model the San Francisco street prostitute Rhonda, who clings to building-sides, drumming her fingers rapidly against the cold dirty bricks to keep from twitching; she tries to smile but her scarred skullface can't do more than bare its rotten yellow teeth which resemble maggots gleaming in a death-wound. I can scarcely recall a single American street prostitute who wasn't an addict or a thief, who didn't have bad skin, who wasn't desperate, or who didn't stink. Rhonda possesses all of these characteristics. She taps her high heels, and her skinny, skinny legs begin to shake. Yes, she smiles; she knows she's supposed to do that; she twitches her face into a lava-fissured grimace.

The first time I met her, back in 1988, she assured me that she wasn't really a prostitute; she'd just fallen on hard times; then she added that I could stick it in any hole I wanted. She wasn't from here anyway, she went on in a rush; she usually stayed up in Santa Rosa, and that convulsive, shivering, twitching habit wasn't really hers, either, because her father had been stationed in Ankara when she was young, which was why her mother had hooked her on heroin when she was fourteen. That was how Rhonda's autobiography went. And her real biography? She'd never been in Ankara in her life, as she laughingly admitted a year later when I saw her among the dark-toned figures who sat motionless at twilight in the sunken plaza feeding into the Powell Street subway station, toward which lines of dark-suited salary workers descended quietly, tired-eyed, sweating and weary, gazing away from one another. In fact Rhonda had never even seen heroin until she was twenty-two. Her mother had nothing to do with her sadness and badness. Never mind. —Accost Rhonda, and she'll say, "What's up?"

"You wanna take a walk with me?"

"For what?"

But by the time you begin to explain, she's already sweating and shaking. "I don't know," she croaks. "Hurry up, please. Where's your twenty?"

For Rhonda is Collette writ desperate. Rhonda sucks strange men's penises in fear, and for need, always craving her heroin so that she can "get well" and let her mind clear long enough to remember firstly that she's hungry and has nowhere to stay, and secondly that a tall demonic whore on Sixteenth Street whom she knows only as Big Lips has sworn to slit her belly open with a dirty razor blade because Rhonda once stole one of Big Lips's dates. By the time she's remembered these two facts, the heroin's already worn off; she's in an alley, vomiting; she'd do anything to "get well"; she croaks, "Hurry up, please. Stick it anywhere. I don't care. Just . . . I gotta . . ."

5

And so for Rhonda and Collette it's sex-for-money, period. And because they're only in it for the money, taking little pleasure in the act itself, the standard definition of prostitution glares harsh and clear and seemingly true, a perfect jumping-off point for the next definition: *Prostitution is exploitation.* (In one Montréal nudie bar I remember seeing a stripper who threw her underpants to a man in the front row who then hastily and greedily clapped them to his nose. Later he gave her two hundred Canadian dollars. Who was more needy in that relationship, and who did better out of it?) Sometimes the American prude argues that whores are evil, dangerous, beyond the pale. At the moment, he's more likely to say that she's *exploited.* (Would a million dollars just to rub noses with another human being still be exploitation? To the prude it would, because prostitution is *dirty*.) The compass needle of blame swings south rather than north, pointing to the customer, but the category of prostitution remains equally blameworthy. And much of the blame derives from our first definition. *A prostitute is someone who exchanges sexual services for compensation.*

What if her services weren't sexual? What would the prude say then? Let me cite Sherrice, an old heroin-addicted San Francisco street prostitute—a grandmother—who became my friend and model. I sometimes let her sleep in my hotel room when she was unable to suck enough penises to pay her rent. This very witty and intelligent woman always stank, in part because when business was slow she rummaged through trash cans. She would gladly have serviced me out of friendship or gratitude, but I preferred to sleep on the floor and let her take the bed, where she spent hours groaning, trying to put the needle in. The only thing she ever stole from me was just a smidgeon of my cadmium red watercolor to use for lipstick. I told her that cadmium was poisonous, but she said she had more important worries, as indeed she did, for one day she disappeared; the other girls on Capp Street said she'd been strangled. One of her regulars was an impotent widower who wanted nothing more than to take her out for dinner once a week and have her smile at his jokes. He paid her $20 for that, and for her as for me it was the same as if he'd paid her $20 to blow him; prostitution is not only about sex, but also about companionship; the longer I study prostitution and marriage, the less difference I can see between them.

The trump card of the marriage fetishist: "Whatever one spouse does for another gets done out of love, or duty, not for a reward. Therefore, marriage isn't prostitution." —This may be true (I certainly hope it is). But whenever anybody does something voluntarily, he believes that he'll be better off doing it than not doing it. In other words, he expects to be *compensated*—with sex, or gratitude, or the praise of his own conscience—or with a banana. —Tell me, did the widower exploit Sherrice? She didn't think so. —Did the other men exploit her? Some did and some didn't. She liked many of them, and not merely the big tippers. Some men compensated her with good money (and of course, just as do I when I write essays for pay, she always tried to get as much money as she could), and some compensated her with respect and kindness. Some were callous, a few were cruel, and one, I fear, was a murderer.

6

So I prefer the following working definition: *A prostitute is someone who exchanges sexual services or intimacy for compensation.* —Yes, prostitution does differ from marriage in two ways: It's shorter term (probably), and it's more aboveboard. In a legal Nevada brothel called Angel's Ladies, seventy-seven acres of desert with its own hot springs, rare frogs and crashed propeller plane, there lives a lady named Jennafer, plump, blonde, happy and easy, who told me, "I think I can trust a man more in a brothel because this is a business transaction. It's exactly that: money for sex. And that's what I want out of it. And if I get an orgasm out of it, that's a bonus."

"Why did you become a prostitute?"

She leaned back, licked her lips, and replied, "Finances. I said to my sister, out of the blue, 'I wonder what the Mustang Ranch is like . . .' That was the first brothel I worked in. And they gave me the opportunity, and it was *fun*. Not only am I bein' paid, but I enjoy what I'm doin.' Gettin' a man off gives me such pleasure."

7

Such pleasure! A prostitute having *fun?* How could that be?

To be sure, *her* fun might not have been the point of the job, but isn't that the case for other paid professionals? What I do for money I try to enjoy; when that fails, cash solaces me. And Jennafer was a businesswoman first and foremost, which is why her conversation evinced a wise preoccupation with money. Once she ruefully said, "I've destroyed two men of my clientele by bein' friends with 'em, by goin' on the outside, by goin' to concerts, and then they just wanna be friends. Sometimes they don't even wanna have sex. Either way, the money just goes out the window." Sure, money was the point, but that didn't mean that Jennafer cared nothing about anything else. When I asked her how many of her customers appeared to want only sex, no intimacy, no affection, she replied, "Well, it's mixed. The men who want to have a good party—two to four hours—they need the sex, but they need to be loved and hugged even more. They need to feel welcome." And here I thought again of Sherrice with her courtly old widower.

"Well, Jennafer, what if you start getting sore and the man wants you to go on?"

"I'll tell him I need to take a break. If I'm in pain, he can give me a back massage, or . . ."

"Have you ever met a client who was very nice but physically repulsive—say, he smelled bad—so that it was hard for you to have sex with him?"

"I'm not gonna make a person feel bad about himself because he doesn't look the way other people do. Maybe he was born lookin' that way or he doesn't have the finances to fix himself up. Beauty is on the inside. But it depends on the disability. If I get a man with four balls and two cocks, I gotta worry!"

"So most of the time the work is okay for you?"

"Let's put it this way," the blonde said. "I'm a very promiscuous person. I love sex. I love myself, and I love a lot of people, including my customers. You, for example."

Whether one takes that statement as evidence of autonomism or as evidence of an immense and spontaneous capacity to give of herself, it would seem that what Jennafer offers to her customers she offers readily and naturally, and that it pleases her to offer it.

"Had you had a lot of sexual experience before you went to work?"

"I wasn't a virgin if that's what you mean. The very first time it was perfect. I think because it was my first experience and it was his first experience, and he was just the nicest man I've had in my life. And the first time I went to work in a brothel, it was almost the same feeling. See, at the Mustang Ranch all the girls will line up at the bell side by side and the guys will come in and they'll be like stunned, I just died and went to heaven. On my first night there, I got picked right away, and I was thinking, like, with all these other beautiful, slender girls, you want me? It was so flattering."

"How did it go?"

"He was really nice and wanted to marry me. I told him I couldn't, on account of my financial goals. A week later he called me. He got seriously angry when I didn't remember him by his voice. He never came back again."

8

That story of Jennafer's suitor is such a classic tale that it might as well be written on the walls of brothels or freeway underpasses. Jennafer never forgets her finances, and neither does Collette, who boasted, "After I put my money in my purse, I turn into a real bitch. My smile comes right off." But the man who pays is free to fall in love. It's his party. If Collette thought she could make an extra $100 by saying, "I love you," do you think she'd hesitate? And if her customer were paying for affection as well as for sex, might he not possibly feel confused as to whether Collette truly loved him or whether he were merely getting his money's worth?

Do you believe that prostitutes can fall in love? If not, then you must think that prostitutes are not like anybody else on earth. Granted, they may share themselves with men who'd repulse other women. ("Their appearance never gotten to me, 'cause I been a cool person," said the call girl Snow. "Only I don't want to be in a situation where it's like a lot of people. One man, he wants to see like a show, and I don't mess around like that. One-on-one, nobody's blockin' your way and no one's tryin' to get more money than you.") Can prostitutes fall in love? Why not believe it? I remember a woman in Africa who never once asked me for money (but whose house rent I sometimes paid). She said she loved me, as I believe she did. I loved her, too. She treated me as well as any woman I've ever been with, braved real dangers for my sake, and wrote to me twice a month for years—although once, it's true, she mistakenly enclosed a love letter to one of her other husbands.

And here we should render the angry, beautiful Collette her due: Ice-maiden though she might have been, she was not entirely unsusceptible to romanticism. When I asked her whether she'd ever dated anybody nice, a smile sweetened her face and she told me about the man who'd stopped her one night at the Rio Hotel and wanted her phone number—a stupid out-of-town man, I should add, who didn't comprehend that Collette was a prostitute even though she'd snappishly proclaimed herself to be a *dancer,* which any local would know to be code for *I spread my legs for pay, or at least will tantalize you with that possibility for pay,* —he still didn't get it! Well, Collette was too busy for his nonsense that night; she clippety-clacked away on her high heels. But three years later she entered a hotel room on a call and it was as if the shining, flashing, multicolored numbers on slot machine banks had finally lined up in her favor, for she found herself sitting down face to face on the double bed with the very same man! She didn't recognize him at first, but he remembered her right away, as if he'd fallen in love with her face. During that hour he respected Collette; he was kind to her. "You know," she told me, "I liked him so much that if I'd met him in another context I would have had a fling with him for nothing. I would have had sex with him—not that I ever told him that, of course, 'cause I was havin' sex with him for money. But he's a very cute, very cute guy," she said softly.

9

Collette was almost ashamed of this confession, I think. Unlike Jennafer, who could lie back and happily climax, she seemed distressed at the possibility of losing control, even if the reward for doing so would have constituted a lyrical experience. I was trying to figure out why, when Collette very primly said, "I don't associate with dancers. I don't get along with 'em 'cause they have pimps. They get their kids taken away but they don't care since they have million-dollar houses. And they seem to kind of sort of *enjoy it,"* she added with contemptuous loathing, "'cause they're exhibitionists. *They'd probably have sex for $50"* —which to Collette was evidently the ultimate insult. (Sherrice and Rhonda, of course, would have done it for twenty or thirty.) I then understood that Collette looked down on her own profession, and perhaps by extension on herself.

10

Why should she be? What had she done wrong, in making men happy? She wanted money. Well, money is admirable. And what was my African wife after? She hoped to marry me, or somebody, anybody; she wanted me to come back (which I did); she wanted to retain herself in my memory in case she might need my help (which I gave); above all, she genuinely cared for me. She was my darling. And how did her motives differ from those of any not-prostitute? But when I try to explain all this to my fellow citizens, they're scandalized—oh, the shame, the bloody shame! Prostitution *must* be shameful, because the body is shameful.

11

In the Book of Genesis we read that until Adam and Eve ate of the Tree of Knowledge, they were naked and unashamed, like my six-month-old daughter, who shrieks with glee to see her mirror image clothed or unclothed. But once they'd committed the Promethean crime of enlightening themselves, Adam hid from God, because his uncoveredness made him afraid. Hence in the dozen underground blocks of nineteenth-century Havre, Montana, with its plastery, moldy cellar smell, one passes the speakeasy's round tables laid out with dingy cards and red, white and blue poker chips and finds the brothel's beds perforce all together for reasons of space, but each bed's guarded by curtains on strings, and there's a loud piano to cover up the moans. Adam's still hiding from God. Even Jennafer admitted, "A lot of the girls who work in a house, they do feel ashamed. If they've just finished spendin' their money like wildfire, they sometimes don't know who they are."

After World War I, dispossession went further,* the brothels themselves comprising an American Eden from which the girls and their clients got expelled by moral crusaders: Prostitution is exploitation, so close down the whorehouses! A few legal houses such as Angel's Ladies keep the faith in Nevada; some exist on the sly, and we shouldn't forget that massage parlors may offer more than massages, but nowadays in the United States one usually finds only call girls or street girls. Eve runs through the night, terrified of God's squad car and silver badge. Moreover, Eve knows she's naked, and is ashamed. That's why that black transsexual call girl named Snow said in her low, gentle voice, "I don't think it should be legalized. A lot of people really depend on sellin' their bodies, and bein' from the South I just don't feel comfortable with that."

And throughout the world, wherever there are People of the Book—Jews, Christians or Muslims—this tradition of shame haunts and taints our bodies, which is why Prostitutes of the Book so often suffer from scorn. As an aboriginal woman in the Redfern ghetto of Sydney, Australia, once said to me: "You get punched for doin' that stuff. By your sisters and by your aunties."

In Buddhist Asia it's not that way. I have spent many happy hours among the prostitutes of Thailand, Cambodia, Burma and Japan.

*Until around 1917–18, prostitution as such rarely appeared in American statute books—laws against adultery, "crimes against nature," and the like succeeded in repressing sexuality quite conveniently; laws against vagrancy criminalized sex on the street.

Some hide their professions from their families. Many do not. Almost without exception they are clean, personable, affectionate. They enjoy dancing, travelling, sightseeing. They're girlfriends, wives. If you are affectionate and kind, they'll stay with you. They'll bargain down the taxi drivers, patch your clothes, translate for you, fetch medicine when you're sick. And if you don't respect them, if you fail to cherish and take care of them, they will leave. They belong to themselves.

12

In America, many call girls and legal prostitutes comprise a corps of similar cleanliness; they're the sort that Jennafer called "the classy girls, the ones who care about themselves." And black Snow lived in a similarly comfortable conceptual world. "Call girls do it a little more classier, you might say," she opined. "They do it off pagers and cell phones and they don't have any real danger. Streetwalkers, the police will come by. I done that for two month; I was scared shitless." She'd been a call girl for eight years. Once she was a man. Now she had breasts and a penis. Her husband was a lesbian. "The people I normally get is really nice, although I've had a couple of assholes. Normally they're over forty-five or fifty-five or whatever, and obese, so they have to pay for it."

Snow was safe—she so much wanted to be safe! In the back of so many high class hookers' minds whispers a demon called Fear—fear that they'll end up on the street. The Southeast Asian prostitutes almost never express this. They tend to save up their money quietly, marry and retire. Sometimes, if they get a yen for expensive jewelry and want to cheat on their husbands, they might make another foray into what's called "the life," but it's a measure of the stability of their situation that they can often stay married. I'm not saying they have it vastly better; many of them fear the life they came from, the backbreaking rice field life they'll never permanently escape. But every American prostitute I've ever interviewed who *didn't* work the streets looked down on those who did—and when I say "looked down" I imagine an elegantly dressed woman on the deck of the *Titanic,* staring at the fatally cold sea into which she must inevitably fall. Sometimes she'll crack jokes about her fallen sisters, as if in fun, but those jokes are as boisterous yet secretly indignant as a party of Arabs watching a stripshow. "I can never, never work the streets," Jennafer said. "Just 'cause it's too damn scary." She knew three prostitutes who after hiring themselves out at the Mustang Ranch had tried to go into business for themselves and wound up dead. "Not to mention how disgustin' it is," she went on, "'cause they go from car to car, suckin' off men with no place to clean up in between. More than likely, they got either a drug habit or a goddamn pimp. I can't stand women who are so stupid they got to give their money to a goddamn man. I can't understand why a woman would want to support a man by fuckin' a bunch of other men. Those women should be shot in the head." (By the way, my dear friend Athena, a beautiful, triangular-faced Chicago call girl who sometimes takes me out to expensive Italian restaurants, might beg to differ. She supports a certain artist who has not yet realized his possibly hypothetical commercial prospects and who happens to be her husband. Athena requires all her customers to don *two* condoms. Her husband has to wear only one. She says, "I love my husband. I have no complaints. It's between us." And she does not fear the street girls, but she pities them, and often volunteers for "outreach" work, which means passing out free condoms. It just goes to show as the saying goes, "all girls are different.")

Jennafer probably was safe. Snow was fairly safe, and Collette, too. That strung-out call girl named Nikki, who worked for the same agency as the other two, insisted: "Some people are desperate, you know. But this is *different* from the street." (She was one of the most desperate women I've ever seen.) "You have bachelor parties, just shows, you know, tittygrams; it's 98% okay. Just the drunk assholes . . ."

Nikki was frightened of me. She might have been a paranoid schizophrenic. She expected me to shoot her at any minute. It did not surprise me that she was on probation with the agency, because her skinniness and half-coherent panic befitted any street prostitute on her way downhill. I can hardly bear to imagine what experiences Nikki must have had in her furtive life. And yet she too had enrolled herself in the comforting ranks of "the ones who care about themselves!" She was proud of her life! "Every time, you meet somebody different," she sighed, slowly, mechanically beginning to strip. "Every time, you meet somebody interestin'. There's stars that call. You go out with 'em. It's good out here. This is the big money town that won't ever go. There's guys out there, you don't do nothin', but you still get the money . . ."

Nikki was right. The escort agency business is basically a shuck. Pay your $250; tip the girl $300 more, and then if she won't blow you, what are you going to do? Call the Better Business Bureau? This is why many call girls describe themselves as "entertainers" instead of prostitutes and look down on street-whores or the inmates of legal brothels with equally righteous shudders. When I asked Collette what she thought of the Cottontail Ranch, she said: "I heard they were nasty and dirty and rundown, and they don't get tips and for one hour they have to be in some little room with a man doin' whatever he says." (And yet practically in the same breath she could say about her own subprofession: "I been too lucky in this business. I never been arrested or even eighty-sixed from one of the big hotels. I have a really good chance of getting into workin' reception at the Mandalay Bay Hotel . . . I got to get out of this.") And Snow said: "That would feel like an awkward situation, sittin' in a house, waitin' for someone to pick me to do whatever they want. Me, I think I'm old enough to pick myself." (But the agencies which she worked for ran ads in the yellow pages such as **TWO GIRLS ARE MORE FUN** and **U-PICK-EM.***) As for Nikki, she reiterated: "They have to give half to the house. They're always bein' monitored, but sometimes they stash some money in their shampoo. You gotta stay in that room, too. You can't complain. If you work there, you gotta fuck; you gotta suck dick. But me, I don't have to do nothin'."

Jennafer for her part claimed that a call girl's life was "just as dangerous as bein' a street hooker. You don't know who you're meetin.' You don't know if they got devices in the room. If they want sex, that's a hush-hush deal."

"And how dangerous is what you do?"

"It's less dangerous, in my opinion, than at a bar, where you're gonna drink your ass off and wake up God knows where. Pregnancy's the only sexual disease you can cure. But we check 'em. If they come in all sweaty,

*On one page, Kitty's ranch girls, Sheila's biker girls, Kristina's crushed hearts and Cheerleaders all had the same number, 253-6969. "I don't even know which agency I work for," one call girl mumbled. "It's better not to ask too much. I just do my thing. I know it by the name the Stripper Agency but in the phone book it's lots of other agencies."

we make 'em take a shower. I'll shower with 'em if they want me to. After all, I'm gonna be having sex with 'em, so what's the difference?"

"We want this to be a real family-related place," her employer told me over dinner. "It's just a big family where everybody trusts everybody. In fact, I find these girls nicer than the church people I used to work with." Jennafer refilled my glass of homemade strawberry juice, then Mack went out to weed his tomatoes before darkness came.

13

Paradoxically, illegal prostitutes may possess more freedom of choice than legal ones, because they are not monitored (unless they have pimps). I remember so many street prostitutes in San Francisco who rocketed down the sidewalk with happy stars in their eyes (many were young and on drugs, of course; they tended to lose their energy before they were thirty). They did a dozen deals an hour, running back and forth to keep their customers, pimps, and pushers all pinned, while like good stock marketeers they bought and sold shares in their own commodity futures; many of these whores were excited, free, maybe even happy. They went to jail and died young, sure, but can we say the mayfly's life is less valuable than the elephant's merely because it's shorter?

In the legal brothels such as the Cottontail Ranch or the Shady Lady, pink light bulbs demarcate surprisingly compact, lonely structures set off from the open road. Jennafer was very happy at Angel's Ladies, but that establishment might have been an exception. "Things just weren't as nice as they were here. And I have my animals. And Mack and Angel are so *nice,* they are. At the A__________you're pretty much locked down and they charge you $31 a day. You can't take a walk. I worked at the B__________ and the C__________, but the things they did to me were very unkosher. Like, my dog wasn't allowed to go in, but theirs was. And they sprayed my dog in the eyes with ammonia. At that time I didn't have anywhere to go to. And one of the women, she got impregnated by her boyfriend, and it was a tubal pregnancy, and they refused to take her to the hospital, so I did, and I got fired for it."

But the call girl's profession contains its own counterpart annoyances.

Yes, during that paid hour, the client's bedside phone is constantly ringing (calls from the agency), and the cell phone in the lady's purse keeps going off; like the shouted endearments and blown kisses of the fast-flitting street prostitute, it's all busy and rather jolly, but those telephones assert *control,* which is personified by the phone girls who in one prostitute's scornful description "sit behind the desk all day." They can torture the call girls in numerous petty ways. Snow, for instance, liked the *nom de joie* she had chosen, but her phone girl changed it to Sugar just to annoy her. Yet she still had to tip her phone girl when she got back from a job; otherwise the phone girl might not send her out again. The agency charged a base fee of $250, out of which Snow might get $50, but then that $50 had to go back to the phone girl as a tip; and sometimes the customer might (as did I) bargain the agency down to as low as $125, in which case the call girl got nothing. Snow's only sure money came from client tips, meaning that she had to perform extra special services. But that wasn't always so bad.

At Angel's Ladies, Mack and Angel just took a straight fifty-five percent and gave each prostitute a room of her own with a satellite dish, kitchen space and one free meal every day. But they were supposed to report all tips, no doubt for tax purposes. (Did they? I didn't ask.) Snow once made four grand on a single party call. When she said that only her husband could make her penis hard, the client allowed her to summon him, then said, "Hey, you two just have fun." And so all Snow and her husband had to do was make love. They kept every cent.

14

Earlier I said that the conventional understanding of a prostitute's client envisages a man who rents a woman's body as if it were a machine. Never mind the many men I've met who weep when the street-whores they love go to jail. Never mind the case of the man who would run to buy a hamburger and fries for his favorite bar-girl whenever he saw her drunk; he'd help her eat; he'd spoon-feed her black coffee right there at the bar; he'd drive her to her mother's house. Never mind the many suitors of a certain introverted alcoholic lesbian whom none of them really knew because not even her parents knew her; she'd told everyone her parents were dead, and so it was strange to meet them at the hospital where after a car crash she lay in a coma for weeks. Many of those suitors found their way to that hospital room and gazed down at that swollen jaundiced body in embarrassment and grief. They went back to the bar and told everyone else that she'd gotten through the tracheotomy, that she was off oxygen now, that the swelling was going down, that she was conscious, that she could speak in a whisper, that her parents had taken her home. Never mind all that, because it's perfectly true that some men do rent prostitutes as if they were machines. Collette can certainly vouch for that. Let's give in to the prudes for a moment and pretend that it's always so. But I remember a former prostitute named Gladys who now worked in a stuffy little paralegal office without windows; the baby seat, filing cabinet and paired desks occupied most of it. Gladys had succeeded; she'd been rehabilitated after one arrest too many. She wore a blue dress. Her unbeautiful but serene round face moved like an office appliance. Wearily she made notes on a yellow pad. The phone rang, and she said into it, "Hi, Mr. Smith, how are you; I'm a little harried but I did call him today." Why didn't I feel happier for her? Her trick name had been Joy. "Mainly all I did was basic flatbacking," she said in a bored hard voice. When I pulled out the stipulated $20 bill, she took it and prestidigitated it into her bra although her purse hung handy from the back of her chair. Was it habit, or did she mean to give me a thrill, or did she actually miss being in the life? At least it offered independence and excitement, and the income was tax-free. As for the rest of us, in doctor's offices and at airline ticket counters, don't we use each other like machines? When I reenter my country and some customs official humiliates me by commenting on yesterday's dirty underwear, or commands me to count out all my cash in sight of all the other passengers on my flight, or strip searches me, I can hardly be so presumptuous as to compare myself to Gladys on one of her bad dates, but if the mercantile character of prostitution taints it, then isn't our whole society likewise bad and sick and rotten with swimsuit models on billboards and golfers who treat their caddies like the dirt beneath the fine green grass, and customers and salesclerks who don't ask each other, "how are you?" All I can say is that I would rather be a Jennafer than a Gladys anytime. "Mack, he really cares about the girls," she said, putting more lasagna on my plate. "He and his wife are both swingers. They used to own mortuaries. And they're havin' a good time with it. They're really nice." As for Collette, maybe she already is Gladys. In practically the same breath that she was denouncing exotic dancers for renting their bodies at democratic prices and even climaxing when they did it, Collette cuttingly related the tale of a woman whom she despised even worse: "There's this girl in the business and *she does not have sex*. Personally, I think she's in the wrong business. She's not gonna make money. She made *me* lose a call. We were on a party together and I called her into the bathroom and said, look, he just wants two girls. All you have to do is give him a hand job and I'll do the rest. And she said, oh, no, I won't do that. I said to her, just touch it, just play with it a little, and I'll finish him off. And she still wouldn't do it! So I lost that money. I wanted to punch her head . . ."

"Collette, do you think prostitution should be legalized everywhere in the U.S.?"

"Should they legalize it? Absolutely. Personally, if they're givin' out AIDS tests and drug tests once they legalize it, more power to 'em. If it's two consentin' adults, that's nobody's fuckin' business."

(But Jennafer answered like the honest businesswoman she was: "If it's legal elsewhere, it's gonna take away a lot of money from us.")

If by some prodigy prostitution were suddenly legalized tomorrow in the United States, generations would fall away before the wounds wrought by prudery and hypocrisy in whores' spirits could heal. In the fact that prostitution is criminalized, prosecuted and persecuted lies the real shame of it all.

Postscript

Recently one of the city councilwomen where I live proposed a new measure in the war on prostitution: Confiscate the cars of men who solicit prostitutes. I wouldn't be surprised if her idea got enacted some fine day. To ignorance, scorn, fear and punitive prudery, why not add greed? The technical details have already been worked out in the war on drugs. Let's say a police department wants new squad cars. All they have to do is go out and bust people, then keep their money. (Human nature being what it is, I'd imagine that there are some police officers who do this to get pocket change.) Once enforcement becomes profitable on a commission basis, so to speak, we can expect zealous enforcement—with or without good cause. I quote the Marquis de Sade: *It's this multitude of laws which is responsible for this multitude of crimes.*

Philosophical Sidebar

If we could give prostitutes all the money they ever wanted, there would be no prostitutes anymore. — False.

If we could give johns all the love they ever wanted, they wouldn't go to prostitutes anymore. — False.

Nicole

From *Whores for Gloria*

This excerpt is reworked by Vollmann in the scene from his screenplay for *Whores for Gloria* included here as "Decisions, Decisions."

THE NEXT THING JIMMY knew, he was on the street and it was dark and he was whore-hunting. He saw women dancing on the sidewalk; he was sure that they offered both acute and obtuse triangles; but they would not go to his hotel and he did not want to go to theirs because he did not like to feel trapped at the same time that he felt dizzy. —How fine the moonlight was, though! It made him retch. —He saw a whore leaning against the side of a reflective building, waggling her skinny knees although her high heels and her butt did not move and her head was cocked against her shoulder so that she could watch men out of the corner of her stupid little eyes. She said doll you want a date? and Jimmy said thank *you* for the offer but tell you the truth I'm looking for my friend Gloria you know the one with the big tits? —Oh that's just an *excuse!* sneered the whore, at which Jimmy cocked his head very wisely and said I never excuse myself except when I burp. Do you ever burp? Gloria doesn't. —Oh Christ, said the whore, who was as slender and unwholesome looking as a snake, and she stalked around the corner, heels clacking angrily. —Next he had several offers from a pimp who said he *knew* Jimmy would be satisfied, so Jimmy looked as dumb as he could and said wow pal sounds like a good one and you'll never believe this but I left all my money back at my hotel. —Don'tcha even have twenty on ya? said the pimp. —Jimmy said don't I wish but God's truth is I got one hundred two hundred dollars back home in fact I got *lots* of money in fact I think I may even be a *millionaire,* so bring her by pal I only live two hours away from here what do you say? —When the pimp heard that, he didn't even bother to answer. He crossed the street, shaking his head, and Jimmy stood leaning up against a wall and laughing inside himself with snotty little gurgles like a bottle of Scotch pouring down the toilet. Finally he found a whore who would go with him. He looked around to make sure that the pimp wasn't watching and showed her forty dollars. Her name was Nicole, and she looked rather more old than young, twenty-five maybe and strung out, but not sharp and hard like a piece of broken glass, only used up like a dirty eraser, so he figured she would be OK with her lank hair curling around her ears and her ear-rings of white plastic pearls, so he said Well come on and Nicole looked at him tiredly with her skin stretched dry and tight across her forehead and Jimmy said Nicole your blue eye-liner's smeared you should fix it if you want to stay beautiful and Nicole rubbed her forehead and said she had a headache. He said well come *on* baby come with me then you can buy yourself a painkiller.

I don't usually go to the man's place, Nicole said. You promise you won't hurt me?

I promise, Jimmy said. If I wanted to hurt you, he explained to her very logically, you couldn't get away from me anyway.

That's not true, said Nicole. I could kill you easy.

Well see, said Jimmy grandly, you have nothing to worry about. You can kill me easy, so why be nervous?

He took her up the street and she kept asking how far it was. Three more blocks, said Jimmy. The light glowed in her hair.

The first thing she asked to do was use the bathroom. He heard her shit. I suppose she must be nervous, he said to himself. Jimmy had once been a reader, so he knew how in Auschwitz or Treblinka there was a ramp leading up to the gas chambers called the Road to Heaven where all the women had to wait naked and squatting while the men were finished being gassed (they went first because they did not need to have their hair cut off for the submarine crews), and while the sheared women waited they usually emptied their bowels and the guards laughed and laughed like hooded pimps in an alley and now history repeated itself as Jimmy stood nipping on a fresh beer and waiting for Nicole to complete the preparations for her little ordeal.

Well, he said to himself, *I* can't help it if she's nervous. She's got a job to do.

Silently he said Gloria, are you still there? Gloria?

When Nicole came into the kitchen she was naked except for her red shirt. —You want a half-and-half? she said.

Sure, Jimmy said.

Will you *take care of me* first? she said smiling; her face glowed, she seemed so sweet like Gloria.

Sure I will, he said, what do you want me to do? (He thought she meant for him to jerk her off or otherwise *affect* her. He sometimes liked to fool himself.)

Will you pay me first? Nicole said patiently.

Oh fine, Jimmy said. He got the forty dollars out of his wallet and gave it to her.

Then Nicole sat down on the chair in the kitchen and took his penis in her hand and he saw how her arms were discolored everywhere with abscesses and needle tracks and he leaned forward a little so that Nicole could put his penis into her mouth and she began to suck at it smoothly, rapidly and Jimmy looked down at the top of her head and wondered if her eyes were open or closed and then he looked at the wall and watched a cockroach crawling down between the gas pipe and the sink, and he listened to the noises that her lips made sucking his penis, and he listened to the loud ticking of her cheap plastic watch. Jimmy was not thinking about anything in particular, but his penis began to get hard right away. As soon as it was entirely stiff like some dead thing, she took it out of her mouth and rolled a rubber onto it with her lined and grimy hands. —Now take your shirt off, Jimmy said. —He stepped back from her and dropped his clothes to the floor. Nicole sat wearily on the chair, rubbing her forehead. When she pulled her shirt over her head he saw that she had a cast on her left wrist. Her breasts were big and sad like owls' eyes.

You want my coat for a pillow? said Jimmy.

Nicole shook her head.

All right then, he said, get down on the floor.

The kitchen floor was black with dirt. Nicole lay down on it and raised her legs to make her cunt so nice and tight for him, and Jimmy stood over her watching the groping of those legs, which were speckled with boils and lesions, until her left ankle came to rest on the chair that she had sat on, while the sole of her right foot had to be content with bracing itself against Jimmy's refrigerator. Her breasts lay limp on her belly, as round as the faces or polished brass pendulums of clocks. Jimmy stood enjoying her for another moment, liking the way she looked as she lay there between the refrigerator and the wall, brown-skinned and almost pretty, with a white plastic cross between her tits.

Are you Catholic? he said.

Yes, Nicole said.

Jimmy strode around naked except for his socks, inspecting her cunt like an emperor. This was the best part. Nicole gazed up at him and pulled the lips of her slit taut and up to show him the ragged pear of pinkness inside, and her cunt-lips glistened under the kitchen lights with the brightness of metal foil. —Your pussy is just like a flower,* Jimmy complimented her; all the same he did not want to get his face too close to it. He got down on his knees; he leaned his weight on his arms as if he were doing push-ups (for Jimmy was always a gentleman who would not hurt a woman with his weight); then he stuck his penis into her. She had told him that he was her first date of the night, but her cunt seemed to be full of something viscous like come or corn syrup. Maybe it was just the lubricant she used. Anyhow, it stank. She had great black spots on her thighs that might have been moles or more probably the subcutaneous hemorrhages of Kaposi's syndrome as Jimmy well knew from his profoundly intellectual studies. Every time he thrust into her she grunted. He could not tell whether this was because he hurt her or because she did it to excite him and so get it over with faster. He did not feel that she hated him and her body was trying to expel him; more probably she just endured him and trusted to the frictionlessness of the corn syrup or whatever it was to protect her from being hurt by his thrusts (in direct proportion as *his* sensation was diminished), but the corn syrup did not much work anymore to soothe that red raw-rubbed meat between her legs, so Nicole just tried not to think about what was happening and grunted at Jimmy's every painful

*"I still remember the effect I produced on a small group of Gala tribesmen massed around a man in black clothes," wrote Vittorio Mussolini. "I dropped an aerial torpedo right in the center and the group opened up like a flowering rose. It was most entertaining."

thrust and bit her lips whenever he grazed an ovary. She gripped his balls tightly all the time so that the rubber wouldn't slip; she dug her fingernails into his balls, either by mistake or to make him come. But after thirty seconds Jimmy knew that he wasn't going to be able to come. Maybe if she'd just sucked him off he could have done it, but what with the rubber and the stuff in her cunt he couldn't feel much. Jimmy fucked and fucked until he got bored and then told her that he was done. —Call me, he said politely. —Later his prick started to itch, and he worried about disease.

Decisions, Decisions

From
The screenplay *Whores for Gloria*

This is an excerpt from Vollmann's unpublished and unproduced screenplay *Whores for Gloria*. It is interesting to see that besides novels, stories, essays, poems, and journalism, Vollmann has tried his hand at this popular and conventional form of writing: a script for the silver screen. To this date, none of Vollmann's works have been made into films. —MH

CUT TO EAGLE'S-EYE VIEW

of the Tenderloin at night, whores getting in and out of cars, PIMPS and DEALERS lounging, etc., all in incredibly fast motion as the night waxes and wanes and gives way to morning (everything almost deserted, then the rush hour) while we swoop above the streets, in no more time than it takes to say the following lines:

NARRATOR

When everything—<u>EVERYTHING!</u>—about life makes you want to grin, and it just gets sunnier and funnier until after awhile you can only see the teeth in the smiles and then you feel . . . —well, not "on the edge," exactly, for the world has no edge; but as if you have always been over the edge, and the smiling and laughing is a sort of spastic reflex like crying or retching (really, it's all the same); when everything is so confusing that you can never be sure whether or not your whore is a woman—

until she pulls her underpants down; when you get drunken crushes on women whose drunken mothers used to try to stab them; when only the pretty shapes of women have integrity and when you close your eyes still see them leaning and crossing their legs and milking their tits at you, THEN you may on occasion like Jimmy find yourself looking down a long black block, down the tunnels of infinity to a streetlamp, a corner and a woman's waiting silhouette. —Or else like Jimmy you may have another drink.

SMASH CUT TO:

JIMMY goes around the corner and sees NICOLE, who looks rather more old than young, twenty-five maybe and strung-out, but not sharp and hard like a piece of broken glass, only used up like a dirty eraser, so he figures she'll be okay with her lank hair curling around her ears and her earrings of white plastic pearls.

NARRATOR

Finally he found a whore who would go with him. He looked around to make sure that the pimp wasn't watching and showed her forty dollars.

Simultaneously we see JIMMY doing this.

NARRATOR

(continuing without a beat)

Her name was Nicole.

JIMMY

Well, come on!

NICOLE looks at him tiredly, with her skin stretched dry and tight across her forehead.

JIMMY

Nicole, your blue eyeliner's smeared. You should fix it if you want to stay beautiful.

NICOLE

(rubbing her forehead)

I have a headache.

JIMMY

Well come on baby come with me then you can buy yourself a painkiller.

NICOLE

I don't usually go to the man's place. You promise you won't hurt me?

JIMMY

I promise.

(very logically)

If I wanted to hurt you, you couldn't get away from me anyway.

NICOLE

That's not true. I could kill you easy.

JIMMY

(grandly)

Well, see, you have nothing to worry about. You can kill me easy, so why be nervous?

They start walking up the street and the camera follows.

NICOLE

How far is it?

JIMMY

Three more blocks. That's why the light glows in your hair.

CUT TO:

INT. HOTEL ROOM

A relatively upscale one for the Tenderloin, with its own bathroom and a small kitchen alcove scaly with shrill white plastic tiles, which are stained yellow and brownish-green here and there. There is no mattress on the bedframe, just a piece of foam rubber. NICOLE and JIMMY have just come in.

NICOLE

I gotta use your bathroom.

JIMMY opens the door for her with a lordly gesture. We glimpse a small toilet of indescribable filth. The door closes behind her. JIMMY reaches under the bed and brings out a can of beer covered with something like doghair and lint. He winks at himself and cleans the can off on his shirt, mouthing rapidly, gleefully, and silently. We hear NICOLE trying to lock the bathroom door from the inside and failing. Then we hear her shit.

JIMMY

I suppose she must be nervous.

FADE TO:

HANDSOME JIMMY (who is JIMMY's younger self—much younger), sitting in the San Francisco Public Library reading. His eyes are intense, but not staring the way JIMMY's eyes do. His lips are still.

NARRATOR

Jimmy had once been a reader . . .

ZOOM IN to the book that JIMMY is reading: a series of black and white pictures of atrocity scenes in the Nazi concentration camps. In the background we hear the Blue Danube Waltz.

NARRATOR

. . . so he knew how in Auschwitz or Treblinka . . .

The photographs come alive: grainy black-and-white death camp footage.

NARRATOR

. . . there was a ramp leading up to the gas chambers called the Road to Heaven where all the women had to wait naked and squatting while the men were finished being gassed . . .

SLOW PAN across a group of naked Jewish women about to be exterminated. We recognize CECILY, REGINA, GLENDA, THE UGLY WHORE and especially NICOLE. Beside Nicole is the woman we will eventually learn is GLORIA.

NARRATOR

. . . (they went first because they did not need to have their hair cut off for the submarine crews) . . .

We hear NICOLE flush the toilet. More death camp footage.

NARRATOR

. . . and while the sheared women waited they usually emptied their bowels and the guards laughed and laughed like hooded pimps in an alley . . .

FADE TO:

JIMMY finishing his beer, sliding the empty can under the bed with a furtive triumphant smile, beginning to mouth silently again.

NARRATOR

(as Blue Danube Waltz fades out)

. . . and now history repeated itself as Jimmy stood nipping on a fresh beer and waiting for Nicole to complete the preparations for her little ordeal.

JIMMY

Well, I can't help it if she's nervous. She's got a job to do.

(mouths silently and unintelligibly, with a desperate and urgent look on his face)

Gloria, are you still there? Gloria?

Nicole comes into the kitchen, naked except for her red shirt.

NICOLE

You want a half-and-half?

JIMMY

Sure.

NICOLE

(smiling as she says this; her face glows; for her this is the most important moment, so she tries to seem sweet)

Will you take care of me first?

JIMMY

Sure I will. What do you want me to do?

NARRATOR

He thought she meant for him to jerk her off or otherwise <u>affect</u> her. He sometimes liked to fool himself.

NICOLE

(patiently)

Will you pay me first?

JIMMY

Oh fine.

He gets the forty dollars out of his wallet and gives it to her.

Then NICOLE sits down on the chair in the kitchen and takes his penis in her hand and we see how her arms are discolored everywhere with abscesses and needle tracks. He leans forward a little so that NICOLE can put his penis into her mouth and she begins to suck at it smoothly, rapidly. JIMMY looks down at the top of her head and then at the wall where we see a cockroach crawling down between the gas pipe and the sink, and we hear the noises that her lips make made sucking his penis, and we hear the loud ticking of her cheap plastic watch. As soon as his penis is entirely stiff like some dead thing, she takes it out of her mouth and rolls a rubber onto it with her lined and grimy hands.

JIMMY

Now take your shirt off.

He steps back from her and drops his clothes to the floor. NICOLE sits wearily on the chair, rubbing her forehead. When she pulls her shirt over her head we see that she has a cast on her left wrist. (NOTE: This easily recognizable feature should also appear above in the pan across the doomed naked Jewish women.) Her breasts are big and sad like owls' eyes.

JIMMY

You want my coat for a pillow?

Nicole shakes her head.

JIMMY

All right then; get down on the floor.

The kitchen floor is black with dirt. NICOLE lies down on it and raises her legs to make her cunt so nice and tight for him, and JIMMY stands over her watching the groping of those legs, which are speckled with boils and lesions, until her left ankle comes to rest on the chair that she was sitting on, while the sole of her right foot has to be content with bracing itself against JIMMY's refrigerator. Her breasts lie limp on her belly, as round as the faces or polished brass pendulums of clocks. JIMMY stands enjoying her for another moment, liking the way she looks as she lies there, a white plastic cross between her tits.

JIMMY

(just making conversation)

Are you Catholic?

NICOLE

Yes.

JIMMY strides around naked except for his socks, inspecting her cunt like an emperor. For him this is the best part. NICOLE gazes up at him and pulls the lips of her slit taut and up to show him the ragged pear of pinkness inside, and her cunt-lips glisten under the kitchen lights with the brightness of metal foil.

JIMMY

(in his most courtly manner)

Your pussy is just like a flower.

He gets down on his knees; he leans his weight on his arms as if he were doing push-ups; then he sticks his penis into her. We see great black spots on her thighs that might be moles or more probably the subcutaneous hemorrhages of

Kaposi's syndrome. Every time he thrusts into her she grunts.

ZOOM IN ON:

NICOLE biting her lips with pain.

ZOOM IN ON:

JIMMY rolling his eyes and winking.

NARRATOR

But after thirty seconds Jimmy knew that he wasn't going to be able to come. Maybe if she'd just sucked him off he could have done it, but what with the rubber and the stuff in her cunt he couldn't feel much.

ZOOM OUT TO:

JIMMY rolling off her. He stands up, then lowers his head and clasps his hands; his lips move as if he's saying grace. Then he looks straight down at her. She's lying there watching him.

JIMMY

(very genially and naturally)

Call me.

The Hermophrodite

From
The Ice-Shirt

The *Ice-Shirt* is the first book in Vollmann's *Seven Dreams* sequence, and his only title to be selected by Book-of-the-Month Club. This excerpt interweaves the Inuit creation myth of Elder Brother and Younger Brother (and the mysterious appearance of the female sex) with modern day San Francisco and transvestites, gender bending, and sexual identity. This rather surreal and non-linear form of story telling is a recurring motif in all of the published *Seven Dreams* volumes—i.e., progressions of the never-ending reverie, history commenting on the present and vice-versa. —MH

??-ca. 30,000 BC

God has made everything out of nothing.
But man He made out of everything.

Paracelsus, *ca.* 1590

ELDER BROTHER AND YOUNGER Brother lived on the ice without knowing where they had come from. Elder Brother supposed that maybe the ice had given birth to him through a seal-hole, because that was how Younger Brother had been born; but whether or not that was the case, many questions lay underfoot, like frozen tussock-beds. He had no memory of how he had learned to be himself, striding about so utterly at home upon the black ice; he could recollect many hunts and moons before the time of Younger brother, but whether his aloneness had ever had a beginning he could not say. Sometimes he had a dream of another Brother, who had turned his face from him and gone southward into the ice-mountains, crying out and tearing at himself with his *BLACK HANDS*; and there were other nights when he was certain that in the ice-combs far beneath him many other brothers lay curled in frozen sleep, waiting to be born; but when he thought upon them those fancies seemed to him fantastical, for on that entire world of ice there were to be found but two souls: Self and Other; and between two and many there lies a gap as wide as between one and two. Thus, Elder Brother could never believe in a multitude of men corresponding to the seal-multitudes he fed on; nor did it seem to him wise to make any presumptions. The ice had taught him that: each step he took upon that surface must end with the weight of heel and toe placed firmly upon *known* ice, never *presumed* ice that might be no more than a film, shattering beneath him so that he fell into the black dead sea beneath, never again to be born, perhaps . . . So he became by degrees even more practical, and stern and stately in his knowledge. Younger Brother feared more than loved him. But this was a matter that Elder Brother considered of no importance. The only important thing was getting enough for them both to eat. Being accomplished in this, he felt content that he did his duty; after all, without him Younger Brother must perish. The truths that he learned from the ice were not simple, but neither were they ambiguous. So Elder Brother strode with sureness through his ice-life.

Younger Brother was less sure who *he* was. Sometimes he thought he was a seal, and lay on his stomach barking. The wind was cold, and Younger Brother wept even as he barked, but he would not move because he wanted so much to be what he thought he must be; there were so many seals that he was sure that they were his relatives. Once when Elder Brother returned from a hunt he found Younger Brother almost buried in the snow, so long had he been there. —"You are not a seal, you know," said Elder Brother. "You are a boy." —But Younger Brother did not know what a boy was. Elder Brother was a grown man, and there were never any other people.

At other times Younger Brother was convinced that he must be a polar bear. He strutted about on his two little legs, growling and seeking to kill the seals. The seals said, "First he barks like us, and now he tries to bite us. What sort of fool is he?" They spanked him with their flippers. Younger Brother cried because he was too weak and slow to kill the seals.

One day he was sure that he must be a gull. He waited until a strong wind came; then he flapped his arms. The wind said, "What is this? A cub-animal? Good, I will pick him up and then drop him. What fun it will be to watch him fall!" —The wind seized Younger Brother and bore him high above the ice, so that Younger Brother screamed, and all the other gulls screamed back at him. They were trying to instruct him in the important skills of screaming and flying, but he did not know their language. In his fear he wet himself. The wind was disgusted at this and dropped him at once. By a fortunate accident he landed in soft snow.

After this, Elder Brother decided that it was dangerous to leave him to himself. Really he was too young to begin hunting, but there was no one to take care of him. If he continued to think that he was not human, one day he might turn into something inhuman.* So Elder Brother put him on his back and took him hunting. Younger Brother always cried.

Elder Brother was very skilled at walking on the ice. He could tell from its color how safe it was to walk on. "Never walk where the ice is black," he told his brother. "That ice is young ice; it is weak ice." And Younger Brother listened because he wanted to be like his brother. —"Never walk on snow-covered ice," said Elder Brother. "You cannot see what color it is. Sometimes the snowdrifts will float on open water. That is called *mafshaak*. If you walk there you will die." —And Younger Brother listened, remembering every word.

"Sometimes you will see me walking on black ice," said Elder Brother. "Do not try to imitate me. You are ignorant and weak. I can walk on ice so thin that my foot breaks through it with every step. If you try it you will die." —Younger Brother listened without saying anything.

"See this pole with the bone point?" said Elder Brother. "This is called an *unaak*. When you mistrust the ice you walk on, use your *unaak*. Jab the point firmly into the ice. If it punctures through, the ice is not safe. If it does not go through, you may proceed." —Younger Brother listened well to these words.

*In those days you had to be careful what you thought, because your thoughts would come true. Nowadays you have to be careful what you think because if you think it, it will never happen.

The Bear-Shirt

One day Elder Brother carried Younger Brother on his back to hunt seals. For a long time they had gone hungry. They saw a breathing hole on the far side of a region of black ice. Elder Brother set Younger Brother down and told him to wait while he went to stalk the seal.

Younger Brother sat very still on the ice. The sky was seamlessly grey. The wind was blowing. He could see Elder Brother sitting beside the seal-hole, his spear resting on his knee. Elder Brother never looked away from the hole. As Younger Brother sat watching him across the black ice, he began to feel very lonely. He felt that his brother did not understand him or care about him. He began crying softly. He wished that he was something else than a boy. As he looked around he saw a polar bear crossing the black ice. The polar bear spread his legs wide and moved slowly and steadily across the dangerous ice. When the ice groaned, the bear got down on his belly and began to swim upon it. As Younger Brother watched, he became convinced once again that he was a polar bear, for his thoughts were but a succession of stars that wheeled about in his skull-sky like the moon and the sun, chasing each other through all the lovely hells. He stood up, spread his legs wide, and took his first step onto the black ice. He heard Elder Brother shouting at him, but he paid no attention. He was sure now that he was a polar bear. He felt comfortable, ferocious. His hands had become furry claws. He decided to kill Elder Brother and eat him.

Elder Brother ran toward him. There was anguish in his face. —"Stay still!" he shouted. "That ice is not safe!"

Luxuriously, Younger Brother opened his mouth and growled. Then the ice began to crack beneath his feet. At once he forgot that he was a bear. —"Help, help!" he wailed. —Then Elder Brother was there to lead him back to loyal ice, and he loved Elder Brother more than ever before; and his tear-streaked face made Elder Brother laugh. —"Now we must listen by the seal-hole," said Elder Brother. "If you have no attention for that, watch *Nanoq* and learn how he walks."

Polar bears give an impression of white snowiness, but incongruous with this is the almost triangular head, which the bear nods like a napping seal, in order to deceive other seals into thinking that he is one. Most of us want to be what we are not; but the clever ones, the predators, *pretend* to be what they are not, stalking and sneaking until their victims discover the deception too late.

Although the bear nodded like a seal, he often upraised his head for his own purposes, as if to gaze upon the evil spirits in the stars. When no seals were near he was his real self, and prowled and stalked upon the ice, uplifting his head; —and when he padded so springily upon his black-toed feet, Younger Brother understood for the first time how quickly a polar bear could move, and was frightened. The snow-bear licked his feather-arrow fur. He grinned with his black mouth. His round nostrils dilated. He rushed back and forth upon his iceberg.

"Elder Brother, can one create an ice-bear from one's thought?"

"I cannot say for certain," said Elder Brother. "So my advice to you is to not think on ice-bears." He strode on his way. —Younger Brother hopped feebly in the snow, but he could not by any means go as fast as his leader.

"Elder Brother, Elder Brother, where are you going?" cried the little one. "Please don't walk so fast or I'll be left behind."

"You must learn to keep up," said Elder Brother, turning his face away. He strode away across the mist-blown ice. Younger Brother ran after as quickly as he could, but his legs were fat and little.

The Storm, the Spirit Woman and the Island

"I feel a ringing in my ears," said Elder Brother. "A storm is coming." —That night the stars began to dance in the sky, as if they were being blown about by a strong wind. A ring formed around the moon. The next morning long clouds streaked the horizon. They came closer and closer. They were solid black; they did not reflect the white color of the pack ice. The seals lowered their heads in the water. The clouds became tinged with red in the south. A light breeze sprang up. As the hours passed, the breeze became stronger and stronger. Soon it was a stiff wind, then a gale. The sound of it was terrifying. Elder Brother could hear it coming down from the mountains before it reached him. When that far-off whistling came to his ears, he braced himself, holding Younger Brother as tightly as he could in his arms.

There was nowhere to run to, because the wind was everywhere, and the two brothers had no home. They huddled together, unable to see or hear each other but taking comfort from each other; and still the storm increased. Presently the furious chill of the sea-peaks, which could burn their flesh white, became a shelter to be desired (although they could not reach it now), because nothing else but ice-walls could break the force of that dread wind, which did not seem white to them, although it raked them with such great quantities of snow that they were almost suffocated; nor was it black, although there was such darkness in it that they could see no more with open eyes than with closed; it shattered the icebergs' bristles, splitting ice from ice so that snow gushed through the rifts like white blood foaming down cliff-sides; and the sky screamed through every crevice that it could find or make until the ocean, frozen though it was, was creaking and crashing, wrecked upon the second sea, the wind-sea. And then snow fell and snow blew and the sky's light vanished into cold opacity; the greedy storm had swallowed the sky.

At last there came a lull, although the clouds still rolled evilly about their heads. When Younger Brother looked up at his guardian, he saw that the frost had made his face into something strange and terrible. Elder Brother had great white moustaches, weeping with icicles. His eyebrows were frostbrows that went all the way up his forehead, as if Elder Brother had died and ice had begun to grow and grow on him forever until after a million years he would be buried at the heart of some new frost-continent for a shroud, as in warmer climates dead faces quickly become overgrown with pale white mold until they are patchy and spotted like dogs' faces. To the very ruff, Elder Brother's hood had frozen into a creaking helmet of ice-hardened fur.

"I'm afraid of you!" cried the little boy.

"No, be afraid of the storm," said his brother. "Unless you are very attentive and obedient to wind-songs, you will die."

At this, Younger Brother began to cry, but his tears froze on his cheeks. The wind was rising again. Impatiently, Elder Brother cut off a strip of sealskin from his parka and tucked it around Younger Brother's face. —"Tighten the drawstring of your hood, or your face will turn to ice," he said shortly. "Now come with me. We must find a sleeping-place before the wind sings again."

After this they spoke no longer, for the storm-scream made hearing impossible. They staggered about all through that night-devouring night, but Elder Brother could find no protected spot. The little one came behind him wailing. Sometimes he could not go on; then Elder Brother had to carry him on his shoulders as he went. They were both near the end of their strength. They had eaten nothing but a little bit of frozen fish for five sleeps.

At last Elder Brother stopped in the shelter of an overhanging ice-drift. —"Here we must rest," he said.

He sat down on a rock. Snow was blowing in his face. Younger Brother fell down beside him. His mouth opened, and his eyes closed. Elder Brother pulled the boy to him and set his head in his lap. He breathed gently in his face to warm him. He himself felt already rather warm. His face glowed with frostbite. He stroked his brother's cheek. Patiently, he waited to be killed.

Then suddenly a Spirit Woman came flying down from the sky. Her eyes shone like moons. —The two brothers were astonished. They had never seen anyone other than themselves.

"Spirit Woman, Spirit Woman, who are you?" said Elder Brother.

The Spirit Woman laughed. "I am the blue snow-shadows all around you. You can always hear me; you can sometimes see me; you can never kiss me.

She bent down; she struck the ice. *An island sprang up!* It was vast and white, and there were mountains on it. The two brothers crawled feebly onto the shore, where they lay half-dead. —The Spirit Woman clapped her hands, and a snow-house sprang up around them. Then she bent over Younger Brother and did something to him, but he did not know what it was. —"Live together," she said. "I have fitted you for each other." After saying this she flung her arms up and rose through the roof of the snow-house.

Younger Brother raised his arms; he bent them upwards at the elbows; he wanted so much to be a bird! —but he could not follow the Spirit Woman. He cried.

For a long time the two brothers slept. They did not hear the voices of the birds, or the steady wind. They lay encased in sleep, which melted slowly. When he awoke, Younger Brother felt a warm wetness between his legs that had never been there before. His fresh boy-strength became as feathers whirling in the air. (But Elder Brother's arms still cut through the air like knives.) The nipples flowered on his chest, and bore fruit. Then his brother looked at him as men look at women. He pulled him to him; he kissed him.

"I won't! I won't!" cried Younger Brother.

But of course he had to.

San Francisco Transvestites 1987

Jerome had a long thin body. —"I look like an anorexic girl," he said. "Men are easily fooled. They're so stupid. Usually they just look at my hair." —He put his soft foam-rubber falsies tight up against his nipples.* He combed his long blond hair. He worked the black fishnet stockings up over his toes, his knees, his waist as if he were wading cautiously into female water. He rose; he put his high heels on. —"I should *really* get my fresh undies," he said. —His hair shone so beautifully gold and coppery on his shoulders . . . —"I like comfort," he explained. "I'm not that concerned with looking like a woman, —Oh, *where's* my black bra? That's *such* a nice outfit! Let me go look in the closet. That's where I keep my little *lingerie* bag. —Oh, good, here it is. La, la, la . . . This petticoat is really lush. I *do* have to take these undies off, though. I *have* to feel nylon against my skin." —And so he took his clothes voluptuously off to start over, kneeling thin and naked on the bed to sort through his flimsy things. At last he chose a fluffy black dress; lovingly he slid himself into it, but presently he bent himself on the bed and pulled the dress up to expose his buttocks . . . He was famous for his paintings in nail polish. Ranks and rows of nail polish bottles of all colors stood by the window. He lay stroking his lovely clothes . . . At his request he was gagged with a black scarf and a sock in his mouth. His wrists were tied to his ankles. He stared ahead of him a little desperately, it seemed, with his big blue eyes.

Despite these efforts he did not in fact become a woman until he went into the bathroom with Miss Giddings, dancing into an ecstasy of appliqué and eye-liner and rouge because the pair of them were trying for the look of weary whores. They helped each other on with their

*Being a guest, I was permitted to try the dried orange peels.

lipstick, each one the all-wise Spirit Woman to whom the other could turn for advice, for eye and lip correction. Miss Giddings made perhaps the most remarkable transformation, her lush black wig so sweet around her clown-pale face with its white makeup. But Jerome (now Miss J.) was just as much of a lady. "I *always* look good in red," she whispered to the mirror, when she thought that no one could hear. Then she made her debut. "I'm the Red and Green Girl," she announced. "I'm Miss Christmas Tree." —"*I* feel like a gift" cried Miss Giddings. —"You *look* like a hallucination," said Miss J. —"Oh, I *love* to hallucinate! Hallucinations are my *favorite* things!" —When they had drawn on their black and gold evening costumes, they became so stately, those two, and so beautiful . . . "Oh but our clothes simply *reek,*" they said. "You see, we've been having such *excitement* . . ." They told each other that they looked stunning. They clacked about in the garden in their high heels. With sublime contempt, they decried what they had evolved from: —"Boys?" they said. "They're *meat.* They're less than *objects!* They're things you *eat* and *poop out.*"

Outside the Black Rose Bar (*The Friendliest Girls in Town,* said the pink matchbox), a woman looked at her reflection in the window as she brushed her hair before going into that place of pink lights and mirrors where women who looked like angels would take you by the hand as you walked down their row to the bathroom (the floor of which was often covered with piss to the depth of your shoe-toe), and these women would let you kiss them and put your penis in the slits where their penises used to be, provided that you paid them money—this woman, then, finished brushing her hair and suddenly yawned, and her face fragmented into a hundred lumps for a moment, becoming again a man's face, and then she licked her lips and smiled and became a woman again.

The Woman-Shirt

Before, Elder Brother and Younger Brother had been the same. Now they were different, and difference called to difference, so that they needed each other, but at best this yearning could only unite them for a space; it could not reconcile them. *She* was more capable of loving constancy than *he,* for, having been the younger, the inexperienced, having trembled so often in the face of his quick intolerance, she now basked in this new need of his for her. Whenever he wanted, she laid her head down for him, smelling the bitter smell of dead leaves and earth. Smiling, she chewed a tender, bitter willow-bud. He took her hand; the wind blew, and the water trickled between the stones. —To him her youngness had always been an annoyance. But now her young eyes, her taut young shoulders, and those brilliant black eyes in her pale face, hurt him so happily. It was his *need* that he enjoyed, however, not her herself, although in that first moon he thought that she was everything to him. Looking at her, thinking of her, transported him, which struck him as vile because now it was hard for him not to despise the icy serenity of their earlier relations. And he knew that he should not love her, for she had been someone else whom he had been supposed to love differently. —What is loneliness? Does the lonely space between two rocks vanish when spanned by a spiderweb?

At first they did not know how to tell each other about their new feelings. They hung their heads shyly, like flowers in the wind. They thrilled sweetly to each other and kept their thrilling secret.

They decided to live on their island forever. They built a house out of earth and stones, never having seen trees to build from (even driftwood was so rare that they thought that forests, like seaweed, grew upon the bottom of the sea). From their rocky world they stood watching the sun wheel round and round in the sky, vanishing only when watery blue vapors blew over from the volcanoes of the south. Spring came, and clouds puffed their bellies just above the moss, and streams appeared everywhere, grinding and groaning and laughing and sighing, and birds sang in the rain and insects buzzed beneath the moss, which, wet, sank deep beneath Elder Brother's step when he went hunting, and the sun was a white disk in a white sky, and the weather was cold and cool and cold and warm. They tried to live quietly in that beautifully terrifying spring landscape, with its chips of blue sky whirling in the icy cloud-sea as the wind blew and the rivers roared and ground stones together (being the motors of geology), and the ice-floes seemed to form such a delicate white puzzle-set, unmoving in their matrix of black leads, more white than bleached bone, and in the fjord was an island besieged by floes and behind that rose the grand black slab-mountains of Slab-Land, halfway up which swam cloud-spears as the birds sang and new storm-clouds rushed in and the cold wind screamed and grey clouds fell as low as Elder Brother's head, with more clouds behind them, and it rained, and storms trapped the man and woman and tortured them without meaning to or not meaning to, and as the rain began to fall in earnest the stream-tones increased in pitch and boulders stirred in the riverbeds and the rivers began to groan as the birds sang and the cold rain fell, sometimes freezing as it fell, sometimes not, and Elder Brother could not hunt, and for days they had no food, and the air was so cold, so frightening, so beautiful. —Presently summer came. Pink and yellow flowers sprang up along the sides of moss-cushioned waterfalls, and other waterfalls played in rock-clefts, and the moss embroidered itself with spiderwebs. It was sunny on the ice. The seals lay on their backs and folded their wet black flippers over their bellies. The great slab-landscapes of sea-ice were stitched with white seams and stamped with fine blue granule-lines, as if they had been yards of calico. Elder Brother and his wife sat on the steep and rocky shore, watching the melting of the last dirty drifts of ice, which were weak and rotten, speckled with dead leaves, sun-wrought to treacherous pointed ridges along which it was almost impossible to walk without mishap. Water dripped from them and gathered in dirty puddles underneath them and ran into the clear brown water of the fjord with its light-lines and ripples that softened the greenish-brown outlines of reflections of peaks of the blue knife-slab ridge across the fjord, and the little floes drifted across the image. A gull stood on a rock in the water for a long time. A floe broke in two. On the northern horizon lay a white line of seemingly solid ice, in which was reflected a mountain made blue by the storm-cloud over it; and Elder Brother and his wife saw themselves reflected in each other's faces. The sunshine warmed them, and they were very happy. Stalks of golden grass moved in the breeze in stiff increments, their seed-crowns a precious but heavy burden. Closer to the moss, the little plants with penny-shaped leaves did not move.

Sometimes when he was away hunting, Elder Brother pictured to himself his wife's firm buttocks, which he liked to grip in his hands when he was making love to her. But then he would think to himself: My buttocks are also like that. And this thought would throw him into confusion. He could not understand the *otherness* of his wife.

List of What Porn Is (and Isn't)

This list appeared under the title "Pornography's Top Components" in the FORUM section of a special double issue of *Fiction International* devoted to "Pornography and Censorship" (1992). As usual, underlying the specifics of Vollmann's treatment of pornography is the view that people should be allowed to do whatever they want to do so long as it doesn't hurt anyone else.

1. Pornography has two components.
   A. The aim of the pornographer, which may or may not be realized: to give pleasure.
   B. The effect which it inevitably has on some people (who may or may not be distinct from the pornographer's intended group); it offends. Both these elements must exist for a work to be pornography, just as both sex and compensation must be present to constitute prostitution. A work which sets out only to offend cannot titillate, and so is not pornography. A work which titillates everybody cannot aspire to pornography's underdog status.
2. Pornography need not be sexual in content. The vicious mendacity of President Bush and his managers on the subject of the Gulf War is a good example of political pornography. These statements gave many Americans pleasure and disgusted me. By my standards they were obscene.
3. Because pornography as I define it must produce opposing feelings in people, it's clear that any definition of pornography must be relative. (Examples of the problem: certain Inuit folktales which even ethnographers have bowdlerized; the painting *Déjeuner sur l'herbe; Mein Kampf;* the

Kama Sutra.) Since the term is pejorative, it is those who are repelled by the work who will apply it, not those who are pleased. But since there must also be people who are pleased and since, being pleased, they will prefer the word "art" or "sexiness" or "patriotism" or "Holy Writ," it becomes clear that nothing is inherently pornographic.

4. What this means is that each of us has the right to define pornography as we see it. No one has the right to regulate it.
5. When I look at a human body, I make aesthetic judgments. I think most of us do. I see nothing wrong with looking at a cunt (on a real woman or in a photograph) and deciding whether it's pretty or not. I've never seen a girlie magazine or a self-styled dirty book that I thought shouldn't exist. I've seen plenty of "pornographic" products that don't interest me, and in general I prefer to get my sexual gratification from sexual acts, but live and let live.
6. When a "feminist" tells me that I have to say "woman" instead of "girl," I immediately say "girl." I think "girl" is a prettier word, and sometimes it's a more appropriate word, too. No one word can substitute for another word. The "feminists" seek to impoverish our language, and I won't stand for it. They are free to be offended or insulted by what I say, but I'm free to say it. Forbidden words are like guns. No one should be denied the possession of them a priori, and no one should use them carelessly or viciously. If they do happen to be abused (for instance, to yell at a passing woman, "Hey, cunt!" instead of using the word "cunt" in an innocuous context as I did in #5 above), the abuse can be condemned, but the word itself shouldn't be prohibited.
7. Well, what SHOULD the reaction be to "Hey, cunt!"? I don't know if there could ever be a general rule. It depends on how much you think you can do. (I've written about this in my "Epitaph for a Coward's Heart" in *Thirteen Stories and Thirteen Epitaphs.*) In any event, that's not pornography, that's hate speech. It almost certainly doesn't titillate anybody, even the man who yells.

8. And what should the reaction be to pornography as you define it? I'd say, if it doesn't appeal to you, leave it be; don't censor it. If you can admit that there might be another side to the issue, leave it be. If it's a work of words or images or plaster or whatever, not a real life situation, not a "Hey, cunt!", then leave it be.
9. Are you a censor? Do you tell people not to say "girl"? Shame on you! If nothing offends you, you're a saint or you're psychotic. If a few things offend you, deal with them—fairly. If you're often offended by things, you're probably a self-righteous asshole and it's too bad you weren't censored yourself—by your mother in an abortion clinic.
10. A friend of mine who used to be a Nazi gave me his authentic swastika armband. I was touched that he would give me something with meaning to him, but embarrassed by my ownership of that particular object. I still have it, locked up where it can't hurt people. Many people wouldn't want a swastika armband in their house. But I'd have to say that it's no one else's business whether or not I have one in my house.

Sunflower

From
The Royal Family

In Vollmann's letter to his editor Paul Slovak defending the length of *The Royal Family* manuscript he'd submitted to Viking (see "Crabbed Cautions"), Vollmann summarized the significance of this crucial episode in Henry Tyler's moral and spiritual development as follows: "Sunflower's pain and crucifixion is emblematic of the theme of the book—in fact, central. The Dostoyevskian notion that suffering and degradation is paradoxically ennobling, perhaps even sacred, first gets illustrated to the unbelieving Henry right here. The whole book is about how he learns to follow Sunflower's path." This excerpt originally appeared in Book VIII of *The Royal Family.* —LM

Down the hall from the room upon whose door a sign read DO NOT DISTURB—I DON'T HAVE NOT A THING—PLEASE DON'T KNOCK there was a room on whose door somebody had written and taped a sign which read IF YOU WANT SOMETHING, DON'T ASK. IF YOU REALLY NEED IT, GO ELSEWHERE and across from that door was a door charred and kicked and smeared and scraped, whose upper half had been replaced by plywood already splintered by abuse, and whose doorknob had given way to a handle held in place by two Philips head screws now worked half out; Tyler had had to turn them in again with the point of his pocketknife; and inside that room, rendered holy by an incandescent doughnut in place of any lightbulb, Dan Smooth was sitting at the foot of the bed like a wise grave doctor; and the junked out whore named Sunflower, who'd a quarter-hour before stirred the white lump into the rust-colored liquid in the bottlecap, heaped it to bare lukewarmness, and fed it to her hungry arm on the second stab, now lay on her side mumbling so sadly in a soft hoarse voice; she was naked because Tyler had given her money for the dope, and so when she came with him she'd stripped by habit; it was likewise by habit as well as concern that Tyler sat stroking her pimpled buttock as he would have stroked the forehead of a good dog or a sick child, as he would have had somebody stroke him if he could have found anybody like Irene, whom he could have been a good dog to.

'Cause I slept there all night, he bought me a burrito and then he told me: That's four dollars right there. That's how he treated me, the whore said. Are you listening to me?

Yeah, I'm listening, sweetheart, said Tyler.

Sighing, Dan Smooth got up and began to piss gently into the sink. When he had finished, he stood there for a moment buttoning his fly. Then he lightly tapped his fingernail against the faucet.

The whore's eyes jerked open in terror. —Is that a knife? she said.

It's okay, Tyler said.

What is it? Is it a gun? Is he loading a gun?

No, honey. He's just making music in the sink.

Oh, said the whore, subsiding. He heard her weary breathing. He liked her and was sorry for her. She was twenty years old and looked fifty. She was ruined.

I have so much respect for you and the both of you that I trespass with, she said with an effort.

I respect you, too, Sunflower, he said.

Hey, can you pop this zit on my butt?

This one? It's pretty flat.

I want the white stuff to come out, the whore fretted. Can you pop it for me, please?

Okay, said Tyler, setting thumb and forefinger pliers-like about the red spot and digging into the flabby flesh. Nothing came out.

Is that better? he said.

Yeah, that's a lot better, she sighed. Feels like lots of white stuff came out. You wanna know me? You wanna listen to me? Are you listening to me?

Here I am, Sunflower. Here I am listening.

My father fucked my sister first time when she was five. He fucked her doggy-style, and he put his hand over her mouth so she couldn't scream. Her pussy was all bloody and her asshole was all bloody. There was blood coming down to her knees. Then he fucked me when I was five, and then he fucked my other sister when she was five. But my other sister went and told on him. So me and my sister told my father not to do that no more . . .

And he listened to you?

Yeah, the whore said. Tears boiled out of her eyes.

He stopped fucking your sister? said Tyler gently.

Yeah. He, uh, well, he . . . he . . .

He fucked you and your older sister instead?

Just me, she sobbed. My sister couldn't take it. Said it hurt too much. But I—I heard the youngest crying, and when I saw the blood, I knew . . .

It's okay now, sweetheart. It's okay.

I wanna be a shield, she said. I was a shield for my sister, and now I protect all the men who come to me. They give me their pain. It comes out their cockheads. It just hits me. It just hurts me. It stays with me. That's all I wanna do. I wanna be a shield for all the men in this world, and all the women, and all the kids. They can come and shit on my face if they want to; they can even shit on my goddamned face. You wanna shit on my face?

No thanks, said Tyler, squeezing her hand. That wouldn't make me feel happy.

But did Maj spit in your mouth?

Yes, she did.

I knew it. I could see it.

She lay still for awhile. Dan Smooth opened the tap but no water came out.

Hey, how much did you gimme? she said.

Twenty.

And what about your friend? Why's he here listening? He was supposed to gimme thirty, and he didn't give me squat.

He'll give you ten.

I love you, the whore wept. I love you. I'm so alone and I have so many contacts.

I love you, too, said Tyler, because he would have been her shield, too, if he could.

No! she screamed. Don't say that! I'm here and you're not here—

She fell asleep, and began snoring loudly. Mouth open, face flushed, she opened and then re-closed her eyes, sinking into the earth of dreams, her knees studded with immense white circular scars, her black-grimed toes faintly twitching, and in her sleep she continued to scratch at those angry speckles on her buttocks.

Four knocks, and they let the Queen in. The Queen was alone, but three tall black men stood waiting in the hall outside. She was wearing a man's hooded sweatshirt which shadowed and overhung her dark old face into anonymity. Dan Smooth bolted the door. She put her left arm on her hip, threw her head back and extended her right wrist to be kissed. Tyler got down on his knees to do the honors. —You brown-noser! laughed the Queen, pleased. You heard what our friend says about noses? Hah! Now what about you, Danny boy? Dan Smooth bent over the Queen's hand.

The Queen shook her hood off and stood there for a moment, smiling almost grimly. On the bed continued the long, slow, gasping breaths of sleep.

You gentlemen owe me twenty in visitor fees, she said.

This dump charged you?

They always charge me. They don't know.

One Queen, three bodyguards, cackled Smooth, pulling a twenty-dollar bill from his sleeve.

Good arithmetic, said the Queen. But why can't you multiply?

They're not old enough to bleed when I fuck 'em, said Smooth.

Did you get off on Sunflower's story? said Tyler challengingly. She bleeds from both ends.

You don't need to pick on him, Henry, said the Queen. Danny's a good man. Sunflower's daddy wasn't. We would have taken care of him but Sunflower didn't want that. Sunflower's my baby, she cooed, kissing the woman's dirty toes.

She turned to Tyler and said: You see what she's about? You see why she's good? Jesus Himself ain't fit to pop her zit like you done. Jesus on the very cross of torture and shame never suffered like she suffered. And I don't care how much He gave. He never gave like she did. I know her so well. Queen's come to give her little baby her reward. My baby, my darling little baby. Queen's heart's gonna break.

And between the naked woman's legs she laid five one hundred dollar bills and a baggie with enough China white for Sunflower to kill herself ten times over.

Tyler said nothing. The Queen looked him in the eye and said: It's up to her. Gotta give her some happiness. If she don't O.D., she can come back to me for more favors. Queen'll always take care of her. If she wants to go into rehab she can. If she wants to sell that powder she can. But I know she gonna wanna take that happiness. I know she gonna wanna go home.

From "The Best Way to Smoke Crack"

From
The Atlas

This excerpt from "The Best Way to Smoke Crack" finds Vollmann's john smoking crack with an aging black prostitute in a surreal, run-down hotel room, a scene animated with a horrific vibrancy by his introduction of poetic similes and descriptive details that are too grotesque to be anything other than the result of personal observation.

Here, Vollmann wants to provide us with the opportunity to witness the horrors and beauty and banality of the real, stripped of condescension, sentimentality, political correctness, moral piety, or any other authorial stances that allow him or his readers to feel superior to, and hence comfortable about, the truth of the world. There is a desperate, throbbing honesty that runs throughout all of Vollmann's writing, an old-fashioned determination to seek out regions of geography and the human heart that most other artists consider inaccessible—and then, once there, to "tell it like it is" with as much honesty and empathy as he can. This isn't to say that Vollmann's version of "telling it like is" is mere unadorned, objective reportage: as in all of his best work, moments of humor emerge where you least expect it, as do memorable sentences that gather momentum until they smash through the walls of our habituation and allow us entry into places no one else dares take us.

These efforts bring us close to the scene in a way that is, at times excruciating, but is always memorable and believable. Early in the story, we are probably startled when Vollmann matter-of-factly says of his alter ego, "the john," that "he didn't care how old or young [the prostitute] looked because he loved her"—startled, and yet we believe him. Of course, we also want to know what basis he has for loving a woman who is most definitely *not* the familiar prostitute-with-a-heart-of-gold, but an aging whore with a sick and glowing face, and an addiction to crack, and an abscess that won't heal, and a right eye that is blind due to a blow she received while being raped. In other words, Vollmann convinces us that she is not a cliché to be consumed and discarded, but a real person. And this is why it seems so believable: the john loves her because she is willing to share herself with him so utterly, and because he doesn't have to be afraid of the excitement he feels when he is with her, and because despite everything that has happened to her she still makes an effort to clean her apartment and make herself look desirable and she can still laugh—as these things are revealed, we believe his love. Perhaps we even love her ourselves. —LM

San Francisco, California (1992)

THE CRACK PIPE WAS a tube of glass half as thick as a finger, jaggedly broken at both ends because the prostitute had dropped it. She kept talking about the man down the hall, whose pipe still wore a bowl. She said that his pipe was for sale, but the john figured that he'd already spent enough.

The john was of the all-night species, family Blattidae. Having reached that age when a man's virility begins to wilt flabbily, he admitted that his lust for women grew yearly more slobbery and desperate. Every year now he fell a little farther from what he had been. In his youth he had not considered himself to be anything special. Now he recollected with awe how his penis had once leaped eagerly up at the merest thought or touch, how his orgasms had gushed as fluently as Lincoln's speeches; those were the nights when ten minutes between two trash cans or beneath a parked car had sufficed. His joy now required patience and closeness. That was why he'd paid the twenty-nine dollars to share with this woman whose brown body was as skinny as a grasshopper's this stinking room whose carpet was scattered with crumbs of taco shells and rotting cheese; among his possessions he now counted the sheet which someone had used to wipe diarrhea, the science fiction book called *The Metal Smile,* a gold mine of empty matchboxes, and all the wads of used toilet paper that anyone would ever need to start a new life. He'd bought the room for the night, and after that he was going to go back to work and the prostitute would live there.

Maybe that was why she worked so hard at cleaning up, hanging the diarrhea-sheet over the window for a curtain, picking up the hunks of spoiled food and throwing them out the window, sweeping with the broom without bristles, sprinkling the carpet with water from the sink (which had doubled as a urinal) so that the filth would stick better to the broom. Maybe that was why she cleaned, or maybe it was because she had once had a home where she'd raised her children as well as she could until jail became her home, and although they took her children and turned them into somebody else's (or more likely nobody's) it was too late for her to shuck the habit of making her surroundings decent; or maybe she worked so hard just because she was fond of the john (who was generous), because she wanted him to he happy and comfortable with her.

If it wasn't for whoever left this mess, there'd be no roaches, she said. I've lived in this hotel all the time and never had no roaches.

He sat on the mattress with his arm around her while they smoked a rock, and a cockroach rushed across his leg.

I'm not afraid of any human being, the prostitute said. I'm a single female out there, so I gotta be ferocious so they be respectin' me. And I'm not afraid of any animal. But insects gimme the jitters. All them roaches in here, it's 'cause whoever was in here before was such a slob. If I ever meet that motherfucker and he pisses me off, I'll say to him: You know what? You remind me of your room. Ooh, look at that big fat roach!

Certainly the big fat roach was blameless for being what it was. And the prostitute was likewise faultless for not wanting that roach to crawl across them later that night, once they turned out the bare bulb which reflected itself in the greasy window. Biting her lip with disgust, she slammed her shoe against the wall over and over until the bug was nothing but a stain among stains.

I really hate them roaches, she sighed, loading her blackened pipe with more whiteness. They just gimme the creeps. You know, in the Projects, you catch 'em with crack. If you cleaned up your place too good and stuff and you can't find 'em, just lay a rock out on the table and they'll be swarmin'! Shit, there's another one!

She snatched up her shoe and pounded the wall.

She was picking bits of rancid cheese out of the chest of drawers with three drawers gone while the john lay watching the roaches. They seemed to he accustomed to the light. They scurried up and down the walls on frantic errands, ran across the carpet, whose water-stains and burns resembled the abscesses of half-Korean Molly down the hall (another whore said she kept picking at herself); and one roach even climbed that foul bedsheet draped over the window as a curtain.

The prostitute came back to the mattress and they smoked another piece of rock. She'd loaned the pipe to a whore who'd bought bad stuff, so it stank of something strange. Now she kept running water through it, but that didn't do any good.

Nudge that rock down into the end that's burned blacker. The john knew that much. Don't push it in too hard, or you'll break the mesh which is already almost gone. She'd taught him that. (You'd better not inhale too powerfully for the same reason.) Just tamp it lovingly in with the black-burned hairpin. Lovingly, I said, because crack is the only happiness. The prostitute celebrated whenever she got a big rock by buying a lighter whose color matched her dress. She held a red lighter tonight to keep her red dress company. She was wearing red shoes and a red headband: red was her favorite shade. He'd seen her in the black cocktail dress that she put on when he knocked at her door and she was embarrassed because she thought she looked old; he didn't care how old or young she looked because he loved her, but she closed the door and wouldn't let him in until she was beautiful for him in the black dress which thirty seconds later he was urgently helping her pull off; and he'd seen her in the foxtail outfit that reminded him of women he knew at the horse races, but most often he'd seen her wearing the hue of vibrant blood. She lit the rock and breathed in even though the tube of glass had been broken so short that it burned her lips and tongue when the rock was only half cooked; she breathed in because when she was eighteen her first husband had brought a two-by-four smashing down on the crown of her head, and after that she'd never had very good balance; that was twenty years ago now. And one of her daughters (she'd been very little then) had said: Mama, don't ever worry about falling, 'cause I'll always be next to you, and if I see you start to go down, I'll throw myself right down on the sidewalk so you can fall on me! —It made her cry sometimes to remember that. Her daughter didn't walk beside her anymore, and so she smoked crack.

The john was looking worried. —Crack isn't addictive, now, is it? he said.

Oh, no, honey, the prostitute smiled. It's just a psychological thing.

And later in the night, when she spread her legs for him and he worried about AIDS, she said to him: Oh, don't worry, honey. You can only get AIDS if you're two homosexuals.

There were two roaches on the wall, and she got them both with her shoe in a slamming blow like the one three months ago that had left her permanently blind in her right eye when she was being raped: now she couldn't read a menu anymore.

Inhale it slowly, hold five or six seconds, expel it through the nose. That was her way; that way was more mellow. If you did it too fast you might get tweaked. First the head rush, then the body rush.

Don't inhale so hard, she said. That's the difference between white boys and black boys. White boys always inhale too fast, 'cause they think if they do they'll get more high. You white boys are just greedy sometimes. Black boys know better.

He felt the smoke bite in his chest as he held it in, and then the rush struck him behind his eyeballs. Now his heart began to pound more fiercely. His lips and tongue swelled into a numb clean fatness like a pussy's lips. The feeling that he had was the same as long ago at the high school dances when the boys and girls had stood on opposite sides of the floor and the music had started but he was too afraid to cross that open space where all the girls could see him as he came among them to ask one of them to share her beauty with him for a dance, so his heart pounded faster and faster, and suddenly he was going to the girls anyway and he said: Will you dance with me? and the girl giggled and her friends giggled and she looked quickly at her friends and then at him and said yes and he was going into the music with her holding her hand. It was in exactly that way that his heart was pounding, except that there was no fear in his excitement this time; no matter how rapid his happiness became it remained tranquil.

Well, laughed the prostitute (who always became more talkative the more crack she did), another main difference between white people and black people is white people have reputations to protect when they buy drugs. Black people don't care. —And she laughed.

Ahead waited the long night of her going in and out to do her business which she pretended not to be doing, believing that pretending would keep him from feeling hurt, when actually he wasn't hurt at all: she was trying to be loving by protecting him from what she was doing, while he was trying to be loving by letting her do whatever she needed to do. Meanwhile they both smoked crack. Ahead of that night loomed the night when he took her out for dinner with his friends and she was late because she had to smoke crack and then at dinner she excused herself to go to the ladies' room where she smoked crack and came out weeping as though her heart would break because she was convinced that all his friends looked down on her, so he embraced her outside as she soaked him with tears begging him to return with her to that hotel on Mission Street whose gratings and buzzers were like airlocks, so later that night he did come to her, and when he lay beside her on the dirty mattress and took her into his arms her face was burning hot! Her forehead steamed with sweat that smelled like crack, that delicious bitterclean smell even more healthy and elegant than eucalyptus or Swiss herbal lozenges: she buried her face in his chest and whispered something about the Bible as her sick and glowing face burned its way to his heart. —There was a woman whom he loved who was a scientist. When he told her what had happened, the woman said: That fever, that night sweat, that dementia about your friends, well, it sounds to me like AIDS, particularly the very early stages. —But another friend just rubbed his stubble and said: Her sweat smelled like crack, huh? She must be O.D.ing on crack. Happens all the time! —Ahead of that night crouched the night when the john woke up in his own bed wanting crack. It was the middle of a moonless time. He had no crack. He said to himself: If only the moon was here maybe that would cheer me so that I could sleep again: but ahead of that night laughed the night when he woke up from a dream of crack with the moon outside his window as big and round as the abscess on the prostitute's foot which would not heal, and he lay wide awake needing crack.

They smoked crack, and he lay in her arms staring up at the long lateral groove-lips of the moulding reflected in the mirror of the medicine cabinet, whose shelves had all been wrenched out, and he began to smile.

Look a that! he cried. Look at all those roaches running crazy across the ceiling! I guess they must really be enjoying themselves.

The woman cackled. —I s'pose they be gettin' a contact high from all the smoke up there. But it kinda pisses me off, 'cause they can't pay me no money!

They both laughed at that, and then they did another piece of rock in the best way, she approved of how he smoked crack now; the best way to smoke crack is to suck it from the tube of broken glass as gently as you'd suck the crack-smoke breath from the lips of the prostitute who's kissing you.

Prayer Against Angels

From
The Book of Candles

This is taken from a longer cycle of related poems, a CoTangent Press book object that has been in progress since 1995. It is in that classic, romantic vein of a time gone by. The influence of Blake should be noted—the rhyming scheme, the use of Biblical imagery, the grandiose importance of love, heaven, beauty, and paradise lost. —MH

From the Sea of Candles to the Peppermint Sea
swim the islands of my destiny.

Now the Mount of Prayer grows from the Isle of Breath
and on the Isle of Good Fortune blooms the Flower of
Death

whose blue-eyed blossom preserves me in the way
of justice, that I may outstay
temptation's flicker, temptation's fire—

O, how the monsters do conspire!

For in the Sea of Candles go the Boats of Light
cargoed with flames and prayers against the Night
of Salvation, which is the Night of Sleep,
which safely blinds me while dream-crabs creep
upon my eyes. But even dreams may devour
my unburned soul! Safer than safety blooms the blue
flower.

From the Mount of Prayer I beg the dark to crawl
upon the candles, quickly, lest I fall.

From the Peppermint Sea shines the Angels' Isle
where eyes like candles feed upon souls' wax. Defile
me not. I pray! I pray for holy blindness,
lest I fall in love with angels' kindness.

Candle-emissaries come and go
upon my Sea of Candles, my Sea of Woe.
I will not answer—from love I lurch.
Darkness, arise! The world is my church.

Amen.

Part IV

On Travel

Antarctica

From
"The Land of Counterpane"
in
An Afghanistan Picture Show

BUT I WANTED TO go to Antarctica. In New England there was the snow and the woods, but it was gloomy among the trees and when I went sledding with Julie we would always crash into old stone walls. Antarctica sounded much better; my father told me that hardly anyone lived there. I imagined a sunny space of snow, a smoothness of ice that sparkled blue and green. There were penguins, of course. Icebergs moved through the ocean like ships, and far away could be seen jumping porpoises, and I could build snow castles and have my own ice-cream mine. One needed a parka to live there, but it was not too cold, especially when the sun was out in the afternoons and the ice was like a mirror. I would come out of school sometimes in February or March, almost understanding fractions. Those were warm days for winter; the snow was a little sticky, and it packed perfectly. They were building tall snow sculptures on the green. On my way home I walked past fields with the grass coming up golden through the snow, and that was territory belonging to Antarctica.

The Conquest of Kianazor

This is an excerpt from an unpublished work by Vollmann when he was a student at Deep Springs College. Here, the astute Vollmann reader can see the early direction of style and syntax, and an interest in the history of exploration and travel, that would guide the writer's future projects and obsessions. It is always telling to look at an author's youthful prose: we see the seed that grew into the tree. —MH

Then felt I like some watcher of the skies
When a new planet swims into his ken;
Or like stout Cortez when with eagle eyes
He star'd at the Pacific—and all his men
Look'd at each other with a wild surmise—
Silent, upon a peak in Darien.

—KEATS

IN 1427, THE EXPLORER Juan-Paolo Fransisco García de Paolo discovered a city of gold in the mountains of Africa. He was not surprised to find it, for there had been tales of such in many story-books in Portugal, his native country, and he was wise enough to know that story-books never lie. To the dozen men who remained with him he said, "Behold; we see that which is the end of our quest. Since cities of savages are always named with barbaric exoticism, let us call this one Kianazor." And he bade his scribe record the name.

In truth, it was a fine city. To the north and east the mountains rose impassably high, robed in snow and ice like an Oriental beauty in her veils. South there was only a precipice (in the caves of which giant birds nested) which met the jungle many miles below. To the west were the dangerous slopes which they had traversed for months, and, beyond the horizon, the Jungle and the sea from which they had come. The city itself stood almost in the shadows of the northern mountains, in a valley bright with blossoming trees. Its golden bridges spanned two small lakes; its domed towers reflected the light with the intolerable perfection of mirrors. It was surrounded by gardens. The breeze that blew across the valley carried to the explorers the sounds of laughter and festival, the scents of many sweet incenses.

Juan-Paolo Fransisco García de Paolo raised his seeing-glass (the construction of which had been a family secret for three centuries) to his eye, and surveyed the streets of Kianazor. With the aid of its power he was able to discern many dark-skinned folk in robes whose splendor rivalled that of the peacock, dancing and performing religious rites. All about were maidens seated at stands piled with melons and other succulents, and on the steps of the temples could be seen priests serving cups of a thick golden liquid which the story-books helped to identify as ambrosia. Juan-Paolo Fransisco García de Paolo studied the people of Kianazor until he had arrived at three conclusions:

(1) the maidens were beautiful in their way, and hence deserving of his attention;

(2) the city seemed as though it had an abundance of riches; and

(3) none of its people were carrying weapons; there were not even any sentries in evidence.

All of these made Juan-Paolo Fransisco García de Paolo reflect that perhaps the city of Kianazor should be conquered for the greater glory of his country.

He turned to survey his own party, assessing its strength. From an original size of one hundred and twenty devout souls, it had dwindled through desertion, shipwreck, venereal disease, vampire bats and the reptiles of the jungle to its present number of twelve. They were all loyal and hardy, those twelve. They had endured these decimations with Christian meekness, knowing that there would thus be more booty for them, and never had they questioned his orders (after the executions in Malta). They had not flinched at the grim cliffs which they had just ascended, and he knew that they would not flinch now. Good Portuguese that they were, each was surely worth a thousand soul-less savages, especially now that they had the trick of the exploding powder which the Moorish sage had shown them.

"Men," Juan-Paolo Fransisco García de Paolo began, and his scribe dipped a quill in ink, and held it poised over a parchment to record his words. "Men, let us add to the tales in the story-books, and take the city in the name of our beloved home."

"And shall we teach the heathen to know the greatness of God?" asked his lieutenant, Alonzo Giovanni.

Juan-Paolo Fransisco García de Paolo considered. "Let us promise to spare the ruler for conversion, on condition that he empty his treasuries into our hands. But in truth I suspect that a heathen is incapable of hearing the word of God with understanding, and it would perhaps be more merciful to slay him afterward. Let us attempt to teach only those maidens whose persons attract our fancy, and who are robust enough to bear our baggage home."

To this the men murmured their approval, and Alonzo Giovanni instructed them to prepare the Moorish powder while the leader planned the taking of the city. The powder was removed from its skin pouch and distributed among the conquerors. Each had a bronze tube into which he poured a bit of powder, and placed a metal pellet before inserting the long wick which was used to ignite the powder. The explosion would send the projectile forth with enough violence to remove a heathen's gibbering spirit from his body. It was an excellent device. Juan-Paolo Fransisco García de Paolo had required his men to keep its secret so that no other nation would be able to utilize it unwisely. He was a man of much foresight.

He planned the attack with care. It seemed best to commence with the destruction of the bridges which spanned the two lakes; this would isolate each section of the city, and allow a concentration of might upon each. His eyes, trained by many pictures in the story-books, picked out the palace without difficulty. It would be necessary to search it carefully. Juan-Paulo Fransisco García de Paolo made many calculations of strategy. When he knew that he had taken all necessary factors into account, he explained his pattern of tactics to his men, and all applauded. "Glory to Portugal!" they cried.

The attack was begun. It was a great success. But when Kianazor had been subdued, a thing occurred which was not in the story-books; the ruler made apologetic signs to indicate that he had no gold. Annoyed, Juan-Paolo Fransisco García de Paolo clove him in two with his fine sword and similarly dispatched his screaming queen after taking his pleasure with her. Then he searched the city for treasure. The bridges and towers, unfortunately, were not constructed of gold after all, but rather of the trees that grew about the valley. They seemed to have been varnished with a peculiar kind of yellow sap which gleamed in the sunlight like gold. The palace was painted with beautiful artistry, but it had no vaults filled with gems, no hidden coffers (the conquerors made sure of that). Juan-Paolo Fransisco García de Paolo wished to learn the system of currency which the savages of Kianazor had employed, but, to his regret, none of them remained alive, the maidens who were to have accompanied the expedition back to Portugal had been inadvertently killed while the men sported with them. Alonzo Giovanni thought that a few more might be hidden about, but this was impossible to ascertain through the smoke of the burning ruins.

Three of his men had been murdered by the heathens during the battle, and the nine who remained studied Juan-Paolo Fransisco García de Paolo with gravely mutinous looks.

"Remember the glory of Portugal," he said. "At the very least we have the secret of ambrosia."

But what he had been certain was ambrosia was discovered to be nothing more than melon-juice.

"Very well," said Juan-Paolo Fransisco García de Paolo. "It is clear to me that we are yet destined to trial before finding the golden city." And he led his men on to further glory.

The Advantages of Space (1978)

Vollmann penned this letter to Freeman Dyson (a visionary physicist at Princeton who was attracting attention in the seventies with bold plans for establishing colonies in outer space—and whom Vollmann himself labeled a "crackpot" in a presentation he later gave at Deep Springs College) on behalf of himself and fellow Deep Springer, Jake Dickinson. As with the letter he would write to the Saudi Embassy the next year, the even-handed, dead-serious tone of this letter of inquiry is genuine—and may seem hilarious today. But it is also a good example of the almost casual manner with which Vollmann has embarked on only slightly less extraordinary adventures over the years. —LM

1013 Woodbine Court
Bloomington, Indiana 47401

28 June 1978

Dr. Freeman Dyson
Department of Physics
Princeton University
Princeton, New Jersey 08540

Dear Dr. Dyson,

ABOUT A WEEK AGO I read Kenneth Brower's biography of you and your son and found myself highly interested in your ideas. I doubt that Dyson Spheres will be constructed in my lifetime by creatures in this biosphere, but perhaps some of us could set up something on asteroids or comets in a couple of decades . . .

As I see it, there are currently three possible environments for settlement: the sea, Antarctica,* and Space, in ascending order of preference. Building ocean settlements strikes me as risky because we would probably be close enough to land to be controlled by various overwater interests. Even if we're based in some great abyss (which would be unlikely for a first attempt), we're still at the bottom of a gravity well, down which fall canisters of radioactive wastes, industrial byproducts and the effluvium of toilets. It seems unfortunate to have to trust in other people to keep our environment uncontaminated when that trust has been so far without ground (dry or otherwise). Antarctica seems an order of magnitude better. It's remote; we could get out of sight of military bases pretty quickly and settle down with penguins or springtails. We certainly wouldn't have a gravity well problem on one of the 16,000-foot mountains. Antarctica would be a perfect place to set up a space launch site without strings. (And if we can fuel up with ice . . .) There's even air around to play with; it would be a good jumping-off place. On the other hand, if we didn't jump off within a century or so we'd probably be jumped on by nations looking for new material to exploit. Antarctica would also be rather dull compared to space. I won't be so condescending as to tell you what I think the advantages of space are; you've probably thought of it more than I have.

So . . .

Are we working on another version of Orion? Do you have any new plans? (Brower sort of left all that hanging.) What about finances, or the bone-calcium problem? Have you planned out any directions for the society up there, or would you leave it to evolve by itself?

You see, Dr. Dyson, I'd really like to come along. And I have a couple of friends who might be interested. None of us are brilliant physics or engineering minds (I'm eighteen, puttering with differential equations and may stop there as far as math is concerned), but I wouldn't say we're worthless, either. What sort of preparation would you suggest; how can we help make the whole thing happen?

*North Pole's not all that solid.

A Bizarre Proposition (1979)

Although this inquiry met with no response from the Saudi Embassy, it certainly speaks volumes today about the author's urge to travel to the most distant and exotic and *dangerous* places possible—although in this case, it wasn't quite possible. The magic of this query volunteering to be shot off by the Saudis to the asteroids, where he will commence mining operations, is that Vollmann—who had been devouring and writing great amounts of science fiction during this period—is dead serious. His mission failed, but at least he tried. —LM

Dear Sir,

We have a proposition for you. It sounds a bit bizarre, but we are confident that you will not dismiss it from your consideration for this reason.

We are two American college students whose interests lie in space. It seems to us that space settlements are not only technically and economically feasible, but desirable. It is certainly clear that they will add to our knowledge of matter-vacuum systems, and in particular the solar system and the earth. This is bound to be useful when we are ready to apply it. But the capital expense required demands more immediate benefits. We see these benefits as being regularly available. Consider the following.

Between Mars and Jupiter is a large gap where a planet or planets is thought to have orbited. After some titanic accident, the gap became filled with fragments which we now call the asteroids. There are thousands of them; 1600 have been tracked. The larger ones are big enough to have gravity sufficient to allow settlement and exploitation: Ceres is 480 miles in diameter, for instance, and Eros is the size of Manhattan.

The smaller ones are like floating chunks of ore, rich in nickel, iron and other elements. Many seem to contain usable ice. The vacuum conditions needed for many processes are ubiquitous.

It seems to us that as resources on earth continue to dwindle, the people who can afford the outlay necessary to replace them from elsewhere will realize enormous profits and at the same time prevent industrial collapse. That outlay will certainly be large, and transportation costs will also be high. However, supply-demand theory indicates that eventually that expense will be justified. This should occur within fifty to a hundred years, unless radically new technologies are developed on earth and implemented immediately. This strikes us as unlikely, since all technologies need raw materials, and the only other raw material around which might be able to replace ore is oil, which is also beginning to decline. The plastic industry is bound to be in trouble eventually.

Our proposition, then, is to design a feasible arrangement in conjunction with whomever you choose, and then to mine the asteroids for you. We hope that you will consider us seriously. Please write if you would like any elaboration.

Thank you very much.

Yours sincerely,

William T. Vollmann

Subzero's Debt, 1991

From
The Rifles

In this extended excerpt from "Subzero's Debt, 1991"—one of the sections of "Peel Sound" (Chapter 6 in *The Rifles*)—Vollmann describes what may well be the most astonishing and risky adventure of his life: the dark winter days he spent alone on the Isachsen Peninsula of Ellef Ringnes Island near the magnetic North Pole. Determined to experience first-hand the sort of hardships endured by the crewmembers of the Franklin Expedition during their doomed search for the Northwest Passage, Vollmann arranged to have himself dropped off at Isachsen during March 1991. As these scenes vividly demonstrate, Vollmann avoided sharing Franklin's fate only by the slimmest of margins. —LM

SO THE ICE AND darkness curled round them ever more tightly. —Very good. —In March of 1991, one Captain Subzero, seeking to peel the frozen Franklin flesh-mask away from his FULMAR-skull, spent twelve days at the abandoned weather station at Isachsen, Ellef Ringnes Island—that way he'd know everything!—Well, I won't eat lead, of course (thus Subzero, to himself). I don't want to ruin my brain for other projects. After all, who knows what I'll be once this Dream is over? But I'll understand what death is like, at least . . . I think I have it straight: Mr Franklin is now suffering severe mental impairment and psychosis; Mr Gore exhibits labile affect, persistent abdominal pain and paranoid thoughts like the crooked row of boats drawn nose-up on the narrow beach at Pond Inlet where day by day he can see the dwarf willows growing higher, bud by bud, shivering in the wind, but each bud growing tall and narrow nonetheless above the hairy green leaves; has he started to contemplate eating people yet? As for Mr Fitzjames . . . No, it's hard to imagine that third winter; I'm not sure I can do it. Better go to Isachsen.

In vain did Mr Franklin use every argument which he could adduce to persuade his grave-twin against this mad scheme: Your place, sirrah (thus Mr Franklin) is here with me, where I am compelled to remain. Mr Watson, the Carpenter's Mate, has already engaged to make your coffin. What next, you ask? Ah, that I know well. Remember, Subzero, I'm a very close neighbor of yours. Our ships will be stiff and still in the ice. Capt Crozier will read the funeral address. (Jane and Reepah would be there if they could, but let's keep looking at the bright side of the question.) They'll lower the colors, my friend. They'll wrap your coffin in a flag and chisel out your grave with painful effort. The FULMAR will fly overhead. I know He's been urging you to get rid of me, but that would be as if I were to leave poor Jane. You're upright, Subzero; you're a good popsicle. Anyhow, it'll be too late then. Leaning on picks and staffs and rifles (can't you see it?), they'll bow their fur-hooded heads as you're lowered into the ice. And you won't change, perhaps, for centuries! Your shoulders will be as a rock whose original color was grey, but after the black lichen makes lacy islands all over (say, half a thousand years from now), the whitish-green lichen will affix itself in clumps of phosphorescent rivalry; then come the mineral-green lichen to speckle densely in most of the remaining spaces, so that the rock of you will become an unreal patchwork of softness nestled among the feathery mounds of other lichens and mosses. Later still, when continents move and England is forgotten, then maybe a bud might grow from your frozen heart; spokes of tough willow-root might reach out from an empty center, terminating in trees an inch high, unbowed despite the heaviness of their soft black-flecked buds . . . And for all that time you'll be with me!

But Subzero had to be Mr Franklin in his own way; he had to die alone.

Do you know where Isachsen is? Mr Franklin didn't—how could he? Ellef Ringnes wasn't discovered until 1900 or so . . . Unroll the polar charts, my Arctic Friend! Do you see the massive white dog's head of Greenland? Now look west to Canada. There's Ellesmere Island, lobed and convoluted like a brain stood on end. At eighty-two thousand square miles she's only a tenth the size of Greenland, but since Greenland really ought to be called a continent, Ellesmere remains one of the great islands of the world. Mr Franklin's sailed in sight of her, and so has Sir James. Nested in her western concavity is Axel Heiberg Island, which they say has spectacular petrified forests; I've seen her from the edge of Ellesmere but I have never been there. At the southwest foot of Axel Heiberg is a channel, across which lies Amund Ringnes Island, a little bullet pointing north. Amund, like his brother Ellef, was a brewer in Norway, and I hope that the discoverers succeeded in toasting them both with unfrozen ale. After all, what other cheer could there be on this gravelly mudbank, which is so far north that the map screams with loneliness? She's three islands north yet of Resolute! Now, west of Amund Ringnes is Ellef Ringnes, a somewhat larger puzzle-piece canted north by northwest. This island is one of the stones in the dreary western wall of the Arctic archipelago, which runs northeast from the mainland as follows: Banks Island, Prince Patrick Island, Brock Island (a muddy punctuation mark), Borden Island, then Ellef Ringnes, Meighen, and so back to the northern corners of Axel Heiberg and Ellesmere. Cross this line, and you've come out the Northwest Passage at last! Thus, while Amund Ringnes is lonely enough, Ellef Ringnes faces true nothingness, islandless sea frozen all the way to the Pole, empty for a hundred degrees of longitude going west, until at last one approaches the New Siberian Islands—which are hardly a very good approximation of the Spice Islands that were the Northwest Passage's *raison d'être,* but they'll have to do, just as sometimes Jane has to do for Reepah.

To people like Jane, who have never been there, Arctic islands are much the same. —Perhaps by now I have conveyed a little of the emptiness of Resolute. The relocatees' children, who died here of tuberculosis, might have wept at the last, remembering the moss and berries of Inukjuak. Their parents surely did. —Well, Isachsen is emptier than Resolute. At Resolute there are seventy species of vascular plants. On the northern tip of Ellef Ringnes there are only two. At Isachsen, forty miles away, some zealous soul has found forty-eight species, a respectable number, but I would still rather be at Resolute. (Down at Hudson Bay, Churchill has four hundred species. The figure for Inukjuak is probably similar.) —Next statistic: At Resolute there are about fifteen birds per square mile. At Isachsen there are ten. When I was there I never saw one, but of course I was not wearing my glasses.

(Pond Inlet has four hundred. The temperate forests have one to twelve thousand.)

Isachsen lies at longitude 103° 32' N, latitude 78° 47' N. March is the second coldest month. The sun has only just returned (the first sunrise for 1991 was the 21st of February), and temperatures for that month generally move between -30° and -40° Celsius. An ice island occasionally manned by the personnel of the Polar Continental Shelf Project lies fifty miles or so to the north of Ellef Ringnes. The nearest permanent community, however, is Resolute, which is three hundred and eleven miles to the southeast, and I think we've heard of Resolute before. At a similar distance northeast, Environment Canada maintains a weather station at Eureka, Ellesmere Island. In short, Isachsen is quiet. An auto-station continues to report temperature and windspeed every hour from a shed on the runway. Otherwise, the island is left to itself. No planes fly over. Isachsen freezes year by year in the permanent pack ice.

[. . .]

Isachsen was so cold and still that his footsteps echoed all the way to the horizon. The corrugated metal passageways of the station were like tomb passageways. His steps rang and groaned terrifyingly in that dry and pitch-black coldness. He had to wear his headlamp, and it gleamed cheerlessly ahead, reflecting his own black shape in the glass of dead exit signs so that some monster was always coming toward him. The rec. room was particularly dark and horrible like a vault full of corpses. Armchairs, piled with snow, seemed to stretch and torment the darkness with their high pale burdens. Icy wires dangled from the ceiling. He pulled his gloved hand out of the mitt for a moment and tried to persuade himself that it was fun to watch the moisture rise like smoke from every fingertip—

* * *

He did not sleep at all well that first night. He could not get warm. Although he had dutifully removed his outer suit and VBL and brushed the frost from his underclothing, his back and toes remained cold all night. It was often the case on his Arctic trips that the first night was unpleasant, so he did not feel seriously alarmed. The following night, being both tired and acclimated, he would surely sleep better. Then the third day he could go exploring—without his glasses, it is true, and his $300 North Face backpack, which had gone on the Trans-Antarctica Expedition at eighty below, they said, had showed its true worth at Isachsen within the first half hour when the Fastex hip belt buckle shattered. But he was still quite confident. In the morning, when he went outside to chop snow for the stove, he found that the little toe of his left foot had entirely lost sensation. He tried putting his glasses on to examine it, but they were too thickly coated with ice. Was it frostbitten? Fortunately, chafing it for half an hour inside a felt mukluk liner restored it to feeling.

It was a sunny, foggy day at -32°. Needles of hoarfrost clung to lumber and cables. The sun sported a white corona that brought spots to his eyes. He was very optimistic. His breath froze instantly on his facemask, scratching his nose with needles of ice. The luminous haze permitted a few low snow-mountains to be seen at the horizon, and he was sure that he would be scaling them soon. He had his own island! He laughed out loud.

For lunch he dumped a quarter of a desk drawer of snow into the pot already conveniently enriched with the remains of last night's dinner, pulled up a chair, brushed the new accumulation of ice crystals off his face, started the stove (the pump handle, being plastic, had already shattered from the cold—supposedly Steger had taken that model to the Pole—but Subzero had saved enough of the shaft to suffice), and then for the first time he broke out the 3.5 pound wheel of cheddar cheese, split a few chips from it with his ice axe, picked them up off the carpet and tossed them in with his vegetables—delicious! For dessert he dipped into the bag of fruit pemmican left over from his Inukjuak trip and munched. It was not hard at all, but soft and very very cold, like ice cream.

* * *

Later that afternoon, remembering that he had been a little cold at night, he decided to make himself a sort of heat bunker with the best materials available. There was a bed with a mattress in the adjoining room. Taking some squares of lumber from the boarded up windows, he walled the bed in and then roofed it with his groundcloth. Although he had now been at Isachsen for almost twenty-four hours, he had done no exploring, but he didn't believe that that was odd at all. He was shivering, but he did not think about that much. He convinced himself that he was simply doing something that ought to be done sometime, instead of admitting that it was something that had to be done now. He scoured rooms, looking for blankets. The Polar Psychology Project man had said that there were emergency blankets in bags, somewhere in the Ops building. He couldn't really tell where the dorm building left off and the Ops building began. Anyhow, he didn't see any blankets. —No matter. —He wiped his nose. The snot pads on his mitts were frozen to the texture of coarse emery paper.

He climbed into the bed, zipped his sleeping bag around him, and lay there. Since he continued to shiver, he got out, put on his down parka and down pants, and then got back into bed, looking forward to his nap. Two hours later he was still shivering.

* * *

In Resolute his friend David had loaned him a heap of spare clothes. Take spare everything, David said. At minus thirty, minus forty, you'll need it after a week. It was those spare clothes, among other things, that helped to save his life.

* * *

The Bradley man had given him a radio. He was supposed to call in every evening, to keep them happy. They'd set up the radio for him when they dropped him off, and it had worked. But this time when he called alone there was no answer.

* * *

He did not want to admit to himself that the sleeping bag was no good because if it did not work there was nothing that he could do about it.

In New York he had considered bringing his old bag as a spare, but there simply was no more room left in the backpack. Most winter expeditions make use of sleds anyhow, but, as I have mentioned, air freight to the Canadian Arctic is so unreliable as to be useless—at least for marginal solo expeditions on a budget. As it turned out, Environment Canada in Resolute lent him a sled for toolboxes, which proved very useful. He could have lashed an extra bag onto the sled easily. But getting it to Resolute, that was problem. So he was stuck.

* * *

He managed to get two or three hours of sleep that night and woke up chilled. It was 4:20 in the morning. There was a degree of blue visibility that turned his breath-steam into shadows, and he went out and walked around to warm up. At half past seven the sun began to clear the blue-white sea-horizon; it was large and seemingly oval, a reddish-orange entity that gradually yellowed. Outside of the station, in the happy expanse of that day, the sleeping bag problęm hid again and he was certain that he would have a wonderful time. The ocean, unspeakably inviting, showed him its inch-high knife-ridges of snow; the side away from he rising sun was a very pretty blue. The low blue trapezoids of locked floes or distant mountains (he really couldn't tell without his glasses) were begging him to swarm happily up them all, shouting, shooting, swigging hot chocolate from his thermos—

* * *

Ah, yes, the thermos. A glass one would have broken, so he'd bought a steel one. He had to take off his mitts to open it. The conduction of the metal against his undergloved fingers was agony. When he drank from it, he had to remember to breathe on the place where his mouth would be, to prevent his lips from freezing to it.

At -35°, the average temperature during his stay, a liquid poured boiling into the thermos at breakfast would be ice-cold by dinner, and ice-crusted an inch thick the following morning. He could not take the thermos into his sleeping bag to warm it, since the sleeping bag was not warming him.

* * *

Seen without glasses the landscape was of course greatly softened. In a way this made it even more enticing, like some long view of desert fading into smoky blue horizons of dust. He was sorry, however, to have no choice in the matter. His visibility was restricted even further by the down facemask David had lent him—a godsend against cold and wind, but it had frozen long since into owlish armor, the eyeholes then further diminished by the carbuncles of frost that rimmed them. From time to time he'd un-mitt a gloved finger and scrape away what he could. If he squinted, that eye would freeze shut, and then he'd have to pick and pull at the frozen eyelashes before it could open again; then he'd need to blink vigorously half a hundred times to dissolve the gluey white ropes of half-congealed tears that latticed his vision. Still, there remained a heaven of things to see, things snowcrusted, things hoarfrosted like boards porcupined with splinters, snow-edges that gleamed in the rising sun like sweet yellow butter . . . and then, on that windless morning, he heard something crunch. He was on a ridge overlooking the sea ice. Something crunched again. Again. Footsteps. If he had had either his glasses or his sleep he doubtless would not have been so alarmed, but you must imagine for yourself the shocking effect of a foreign noise, repeated, in that silent place. He thought he saw a yellow shape on the ice, moving. His heart began to pound. He had left his shotgun at the station, so he deserved whatever he got. He began to walk back toward the station as quickly as he could. In a bright orange stuff-sack he had his headlamp and thermos. He took out the headlamp, which he would need, and dropped the stuffsack, to distract the bear in case it followed his track. Then he began to walk even faster. It was very disquieting not to be able to see whether anything was coming behind him. I do not think that there was any bear, actually, but only his anxiety, formed into a bear as in his dreams. Later, when he'd traversed that very gently sloping hillside of snow, which was landmarked by pointy drifts, oil drums and red buildings, all the same size, it seemed, when he'd reached his sled and calmed down, he returned to retrieve the thermos, shotgun on safe but with a chambered round; and after that he was more conscientious about carrying the shotgun with him. It was more concrete, and so more comfortable, than any number of imagined polar bears.

* * *

So he had not yet begun seeing things or hearing things; he was only a little tired. Now, if I were to describe to you Captain Subzero's exact situation and location while at lunch, it would be this: seated by the window, leaning over the desk, with his right forearm resting on the block of cheese (which had not been much used, since cutting it was little easier than carving a block of jade), but his arm was already aching with cold from cheese-conduction even through his suit and parka; his right hand, clad in a skinny glove, held a spoon (which was usually kept in the plastic cup of frozen milk powder, which in turn rested in the drawer of snow, just behind the cheese); in front of him was the stove; to his left the can of sterno for softening his facemask . . . —why, he had everything! He was a little colder than he had been the day before, but he'd make up for that now with extra soup and potato buds . . . He could not see out the window anymore. It was frosted with condensation from his cooking. But the little room seemed wider than it should be. And sounds kept tricking him. A piece of dental floss, dragged between his gloved fingers, squeaked with an echo that deafened him. The steady rubbing together of the legs of his down pants when he walked sometimes convinced him of the existence of an approaching airplane. The echoes of his own breathing in the facemask made him certain again that a polar bear was making crunching footsteps behind him . . . He went out with the shotgun and looked around, just to be sure. Well, without glasses of course he could not see much.

* * *

The light was always like late afternoon, only sometimes a little brighter or a little dimmer.

* * *

He had a feeling of well-being that day. He had begun to know how to wear the clothes, how to pace himself; it was only when he stopped that he became cold.

* * *

The sound of something creepy coming down the hall was only the sound of his stove pressurizing. Likewise the sound of police sirens. The sound of bells was the sound of his frozen zippers clinking together when he walked.

* * *

It was difficult to light a match. The spark would form on the tip, and then maybe it would catch or maybe it would go out. Even the heads of hurricane matches ignited (if at all) in slow motion.

* * *

Every night now he wondered if he would live until morning. He'd read in Stefansson that there was no danger in sleeping when it was cold, that one would wake up when one was chilled, and that was exactly true. But it was still unnerving, to lie down shivering, on the near edge of a dark night, and to know that he'd only get colder and colder. Lying still in the darkness, waiting for the next shiver, he did his best to thrust beyond notice the collar of iron around his neck, the helmet of iron on his face, and the frozen hood behind his head. After awhile, the first drop of ice-cold water ran down the mask and across his nose. The iron collar began to limpen, and water ran down his back. Meanwhile, inside his clothes, the opposite was happening. The sweat on back and buttocks and belly turned to ice. During the day he faithfully vented his perspiration whenever he could, but he could not get rid of all of it, and he was now too cold to remove the VBL at night as he had originally done. In any case, the ice inside it clung too ferociously to be scraped off with a fingernail or a knife . . . So he continued to sleep only an hour or two a night. He composed his epitaph: *I died for the advancement of Vapor Barrier Liners.* But in the morning, when he got up and walked around, he became warm and confident again. He tried to think happy thoughts. He tried not to think about night very much, since to think about it was only to dread it. On the fourth day, having become accustomed to using his eyeglasses only for special occasions, as others use binoculars, by lifting them once or twice a day to the rime-choked eyeholes of his facemask, and peering through them for a few seconds, holding his breath, he set off for Don't Point, which was five miles west of the runway. The strangeness of the sounds continued to haunt him. As he bent nearsightedly over his notebook, on which his breath-steam congealed, the scratching of his pencil suddenly echoed distantly, and he was sure that a polar bear was scrabbling softly down the hill to get him. He touched the gun like a magic charm, and felt better. (It is always better to look on the bright side of the question.) With lack of sleep, his eyes were not focusing as well as before; but he could see adequately; the sunlight was good . . .

The ground was flinty with frozen mud-clods. Lovely white hills surrounded him. The sun was low and white (it was 1:30 P.M.) and its rays were jagged. Tiny grass-stalks were hoarfrosted into flowers. The shotgun tired his neck a little as he walked, and the coldness of it gradually began to burn his neck right through the down collar. Beating his mitts together for warmth, he stopped for a moment to read the names on the 1964 cairn of brown rocks, lichened black, red and green, and then he went over that little hill and raced down the smooth snow to the sea ice of Parachute Bay, which was balding with grey spots here and there, thanks to the wind, but balding only meant showing the underlying steel. He could walk across it; he could ride a horse across it; it held Franklin's ships nice and fast. The sun was friendly. The ice was not unfriendly. It acted as it always did.

He stepped onto the ice, timidly at first, and then he began to laugh with delight because it had been the dream of his life to walk upon the frozen sea . . .

[. . .]

That night again he thought that he might not survive. The pad of the sleeping bag felt like ice, and probably was. The down was clumped into frozen pebbles whose sharp edges had worried holes in the nylon shell of the bag. He closed his eyes, and saw a fire in a fireplace, with andirons; he dreamed of a warm woman hugging him. When he woke up, he'd slept three hours. The collar of his sleeping bag, thick and white with frost, stuck painfully to his throat. He was suffocating in his own breath-ice. In the darkness he could not feel his arms and legs. His back and buttocks ached sharply with cold, and he was shivering. He was cold deep inside his belly.

He put on his boots and went outside and walked a mile until he was warm enough to think.

I need hot chocolate, he said to himself.

He chopped snow with his ice axe and melted it and boiled it over the stove. By then, sitting still, he felt half dead with cold. Pulling off the facemask to expose his wet skin to the cold was very unpleasant; so was putting the mask back on, after he'd gulped the cooling liquid. The mask had crumpled and hardened in that position; he gritted his teeth as he worked the ice-vortices over his face.

I guess I'd better get warm in my sleeping bag, he said . . .

* * *

In the morning he decided that before all else he must find those emergency blankets. His down parka was becoming stiff and crackly with ice; he had another one from David but this was a bad sign. He felt very weak, and the sun was in his eyes and for a moment the ice seemed to him like the costumes of Greenlandic women, brightly beaded with diamonds and crosses. With his shovel he dug out the snow from a doorway that might be the Ops building and there was another door half-open, drifted high; he climbed over the hard whiteness and into a dark wood-ribbed corridor going right, snow lovingly cushioning the stained light bulb, snow bulging out from the walls . . . That door at the far end must lead to the dormitory building. No need to clear it. Let's go straight ahead. He shoveled out the next door; there were icicles on the ceiling that did not tremble as he kicked the door open; it took him a long time because he was very weak. The string of his mitts caught on the inner knob and for a long time he could not figure out what had happened. He kept saying to himself: Now, if I can just solve this sleeping bag problem I'll be much happier. He shambled into the darkness, fumbled, switched his headlamp on. He saw the guts of a fuse box, some upended buckets, boxes of nails, and then a third door, behind which a corridor went left and right . . . Try right first. On the wall was a poster of a woman in a bikini, dancing on a tropical beach, her head thrown back as she laughed or screamed. She was spotted with mold. In the next room he found mattresses, a hammock under a swinging lamp held together with masking tape—very World War II, somehow. One grand puff of breath-steam followed the next, on an endless parade into the wall's oblivion. He switched off the headlamp. A little light came through the snowy pane behind the stovepipe. Yes, a stove. A box of matches beside it. He found a piece of paper, put it into the stove, and lit it. That took a long time. The matches were the old wooden kind, with a white dot of phosphorous on a red head. The white part would sometimes ignite, but it was so cold that the red part wouldn't. Finally he got a match going and touched it to the paper. The stovepipe valve was open; all was ready. But smoke came out of the masking tape patches on the stovepipe and hung in the room, spreading horizontally an inch or so below the ceiling. That stove would never do. He looked around, needing blankets. He saw shelves, a dart board with most darts in the inner ring (pretty good, dead men), a table stacked with *Scientific American* and *Popular Mechanics* (the latest issue 1974). A dark little carpeted room, empty aside from a useless lamp. —I note some mental deterioration, he said to himself, but I'm not shivering, so I must not be hypothermic. Maybe I have the flu. —A big armchair by the stove, facing the steel-grey communications panel whose dead phone and microphone, silent round speaker, rows of red and black plugs and switches, each awarded its little portion of snow, cried out to him in desperate silence. The power booth behind this bulkhead was a little niche from which he could see, as if in some museum, the inner involutions of radio lifetimes, batteries the size of salt shakers, grilles and wires and snow and darkness . . . He stumbled over a discarded metal panel. That was all. —Now the left way. He was very weak and slow. Much darker now. Little cubbies of darkness. A room with long snow-covered tables like pool tables or autopsy tables . . . the headlamp flicked onto a frozen bottle of ketchup. It was so cold that his breath-steam fell instead of rising. The next room contained steel sinks, darkness, vastness. There were plastic bags in the sink. Blankets.

He loaded all the blankets and pillows onto his sled and said to himself: If this works, I'll live and all my troubles will be over. If not, why, I'm in big trouble.

He decided to move up to Marv's shed on the runway. It was so small that the building might retain a little body heat. And there was a tank of propane in there. Marv had given him the key and showed him how to use the little heater.

It took him a long time to walk that three-quarters of a mile. He was very dizzy. First he let himself rest every hundred steps. Then he had to lower the requirement to eighty. He said to himself: Interesting how soft snow is more featureless. When he finally got to Marv's shed it took a very long time to undo the knots. He dragged the blankets in and said: Now we'll see. He got into his sleeping bag. He became very cold as the ice on him melted. Then he stopped getting colder. When he saw that he was going to be all right, he closed his eyes and saw swarms of black dots like midges, and he tried to count them but couldn't. Then he saw a hillside of trees. And he sobbed once.

A fever burst out on him, and he laughed, because now it was patent that it wasn't hypothermia, but only the flu; he must have gotten it in Resolute—

* * *

Marv's shed was never meant to be lived in. It was like an ice-house. The walls and ceiling bristled with frost. It would have been just large enough for two people to lie side by side on the floor, heads touching one wall, toes the other. But almost half the width was taken up by the automatic weather station transmission boxes, together with various crates. Catty-corner to one another were two hundred-pound propane cylinders. The one in the corner of the front wall away from the door was at his head. The one against the crates just opposite the door was by his feet. He'd packed pillows around the base of each so that the metal couldn't steal his heat. More dangerous than they was the fact that Marv had weather-stripped the door very tightly. It opened outward, and could not be closed except from the outside, and then only with the greatest effort. It could not be closed from inside at all. He tied a piece of webbing from the door to its hasp so that he could pull it toward himself when he entered the shed at night, but this left it ajar almost two feet. Worse yet, the fact that it opened outward meant that if a wind blew snow against the door he would be trapped inside.

* * *

He slept and fever-dreamed all afternoon, safely warm for the first time. His breath-ice plagued him no more than that pretty mesh of frost that guarded his window at the Narwhal, crystalline strata curving in the illusion of a well shaft. When he awoke, he checked the barometer (a mildly miserable thing to do, since reaching his arm out let the cold in, and it would take another quarter-hour to get warm again) and he saw that the pressure was falling. It had been falling all day. He leaped up, put on his mitts and boots, slung the shotgun over his shoulder, and went down to the station to get the nails he had seen in the Ops building. There was a piece of lumber there that might have been used to board up a window. He dragged that back up the hill with him. His friend David had worked at the station once. David had told him that the winds at Isachsen were like nothing on earth. The door to Marv's shed opened outward. If a wind should heap up a good hard drift in front of the door, he'd be trapped there. He had to build a windbreak. He began prying up great chunks of hard snow with his shovel. As a boy he had helped his father rebuild one or two of the old New England stone walls on their property. Since he did not have a saw he could not cut even blocks as an Inuk would have, but he could at least stack up the snow-boulders in overlapping rows, chinked with soft snow, conscientiously mortared with urine; he found himself greatly enjoying the building work because it was something with a beginning, a middle and an end which he had control over, unlike almost everything else, and so he heaped up a tumulus of snow in front of the door, just far enough from it so that it could open half-way (enough for him to go in and out with a little gear); and then if the wind were to blow parallel to the wall he could close off the little alley between door and wall with the big board. Already he could see a cloud-knife coming toward him from the frozen sea. He nailed a piece of tarp to the door-frame, so that the door could stay a little ajar even in the face of a wind. He was getting hot, so he pulled his coveralls down off his shoulders to vent the sweat-steam, at which his capilene innerwear frosted up instantly, and he could feel it pucker up on his back as it froze . . .

* * *

He didn't sleep much. Evidently it was the fever that had kept him warm, and that had broken. All night he shivered. The sleeping bag was cold and wet. His chest and stomach were the coldest parts of him. He was becoming very sleep-deprived, and his thoughts were not as clear as they should have been, but he told himself that he'd devote the next day to searching the Ops building for heaters. Even if there were other blankets they wouldn't do him any good. He needed something to warm him up, not just insulate him.

There was no wind. A little snow was falling.

His first stove, the one with the shattered pump, was now out of fuel, and that morning he switched to the second. Simply filling the gas bottle and re-inserting the pump was out of the question at these temperatures because the O-rings could not grip properly. As a matter of fact, the second stove, even though he'd put it together almost as soon as the plane had landed him, was leaking gasoline a few inches from its own open flame. He didn't like that. He poured a little soup on the O-ring and it froze right away and the dripping stopped. He wiped up the spilled gas with a block of snow.

The stove was not pressurizing properly. He had to keep pumping it, which made his fingers ache with cold, and his teeth were chattering as he sat there. When he finally got it going, he had to get up and run half a dozen times up and down the black corridor until he could think again—

Breakfast over, fingers and toes dead, he pulled his mask of iron ice back on and returned to the Ops building. In the room where he'd found the blankets he found the other diesel heater, a tall black cabinet with a louvered door. The PPP man had said that it was connected to a thousand-gallon feeder drum just outside. He went outside and cleared the snow away from the drum with his shovel and ice axe. There were two valves. —Just open the valve, wait a minute and light it, the PPP man had said. He opened both valves as far as they would go. Nothing happened. —What next? He had to do whatever he had to do, rapidly. Already he was getting cold again, and his mind was becoming confused. He did twenty jumping jacks, singing a loud song to hearten himself, and then he was able to think again. Not far from the window he found a yellow drum of jet fuel which was almost empty, as he could tell by rolling it a little on its cradle; a full drum weighed about 400 pounds. To open fuel drums you were supposed to use a barrel bung. He'd discovered that the curved point of an ice axe worked just as well. Gently he hooked the point in and unscrewed the cap. Then he poured out what was left into a wastebasket. He carried the wastebasket back into the darkness and poured the diesel in through the stove door. He heard it trickling deep inside. Now he hesitated to strike a match, because he dreaded burning the whole building down or worse, but he was shivering again; he had to do it. He took a roll of toilet paper from the nearest dark and frozen washroom and rolled it down into the chamber where the diesel was, keeping hold of an end which he could use as a fuse. The matches were as hard to light as ever, and his eyes kept closing, but he struck match after match, each one vainly sparking half a dozen times before the head wore away, until he finally got one to make fire. He held his breath until the toilet paper caught. Then he let it fall into the chamber and closed the door. The stovepipe valve was already open. He waited. The fuel caught, and began to burn calmly and steadily.

* * *

The feeling was wonderful. The collar of ice around his neck began to melt, and he saw steam rising from himself. The snow on the carpet did not melt, but the room became perceptibly warmer. For the first time in he did not know how long, he was able to sit still without getting colder and colder. He did not have to desperately scheme and plan and consider. He could simply be, doing nothing. The sensation came back into his fingers. He was the happiest person on earth.

* * *

A wastebasket of fuel lasted about an hour and a half. He found another drum in back of the station, a full one, and collected more fuel. He cooked lunch over the heater, melted snow for drinking water in a nice slow diesel way so that it wouldn't taste scorched as usual, softened the O-rings of his stoves, unzipped his jumpsuit and VBL suit to melt the dirty sweat-ice inside.

The next order of business was obviously to go back to Marv's shed for his sleeping bag and dry it, too. That would make the nightly ordeals much more endurable. As he ran back up the hill, he luxuriated in his exultation. All his problems were solved now. His hands and his mitts were too stiff to permit him to roll up his sleeping bag very well, so he had to lash it on his sled. He was stumbling and he sloshed diesel oil. He said to himself: You're in an abnormal state of mind. Calm down. Your judgment is gone. —But he could not believe himself. Just as a gun can become so cold that it slowly burns through your double-lined leather expedition mitts, so the sleeplessness had finally reached him. It seemed to him that he would have no responsibilities anymore. The ice in the sleeping bag would melt, and then he would get in it and sleep and be warm, and then the plane would come. There was nothing to it. He lit the diesel heater as usual. The sleeping bag began to steam promisingly. He closed his eyes. Then he smelled smoke.

* * *

He saved the building fireman-style, by running outside, smashing the window with his ice axe, hurling chunks of snow down against the flaming wall, knocking out a segment of stovepipe, and smothering the fire in the heater itself by cramming in newspapers, snow-chunks, an old boot, and whatever else he could find. When he had finished, the room was a shambles. The floor was slick with diesel oil (it was in his eyes and all over his clothes, which henceforth would insulate him even less efficiently), and it had soaked his gloves, which no doubt contributed to the later state of his fingers, and snow and soot were everywhere. He didn't realize until a long time later that it was then, when he put the fire out, that he lost his eyebrows.

* * *

He got on the radio and called Bradley. There was nothing but static, of course, but he convinced himself that he could hear a voice saying: . . . are you O.K.? . . .

Yes, I'm O.K., he said, but I'm concerned about the diesel on me. I'd like to be picked up tomorrow or the next day, please. Over.

He was very happy now. He knew they'd pick him up tomorrow.

He went back up to Marv's shed with the sleeping bag. He heard children playing outside. It was summer, and they were playing ball. He knew perfectly well that there were no children there, but he enjoyed listening to them. There were two or three of them and they were very excited. He could not hear what they were saying, exactly; they were a hundred yards or so away, playing catch or kickball. He smiled not to be alone.

* * *

He slept a little; he wasn't sure how much; and when he awoke he was so cold that he couldn't even shiver. When he went outside to defecate (a process requiring twenty minutes, thanks to numb fingers, frozen zippers, and brittle shrunken nylon), he felt lumps of ice frozen to his buttocks. He stumbled down to the station and made his breakfast. Then he came back weeping.

There was a propane tank and a little space heater in Marv's shed. Marv had told him he could use it if he had to. To ignite it it was first necessary to open the valve on the tank by about thirty turns—a procedure which hurt his fingers so much that he had to warm them in the middle—then to turn the valve on the heater from off to low, then finally to hold a lighted match to the grille with one hand while pushing in a metal button at the base with the other. It took him about a quarter-hour with his already numbed fingers to get a match to light. By then the fingers were somewhat worse. Pushing the metal button was the worst part. It had to be held for twenty seconds or more, until the grille glowed cherry-pink; and when the heater sputtered it had to be held again. When one joint of his finger had been sufficiently burned by the cold, he'd slide the next joint against it, and then be ready to use the adjoining finger. As he stared at Heater's friendly round face, almost pressing his cheek against her, as he drank in her happy red lattice-face behind the grille, he knew that she was his friend and he knew that his fingers were his friend, sacrificing themselves to save the rest of him, and he did not even wonder what his fingers would be like later because they were only doing what they had to do as Heater's cruel cold button burned them again and again.

He spent all day drying out his sleeping bag. He melted all the ice. He also scorched huge holes in it with his weary hands so that the down started coming out and Marv's shed looked like a chicken factory. He scorched holes in his down parka and in his down pants. When it was evening he had finished. He heard the children again. He got into his sleeping bag with the blankets over him and he was so warm when he heard a woman's voice saying: Get your gun. —he lay there for a long time, wondering why he needed to do that. He had hung it outside so that Heater's warmth wouldn't cause moisture to condense on it. Finally he opened his eyes and decided to get the gun. He saw that the door was wide open. He got up and brought the gun in. Suddenly he saw that he was in his socks and under-gloves. Too late now. He closed the door and got back in his sleeping bag. His hands didn't hurt anymore; they were numb. He couldn't work the zippers on his sleeping bag. He lay there patiently. After awhile two fingers on his left hand began to feel strange. There was nothing to do about it but beat his hands together and be cheerful, which he did. Then he commended himself to GOD in case he didn't wake up, and closed his eyes. He seemed to see an angel, who wanted him to come up with her. He told her that he had someone he wanted to marry and be with awhile; he wasn't ready to come with her yet. The angel was disappointed, but let him back down. He could see her crying as she flew away.

It was 7:00 P.M. At ten he awoke shivering. He tried Heater but she wouldn't glow. He hurt his fingers a great deal trying. But the effort warmed him a little, and he went back to sleep. That night he awoke twice with numb hands and feet, but he exercised in the sleeping bag until feeling returned to them, and then he was able to sleep again. He told himself that when the sun came up he'd go down to the station and have a hot breakfast. (His way of comforting himself in Marv's shed was to promise himself food-warmth at the station. His way of comforting himself at the station was to promise himself sleeping-bag-warmth in Marv's shed. He always believed his own propaganda. What actually kept him the warmest was going from one place to the other.)

* * *

That next morning it was -40°, which was the coldest yet. This temperature is not exceptionally cold if one's sleeping gear and clothes are warm. But even the Inuit do not go out in it for prolonged periods of time. They stop frequently for tea breaks in heated shelters. In this case, there was no access to any heat source. The heater didn't work; the diesel stove was wrecked; the sleeping bag, while dry, at least, remained marginal.

He couldn't get warm.

There was a light wind. He went walking in it to try to warm up, and the corners of his eyes went dead in the facemask. The facemask itself was now so frozen that his breath could not get through it, and his face was cold and wet.

He walked down to the station and had breakfast. Taking the facemask off was so horrible that he wished he'd skipped it. Putting the facemask back on was almost as bad.

He walked back up to Marv's shed, just to do something that would warm him up so that he could think. His mind was stifled and coiled in upon itself. He paced the runway, and each lap made him colder and colder.

He decided to get back into his sleeping bag to wait it out.

He went into the shed and took a look at the sleeping bag there, shriveled like a frozen squid, and the squalid darkness with the frost on the walls and ceiling, and he felt an unbearable repulsion, and went to walk the runway once more, and then as he drew near Marv's shed again something told him that if he entered that shivering bag of ice it would be his grave. He decided to go back down to the station again. Maybe his mind would clear on the way.

His fingers were dead. He kissed them through the ice-filled mitts. His fingers, hands, zippers were all each other's friends.

He took the shovel with him, but not the gun. The gun was too cold. Digging out a building full of moldy mattresses, he lay on top of one and pulled another on top of himself to see what would happen. Pretty soon he started to shiver. It wasn't too surprising; the mattresses were frozen inside.

He got up and looked into a room with a sign on the door that said URINAL—PLEASE DON'T USE UNLESS YOU HAVE TO. Under the urinal was a mountain of yellow ice.

He went outside into the sun and started to laugh. After all, it would be pretty stupid to die in a place full of shelter, fuel and matches. Why, if need be he could burn down all the buildings for warmth, one at a time!

He kept laughing, and it seemed to him that he had never been in any danger.

He went to the dormitory building and made himself some soup. He hated pulling the facemask off to drink it, but so what. He drew his underglove across his running nose, and the glove froze instantly. He swallowed the last cold mouthful of soup. Holding his breath, he pulled the crumpled mask of ice back on so that once again he had eyes inside his own skull to see the inside of his nose, garnished with crystals, and far below he could look out his own mouth and see snow at the edge of the light. He wandered into the balloon shed and found a soccer ball and started kicking it and it danced ahead of him and he followed, kicking it and laughing, and the soccer ball rolled down and down and came to the edge of the polar sea and he kicked it and it shot across the snowy ice and he went after it, loving the fog-hued ice stricken with blue riddlings, kicking the ball between the hard low swellings of that endless sea-plain that resembled bluish-white plaster irregularly daubed, and the world opened up wider and wider before him with all its goodness; he traversed the blue-white sheets of ecstasy, kicking the ball toward an ice-mountain he'd never reach and he was happy.

* * *

The next morning it had warmed up to -22° and he felt quite warm. He went down to the station and shouted: *I'm as tough as nails!*

* * *

When he got into the sleeping bag that night, he could actually hear his clothing freeze with a *ping!* and then he felt a sharp cold itch, like the bite of a mosquito from Pluto. To distract himself he composed more Arctic Rules, such as:

1. Never wear an inner glove too thick to brush ice from your eyelashes and also pick your nose.

2. Keep your crotch unzipped in the sleeping bag to warm your hands. (Masturbation at low temperatures, however, is most unrewarding.)
3. It's better to wipe your ass with chunks of snow than to fumble with unmitted fingers for toilet paper.

* * *

It was a white day of fine snow which muffled even the silence. The only way to tell sky from ground was that the sky was not marred by his footprints. The barometric pressure was still falling. Maybe the storm would come tomorrow. The sun was a pale yellow egg easy to look on, a polished stone buckle in a belt of light that split the foggy sky. Ice crystals tinkled in his parka-ruff as he paced the hills. The breeze began to be a wind, and the barometer fell steadily. He watched the snow fall on his black mitts in tiny white crystals—

* * *

He'd tried blankets under the sleeping bag and blankets over the sleeping bag. Now he finally wrapped a blanket around himself inside the sleeping bag, and he was almost warm. He could sleep for four or five hours at a stretch now without shivering, then wake up cold, exercise, and go back to sleep. This discovery seemed to him to be very important. He told himself that his next bag would be a custom bag, wool-lined; the wool liners would be replaceable and there'd be a VBL between them and the down; he had it all worked out. This occupied him at night whenever he shivered.

* * *

Touching a bit of chocolate even through his expedition mitts and four layers of glove beneath now made his fingers ache for five minutes afterward. He hunched in a ball against the cold. He knew that cold was only a negation, not a substance, but what sharp teeth it had! It was so cold that steam fell instead of rising.

Blue ground, white sky, white ground, blue sky, and so it went on forever.

The cold crept between his outstretched fingers. Even when he warmed them one at a time, it bit the side of his hand. He started shivering in the small of his back, and between his shoulder blades. It was worse when his belly was cold, too, when his heart and kidneys were cold.

He walked through a beautiful stretch of snow-hills bathed at their bases in snow-white fog; it was so cold (especially with the breeze) that his nose went numb on its first breath.

Heater glowed today. The sound of the ignition rivaled Wagner's opening E-flat major.

* * *

Night. The radio was silent as always. The wind, which earlier had whistled in two tones, now breathed darkly in long hard breaths, not far away, not near, raging down the snow-hills, now getting a little louder, a little closer; its ice-breath came foaming in through the crack in the door. The temperature dropped rapidly. The septum between his nostrils stung with cold when he breathed. His first shiver was not really a shiver. It happened somewhere near his backbone; his muscles scarcely moved. But the real spasm was not far off. His hands and feet were getting cold now. Most of his bodily integrity remained intact—but, ah, now the cold slid a long skinny finger under his parka and flicked once at his heart. That was nothing, really, just a reminder of what the cold wanted to do in the end. His waist was quite cold now, where the parka ended. His belly jerked, but that was still not a real shiver. Now his eyelids became infected, and began to transmit the cold into his skull. His hands would soon be numb. The wind was at the door now, really and fully. He began to shiver.

* * *

. . . And she said: are you coming to me? and he said yes and she laughed with joy and shouted: *I'm happy, happy!*

* * *

The next day was the day the plane was scheduled to come, and it did not come. He'd packed everything up, which took him a long time, and paced the runway until the wind got his cheeks through the eyeholes of his facemask and frost-bit them. Then he went into the shed again. He did not want to go to the station to cook in case the plane came, and it wouldn't be safe to light his stove inside the shed. So he ate his food raw, food without moisture in it, like cereal, that couldn't freeze no matter how cold it was. Maybe everyone else in the world was dead. After all, something like that had to happen sometime. How long could he hope to live alone? It would be his obligation to live as long as he could. There was no way that he could hope to go the 518 kilometers to Resolute. It wasn't permanent pack ice all the way; he'd be bound to fall through a hole in the frozen sea. More to the point, he didn't know the exact angle he'd need to keep the North Star at to get there. He'd have to stick it out here. If everyone else was dead and rotting, how long? The main problem was going to be drinking water. He would run short of matches first. He had used five or six times more of them than he'd expected. When he was down to a dozen matches or so, he'd have to figure out some way to nurse his flame slowly and sweetly. He did not really need to cook his food. But he did need water. Most likely he would die of thirst. The second stove might last another day or two. Then he could make a stove of sorts of the sterno cans. He had plenty of gasoline for another week, but it would probably be safer to use diesel. So tomorrow he'd better make a stove out of some scavenged can punched with holes and crammed with diesel-soaked rags; he'd have to keep that smoldering day and night . . . No, there was a lake not far from here. The ice on it was supposed to be eight or nine feet thick, the weather people had said. He might be able to chop through that for his water, so that fuel and matches could be saved. But then he'd have no shelter. He'd have to build a snowhouse. Who knows, maybe he could last through April, taking heart as the temperature edged up; maybe he could even make it until the summer. His food could last him a very long time if he were careful. Of course, he'd be getting weak on those rations. Maybe there was something else in the station, some stale chocolate bars or something . . . Ah, yes, the frozen scallops. And when the summer finally came, what then? In the days when they manned the station, they'd had to lay down planks between the buildings in the summer, because the island was nothing but mud then. And no animals; nothing to eat. And if he somehow did survive, then it would be winter again . . .

* * *

After returning to the landing strip with a load from the station, he inspected himself in his compass mirror for frostbite, and saw the usual amusing sight. One eye, which he'd squinted, had frozen shut, bearing snow-blossoms on the clustered lashes, for all the world like soapberry blooms. His eyebrows were also white-starred (so thickly that he did not yet realize that he had no eyebrows anymore). The lashes of his left eye were stiff, white, regularly spaced. Below his red nose, white grass-tufts of moustache and mucus grew onto his upper lip. His hair (what he could see of it outside the balaclava) was like frozen reindeer club moss.

* * *

There was a mountain straight ahead of him, soft, white and saddle-shaped. Its base was shaded in snow as in a fog. Above it, nary a cloud. He decided to walk toward it. He'd never have the chance again. The new-exposed strata of snow were hard and off-white like gypsum. There were lemming-tracks in the snow. He followed them. They paused in a wide and shallow hole in which the animal had left urine and a few specks of excrement like sunflower seeds, and then they went on and then a fox track joined them and then both tracks ended suddenly in the new-blown snow. As he walked toward the beautiful mountain, he was suddenly filled with pity for everything in the world, and he cried.

* * *

The following lavender winter morning at half-past four, he saw a lemming scuttle across the snow. The moon was astonishingly bright and yellow. His hands were very cold that day. He didn't dare take off his undergloves to look at them.

* * *

The plane didn't come, and he'd given up and had gone to the station when he heard it coming. There'd been problems with bad weather. As for the radio silence, that had only been sunspots—

* * *

If we were to add to his Arctic Rules a prescription or two against the difficulties that he suffered (all this being typed with fingers that feel as if a thick and invisible layer of tingly velvet lies between them and the world), we might say:

1. Nylon is almost worthless in the cold. So is most plastic. That includes sleeping bags, backpacks that are supposedly good enough for Antarctica, stove pumps, goggle lenses, jumpsuits, parkas, VBLs, you name it. (An exception is polyethylene. Freezer bags become stiff in the cold but not brittle.)
2. Next time, stick to sealskins and caribou skins.

A beautiful blonde came up on the plane, just for the ride. She was managing Pam Flowers's fourth solo attempt on the Pole. She knew Steger. When he showed her his Steger Designs expedition mitts, she said: But Will didn't take those to the Pole. He took beaver mitts.

Oh, he said.

And an Inuk looked at the mitts and said politely: Not bad for a day hike.

* * *

An Inuk girl called him tough when she saw his frostbitten fingers. But he wasn't, really. Consider the despised workhorse, Back, whom Mr Franklin sent on a fool's errand to the Great Slave Lake one winter, Back the plodding, the loser in love, Back the tedious, whose best smile was a bray of big teeth, who was willing to pay the highest price to oblige his loved Commander. Upon the completion of his commission, Back wrote, without either arrogance or false modesty: *I had the pleasure of meeting my friends all in good health, after an absence of nearly five months, during which time I had travelled one thousand four hundred and four miles, on snow shoes, and had no other covering at night, in the woods, than a blanket and deer-skin, with the thermometer frequently at -40° [Fahrenheit], and once at -57°; and sometimes passing two or three days without tasting food.* —Subzero's twelve days of anxiety were, it is true, passed without company, and largely without heat, while Back was never alone and sometimes had a fire. In addition, Back's caribou-skin might well have been warmer than Subzero's failed goosedown bag (the Inuit consider down to be almost useless for winter camping, and he had known that and should have listened to them). Nonetheless, while Subzero did not do terribly, he did not do well, either. His mistakes were all committed at the beginning, when he made false choices. The new sleeping bag, which there was no way to test in advance, led directly to his shivering, hence to his sleep deprivation, hence to his hallucinations. If he had died it would have been his own fault. It is possible, indeed even probable, that if Subzero had gone into the country with a knowledgeable Inuk, just as Back travelled with knowledgeable voyageurs and Indians, then he might have equaled Back in caliber. While not as physically fit as Back, perhaps, he did possess a high degree of endurance to discomfort. And no matter what phantasms he heard and saw, he never lost sight of his own self. —But all that was unimportant, because he did not equal Back. Mr Franklin, who perhaps was as frightened of Back as he was of anything, suffered the same failing. Mr Franklin did not learn from those who knew.

The Water of Life

From *Imperial*

Taken from a chapter from his nonfiction work-in-progress about Imperial Valley, this excerpt omits nearly fifteen additional pages about the levels of selenium and other toxins found in the Salton Sea. A different, heavily edited and rearranged version of this same material appeared in *Outside Magazine* as "Where the Ghost Bird Sings by the Poison Springs" (later included in Ian Frazier's *Best American Travel Writing* [2003]). Vollmann's account of two trips he made in July 2000 along the notoriously noxious, foul-smelling New River becomes the starting point for an extended meditation about the role that water plays in permitting life to exist in one of the hottest and driest places on earth (only Death Valley rivals it in North America). Flowing northward across the Mexicali and Imperial Valleys toward its eventual destination at the Salton Sea, the New River had for thousands of years provided life-sustaining water to Native Americans who settled in the area. But the allusion in Vollmann's chapter title is ironic, for by the time he sets out in a flimsy rubber dinghy, the river is less a source of life than of toxic wastes—due to the raw sewage and industrial-strength chemicals being dumped, untreated, into it from the Mexican side of the border. I'd made the error of repeating to Bill the reports I'd heard that the New River was in fact "the most polluted river in North America," and that for many years no one had been crazy enough to even think about riding a boat in it—a warning that of course served as an irresistible enticement for him, who thereafter wouldn't be content until he'd personally tested the waters. Another engagement prevented me from joining Vollmann on the first, more dangerous leg of the trip, but I joined him the next day for the glorious adventure depicted here—and only glowed just a little in the dark afterward. —LM.

. . . And let him who is thirsty come; let him who desires take the water of life without any price.

—From Revelations 22:17

In the year **1997,** the town of North Shore, a shuttered, graffiti'd, ruined resort which, as you might have guessed, lies on the northern edge of the Salton Sea, was not very different from the way it would be in 2000, the beach literally comprised of barnacles, fish bones, fish scales, fish corpses and bird corpses whose symphonic accompaniment consisted of an almost unbearable ammoniac stench like rancid urine magnified. Fish carcasses in rows and rows, more sickening stenches, the underfoot-crunch of white cheek-plates like seashells—oh, rows and banks of whiteness, banks of vertebrae; feathers and vertebrae twitching in the water almost within reach of the occasional half-mummified bird, such were the basic elements of that district. Meanwhile, the dock was crowded with *live* birds—longnecked white pelicans, I think. Their coexistence with the dead ones jarred me, but then, so did the broken concrete, the **PRIVATE PROPERTY** sign (last vestige of Americanism), the playground slide half-sunk in barnacle-sand. Could it be that everything on this world remains so fundamentally pure that nothing can ever be more than half ruined? This purity is particularly undeniable as expressed in the shimmer on the Salton Sea, which is sometimes dark blue, sometimes infinitely white, and always pitted with desert light.

In 1999 it had been worse—seven and a half million African perch died on a single August day—and in 2001 it happened to be better, on my two visits at least. Oh, death was still there, but matter had been ground down to sub-matter, just as on other beaches coarse sand gets gradually ground fine. The same dead scales, the barnacles licked at by waves of a raw sienna color richly evil in its algal depths, set the tone, let's say: crunch, crunch. Without great difficulty I spied the black mouth of a dead fish, then after an interval another black mouth, barnacles, a dead bird, and then of all things another black mouth; here lay wilted feathers in heaps of barnacles; here was a rotting fish covered with barnacles, but at least there were those intervals between them; the dead birds were fewer; there must not have been any great die-offs lately.* Scum and bubbles in the water's brownishness reminded me that it's not always wise to examine ideality up close. The far shore remained as beautiful as ever. When each shore is a far shore, when Imperial defines itself gradually through its long boxcars, hills, palm orchards, vineyards, and the blue pallor of the Salton Sea beyond, then the pseudo-Mediterranean look of the west side as seen from the east side (rugged blue mountains, birds, a few boats) shimmers into full believability. Come closer, and a metallic taste alights upon your stinging lips. Stay awhile, and you might win a sore throat, an aching compression of the chest as if from smog, or honest nausea. I was feeling queasy on that April evening in 2001, but over the charnel a cool breeze played, and a Hispanic family** approached the water's edge, the children running happily, sinking ankle-deep into scales and barnacles, nobody expressing any botheration about the stench or the relics underfoot. For them, perhaps, this was "normal." I stepped over another dead fish, proof that the Coachella Valley Historical Society's recent pamphlet was right on the mark: the Salton Sea, it informed me, was *one of the best and liveliest fishing areas on the West Coast. Stories of a polluted Salton Sea are greatly exaggerated . . . The real problem is too much salt . . .* In 1994 the author took a drive around the sea with her husband (she'd avoided it for thirty-five years, *believing the largely negative articles in newspapers and magazines depicting its sorry decline)*, and experienced *a wonderful sense of what is right with the world.*

PRELUDE TO A RIVER CRUISE

How many Salton Seas on this planet already lay poisoned—if they were poisoned—for the long term? The Aral Sea? Love Canal? Lake Baikal? Would their new normality become normative for the rest of

*According to Tom Kirk of the Salton Sea Authority, the birds were dying mostly from avian cholera, botulism, and Newcastle's disease. —"We seem to have far too many of these," he said to me in 2001. "But keep this in mind. Twenty thousand birds died at the Salton Sea last year. That's less than one percent of the bird population."

**The woman who used to share Imperial with me remembered them as an Asian family.

us? How badly off was the Salton Sea, really? One book published five years after that Coachella Valley Historical Society pamphlet described the Salton Sea as a *stinking reddish-brown sump rapidly growing too rancid for even the hardiest ocean fish. By 1996 the sea had become a deathtrap for birds . . . They died by the thousands. The coordinator of the [human] birth defect study admitted that her team was stumped by whatever was causing the deformities in the area.* But the authors of that book were not stumped at all. The Salton Sea has three inflows: the Alamo River, in whose bamboo rushes Border Patrol agents play out their pretend-Vietnam cat-and-mouse exercises with illegal immigrants; the rather irrelevant Whitewater River, which flows in from the northwest not far from Valerie Jean's Date Shakes*; and our chief subject, the New River, which, we're told, *claims the distinction of being the filthiest stream in the nation. Picking up the untreated sewage, landfill leachate, and industrial wastes from the Mexican boomtown of Mexicali, the New River swings north to receive the salt, selenium, and pesticides running off the fields of the Imperial Valley . . . It dead-ends in the Salton Sea . . .* There you have it, but according to that confederation of counties and water districts called the Salton Sea Authority, what you have is no more than *Myth #5: "The Sea is a Toxic Dump Created by Agriculture."* The Facts: Pesticides are not found at any significant level in the Sea. Moreover, selenium levels are only one-fifth of the federal standard, and (if I may quote from the rebuttal to Myth # 4), *water carried by the New River from Mexico is not a major contributor to the Sea's problems*. Reading this, I began to wonder, as this leaflet put it, *then what are the Sea's actual problems? The Facts,* and here come the facts: *Bird disease outbreaks* get freely confessed, and if that phrasing sounds euphemistic, well, who am I to say that the stinking bird corpses at North Shore are any "worse" than, say, the sweet-stenched feedlots, with mottled black-and-white cattle almost motionless under metal awnings? Those creatures likewise are destined for death. The next sad fact is *fluctuating surface levels,* which I take to be a reference to Bombay Beach's half-submerged houses getting sunk in salty sand, the mostly submerged Torres-Matinez Indian reservation,

*The Audobon Society's spokesman Fred Cagle characterized the Alamo's fifty-two miles of water to me as "all irrigation runoff" and the Whitewater as "like the Alamo but less of it."

the drowned buildings of North Shore and Salton City. Finally come (and we may as well put them all in a row, since they amount to the same thing) *nutrient-rich water, algal blooms and fish kills.* To me, this phenomenon, which ecologists call eutrophication, seems symptomatic of *Myth #5: "The Sea is a Toxic Dump Created by Agriculture."* What else but fertilizer runoff could produce that "nutrient-rich water?" (Now that I think of it, Mexican sewage in the New River could.) The Salton Sea Authority mentions only a single cause for any of these problems, the one everybody agrees on: salinity—twenty-five percent higher than that of the ocean. Needless to say, salinity cannot explain algal blooms. But, to get right down to it, *we do not know all there is to know about the sea.* There again you have it.

I decided to undertake a course of aquatic exploration. Specifically, I thought to ride the New River, which I'd never heard of anybody doing. How navigable it was, how dangerous or disgusting it might be, not a soul could tell. My acquaintances in Imperial County said that yes, it did sound like a stupid thing to do, but probably not that unsafe; the worst that would likely happen to me was sickness. As for the Border Patrol, they advised against it, calling it "extremely dangerous" and incidentally promising me that should I cross from Southside to Northside by means of the New River, I'd infallibly be arrested.

MEMORY-HOLES

The New River curves and jitters in a backwards "S" sixty miles long from the Mexican border to an estuary (if I may call it that) of the Salton Sea equidistant from the towns of Calipatria and Westmorland. On a map of Imperial County, the towns and road-crossings of its progress are traced in blue, right down to the last demisemiquaver. We know, or think we do, exactly what, or at least where, the New River is. But immediately southward of Calexico's stubby fan palms in bank parking lots, pawn shops, and Spanish voices, runs a heavy line which demarcates the end of California and the United States of America, which is to say the beginning of Mexico, and specifically of the state of Baja California. Here the New River becomes the Rio Nuevo, and if we try to follow it upstream, it vanishes from all but one of the maps I've ever seen, each time in a different way.

Of course it comes from the Colorado River, said everyone I asked in Imperial County. *All* water here comes from the Colorado.

Mexicans, on the other hand, assured me that the New River began somewhere near San Felipe, which lies a mere two hours south of the border by car. They said that the Rio Nuevo had nothing to do with the Colorado River at all.

My plan was to cross into Mexicali, get a taxi to take me to the source, wherever it was, hire a boat, and ride downstream as far as I could. But now that I sought to zero in on the mysterious spot (excuse me, Señor, but where exactly does it start?), people began to say that the river commenced in Mexicali itself, in one of the Parques Industriales, where a certain Xochimilco Lagoon, which in turn derived from Laguna Mexico, defined my Shangri-La. How could I take the cruise? Moreover, the municipal authorities of Mexicali were even now pressing on into the fifth year of a very fine project—namely, to entomb and forget the Rio Nuevo, sealing it off underground beneath a cement wall in the median strip of the new highway, whose name happened to be Boulevard Rio Nuevo and which was a hot, white double ribbon of street adorned by dirt and tires, an upended car, broken things. Along this median they'd sunk segments of a long, long concrete tube which lay inconspicuous in the dirt; and between some of these segments were gratings, sometimes lifted, and beneath *them* lay square pits, with jet-black water flowing below, exuding a fierce sewer-stench which could almost be some kind of cheese—yes, cheese and death, for actually it smelled like the bones in the catacombs of Paris.

What were some of the treasures which the Rio Nuevo might be carrying to the United States today? The following chart gives a hint:

DISEASE RATES (per 100,000)

Disease	U.S. Average	Calif.-Mexican Border	Mexican Average
Amebiasis	1.34	1.38	798.8
Hepatitis A	12.6	37.1	50.1
Shigellosis	10.9	35.3	?
Typhoid	0.2	0.4	36.1

Source: Environmental Protection Agency

(The North American Development Bank, the Border Cooperation Commission, the U.S. Environmental Protection Agency and various other such entities were helping to lead Mexico into a bright new day with a wastewater treatment facility, a pumping plant, and God knows what else. Nobody I talked to seemed to have much idea about any of it.)

A yellow truck sat roaring as its sewer hose, dangling deep down into the Rio Nuevo, sucked up a measure of the effluvium of eight hundred thousand people. This liquid, called by the locals *aguas negras,* would be used in concrete mixing. Beside the truck were two wise shade-loungers in white-dusted boots, baseball caps and sunglasses. I asked what was the most interesting thing they could tell me about the Rio Nuevo, and they thought for awhile and finally said that they'd seen a dead body in it last Saturday. The one who was the supervisor, Señor Jose Rigoberto Cruz Córdoba, explained that the purpose of this concrete shield was to end the old practice of spewing untreated sewage into the river, and maybe he even believed this; maybe it was even true. The assistant engineer whom I interviewed at the civic center a week later said that they'd already found hundreds of clandestine pipes which they were sealing off. He was very plausible, even though he, like so many others, sent me far wrong on my search for the headwaters of the New River. Well, why wouldn't they be sealing those pipes off? My translator for that day, a man who like most Mexicans did not pulse with idealism about civic life, interpreted the policy thus: See, they know who the big polluters are. They're all American companies or else Mexican millionaires. They'll just go to them and say, we've closed off your pipe. You can either pay us and we'll make you another opening right now, or else you're going to have to do it yourself with jackhammers and risk a much higher fine . . . —No doubt he was right. The clandestine pipes would soon be better hidden than ever, and subterranean spillways could vomit new poisons.*

*Here is a revealing excerpt from a California Environmental Protection Agency report. An EPA delegation crossed the border for a conference with Victor Hermosilio, the Mayor of Mexicali, specifically "to discuss New River issues." One of those issues was "monitoring of underground storm drains entering the New River concrete encasement project—prior verification of sewage spills into the New River from these storm drains was possible visually, *but can no longer be accomplished since the entire system is underground*" (my italics).

The generator ran and the Rio Nuevo stank. The yellow truck was almost full. Smiling pleasantly, Señor Córdoba remarked: I heard that people used to fish and swim and bathe here thirty years ago.

Perhaps even thirty years ago the river hadn't been quite so nice as that, or perhaps people had fewer opportunities back then to be particular about where they bathed, for that night, at a taxi stand right in sight of the river, while a squat, very Indian-looking dispatcher lady in a sporty sweatshirt sat shouting into a box the size of a microwave, with the radio crackling like popcorn while the drivers sat at picnic tables under a sheetmetal awning, the old timers told me how it had been twenty-five years ago. They'd always called it the Rio Conca, which was short for the Rio con Cagada, the River with Shit. Twenty-five years ago, the water level was lower because there'd been fewer irrigation canals to feed into the watercourse, and the drivers used to play soccer here. When they saw turds floating by, they just laughed and jumped over them. The turds had floated like *tortugas,* they said, like turtles; and indeed they used to see real turtles here twenty-five years ago. Now they saw no animals at all.

Where does most of the sewage come from? I asked Señor Córdoba.

From the factories and from clandestine pollutants. It's a good thing that we're making this tube, so that now it'll just be natural sewage.

After the first hour, I began to get a sore throat. The two sisters who were translating for me felt nauseous. After the second hour, so did I. (Maybe this wasn't entirely the Rio Nuevo's fault; the temperature that day was 114°F.) Even now as I write this I can smell that stench. Well, in another year or two it would be out of mind—in Mexico, at least. I remember coming back near that place at twilight, and finding a sepulcher-shaped opening between highway lanes, a crypt attended by a single pale-green weed, with the cheesy shit-smell rising from that greenish-black water which sucked like waves or tides. More concrete whale-ribs lay ready in the dust; soon this memory-hole also would be sealed. The assistant engineer at Centro Civico said that his colleagues hoped to bury 5.6 kilometers more by the end of the year . . .

CALL IT GREEN
(PART 1)

The taxi driver followed the Rio Nuevo as well as he could. Sometimes the street was fenced off for construction, and sometimes the river ran mysteriously underground, but he always found it again. We could always smell it before we could see it. Now it disappeared again, beneath a wilderness of PEMEX gas stations. At Xochimilco Lagoon, liquid was coming out of pipes, and foaming into the sickly stinking greenness between tamarisk trees. The water didn't just stink; it reeked. Then it vanished into a culvert. Old men told me how clear it used to be twenty years ago. Twenty years past, people swam in it. At Mexico Lagoon the sight and the tale were much the same.

The end, said the taxi driver, smiling with pride at his English.

That, so I thought, was all of the Rio Nuevo I could ever see except for the federal zone where, in a gulley overlooked by low yellow houses and white houses and dirt-colored house-cubes, the northernmost extremity of the river had been fenced off from the public, and by the same logic allowed to run stinkingly free; the water here was very green.

A digression on greenness: Up the western gulleyside a block or two, on the poor-hill which could be seen from the street by the Thirteen Negro dancehall, a legless man, Señor Ramón Flores, was sitting in the porch-shade of his little yellow house on Michoacan Avenue. He used to be a taxi driver; another driver said that diabetes had done for his legs. —I've been here since 1937, he said. I've always lived in this house. I remember the Rio Nuevo. —Raising his hands like a conductor, outstretching his fingers like rain, he sighed happily: It's always been green! There were *cachanillas* and tule plants. They were all over the Rio Nuevo, but they're not there anymore. And I remember how in 1952 the river overflowed. People were camping around it then, in Colonia Pueblo Nuevo. The gringos threw water into the river on purpose so that people would get out of the area. So the government moved them from Colonia Pueblo Nuevo to Colonia Baja California . . .

So the *cachanillas* and the tule plants are gone, you said. How about the smell? Does it smell any worse than it used to?

Oh, it's always smelled that way, but in the summer it's worse. Have some more mescal. You know, down south there's another kind of mescal that's stronger; three shots and you're in ecstasy; four shots will knock you out.

Thanks, Señor Flores, I will, and we enjoyed a long slow conversation on the subject of exactly why it was that Chinese food in Mexicali tasted different from Chinese food in Tijuana, until the hot evening breeze sent another whiff of Rio Nuevo my way, prompting me to inquire: Do you have any problems with the smell? Does it ever make you sick?

We're used to it, he said proudly.

Does it always smell like sewage, or is there sometimes a chemical smell?

No, it just smells like shit.

Do you think it's justice for the gringos that you send your sewage to America?

They asked for it, he laughed. They use it for fertilizer.

A Border Patrolman told me that the Rio Nuevo will strip paint off metal. Do you think that's true or is it just propaganda?

Oh, that's true, he said contentedly.

Yes, the water was very green, no matter that an elegant woman in leopard-skin pants who'd lived beside the river for twenty years in the slum called Condominios Montealban shook her long dark hair and said: Green? No green. No brown, no black. No color. Just dirty. —White foam-clots drifted down its surface as tranquilly as lamb's-fleece clouds, but it was green, call it green, and green trees attended it right to the rusty border wall, where as I stood gazing at the river one of the two Mexican sisters pointed in the other direction; and between a painting of the Trinity and a gilded tire from which other *pollos* began their illegal leap, half a dozen young men came running from a graffiti'd building to swarm up over the wall, forming that graceful human snake I knew so well, the first man being lifted over by the last, all of them linked, then the ones who were already over pulling the last ones over and down into the United States, while one of the sisters, Susana the gentle sickly one, watched sadly from the taxi, while the other, Rebeca the dance choreographer, crossed herself and said a prayer for them.

CALL IT GREEN
(PART 2)

But *nobody* seemed to know where the New River came from. Mr. Jose Angel, Branch Chief of the Regional Water Control Board up in Palm Desert, seemed to think it was from sixteen miles south of Mexicali, he didn't exactly know the place.

Fitting his fingertips together, the assistant engineer at Centro Civico mentioned "natural springs." He drew me a map which located these springs on the side of a squarish volcano called Cerro Prieto, which was located due west of Mexicali on the Tijuana road. A drain then carried the natural springs' contribution to civilization meanderingly southwest and then southeast to Laguna México, which as I've said drained into Laguna Xochimilco, so my driver for that day sped me off most of the way to Tecate before we found out that actually Cerro Prieto was due south of Mexicali, not sixteen miles as Jose Angel had said, but sixteen kilometers, so we careened back to take a southward turn on the San Felipe road, crossing the Rio Nuevo once at 5.8 kilometers; and we kept on across the Colorado delta sands until from the direction of the broad purple volcano there came a faint but mucilaginous stink. Near the town of Nuevo Leon, trailers and gates marked out the restricted geothermal station; and in a certain air-conditioned office, an engineer looked up from the blueprints on his glass-topped table and said: As far as I know, it has no connection with the Colorado River.

Well, it was true that no direct connection existed. On the last of his blueprints, the one I'd craved to see, the Rio Nuevo evidently began in a complex spiderweb of wriggling agricultural drains in Baja California's hot olive-drab and yellow-drab flatscape, for instance Dren Collector del Norte, Dren Xochimilco and Dren Ferrocarril, the last so called because it partly followed the course of the railroad tracks. We went to Ejido Hidalgo to discover, insofar as we could, the source of Dren Ferrocarril, and found restricted areas of white, sulphurous steam erupting on the horizon between a latticework of pipes, everything guarded by shrugging sentries who had no authorization even to call anybody and who had never heard of the Rio Nuevo. And now for the nearest of the natural springs, oh, yes, here it was: a cement-walled canal in which liquid of an insanely phosphorescent bluish-white glowed in the sun.

MEDITATIONS OVER ANOTHER HOLE

In the United States, the New River is more or less denied and avoided; in Mexico, they were doing what they could to achieve the same bliss; for now, though, the Rio Nuevo remained a part of the human landscape. Begin, for instance, with the wildly spicy-sour smell of a shop which sold dried chilis; then came a concrete ruin, scarcely even a foundation anymore, advertising itself for rent, after which, at the intersection of Calle Mariano Escobedo and Avenida Miguel Hidalgo, the street dipped down into a pale-dry gulley of trees, houses, warehouses, taco stands, this view being centered by the following grime-stained red-on-yellow caption:

Hacienda S.A.
FABRICA DE TORTILLAS

and in this dip there ran two blue-grey dust-sugared ribbons of asphalt between which there seemed to be something resembling a segmented overturned bathtub of endless length; I could see darkness between the segments here and there; that was all. Pedestrians toiled across the dirt; garbage, especially plastic jugs, adorned it; and beside me, from a little trailer with a prison-barred window, a woman's hand every now and then flung out new garbage: a plastic plate with red rice stuck on it, a plastic bag of something, a used condom.

Early one evening, the heat stinging my nose and forehead almost deliciously, I descended back into that gully, half-crossed the road which so many people hoped and believed would be the new straight shot to Calexico, found a square hole, and peered down into it, wondering whether I would stand a chance if anybody lowered me and a raft into it, and while I considered the matter, my latest taxi driver, who enjoyed flirting with my translator, stood on a mound of dirt and recited "El Ruego" by the Chilean poetess Gabriela Mistral. Thus Mexico, where the most obscene feculence cannot prevail over art. —The current appeared to be extremely strong, and there was no predicting where I would end up. At best I'd be washed out into the federal restricted area by the border, where I'd probably get arrested, since even after seeing my press credentials the Mexicans had denied me entry. Should there be any sort of underground barrier, my raft would smash into it. I'd probably capsize and eventually starve, choke or drown, for I didn't think I could swim against that speeding current whose stench was now making me gag, and even if I could, I didn't see how I could clamber up out of any hole. Just to be sure, I knocked on a few doors at Condominios Montealban, whose grimy concrete apartments, home to poor people, *polleros,* prostitutes and car thieves, stood a few steps away. How bad did they think it would be if one had to take a swim?

Well, the kids have respiratory problems just from living here, said one lady who was standing in the broken courtyard. They have coughs, and on the skin some dimples and rashes. There used to be nothing but a fence here. *Pollos* would go in. We used to see them swimming. They used to die. Some of them made it to America, I don't know how many. Now in the Rio Nuevo we see only dead people. They throw people in it like trash. Sometimes it's gays. Two months ago we found a body in there. He was naked. I saw the police and the ambulance, but I didn't go there because I don't wanna look at those things.

How about you? I asked a Chinese woman. Does the river ever make *you* sick?

A year ago, when they tubed this section, we stopped smelling it. I don't know anybody who's gotten sick.

(Some of the taxi drivers at that dispatch stand used to get sick from the Rio Nuevo, they'd told me, but it was better now. None of them got sick from it anymore.)

I went to some knowing-looking, money-hungry, daredevil teenagers who sat in the shade of the old stone lion and asked whether any of them would be willing to ride underground in the Rio Nuevo with me. They shook their heads sorrowfully and said: No oxygen.

That settled it. Since I couldn't spend my own death benefits, I decided to begin my little cruise in America.

FIRST RIVER CRUISE

Señor Jose Lopez, who clerked at the motel where I was staying in Calexico, was an ex-Marine with a cheerful, steady, slightly impersonal can-do attitude. When I told him nobody seemed willing to take me on the New River or even to rent me a rowboat, he proposed that I go to one of those warehouse-style chain stores that now infested the United States and buy myself an inflatable dinghy. I asked whether he would keep me company, and he scarcely hesitated. —Anyway, he said, it will be something to tell our grandchildren about.

The store sold two-person, three-person and four-person rafts. I got the four-person variety for maximum buoyancy (since, as I've said, the idea of capsizing in the New River scarcely appealed to me), selected two medium-priced wooden oars, paid $70, and felt good about the bargain. That evening at dusk, driving past the inky silhouettes of hay bales, I revisited the spot where the New River came through the gap in the border wall and, gazing back into that federal-restricted area in Mexico, I thought some more about what I was about to do, wondering whether I could prepare any better than I had. It was 115°F then, and sweat pattered down from my forehead onto the film holders. Nobody had any idea how many of the New River's sixty American-miles might be navigable; the Border Patrol (one of whose white vehicles now hunched just across the river, watching me) had simply advised me not to attempt any such thing because it was "dangerous."

I'd prevailed upon Jose to bring his father from Mexicali. The old man would drive Jose's truck and wait for us at each crossing of the road that he could, always going ahead rather than behind, so that if we had to walk in the heat, we'd be sure of which direction to go. If we waved one arm at him, he'd know to drive to the next bridge. Two arms would mean that we were in trouble.

I worried about two possibilities. The first and most likely but least immediately serious eventuality was that we might get poisoned by the New River. Should this happen, most likely we'd have a grace period of several hours to achieve the next meeting point before any ill effects overwhelmed us both. The second peril, which seriously concerned me, was dehydration. Should we be forced to abandon the boat in some unlucky spot between widely spaced bridges, it wouldn't take long for the heat to wear us down. Tomorrow was supposed to be not much over 110°F so it could have been worse. My daypack lay ready to hand, half filled with bottled water, juice and sugar-salted snacks. I'd told Jose to prepare his own supplies. He was behind his desk at the motel now, laboriously inflating the dinghy breath by breath whenever the customers gave him a chance, for he had no bicycle pump with him. This was the kind of fellow he was: determined, optimistic, ready to do his best with almost nothing.

His father had first come into the United States as a teenaged *pollo* in the fifties, when a Japanese ranching family, just recently un-relocated from some miserable American prison camp, said that they couldn't pay him except in food and clothing, but they'd teach him everything they knew. Jose's father jumped at the chance, just as Jose had gladly accepted my offer to ride the New River with me in exchange for $50 (I gave him $100 plus the dinghy); and the fact that both of them worked so hard and so eagerly for so little breaks my heart. Jose's father worked through the harvesting season for two years. Each time, he'd walk along the border all the way to the terrible reddish barrenness of El Sentinela (Mt. Signal), which was a journey of about twelve hours, then cross at a certain place he told me about where there were no Border Patrolmen (they are there now). Then came thirty-eight miles in the heat. Sometimes there were taxi drivers who would take the illegals that distance for $10, and you can imagine how much that would have been for a Mexican laborer in the fifties, especially given Jose's father's wages (in 2001, Jose got a $20 speeding ticket in Mexicali, and paying this fee infected him with anguish). In his second year, Jose's father was prepared to spend the $10, less to spare himself the exhaustion of that thirty-eight miles than to limit his risk of being arrested, but some other Mexicans were waiting ahead of him, and the taxi driver took their $10 and then turned them in to the Border Patrol. After this, Jose's father never trusted American taxi drivers; he went by foot. Each year when the last crop was harvested, he gave himself up to Immigration so that he'd get a free ride back to the border. When he arrived at the beginning of his third year, the Japanese brothers began paying him $0.25 an hour. He was ecstatic. His grandfather, who'd been boarding him in Mexicali during the off season, was finally able to go back home to southern Mexico; Jose's father could fend for himself now . . .

Sheep-shaped clots of foam, white and wooly, floated down the New River. (That's domestic sewage foam, explained a scientist from the Environmental Protection Agency. Near Brawley there's a lot of foam as well.) I stood there on the trash-covered bank, inhaling the reek of excrement and of something bitter, too, something like pesticides. Still and all, the water didn't smell nearly as foul as in Mexicali. The cheesy stench was gone; now it was more tolerably sour and rancid, diluted by sun and dust. The Border Patrolman sat motionless in his wagon, watching me. After fifteen minutes my throat got sore and I went back to the motel. Another Border Patrol car followed me slowly through the white sand.

At seven o'clock the next morning, with Imperial already laying its hot hands on my thighs, my shoulders, and the back of my neck, the three of us, Jose, his father, and I, were in the parking lot across the river from the supermarket, squinting beneath our caps, squatting down in the dirt while Jose's father stick-sketched in the dirt, making a map of the New River with the various road-crossings that he knew of; and across the highway, on the dirt road where I'd been the night before, another white Border Patrol vehicle sat. The first place that the old man would be able to wait for us was the bridge at Highway 98, about a mile due north but four miles' worth of river, thanks to a bend to the west-northwest. After that, there might be a safe stopping place for the truck at either Kubler or Lyons Road, or perhaps the north-south overpass of S-30; but this depended on traffic, so the next spot which Jose's father could guarantee was Interstate 8, which looked to be a good ten miles from Highway 98 if one counted in river-bends and wriggles. Perhaps two miles after this came a longish stretch between roads; I hardly expected to get so far; as I said, nobody in memory had been on the river; nobody knew if it was even navigable.

Now we dragged the dinghy out of the back of Jose's truck, and Jose, who from somewhere had been able to borrow a tiny battery-powered pump, tautened his previous night's breath-work until every last wrinkle disappeared. From the weeds came another old man, evidently a *pollero*, for he, after laughing at the notion that Jose and I were going to be literally up Shit Creek, began very knowingly and solemnly to warn us of obstacles. We would not be able to reach even Highway 98 without a portage, he insisted, because there was going to be a culvert through which the wiriest illegal alien could not fit. He gazed at me with begging eyes, hoping, I think, to be hired as a guide. But our brave yellow craft, rated at four persons, appeared barely capable of keeping Jose and me afloat, so I could not encourage his aspirations. We dragged the boat down a steep path I'd found between the briars, and then the stench of the foaming green water was in our nostrils as we stood for one last glum instant on the bank, whose muck seemed to be at least halfway composed of rotting excrement. I could no longer see the palm tree shadow, dark on grey, on the supermarket parking lot. Everyone waited for me to do something, so I slid the dinghy into the river. A fierce current snapped the bow downriver (the flow here has been measured at two hundred cubic feet per second). I held the boat parallel to the bank as Jose clambered in. Then, while Jose's father gripped it by the side-rope, I slid myself over the stern, while Jose's trapped breath jelly-quivered flaccidly beneath me. I had a bad feeling. The old man pushed us off, and we instantly rushed away, fending off snags as best we could. There was no time to glance back.

What a deep, deep green it river was! (It's always been green! Señor Ramón Flores had sighed.) Shaded on either side by mesquite trees, palo verdes, tamarisks (or "salt cedars" as they're sometimes called), bamboo and grass, it sped us down its canyon, whose banks were stratified with what appeared to be crusted salt. An occasional tire or scrap of clothing, a tin can or plastic cup wedged between branches, and once what I at first took to be the corpse of some small animal, then became a human fetus, and finally resolved into a lost doll floating face downwards between black-smeared roots, these objects were our companions and guideposts as we whirled down toward the Salton Sea, end over end because Jose had never before been in a boat in his life. I tried to teach him how to paddle, but he, anxious behind his smiles, could not really concentrate on what I was telling him, and kept dipping the oar as far down as he could reach, then pulling with all his might. He would soon get exhausted. Nor could I help him as much as I wanted to, on account of my obligation to take notes and photographs. Poor Jose! Every now and then I'd see us veering into the clutches of a bamboo thicket or some slimy slobbery tree-branches, and I'd snatch up my oar, which was now caked with black matter (shall we be upbeat and call it mud?). Sometimes I'd be in time to stave off that shock. Often these woody fingers would seize us, raking muck and water across our shoulders as we poled ourselves away. Already we were sopping wet and patchily black-stained. The first few drops on my skin burned a little bit, but no doubt I imagined things. What might they have contained? In the Regional Water Quality

Control Board's poetic words, *the pollutants of major concern are the pollutants identified by the Board in its 303(d) list.* Namely, for the New River, of which seventy percent of the effluent comes from the Untied States, meaning that the contamination would presumably worsen as one approached the Salton Sea, *they are bacteria, silt, volatile organic constituents (VOCs), nutrients, and pesticides. The pollutants associated with agricultural runoff are salts, silt, pesticides, nutrients, and selenium.* Jose kept spraying me by accident. There was not much to do about that; certainly I couldn't imagine a gamer or more resolute companion. He was definitely getting tired now. Replacing my camera, which was now speckled brownish-black from the New River, into its plastic bag, I laid down my notebook between my sodden ankles and began to paddle again. Here the stench was not much worse than that of marsh water. Had I simply grown accustomed to it (I remembered how my friend William had grimaced in disgust one night when we stood high on the bank), or was the New River really not so bad? The stink of a Florida mangrove swamp, or a Rhode Island cranberry bog, or a Cambodian riverbank on which the fishermen have thrown down many a wicker basket's worth of entrails, struck equivalency, in my memory at least, with where we now were. Although it was not much after eight in the morning, the water had already begun to approach blood temperature (the revised forecast for that day was 112°F, and it got a little warmer than that). We rammed into another tamarisk thicket, and when the branches sprang up to catapult more river-droplets on our heads, it felt almost pleasant.

We were passing a secluded lagoon into which a fat pipe drained what appeared to be clear water. We sped around a bend, and for no reason I could fathom, the stench got much worse—sewage and carrion as in Mexicali. The greyish-black mud clung more stickily than ever to the paddle here. I vaguely considered vomiting, but by then we were riding a deeper stretch which merely smelled like marsh again. The water's green hue gradually became brown, and that white foam, which occasionally imitated one of those faux-marble plastic tabletops in some Chinese restaurant in Mexicali, diluted itself into bubbles. Everything became very pretty again with the high bamboos around us, their reflections blocky and murky on the poisoned water. Occasionally we'd glimpse low warehouses off to the side, and wondering whether they might presage the approach of Highway 98 distracted me from the bitter taste in my mouth, which would continue to keep me company for days. Another inlet, another pipe (this one gushing coffee-colored liquid), and then we saw a duck swimming quite contentedly. Black-and-white birds, possibly phoebes, shrieked at us from the trees, fearing that we might pillage their nests. The heat was getting miserable. Narrowing, the river swerved under a bridge, and I got a beautiful view of more garbage snagged under dead trees . . .

I kept wondering when we would reach the pipe about which the old *pollero* had warned us; we never did. My end of the boat, having punched into one bamboo thicket too many, hissed sadly under me, sinking slowly. Since the price included several airtight compartments, I wasn't too worried, but I didn't really like it, either. Meanwhile the river had settled deeper into its canyon, and all we could see on either side were bamboos and salt cedars high above the bone-dry striated banks. A wild, lonely, beautiful feeling took possession of me. Not only had the New River become so unfrequented over the last few decades that it felt unexplored (no matter that every bend had been mapped and we couldn't get away from the trash, the poison and the stench), but the isolating power of the tree-walls, the knowledge that the adventure might in fact be a little dangerous if we continued it far enough, and the surprisingly dramatic loveliness of the scenery all made me feel as if Jose and I were nineteenth-century explorers of pre-American California. But it was so weird to experience this sensation *here,* where a half-mummified duck was hanging a foot above water in a dead tree! (What had slain it? Can we necessarily blame the New River? I thought of one old man on the shore of the Salton Sea who thought that nothing was really wrong there and said about the avian die-offs: How do those *scientists* know that all those birds weren't sick before they got here?) Lumps of excrement clung to the shore. Lumps of reeking black paste clung to my paddle. The river skittered from bend to bend in its sandy, crumbling canyon, and suddenly the sewage smell got sweeter and more horrid once again, I didn't know why. And now another splash from Jose's paddle flew between my lips, so that I could enter more deeply into my New River researches. (How did it taste? Well, as a child I was given to partake of the sickly-salty Salk polio vaccine—an ironic association, I suppose, for one of the thirty-odd diseases which lives in the New River is polio.) Not long afterward, fate awarded Jose the same privilege when a snagged tree sprung out of the water into his face.

At hot and smelly mid-morning the river split into three channels, all of them impassable due to tires and garbage, and here again the water became the same rich lime as the neon border around the Mexicali sign for MEUBLES ECONOMICOS, which as dusk arose, gradually succeeded in staining its metal siding entirely green. Above us, Jose's father waited at the Highway 98 bridge. The Border Patrol had already paid him a visit. They wouldn't permit him to come help us. We hauled the sagging dinghy up the slope and through a fenced-in place where the earth was so pale that a brown jackrabbit, whose hue might in other jurisdictions match the color of dirt, seemed lushly alive. I didn't think we could count on enough buoyancy to make it all the way to I-8, so I called it quits. Even after taking a shower my hands kept burning, and the next day, Jose and I still couldn't get the taste out of our mouths. We used up all his breath-mints lickety-split; then I went to Mexicali for tequilas and spicy tacos. The taste dug itself deeper. A week later, my arms were inflamed up to the elbow and my abdomen was red and burning. Well, who knows; maybe it was sunburn.

ANOTHER RIVER CRUISE

Ray Garnett, proprietor of Ray's Salton Sea Guide Service, was a duck hunter, but he preferred to take his birds in Nebraska. He knew quite a few men who hunted the wetlands around the Salton Sea, and he used to do that himself, but about their prizes he remarked: I don't like 'em, 'cause they taste like the water smells.

How about the fish, Ray?

I've been eatin' 'em since 1955, and I'm still here, so there's nothin' wrong with 'em.

As a matter of fact, he thought that the Salton Sea must have improved, because he used to get stinging rashes on his fingers when he cleaned too many fish, and that didn't happen anymore.

Ray went out on the sea pretty often. He'd been a fishing guide for decades. Now that he was retired, he still did it to keep even. He called the Salton Sea *the most productive fishery in the world.*

About the New River, Ray possessed very little information. He'd never been on it in all his seventy-eight years, and neither had anybody else whom he knew. —Seems to me like a few years back I was down here duck huntin' and then I heard a boat comin', he said. That was why he was willing to hazard this $800 aluminum water-skimmer with its $1,200 outboard motor on the New River. He was even a little excited. He kept saying: This sure is different.

Ray preferred corvina to tilapia, and in fact he'd brought some home-smoked corvina in the cooler. It wasn't bad at all. Probably I was imagining the aftertaste. Thirty-four pounds was the record, he said. Fourteen to fifteen pounds was more average. He could gut one fish per minute.

In the sixties and seventies lots of people came down here, he told me. Then that bad publicity scared people away, but they're startin' to come back.

Today, as it turned out, Ray's boat was going to cover the river's final ten-odd miles. Poor Jose only got $100. I had to give Ray $500 before he'd consent to try the New River.

Stocky, red, hairy-handed, roundfaced, he did everything slowly and right, his old eyes seeing and sometimes not telling. We put the boat in near Lack Road in Westmorland, and the river curved us around the contours of a cantaloupe field, with whitish spheres in the bright greenness, then the brown of a fallow field, a dirt road, and at last the cocoa-brown of the very water which whirled us away from that sight.

The New River's stench was far milder here, the color less alarming; and I remembered how when I'd asked Tom Kirk, who headed the Salton Sea Authority, how much of the Salton Sea's sickness came from the New River, he'd promptly answered: None. People point their fingers at Mexico and at farmers. Neither of these are contributing factors to bird deaths or fish deaths in the Salton Sea.

Maybe he was right, God knows. Maybe something else was causing them.

You think there are any fish in this river, Ray?

Flathead catfish. I wouldn't eat 'em. One time we did core samples of the mud in these wetlands. It has just about everythin' in it.

Swallows flew down. The river was pleasant really, wide and coffee-colored, with olive-bleached tamarisk trees on either side of its salt-banded banks—all in all, quite lovely, as Hemingway would have said. We can poison nature and go on poisoning it; yet something precious always remains. I thought about all the Indian tribes whom we'd forced off their hunting grounds—grazing lands these days, or maybe likely industrial parks—and in exchange we'd awarded them "reservations" where we thought the land was most worthless. And now coal and oil were sometimes found on those reservations. There was always something that our earth had left to give, and we kept right on taking and taking. I wondered what Imperial must have been like, or for that matter the whole continent of North America, in the days of its pre-Conquest glory. Lowering our heads, we passed under a fresh-painted girder bridge which framed a big pipe, probably for water in Ray's opinion. Rounding the bend, we met with a sudden faint whiff of sewage. But the river didn't stink one-tenth as much as it had at the border, let alone in Mexico. Passing a long straight feeder canal with hardly any trash in it, we presently found ourselves running between tall green grass and flittering birds. Villager Peak in the Santa Rosa Mountains was a lovely blue ahead of us. Now the bamboo thickened on either side and rose much taller than head high. Whenever Ray duck hunted, he wouldn't shoot if his prey were going to fall into a thicket like that, because it was virtually irretrievable then.

Have another piece of that corvina, said Ray.

Now there were just hills of bamboo and grass on either side, like the Everglades. Four black-winged pelicans flew together over the grass. The sunken chocolate windings of the New River seemed to get richer and richer. But presently another smell began to thicken, the familiar stench of North Shore, Desert Shores and Salton City. —The sea's right on the side of these weeds here, my guide was saying.

What's that smell, Ray?

I think it's all the dyin' fish, and dead fish on the bottom. It forms some kind of a gas. It's just another die-off. It's natural.

Ducks were flitting happily, and then we saw ever so many pelicans as we came to the mouth of the Salton Sea. Were they contented here or did they just have to take what they could get, since ninety-five percent of California's wetlands were already gone? I could see Obsidian Butte off to the right, and then the promontory of what must have been Red Hill Marina. How many dead fish did I spy around me? I must be honest: Not one.

You get away from the smell when you get out here fishin', said Ray, and he was right, for far out on the greenish-brownish waves (that's algal bloom that made the water turn green, he explained. So there won't be any fish in here today. You don't fish in here), the only odor was ocean.

They've had studies and what have you ever since the late fifties, he sighed.

And did they conclude that water quality was getting worse?

That's what we thought in 1995 when we put four hundred and twenty hours in and didn't catch a fish. In '97 and '98 they started coming back. Whether the fish have gotten more tolerant or whether it's somethin' else, I don't know.

It was pretty salty out here, all right. The Department of the Interior had announced that the sea's ecosystem was doomed unless nine million tons of salt could be removed every year.

Deep in a choppy orangish-green wave, Ray thought it best to turn around. As we approached the New River we grounded on a sandbar.

There were actually three of us in the boat: Ray, myself, and my friend Larry from Borrego Springs, who now in his autumnal years was becoming a natural history enthusiast. He'd come along for the ride. Ray announced that somebody had to get out and help him push. I stared at the sores on my ankles which had arisen during the cruise with Jose, and while I stared, good old Larry leaped into the water; but my selfishness was all for nothing, because we were still grounded.

If you don't mind gettin' your feet wet, said Ray to me, it sure would make things easier.

We pushed. The water seemed to sting my feet, and later that day they might have been inflamed, or maybe once again I was imagining things. Certainly it wasn't as bad as near the border.

Going back upriver, brown pelicans accompanied us overhead, and then there were some bubbles, possibly from pollution or possibly from some geothermal source. A jackrabbit crouched on the bank. Now again came the lush, low banks of Westmorland, and up on either side of us the flat green fields to whose crop yields this river had in part been sacrificed (as a fellow from the Audubon Society told me: Nine million pounds of pesticides a year on Imperial Valley fields have got to go somewhere!), birds under concrete bridges, smoke trees, a fire pit, made perhaps by illegal aliens, beer cans, toilet paper, birds' nests, tamarisks, which choke out anything, and a dead palm trunk. The New

River was turning chocolate-green again. Now, upstream of our starting point, the water grew paler and creamier, greener and foamier than ever, with clots of detergentlike froth merging with the mysterious bubbles. Meanwhile, on the bank near a wall of seasoning haybales, a man stood, getting ready to fish.

Must be somethin' wrong with this water, said Ray, 'cause I don't see any bullfrogs. I been watchin' the bank. I seen a lot of 'em in the canals, but not a one here. No turtles, either. Bullfrogs and turtles can live in anything.

Now came a sickening sweet stench of rotting animals. That stench went away, but presently I got a sore throat and my eyes began to sting. I didn't ask Ray how he was doing. And presently we came to a burned, half-sunken bridge; it was too risky to try to get past it, so that was the end. My feet kept right on tingling. With a kind and gentle smile, Ray gave me an entire bag of smoked corvina.

THE GOLDEN AGE

The article on California in the eleventh edition of the *Britannica* (published in 1911) states that *irrigation in the tropical area along the Colorado river, which is so arid that it naturally bears only desert vegetation, has made it a true humid-tropical region like Southern Florida, growing true tropical fruits*. Wasn't that the golden age? Actually, the golden age hasn't ended even now. I look around me at the Salton Sea's green margins of fields and palm orchards, and spy a lone palm tree far away at the convergence of tan furrows, then lavender mountains glazed with confectioner's sugar; this is the landscape, where all is beauty, the aloof desert mountains enriched despite themselves by the spectacle of the fields. Fertilization, irrigation, runoff, wastewater—the final admixtures of all these quantities flow into the Salton Sea. I couldn't condemn the state of the Salton Sea without rejecting the ring of emerald around it, which I refuse to do. About the continuing degradation of that sump, Jose Angel very reasonably said: It's a natural process because *the sea is a closed basin.* Pollutants cannot be flushed out. You could be discharging Colorado River water directly into the Salton Sea, or for that matter distilled water into the Salton Sea, and you would end up with a salinity problem, because the ground is full of salt! The regulations do not provide for a solution to this. You have to engineer a project. You have to build some sort of an outlet. Now when it comes to nutrients, I think there is a role for regulation to play. We can't blame Mexico for everything, but they certainly play a role in the nutrients. They add to the problem but we have our hands full in the Imperial Valley, too. And what can we do? Because fertilizers have a legitimate agricultural use.

The stylized elegance of a palm grove's paragraph of tightly spaced green asterisks defied legitimate agricultural use, and so did the ridge-striped fields south of Niland, where sheep and birds intermingled in a field, the cottonballs on the khaki plants so white as to almost glitter. Suddenly came a brilliant green square of field on the right-hand side of Highway 111, a red square of naked dirt on the left, a double row of palms in between, with their dangling clusters of reddish-yellow fruit . . . Legitimate use, to be sure, from which I benefited and from which bit by bit the sea was getting saltier and fouler with algae and more selenium-tainted, creating carrion and carrion-stench, which kept sea-goers away, so that it was legitimate agricultural use which created that empty swimming pool in that motel in Salton City with cacti and flying fishes alternately painted on the two rows of broken-windowed rooms. The palm trees danced in a wind that stank of death. Legitimate use made the half-scorched rubble of the Sundowner Motel, whose rusty lonely staircase comprised a vantage point to look out across the freeway to Superburger and then the sparse pale house-cubes of Salton City. On a clear day one could see right across the Salton Sea from those stairs, but if there was a little dust or haze, the cities on the far side faded into hidden aspects of the Chocolate Mountains' violet blur. Year by year, the Sundowner disappeared. By 2000, only the staircase was left, and in 2001 that had also been carried off by the myrmidons of desert time. Meanwhile the Alamo flowed stinking up from Holtville with its painted water tower (that river also commenced in Mexico somewhere), and the Whitewater flowed stinking, and the New River bore its stench of excrement and something bitter like pesticides. Imperial flowered and bore fruit; Imperial hid its excretions behind dark citrus hedges. Through that lush and luscious land whose hay bales are the color of honey and whose alfalfa fields are green skies, water flowed,* ninety percent of it not from Mexico at all, carrying consequences out of sight to a sump three hundred and fifty-two square miles in area. *Pursuant to Section 303(d) of the U.S. Clean Water Act, the Regional Board approved its updated list of impaired surface waters in January 1998 (copy attached). Within the Salton Sea Watershed: the Salton Sea, the New River, the Alamo River, the Imperial Valley Agricultural Drains, and the Coachella Valley Stormwater Channel were all listed as impaired.* From a distance it looked lovely: first the hand-lettered sign of MAY'S OASIS, then the Salton Sea's Mediterranean blue seen through a distant line of palms, and the smell of ocean . . .

*It is heartening to see that the University of California Cooperative Extension and other such entities are preparing new experimental projects to conserve irrigation water and keep more fertilizers and pesticides from running off of the fields. Alfalfa might well be the most water-greedy crop. Furrow irrigation is by far the most wasteful kind.

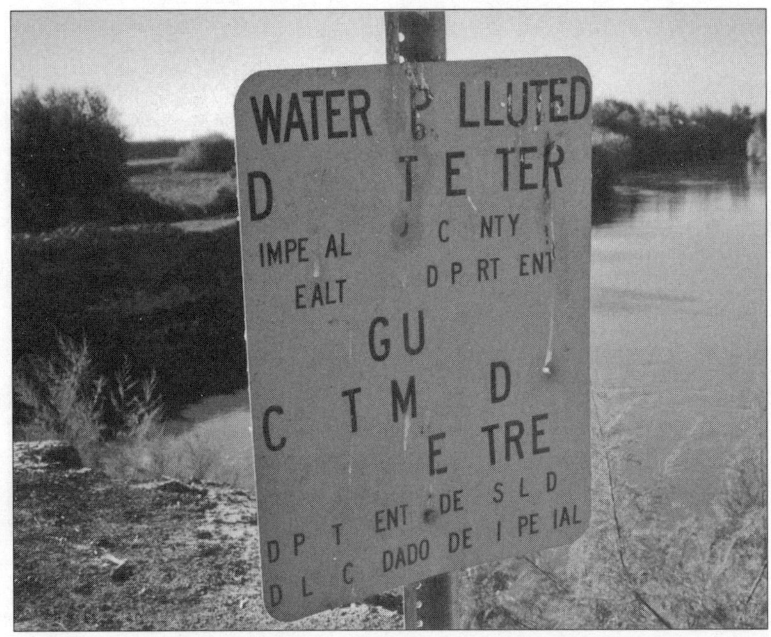

THE WARNING SIGNS ANNOUNCING "PELIGRO" ("DANGER") POSTED ALL ALONG THE NEW RIVER HAVE APPARENTLY BEEN EFFECTIVE: OUR GUIDE RAY TOLD US THAT DURING HIS FORTY YEARS OF LIVING IN THE AREA, HE'D NEVER HEARD OF ANYONE ATTEMPTING TO TAKE A BOAT RIDE ALONG THE NEW RIVER TO THE SALTON SEA. —LM

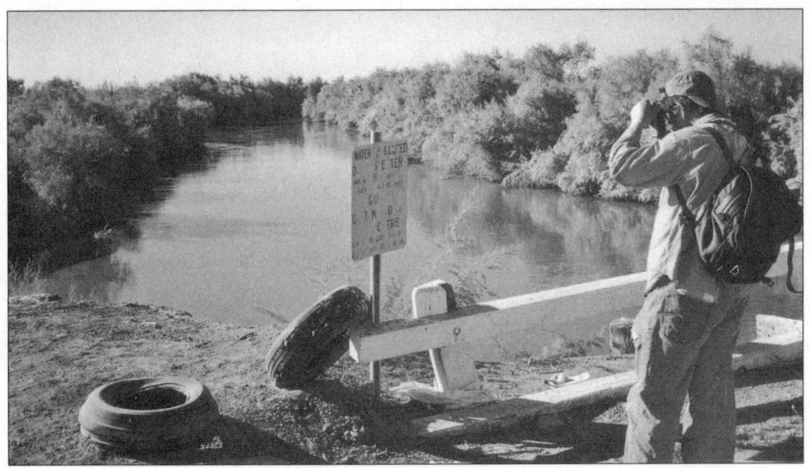

VOLLMANN TAKING PHOTOS NEAR OUR DEPARTURE POINT. —LM

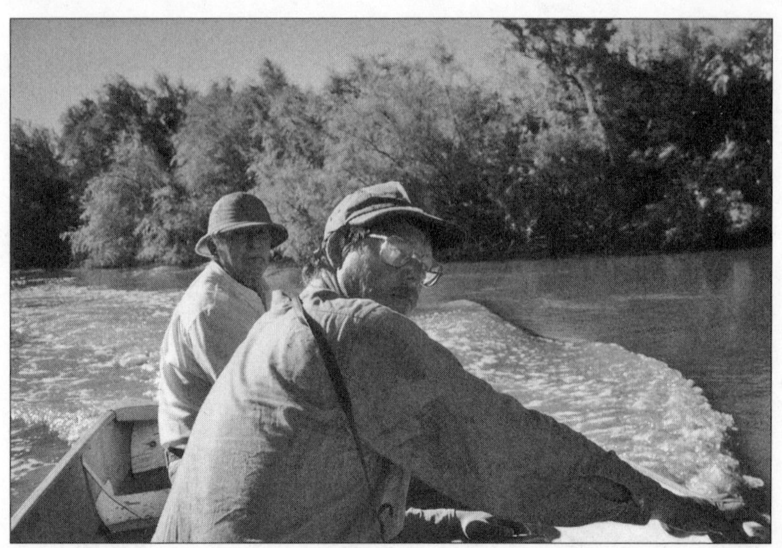

VOLLMANN AND OUR GUIDE RAY. —LM

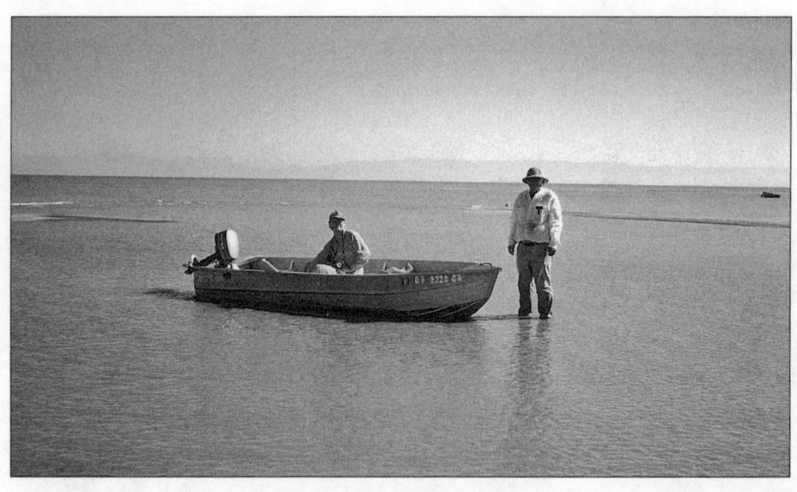

VOLLMANN AND RAY SOON AFTER THE NEW RIVER LET US OUT IN THE SALTON SEA. —LM

Part V

On Writing, Literature, and Culture

Writing

From
Four Essays

This is another section of *Four Essays* (see "Honesty" in the "Background and Influences" section). It originally appeared in *Why I Write: Thoughts on the Practice of Fiction* (Boston: Little, Brown, 1998), edited by Will Blythe.

The way of thinking that you reproach is the sole consolation of my life.
—MARQUIS DE SADE, PRISON LETTER TO HIS WIFE

I WRITE THIS BY hand, with swollen and aching fingers. Sometimes the ache oozes up to my shoulders, sometimes only to my wrists; once or twice I've felt it in my back. Poor posture, they say, or "repetitive stress injury," or possibly carpal tunnel; when for a price of five hundred or a thousand dollars they administered electric shocks to my hands and arms to determine the relative health of my nerve-sheaths (the current made my limbs jerk, in obedience to the highest laws of galvanics, and a premedical spectator laughed), I was told that my case was either moderate or severe. Subject to respites occasioned by voyages or stints of block-printing, I have woken up with pain, and slept with pain, my sweetly constant mistress, for seven years now, ever since my thirtieth birthday. While there have been occasions when I could not close my hand around a water-glass or turn the pages of a book, mostly this pain is an unobtrusive companion, a chronic irrelevance when I am loving my work, a chronic warning when I am not, in either case acknowledged and respected for having so steadfastly guested me, but rarely listened to: pain gives always the same advice, the wisdom of prudes and legislators: stay within the limits. This pain of mine certainly does.

Pain's advice is also that of a loving nurse with long dark hair, of my own heart, which used to tell me when I was in elementary school that if I could only escape the chalkboards and inky desks, running away into sunny fields of milkweed, I would find my destiny. If I weren't writing, who knows what brighter life I would find? My pain respects me, being in no wise related to the shouting tyrant endured by puking heroin addicts in withdrawal, burned children, soldiers gassed or shot in the stomach. When I think of them, I love my pain more for being so undemanding, for letting me do almost everything I want to do. Yes, I worry sometimes about future damage, having met old ranch hands whose hands were but blackened hay-baling hooks. Writing is bad for me physically, without a doubt, but what would I do if I stopped?

The nights of sleepless excitement are almost reduced to memories now. They possess me but once or twice a year. I no longer feel, as I did at seventeen or twenty, that I am an ecstatic vessel bubbling over with words—words gushing from my hands like sparks, forming at my will or beyond my will in armies upon paper and screen, the letterforms themselves beautiful, the combinations of words likewise beautiful to eye, ear, lips and heart. Now I feel instead that the tale is a block of darkness which I chip away at deliberately until I begin to glimpse tiny stars within; I seek to unveil as many of these as I can, leaving just the right amount of darkness behind them to make them shine the brighter by contrast, protecting them from the day. I labor where before I played. In part this change is due to the pain in my hands. But another reason is that what once came easily would now come too easily. The thrill of writing, as of pure animal sexuality, derives from newness. Following newness faithfully must bring us farther and farther out of school, until the milkweeds loom around us. The difficult way is the way that I want to go. I write less and less for "success," although for financial reasons I will always try to write for publication. I write to discover the universe and to discover myself. My writing is thus, for me, a deeply selfish act. Very often, what I discover infects me with sadness, even with anguish. This voyage which I am taking into the block of darkness leaves me night by night more alone.

Example: I am on the verge of concluding a long essay on violence which it has taken me sixteen years to write. My three American commercial publishers have all turned it down, mostly unread. I am sad about this to the extent that the middling advance (thirty thousand dollars, say, spread over two or three years if I were lucky) and the minor increase in "recognition" that publication might have brought me would have benefited my career—that is, enabled me to continue writing in comfort. That is why I will try some academic presses now. I am also sad because I love books as objects, and it would be a pleasure for me to hold my finished work in my hands. I am otherwise indifferent. I am fortunate enough to make money writing elsewhere. If the manuscript remains unpublished in my lifetime, I will entomb it somewhere, out of respect for what I learned in the writing, but without much regret. For the secret (which actually is no secret, since you who read this either know it in some sense already, or you will never know it) is this: Writing is an intense joy, as faithful as pain, as beautiful as love; making beauty is love, is making love; and that is what writing is.

Every joy which I have ever experienced, even the most physiological, ultimately reaches me as aesthetic. Whether writing is knowing or whether it is singing, the love remains, the joy, the daring, the exaltedness when one approaches, at however far a remove, perfection. Shake the greatest art ever, and dross will come out. But honest effort for its own sake is beauty. If the writer is talented and lucky enough, then the result may be beautiful, too. (I use the word "lucky" advisedly. We credit Petrarch's genius alone for his sonnets. But what if he had never met his Laura? Can we credit him for her existence, or for the effect which she had on him?) If the result is beautiful, then others can see it and feel it. But look through a camera at a face or a landscape, and you might see the perfection of it even if you fail to trip the shutter, or if you set the wrong f-stop. Write a bad poem, and you still might have seen God or gained enlightenment at the feet of the Devil.

Sometimes I sit by the ocean in southeast Asia, or walk toward a subarctic horizon glittering with crowberries, and I think: This is enough. I am here; I have seen this; to the best of my capacity I have known this. This is beautiful. —And I let it go. The perceiving was all the writing that I felt called upon to do. And other times I awake from a terrifying or dazzling dream, and I know that if I don't write it down now, its filmy coherence will rupture into a million shrinking droplets, like certain kinds of ink trying to dry upon acrylic. After all, so what if

I forgot that dream? How many faces, flowers and rivers have I forgotten? Maybe they've sunk into me, and I draw from them without knowing it, or maybe I simply have the sense that I could only mar any conception I have of them by trying to translate it into groups of letters. But the dream calls to me, cries out for me to save it. Or a story comes into my head. Or the voice of someone who loves me speaks to me. Or an idea, an inhuman crystal, attacks me with its colors, just as strange ores and fossils attack the rockhound, their possibilities overruling his tranquility so that he must take up his hammer and get on his walking boots.

How could I possibly have the effrontery to say that any of this is significant to you? When I go into a museum I see the clusters of tender, avid or dutiful faces around the fad-pieces of the moment; and then at unpredictable intervals an unknown work will catch somebody's soul (or maybe his feet got tired); and surrounding these hang the crucified legions of the unregarded. Which category will the books I write be placed in? How can I know, and how does it depend on me? Does what I write seem beautiful to me? That is all that I can know and count on, and it is enough. But if it is beautiful to you, too, I am grateful. I like to please people. I like to be, as ticket-collectors say, "validated." I like to make a living.

But I'm beginning to wonder whether someday I ought to prove my love. De Sade proved his in prison. Homes without bookshelves, people who don't mind *le mot juste* but will settle for the oll korrect approximation, readers without enough time to finish a short story—these signs of the times, like the pain in my wrists, which at the moment nibbles at my palms, all remind me that my days are numbered. How long will this world continue to support my easy life? I believe in my sincerity; I believe that I am willing to suffer for the sake of the word; but the pain in my hands is only a promise, not a demonstration like de Sade ranting and masturbating behind the prison door, refusing to renounce his terrifying lusts, or Hans and Sophie Scholl going to the scaffold for writing anti-Nazi pamphlets, or Joan of Arc eloquently defying the inquisitors who will burn her. How can I prove myself? How can I love more? For now, the answer is to keep writing whatever happens, to try to do better, to go where I must, listening to joy. De Sade, the Scholls and Joan didn't choose to be afflicted, and I hope never to be tested as they were. I know that I love what I do. I hope that my life (for which I give thanks) glides on and on, and that, like a good prostitute, I can continue to convert joy into cash.

Letter Against Cuts

In this letter to his British and American editors, Vollmann responds to their suggestion that his manuscript of *Fathers and Crows* needed to be cut by nearly one-third by presenting an eloquent and detailed case for retaining its length. His rebuttal provides a revealing description about his motives and methods in writing *Fathers and Crows,* the importance he attributes to his novel both as an accurate, exhaustively researched work of history but, more importantly, as history reprocessed into literary art—one drawn, as he puts it, "from my imagination—but my imagination appropriately filtered and disciplined." As for the promise he makes at the end of this letter, that "subsequent *Dreams* won't have to be nearly this long," it should be noted that the *Argall* manuscript was even longer; see also "Crabbed Cautions of a Bleeding-hearted Undeleter." —LM

18 February 1991

To: Esther Whitby and Tom Rosenthal
André Deutsch Ltd.
Christine Pevitt and Amanda Vail
Viking

From: William T. Vollmann

Re: Cuts in *Fathers and Crows*

I AM DELIGHTED THAT Viking and Deutsch now stand prepared to sign a contract for the U.S. rights to *Fathers and Crows,* thereby continuing the American appearance of the *Seven Dreams* series. One condition of this accord is that the manuscript be first cut from 1,400 pages to 1,000 pages. I have spent some time looking over what I've written, and respectfully propose the following compromise:

> I can promise to cut *Fathers and Crows* by 200 pages. I can also promise to *sincerely do my best* to trim away another 200 pages. I do not want to guarantee a 400-page reduction, however, for reasons detailed below. If you grant me this favor, I can assure you in return that none of the subsequent five volumes in this series will be more than 550 pages in typescript, and most should be substantially less.
>
> The reasons for my request now follow.
>
> 1. [A reason why this CAN be done.] My typescript is not nearly as long as it looks. For convenience in editing I printed it with numbered lines (which added 100 pages to the length right there), in large type, with generous margins. Therefore, it isn't financially necessary to cut as much as may appear at first glance.
> 2. [A reason why this SHOULD be done.] Most authors, including me, are selfish, lazy and greedy about words amassed. We don't like to cut if we can avoid it. After having let my book sit for a few months, I believe that cutting, say, 100 pages would actually be of some benefit to my conception of the book. Because I want to be flexible and realistic, I have gone a little farther and offered to cut 200-plus pages, which I believe can be done without greatly damaging my conception of the work. So I would appreciate it if you would be flexible, too.
> 3. [A better reason why this SHOULD be done.] *Fathers and Crows* is the length that it is for a reason. Unlike the previous volume, *The Ice-Shirt,* which is essentially a metaphorical history of a five-year event that took place about a thousand years ago, *Fathers and Crows* is a largely factual history of some very complex events occupying the entire first half of the seventeenth century.

Permit me to elaborate on this.

There are three contemporary books on *Fathers and Crows*'s topic that I know of. The first is a novel by Brian Moore called *Black Robe*. At the moment it is being made into a movie in Québec, which will be entered at the Cannes Film Festival. It is about the conversion of the Huron by the Jesuits in 1634–49, and the subsequent martyrdom of both parties. It is a very good book in many ways. But Mr. John Steckley, the only person in the world who speaks the Huron language now, and who is a scholar of some repute, noted in a letter to me that Moore fell into a number of traps of cultural bias which mar the integrity of the book, and debase it almost into a mere work of entertainment. The second is a work of anthropology by Prof. Bruce Trigger, whom Moore consulted, as did I. Trigger's book is called *The Children of Aataentsic*. It is a history of the Huron people from their earliest beginnings (described sketchily, in accordance with the archaeological record), through their first indirect contact with European trade goods in the 1500s, until their destruction in 1649–50. Trigger is careful not to enter much into reconstructions of Indian personalities and psyches, since it is not his task to be speculative, and so instead describes group motivations, both economic and political. It is one of the best works of pure history that I have ever read. The third and final book is Leonard Cohen's novel *Beautiful Losers*, which is about Catherine Tekakwitha, an Iroquois who may soon be canonized. Cohen's book is very good for what it is, but cannot be said to be grounded in Amerindian ethnography.

Fathers and Crows is unique.

First of all, this book is an accurate work of history on an almost unknown subject. In scope it is comparable to Trigger's (it includes much that Trigger does not). Books which tell how Europeans overpowered Indian cultures by force are common. This book tells every move of the five-cornered chess game in which the French killed the Huron with kindness, making them dependent on their trade goods, disrupting their society with missionary ideology, and meanwhile destabilizing the world around them by introducing firearms, which pitted tribe against tribe in bloody and escalating arms races. In the end, when the Huron were rubbed out by the Iroquois (who were supplied with muskets by the Dutch), the French were worse off than before. *Fathers and Crows* is therefore a cautionary history of much the same type as William Shawcross's *Sideshow:*

Nixon, Kissinger and the Destruction of Cambodia. But it is somewhat more ambitious than Shawcross's book, which covers a period of about ten years and only three cultures. *Fathers and Crows,* as I said, covers half a century, and five very different societies: French, Micmac, Huron, Iroquois and Algonkin (with occasional glimpses of English, Dutch, Susquehannocks) PLUS their melding into present-day Québecois.

But I have been able to go beyond histories such as Trigger's by making use of the novelist's tool of character. First of all, I believe I've succeeded in offering a radical reinterpretation of Samuel de Champlain, whom we generally eulogize as a hero, pioneer, bold warrior, etc. I represent him as I think he really was, based on close study of the sources: bigoted, fanatical, paranoid yet paradoxically cocksure, a desperate, unsuccessful social climber, the forty-year-old husband of a thirteen-year-old girl who hated him, a stolid, stoic plodder who could accomplish very narrow miracles for which his puppet-masters took the credit. Second, I feel I've brought the Jesuits and the Iroquois alive by going back to the creation-texts of both societies, showing where both group-characters came from. Third, I believe I've succeeded, more than anyone before me, in getting inside the heads and hearts of seventeenth-century Indians. I feel that someone like my made-up protagonist, the half-Micmac woman Born Underwater, could really have lived, and that her career could have followed the events which I describe. Amantacha the Huron, who really existed, is someone else whose character I'm really proud of—he's different from Born Underwater not only sexually and personally but culturally. I feel that I show what Huron-ness and Micmac-ness must have been like—which adds to the meaning of the history that I tell.

In researching this book I've read ALL the relevant primary sources (including the complete works of Champlain, the appropriate thirty-odd volumes of the seventy-three-volume *Jesuit Relations,* the position documents on the canonization of Kateri Tekakwitha, all the writings of Saint Ignatius of Loyola available to me in translation, the Constitution of the Iroquois, etc., etc.), visited all the important sites mentioned in the story, read a great number of secondary sources, and corrected my text with the vigilant aid of two foremost anthropologists—Trigger for the Huron and Iroquois parts, and Ruth Holmes Whitehead (who performed the same service for *The Ice-Shirt*) for the Micmac parts.

And I've also drawn on my imagination—but my imagination appropriately filtered and disciplined.

I think that that is why Trigger, who is the world authority on my subject wrote me that he believed *Fathers and Crows* to be a work of genius which offers us a new view of the seventeenth century.

So what about cuts?

I hope you see that the complexity of the book is such that too much cutting in any one place damages the rest, not only as a work of art but also as the work of history I want it to be. There are places—especially toward the beginning, and maybe in the early 1630s—when the writing is flabby, and scenes can be tightened or eliminated to great effect. I sincerely look forward to this challenge, because I want to make the book even better than it is. There are other places—such as the life of Saint Ignatius, and the founding of the Iroquois confederacy—where if I prune very very carefully I can respect commercial considerations without losing too much. But after that, every additional cut will take another additional incident from the book, thereby dimming the Byzantine multifaceted glitter of it, and mutilating it.

If *The Ice-Shirt* didn't make you money, *Fathers and Crows* isn't likely to make you money, either. Some of the *Dreams* set in the present may do better for you commercially. But *Seven Dreams* is not like a Stephen King book and will never be. I honestly believe that *Fathers and Crows* is my best work so far, and that it will eventually be recognized as such. In the meantime my other books, such as *Rainbow Stories*, are already recognized, and will only sell better as my name becomes better known. So I ask you to please accept my gesture of cutting not 400 pages, but 200 to 400, and my promise that subsequent *Dreams* won't have to be nearly this long (the state of my wrists wouldn't permit it even if I wanted to). I'd be very grateful, and so would the characters in my book.

—William T. Vollmann

Whores for Gloria: A Note to Publishers

I HAVE HAD MORE trouble selling this book than any other since my writing career began. So far it has been rejected by both my standard hardback publishers (Deutsch and Atheneum), and by Grove and Soho as well. Given this state of affairs, I respectfully ask that you read the following statement.

Whores for Gloria is, in my belief, of the same quality as *Let Us Now Praise Famous Men* and *The Grapes of Wrath*. I realize that many people who admire the latter two books will hate *Whores for Gloria* by reason of the book's subject, which is street prostitution. All three of these books are about the dignity and beauty of being human even when a member of a despised or outcast class. *Whores for Gloria*, of course, labors under a special handicap. Reading about the crucifixion of the Joad family in Steinbeck's book is painful, sad, and that emotion inspires respect for Steinbeck's art. Reading about the mutually inflicted suffering of Jimmy and the prostitutes in *Whores for Gloria* is often repulsive, and that inspires resentment and disgust. That is why I will not be surprised if my book takes years to get published, as was the case with *Let Us Now Praise Famous Men*. And that is why I would be greatly surprised if the book once published were never banned like *The Grapes of Wrath*.

Love and compassion, which I believe that my book has, is not enough. A book must also be informed by knowledge and unflinching honesty. When Stephen Crane wrote his prostitute book, *Maggie: A Girl of the Streets*, he failed because he did not take his subject far enough. *Whores for Gloria* bears FULL witness. It is a documentary in the form of a novel. All of the prostitutes in the book are real people. Most of the incidents and dialogue are genuine. I have done my subject justice.

This required that I depict sexism, brutality, lust, sexual activity, bodily uncleanliness, drunken binges, deviance, and psychosis—and these as simple preconditions for the life of my protagonist. But in the demimonde as elsewhere there are flashes of a secret and beautiful inner life, which I believe exists in almost everyone, winner or loser. Those who read my book with any sort of care will find hints of it. The fact that this goodness is consistently thwarted only makes me admire it more, for it continues to well up—I saw it.

Crabbed Cautions of a Bleeding-hearted Un-deleter— and Potential Nobel Prize Winner

In this letter to Paul Slovak, his longtime editor and supporter at Viking, Vollmann's detailed response to Slovak's recommendations regarding the need to cut the manuscript of *The Royal Family* by approximately one-third provides a fascinating glimpse into Vollmann's views about the long-term value of his work, the compromises he feels he has had to make as a journalist, and his belief that he can live with such compromises only so long as he insists on retaining "the right to republish everything the way it should be in a book someday." In the end, Slovak was able to get Viking to agree to publish the uncut version of the novel—although only after Vollmann had agreed to reduce his royalty earnings. In his acknowledgments in *The Royal Family* Vollmann noted that, "Against his better judgment, Paul Slovak at Viking permitted me to refrain from cutting the book by one-third. Paul, I want to thank you for having stood by me for so long." —LM

December 11, 1998

Dear Paul,

I. Which telleth of Vollmann his gratitude

THANK YOU FOR YOUR kindness regarding the length of this book. Paul, you have always been my friend and advocate in an environment which is alien and probably inimical to me. Time after time you have indulged me, and I am sure that the sales figures of my books must have disappointed you and made it progressively harder for you to defend my projects at marketing conferences (which I imagine as being nightmare rituals where manuscripts which don't measure up are burned alive on altars to Mammon).

II. Of his self-righteous justifications

Thanks to our phone conversation, the directive in your letter is, I hope, moot. But here are my thoughts on it anyway. Your letter speaks of being realistic, which means cutting the book by one third (which I think was also . . . [the] proposal for *Fathers and Crows*.) If we are to be realistic, let's agree that the case is actually worse than this. Looking at my royalty statements, I'm forced to admit that while I might have brought Viking a smidgeon of critical cachet, my books have only barely, if at all, justified themselves financially. Your kind euphemism about the cost of paper, which you also used in the case of *The Atlas* to persuade me to cut a little, is, I believe, meant to spare my feelings. No doubt Stephen King or John Grisham could publish 1,500-page novels if they cared to (and maybe they have). Moreover, as I look around my bookshelf, I see some of the volumes which have been my best friends over the years: *War and Peace, The Tale of Genji, Black Lamb and Gray Falcon, Remembrance of Things Past, Moby-Dick.* I notice that these too are fat books. I believe, rightly or wrongly, that I possess enough talent and skill that at least some of my books deserve provisional admittance to the Society of Fat Books. Whether or not they deserve to stay there, well, as the saying goes, only time will tell. But I would rather not have my books published at all than suffer them to be abridged for merely commercial reasons.

I support myself reasonably well on my magazine work, and, if my books no longer got published, I could get by . . . I have made my bargain with the Devil and don't begrudge it. I write my heart out on everything I do. Then I send the pieces off to the butchers and cheerfully allow them to do whatever they want. Almost never do I read the final product. My consolations are four: First, I'm well paid. Second, I like almost all the people I work with. Third, I get to go to neat places. Fourth and most importantly, I reserve the right to republish everything the way it should be in a book someday.

This is why I am sometimes so difficult to work with at Viking. If I abrogated my responsibility to the books, I would truly have no integrity. I try to make up for my stubbornness where I can, by readily agreeing to any and all cover art and copy, by not fussing if my name gets misspelled on the spine of my own book, by not being a hardball negotiator about contracts. . . .

I fully realize that my own crabbed peculiarities do not run the world, and I cannot expect Viking to tiptoe around them. That's why I am so grateful to you for allowing me to keep the book intact. And when you are arguing for me in some futuristic boardroom whose control panel offers direct communication with the Vatican and the Pentagon, feel free to use the following practical arguments as to why the company might want to consider publishing *The Royal Family* as written:

III. Armaments to fight the Devil

1. Most importantly, it will be a better book that way.
2. We did this for *Fathers and Crows* in spite of . . . prophecies of doom. And it got a starred *PW* review, etc. Maybe it even sold thirty-seven copies . . .
3. This sounds crazed and immodest, but I actually believe I have a shot at winning the Nobel Prize or some other prestigious award someday. If Viking sticks with me that long, I think they may benefit from keeping me happy and by keeping the books intact. I am also getting more and more foreign sales these days. May the company please, please, just be patient.
4. It will be easier for me to help promote the book if I am proud of it.

IV. In which we shew one scribbler his struggles

I did spend a good three weeks rereading and agonizing (two weeks of which were made more pleasant by contrast with the setting: jury duty), and I managed to cut almost a hundred pages, much of it from the last part of the book. The "Coffee Camp" chapter in particular is lighter. Of course this is much less than Viking would like. Sorry. I have restored the "Vigs" chapter for which I had mistakenly substituted a repetition of the Domino material. You can cheer Barbara up by telling her it's ten pages shorter.

It's probably a waste of your time for me to justify everything I kept, but maybe a few remarks on specific sections preserved from the headsman's axe would be of interest.

V. Crabbed cautions of a bleeding-hearted un-deleter

Sec. 114, pp. 309-10: Domino is not a monster sui generis, but a very troubled person whose family is much worse off than she. This section is a fairly economical (elegant) way to show it. We don't want D. to be just a villain.

Book VIII: Sunflower's pain and crucifixion is emblematic of the theme of the book—in fact, central. The Dostoyevskian notion that suffering and degradation is paradoxically ennobling, perhaps even sacred, first gets illustrated to the unbelieving Henry right here. The whole book is about how he learns to follow Sunflower's path.

Book X: Essay on bail. I know how you feel about this, Paul, and spent days going back and forth on it. You're right that the reader won't miss this if it's not there, and it is long and it delays the story. *However* . . . in my state of doubt, I went and reached for *Moby-Dick*. Just consider how much of this book is composed of digressions on cutting up whales. In *The Royal Family* there are three digression-chapters: this one, the short Geary Street chapter, and the description of rush hour in the financial district at the beginning of one of the John chapters. I think that all three are justified. This book is, among other things, a very pointed satire, and to keep those points sharpened these three grindstones are valuable. Domino and many of her colleagues are sleazy petty criminals and worse, to be sure, and yet they are victims also—and not necessarily (perhaps not at all) of their male customers, as it is so fashionable to assert these days, but certainly of the justice system which is rigged against them. What I learned about bail shocked me, and I want the thoughtful reader to be shocked, too, hopefully returning to the tale more willing to cut Domino some slack. And, as you'll see if you have time to read it, I did shorten and tighten this considerably.

Book XVII: Smooth is a very important, ambiguous character. This Dream House section is now more explicitly about him (don't worry;

I added only about fifty words total, and deleted lots more). He is the Queen's best friend and also partly responsible for Feminine Circus. And one of the devices of the book is that almost everybody in her family is potentially capable of betraying the Queen; and maybe they all do, because they are human, weak, selfish.

Book XIX: Meditation on stock market. Here the satire becomes especially pointed. The cab driver, like one of Dos Passos's camera eyes, shines upon us the gaze of America: nononsense, business-centered, not even hypocritical (everyone knows Brady's girls are real; the virtual business is just legal color). Feminine Circus is not even that big a deal to the jaded American eye. Sooner or later Brady will be upstaged. In the meantime, can I get mine? The cab driver offers us one of the few "outside" or "public" views of Brady's achievement.

Anyhow, you get the gist: Even cutting the less than one hundred pages that I did was quite a battle . . .

VI. Exasperating legalities

You asked me whether any part of the book needed to be vetted. Here is all I can come up with:

Daro Inouye (p. 1145), Tyler's friend who happens to be a public defender, is a real person, and appears as such in the bail essay chapter, along with a lot of other real people. These people have all read the bail chapter, corrected all factual errors I made, and signed off on it. I think it is fine to have Daro in his official capacity telling Henry a real story he told me. He likes me fine. What do you think?

I assume that the excerpt from Darwin on p. 247 is fair use (short) and in the public domain.

I guess that's it for now. Thanks again for understanding. I *promise* that *Argall* will be much, much shorter.

Your friend,

WTV

"My Life's Work" (2002)

When Vollmann first sent the several-thousand-page manuscript of *Rising Up and Rising Down* to his new agent, Susan Golomb, he accompanied it with this letter, in which he summarizes the aims and structural arrangement of this twenty-three-year-long project that he refers to simply as "my life's work." Vollmann, who had represented his own work for most of his career, had recently arranged to have Golomb serve as his agent, in large part because of his inability to find a publisher for this massive project. Golomb eventually was able to arrange for the publication of the entire manuscript by McSweeney's Books in 2003 and for an abridged edition by Ecco Press in 2004. —LM

Dear Susan:

In February 1998 I completed a twenty-three-year project entitled *Rising Up and Rising Down*. This manuscript (which approaches 4,000 pages, and is thus only half the length of Routledge's *Encyclopedia of Philosophy*—all in all, a slim volume) attempts to delineate a moral calculus for violence—or, in other words, to determine when violence is justified. I believe this is one of the most important tasks which the human mind can hope to undertake. We read the Bible, Aquinas, Thucydides, Marx, Hitler, Gandhi, Caesar, and so many others to help form our opinions on this question among others.

Viking, FSG, and Grove, who've published my other ten books, have refused to touch a book of this length. Perhaps less crass is the fact that a more academically oriented press would (I hope) do the job right. My bibliography of sources cited in the text lists about 800 items; you can imagine how the footnotes do go on. I require exemplary proofreading, along with a certain welcome insouciance about publishing economics (for this book will obviously be very expensive to produce, especially with its many illustrations).

I am hoping in addition that, as my other publishers have done over the years, I will be allowed to say what I say in the way that I say it—in other words, editors may make suggestions, but all decisions on style and even punctuation must remain up to me. Otherwise I may as well be selling insurance.

What could I offer you in return? I believe that this book is worthy of standing in the shadow of Gibbon's *Decline and Fall of the Roman Empire.* Few people read Gibbon these days, and doubtless few will make it through *Rising Up and Rising Down.* That doesn't concern me much, and I hope that it won't you.

The book is theoretical, journalistic, and, like all my books, literary (which is why I don't much like wording changes). It falls into two parts, one historico-theoretical, and the other more experiential.

The theoretical part sketches moral portraits of Caesar, Napoleon, Trotsky, Stalin, Cortes, Montezuma, Joan of Arc, Sun-tzu, the Heike and Genji warriors of old Japan, Robespierre, Lincoln, John Brown, Martin Luther King, Gandhi, Hitler, the Amazons, the seventeenth-century Korean crown princess Lady Hyegyong, Viet Cong cadres, Lieutenant William Calley, the seventeenth-century Polish Rabbi Joel Sirkes (the Bach), Pancho Villa, Lawrence of Arabia, de Sade, and a few more.

For the experiential part, I have been fortunate enough to have had the opportunity of travelling to a number of war zones and odd places, thanks to a few mainstream magazines who've paid my way over the years. Among the individuals I've interviewed for this book are Biljana Plavsic, now Acting President of the Bosnian Serbs; Khun Sa, the "Opium King," the world's largest distributor of heroin; Bo Gritz, the most decorated Vietnam veteran in America and also the head of an apocalyptic, anti-Semitic survival cult; Hadji Amin Tohmeena of Pattani, who is the leader of the shadowy Malaysian "PULO" terrorist group sponsored by Qadhafi (they especially like to blow up schools and train stations); Khmer Rouge cadres, Japanese untouchables, Guardian Angels, and voodoo practitioners. Maybe half of the case studies in this book have appeared in those magazines, but out of context, with the footnotes removed, and, above all, abbreviated. Their appearance in *Rising Up and Rising Down,* therefore, should not be thought of as opportunistic recycling.

The "point" of the book occurs between its two halves. This is my moral calculus of violence, which consists of numbered axes. Since I am not a professional philosopher or logician, it is in places surely flawed and vague. But it is also honest, not overly complicated, and based on reading and experience, so if a revolutionary or a politician reads it, it may conceivably do real good in the world.

Accompanying the case studies in the experiential half of the text are a number of photographs which I have taken (some of which have appeared in magazines). United Nations "situation maps" are included for certain of the war zones I visited. A gangster in Jamaica's Rema ghetto drew me several maps of friendly and hostile territory in his neighborhood. And many analogous illustrations appear: neo-Nazi leaflets, Thai newspaper clippings, etc.

The theoretical section is be accompanied by counterpart reproductions of historical images: Napoleon at Eylau, Trotsky during the Russian Civil War, John Brown after Harpers Ferry, Joan of Arc, Gandhi, Tolstoy, Alexander Berkman, Heike warriors, and so on.

No illustrations are included with this packet of excerpts.

I have not indexed this book. It probably should be indexed.

I've been advised to provide a brief description of current literature on this topic. Michael Walzer's book on just and unjust wars is one example, but *Rising Up and Rising Down* attempts a much wider scope. I don't really know of any comparable work. The subject of ethical violence remains largely unexplored.

I believe that this book could be used in classes in: ethics, history, philosophy, criminology, Slavic studies, Asian studies, political science, and perhaps military science. In addition, since parts of it read well, I think, and since I have some reputation now as a literary author, it is possible that the English and literature classes which employ my other books might also use this one.

In any event, it is my life's work, and, if it comes remotely close to realizing its aims, it should be classed in the canon of great books.

Please let me know what you think.

Your friend,

William T. Vollmann

American Writing Today: Diagnosis of a Disease

From

Conjunctions (Vol. 15, Spring 1990)

Approximately 90% of neoplasms originate within 2 cm of the anterior midline of the mouth.

—*Dr. Rodney Million and Dr. Nicholas J. Cassisi*, **Management of Head and Neck Cancer: A Multidisciplinary Approach**

As this quotation shows, the mouth is a veritable fount of pestilence, vomiting forth its unclean words to infect all who are not armored with ignorance and earwax. Worse still is when the virus is sealed into a cartridge, positioned with a click of the pen-button, and squeezed through the ball-point onto a sheet of permanence, where spores of words wait gleefully for library centuries until they can attack new victims. Of course there are also saintly books which heal us with word-light, yet these are now sparse. Indeed, the American scene suffers from a plague of writers careless and even putrid. With the assistance of many learned doctors of oral and anal health, I now propose to set forth our responsibility, and some rules for reform.

This first requires that I set right all the woes of the world.

THE FAILURE OF AMERICAN SOCIETY

It is a commonplace that our United States are in decline. On the part of our government we have at best a shortsighted reactive strategy to specific events, lacking in any vision which might influence basic causes. As for the governed, our apathy and misinformation grow hourly. The terrifying increase in random violence and racism of all colors bespeaks a nation polarized halfway to impotence. From homelessness to schools where nothing is taught, from impending environmental disaster to continued environmental assault, our failures illuminate us as Selves incapable of comprehending others.

Our policy toward Nicaragua demonstrates that we cannot put ourselves in a Nicaraguan's shoes. Our laughable War on Drugs does not address the question of why people use drugs, or what people might do instead. Our suppression of abortion is not even hypocritical, it is simply, astoundingly, blind. And we truly have the "leadership" we deserve, for when we see the Other, what do we do? —Suppose that you do not rent whores, and a whore approaches you in the night-lit street, brave and desperate. Suppose that a member of some cult sets out to convert you. Suppose that someone begs you for money. —No, suppose simply that someone sits down beside you in your subway car and begins to talk to you. In how many cases will you answer?

THE FAILURE OF HUMANITY

To fail this test is only human. But survival and happiness depend on knowledge. And knowledge can only be obtained through openness, which requires vulnerability, curiosity, suffering.

The vicious Christian ignoramuses who are determined to end abortions in our country are cousins to the Muslims who preach murder, the Maoists who restore order in China beneath their tank-treads, the terrorists who shoot tourists in Peru or Sri Lanka. These will have their day, because they use force. But ultimately they will be defeated by force, and it will be a force they do not know. Why? Precisely because they will not know the Other. As long as they do not know it, how can they guard against it?

We must take care not to be like them. How can we best do this? By knowing them. By understanding without approving or hating. By empathizing.

How best to do that?

THE GLORIOUS ICE-CREAM BAR

Through art.

A RHAPSODY OF DESSERTS

Art takes us inside other minds, like a space capsule swooping down across Jupiter while the passengers can see strangeness and newness through the portholes, meanwhile enjoying all the comforts of standard Temperature and Pressure.

Of all the arts, although photography *presents* best, painting and music *convey* best, and sculpture *looms* best, I believe that literature *articulates* best.

THE PRESCRIPTION (WHICH MUST INEVITABLY SOUND DULL, LIKE A DOCTOR'S COMMAND TO TAKE MORE EXERCISE)

We need writing with a sense of purpose.

GENERIC DRUGS REJECTED

What about beautifully useless books, like the French *Maldoror*? —They too have their place. But there is too much writing nowadays that is useless WITHOUT being beautiful. —On the other side are those scarcely mentionable works which strive to be useful and fail in proportion to be beautiful: "socialist realism." In our own country we rarely fall into that mistake, but it does happen, as in the spots where *The Grapes of Wrath* is mildewed.

In this period of our literature we are producing mainly insular works, as if all our writers were on an airplane in economy seats, beverage trays shading their laps, faces averted from one another, masturbating furiously. Consider, for instance, *The New Yorker* fiction of the past few years, with those eternally affluent characters suffering understated melancholies of overabundance. Here the Self is projected and replicated into a monotonous army which marches through story after story like deadly locusts. Consider, too, the structuralist smog that has hovered so long over our universities, permitting only games of stifling breathlessness. (The so-called New Historicism promises no better.)

THE RULES

1. We should never write without feeling.
2. Unless we are much more interesting than we imagine we are, we should strive to feel not only about Self, but also about Other. *Not* the vacuum so often between Self and Other. *Not* the unworthiness of Other. *Not* the Other as a negation or eclipse of Self. Not even about the Other exclusive of Self, because that is but a trickster-egoist's way of worshipping Self secretly. We must treat Self and Other as equal partners. (Of course I am suggesting nothing new. I do not mean to suggest anything new. Health is more important than novelty.)
3. We should portray important human problems.
4. We should seek solutions to those problems. Whether or not we find them, the seeking will deepen the portrait.
5. We should know our subject, treating it with the respect with which Self must treat Other. We should know it in all senses, until our eyes are bleary from seeing it, our ears ring from listening to it, our muscles ache from embracing it, our gonads are raw from making love to it. (If this sounds pompous, it is perhaps because I wear thick spectacles.)
6. We should believe that truth exists.
7. *We should aim to benefit others in addition to ourselves.*

Afterword to Danilo Kiš's *A Tomb for Boris Davidovich*

Originally appearing in the Dalkey Archive Press reprint of Kiš's *A Tomb for Boris Davidovich* (2001), this afterword not only displays Vollmann's impressive skills as a reader and interpreter of others' works, but offers some of the most revealing statements he's ever made about his own writing as well. Opening with a backward glance at his troubled youth growing up in Indiana, Vollmann sketches in his early attraction for works such as Kiš's that removed him from this bastion of convervativism by offering "shocking incitements not only to my political development but also to my creative purpose." By introducing people struggling to retain a sense of themselves amidst the most extreme circumstances imaginable, Kiš and other Eastern European authors Vollmann was encountering about this time forced him to consider "the profoundest questions about what human nature is, or means." Intuitively drawn to extremity from a personal standpoint, Vollmann would adapt this approach of consciously using extremity as a means of illuminating the ordinary and make it a cornerstone of his aesthetics. Moreover, Kiš's "block method" of arranging *A Tomb* into a series of brief, highly compressed blocks of text that unfold in a collage-like manner rather than as linearly arranged narrative sequences, provided a structural model that Vollmann found to be enormously useful in his own composition process. As he put it in his *Paris Review* interview, "For me, at least, it's easier to create coherence and beauty on a small scale. Organize a block, reread, and rewrite from beginning to end. Afterward, the blocks can be arranged in a narrative or architectonic way, rejiggered accordingly."

Vollmann then summarizes the way Kiš jolted him out of his complacency by his powerful treatment of several crucial socio-political issues that Vollmann would wrestle with in his own work—the loss of historical memory (and the debilitating impact that television plays in this process in a society where "historical memory and political perceptiveness are attenuated in direct proportion to its commercialism"); the flawed nature of characters such as Kiš's Dr. Taube and Verschoyle (and by extension, himself) who are "romantics in the best and worst senses of the word" in that "both not only wish to do good, but also operate under the half-conscious thrall of aesthetic feelings;" and most fundamentally, the question of whether the reactionary forces of fascism and totalitarianism are inevitable results of human nature, or whether they are constructs that can be resisted and eventually overcome. Vollmann then concludes his summary of this debate between revolutionaries and conservatives in a manner that could serve as a gloss on the dialectic that has raged unabated in his own work, by asking "whether the beaten wives, perished workers and misled children ought to be classified under the same rubric of unavoidable, essential existence, or whether their tragedies, being the results of human agency, may be redressed through a massive change in social structures. What sort of changes?"

Vollmann's dedication in the forthcoming *Europe Central* suggests the impact Kiš has had on his work—"This book is dedicated to the memory of Danilo Kiš, whose masterpiece *A Tomb for Boris Davidovich* kept me company for many years while I was preparing to write this book." —LM

ABOUT TWENTY YEARS AGO, the bookstore which I frequented in Bloomington, Indiana, began to carry the Penguin "Writers from the Other Europe" series. Every title was chosen with care, translated with felicity, and intelligently introduced (the Joseph Brodsky introduction to the volume now in your hands being in my opinion the most impressive of an excellent lot). How can I describe the impression that these books made on me? I was a lonely, homely teenager who felt as stifled by the heartland as ever did any Trotsky or Emma Bovary. Although Bloomington was a college town, Indiana remained a typically American bastion of complacent parochialism, of brutal commercialism, indeed of anti-intellectualism and jingoism. Not far away, the Ku Klux Klan still paraded in Martinsville. The John Birch Society for its part helpfully spotlighted anti-American subversion. I was beaten up on the school bus two or three times by big, tall, stinking boys who called themselves "grits." They explained that it disgusted them to see somebody like me, who wore glasses and was always reading a *book* (this four-letter word, of course, being the worst of the obscenities they threw my way). I hasten to add that on the whole my high school years in Indiana were not unpleasant, thanks to the native friendliness of most Midwesterners. If I had to choose, I'd rather associate with kind people than with interesting or intellectual people who were not kind. Most Hoosiers, after all, were decent enough. And some of my friends had a kindred curiosity about the larger world; I've kept my ties with them to this day. As for the others, if I can understand why Greenland Eskimos or Québecois Francophones want to preserve their own ways of life, how could I fault my own fellow citizens for not being cosmopolitan? It's just that many, many things lay beyond the pale in Indiana. The bigotry and the hypocrisy were far less unnerving to me than the proud and cheerful *ignorance*—an all-American trait which continues to appall me to this day. Our government's military adventurism and capricious acts of repression around the world, our own disproportionate responsibility as American consumers for the degradation of the global environment, the murderous corruption of our "war on drugs," the ongoing domestic war against freedom of speech, and all the other rather unremarkable failings of a given nation at a given time—well, not many Americans waste much thought on them. I did not have the experience to comprehend all this twenty years ago. But I knew that I was missing something. There had to be more than *this.*

The books in the "Writers from the Other Europe" series were thrilling and shocking incitements not only to my political development but also to my creative purpose (for which again I'd like to thank the various translators). What can be said after a first reading of Borowski's concentration camp short stories? These exquisitely detailed vignettes of routine human interaction going on literally in sight of other human beings getting hurled into burning trenches raise the profoundest questions about what human nature is, or means. In my work as a journalist of war I've kept Borowski in mind. People in extreme situations are still, for better and for worse, people. Their doings become magnified. To share a scrap of bread is a heroic act. And to obey the law and denounce a Jew to the Gestapo, well, think of what that one simple act makes somebody!

I could go on at much greater length about Borowski, or about the unearthly beauty of Bruno Schulz's sentences, the spirit of doomed tenderness which shines like a magnesium flare in Jerzy Andrzejewski's *Ashes and Diamonds,* the moral dilemma of Hrabal's *Closely Watched Trains,* the extraordinarily effective study of how memory is tainted by atrocity in Konwicki's *A Dreambook for Our Time,* the despairingly ironic "jests" of Kundera's short stories. Suffice it to say that the "Other Europe" of the series is a sad, cold, terrorized, yet strangely mystical place. By the shadow of Soviet repression and by the gravitational pull of Planet Auschwitz, these other Europeans are compelled to consider the most fundamental questions of human existence. Of course it would be offensive to glamorize the situations in which the characters find themselves. But we can be grateful to the authors who brought them to life. Not only do their hard-learned lessons, or failures to learn, illuminate our own capabilities and limitations as moral and spiritual beings, but the tellings of the tales sometimes become great art.

Such is the case with *A Tomb for Boris Davidovich.*

Why has this book in particular been always on my desk or at my shelf for twenty years? As I said, growing up in a society whose historical memory and political perceptiveness are attenuated in direct proportion to its commercialism, I knew that I was missing something. I vaguely understood that something was amiss in my surroundings, but I remained unable to possess even the falsely glamorized conception of Communism which leads Dr. Taube in "The Magic Card Dealing" to "join the workers." (Nor, therefore, was I in any particular danger of suffering his fate.) In the end I became somebody a little more like Gould Verschoyle in "The Sow that Eats Her Farrow." Verschoyle's character has been formed at least in part by his home city of Dublin, with its "carnivalesque cohort" of "nobly disappointed, aggressive bohemians, professors in redingotes, superfluous prostitutes, infamous drunkards, tattered prophets," etcetera. And so he goes to fight on the side of the left-wing angels in Spain. I myself became a hack journalist.

Both Dr. Taube and Verschoyle are romantics in the best and worst senses of the word. Both not only wish to do good, but also operate under the half-conscious thrall of aesthetic feelings. Was Dr. Taube's desire to become a Communist based entirely on an aversion to "the exploitation of man by man," or did his own town's "quarters of murderous light and damp, moldy shade resembling darkness" (the passage has already been quoted at greater length in Brodsky's introduction) have anything to do with it? In other words, did he, like me, feel alone in a place whose harshly, hopelessly reactionary ethos he took or mistook to be something other than the natural human condition? For if there was truly no getting away from the daily round in which husbands beat their wives, unemployed workers freeze to death in the streets and children get taught lies in school (or watch television), how unutterably terrible life would be! Buddha, we're told, was similarly horrified when he discovered the existence of sickness, old age and death. He rejected things as they were. Much of the unending debate between revolutionaries and conservatives has to do with whether the beaten wives, perished workers and misled children ought to be classified under the same rubric of unavoidable, essential existence, or whether their tragedies, being the results of human agency, may be redressed through a massive change in social structures. What sort of changes? To imagine that in other contexts Dr. Taube and Verschoyle might have chosen to be, say, Mexican nationalists or American animal-rights activists is in no way to trivialize them. *A Tomb for Boris Davidovich* is not about Communism-as-ideology. Dr. Taube and Verschoyle are as real—"round" characters beyond ideology—as is, say, Pierre in *War and Peace*. Pierre wants to be good and do good. In the course of his frequently blundering development, he tries many roles: an admirer of Napoleon, loyal if unloving husband, a Freemason, a Napoleon-hater, and finally a happy family man. In the twentieth century he undoubtedly would have flirted with Communism.

Why is the phrase "do-gooder" synonymous with "naive innocent"? One twentieth-century sourpuss said that only a callow or hard-hearted soul isn't a Marxist at age twenty, and only a fool remains a Marxist at age forty. In the twenty-first century, Marxism will be replaced by an equally fiery -ism. The best thing which can happen to do-gooders between twenty and forty is that they retain and even deepen their desire to benefit the world, while at the same time developing a realistic understanding of the ethics of ends and means. The end does not justify the means and never will. Moreover, some ends and some means, however laudable, are impractical. What to do? Join the workers in a fashion that that will do the workers some good, without unjustly hurting anybody else.

It is debatable how far on this maturing path Dr. Taube and Verschoyle are able to travel before they come to their separate bad ends. Verschoyle perhaps learns more, for he figures out enough to report to his commanding officer in Spain that "coded messages are getting into the wrong hands." Dr. Taube eventually realizes that he is being kept in isolation from the Russian people whose progressiveness he idolizes, but by then it's already too late. Regardless of how we might otherwise judge either of these men, it seems that they are both brave, warm-hearted, benevolent and perhaps even useful to the cause they serve. Under almost any other circumstances, these traits would have ensured their status as instruments of good.

The circumstances which prevailed, however, might be summed up in a single proper name: J. V. Stalin.

A case could be made that the murderousness of Leninism should have been warning enough to steer clear of Stalinism. In spite of all the obstacles to learning the truth—or maybe because of them—Solzhenitsyn was able to denounce the revolution's earliest epoch in the first volume of his *Gulag Archipelago*. To many of us who believed that Lenin was not all that bad, those chapters were shocking. The recent unsealing of old murder files, particularly of the horrifying documents in the "secret archive" presented in translation by Richard Pipes, makes clear the cruelty of Marxist praxis in Russia from, at latest, the civil war onward. But in the epoch of Verschoyle and Dr. Taube, a true believer could have plausibly entertained the idea that the excesses of the Reds in the Russian civil war have been counterbalanced or even caused by the crimes of the Whites, and, moreover, that you can't make an omelet without breaking eggs. Shortly before he was pickaxed to death by a Stalinist assassin in 1940, Trotsky appealed to his readers to give the revolutionary experiment more time. Three decades, he insisted, were hardly enough for the bloody dust to settle. The people of the USSR gave Communism more than seven decades and it never ceased to fail them. By the time I first discovered *A Tomb for Boris Davidovich,* the Trotskyites had had to fall back on the pathetic slogan: *"Defend bureaucratically deformed workers' states!"* In other words, the Communist system stank, but it was still the best around. Millions of people decided otherwise.

In Dr. Taube's time, there was still hope. We must also remember that the encirclement of the Soviet Union by hostile capitalist states was a proven fact (no matter that Stalin made paranoid capital from it), that Communism had been brutally put down in Germany, and that the nightmare of Hitlerism now threatened everything that the Taubes and Verschoyles stood for. No wonder that to a believer in the nobility of socialism, Soviet Communism, even Stalin's Communism, was the last best chance. It would have taken more suspiciousness than most do-gooders possess to fathom Stalin. And maybe, like some of my American friends, they wanted to remain ignorant. Maybe in politics, as in sexuality, a purity of passion exists only in the preconsummation state of half-blind surmises.*

It is part of Danilo Kiˇs 's achievement to have created these two more or less sympathetic characters, who can be accused of no sins more serious than self-delusion. The Communist ideal is of course more fully realized in Boris Davidovich Novsky in the title story. Unlike Verschoyle and Dr. Taube, this man is hardheaded, competent, effective, trusted and even famous—a real hero. Precisely for that reason (such runs the Stalinist logic), he has to get eliminated, for what if someday he got the idea of offering himself as an alternative? His Achilles's hell is pride in his own rectitude. If the Communist Party is the most scientific and advanced vehicle for the salvation of humanity, and if, therefore, it must be considered "my Party, right or wrong," and if it needs me to do anything, no matter how loathsome, which it claims will accomplish the end, then I'd better do it. This is the argument which wins over Novsky's counterpart, Comrade Rubashov, in Koestler's famous *Darkness at Noon.* What wins Novsky over, on the contrary, is being forced to watch the murder of men who physically resemble himself, immediately after each victim has been told: "If Novsky doesn't confess, we'll kill you!" And Novsky, with that failing—or virtue—which afflicts people who care about the world and long to improve it, feels responsible for these deaths. In *The Brothers Karamazov,* Dostoyevsky at one point propounds the doctrine that our only

*For a panorama of Communist sincerity across Europe in World War II, and its various convolutions and involutions, the reader is recommended to read Manes Sperber's novel trilogy *Like a Tear in the Ocean.*

hope of rescuing humankind from its own evil is through acknowledging our kinship with one another to such a degree that we experience guilt and repentance for violence committed by others. This magnificently crazed notion may well be appropriate for lone politician-saints such as Gandhi. For Novsky, it's fatal. He "realized with horror that this repetition" of murders "was not accidental, but part of an infernal plan: each day of his life would be paid for with the life of another man; the perfection of his biography would be destroyed." And so Novsky, like Verschoyle and Dr. Taube, gets duped precisely because he possesses empathy and compassionate impulses (no matter that it's masked by the pretense of cold vanity over his reputation). He agrees to confess.

The more pragmatic careerist Chelyustnikov in "The Mechanical Lions" fares less better than Novsky, for he has fewer ideals. He lives out his term in a prison camp. Whatever false confession he's made to sign, we can be sure that it affects him less by wounding his trickster-conscience than by pricking his apprehensions about his own survival. Likewise, the envious, anti-Semitic murderer Miksha Hantescu in "The Knife With the Rosewood Handle" perishes in the Gulag only through the generalized neglect of his jailers, not through any decree of liquidation. And, indeed, survivors of the camps have often attested that criminals won more success there than politicals. (Miksha doubtless would have met a better fate had he not been a foreigner, hence an unreliable element.) Kiš's warning in these series of parables is horrifically clear: In systems such as Stalin's, people are vulnerable to the ultimate degree of repression in direct proportion to their generosity of heart.

This is why I sympathize with Brodsky's conclusion in the introduction that *A Tomb for Boris Davidovich* "achieves aesthetic comprehension where ethics fail." I sympathize with it, but I disagree with it. It is precisely in such situations as Kiš's characters find themselves that ethics is most desperately needed. One cannot blame the Chelyustnikovs overmuch; certainly one cannot blame them in comparison to the Stalins. But surely by that very token we ought to honor the Novskys who retain sufficient integrity to feel ethically cornered in a context far from entirely of their own making. Granted, Novsky's ethics in his cold prison darkness may be best described as a beacon of light without warmth. Granted, he's misled by them in the end—or is he? Maybe his choice to save the lives of his other doubles by confessing was really the best one. Who can say? At least he made a choice.

As representatives of the various human types and motives which can be marshaled by a given ideology, Kiš's characters are inexhaustibly memorable. Indeed, they're universal. The steady man Chelyustnikov is of a piece with the Khmer Rouge general I once interviewed who joined that gang of Maoist murderers with open-eyed enthusiasm simply because he could see that Pol Pot would win. The poet Darmolatov can be found today in every culture and regime of the world. And Kiš reminds us of that fact with his parallel tale "Dogs and Books," set six centuries before the fall of Novsky.

I scarcely need repeat Brodsky's praises of the style, whose merit would have been apparent without them. The author's economy of language (which Brodsky rightly calls "a poetic type of operation"), combined with equal parts of lyricism and desperate irony, work together to make this one of the great books, though firmly set in a specific time, and could be profitably read and reread when all the Marxist states have become as fabulously forgotten as the civilization of the Etruscans.

Debts and Debtors

From
Fathers and Crows

As he does in his other volumes of the *Seven Dreams*, Vollmann inserts himself into the text and examines what consequences the events of history have on the present—the people, the culture, and the meaning of "history" itself. —MH

A reference, at least, to the missionary efforts of the French, while in the occupation of Canada, ought not to be omitted.

***—Lewis Henry Morgan, League of the Iroquois* (1851)**

Eleven days before the English conquered Québec forever, they burned a little French town. The Captain of the HMS *Scarborough* (Admiralty 1022) sat looking at the flames for a moment and opened the log. Now he made the march back through the foliage of the previous hours' memories which rustled about him like the maples around that settlement: . . . *all the inhabitance was, run in the woods,* he wrote, *where we searched strictly and found an Indian cannue and several other things, but most of their affects they carried with them, so we left 30 men in the ridout all night and had shooting parties out all day . . .*

The Anglophones, they don't know exactly nothing! shouted Pierre.

He wedded his pretty Marie-Claude in the month of Aoˆu t,when the mosquitoes and blackflies were not too bad, so that they could have the reception at their country house. In the photograph, he grins holding his champagne glass, bearing the confetti in his hair, and she is laughing so hard she is almost crying. The forest rises behind them. Confetti spangles his dark suit.

I visited them in Novembre. They lived in Montréal. The Fleuve Saint-Laurent was the hue of a tarnished mirror which split the whole world of Canada in two (all the way to China, as far as the Sieur de Champlain could tell). Over the Fleuve hung clouds fire-red at the edges like hellish essences, votive candles. Below these stretched an evening of white-roofed blocks of houses, brassy yellow eyes of automobiles in the narrow crevices between the house-encrusted plates of ivory. The roofs bore their snow more thickly at their eaves than in the middle. Trees were frosted grey with snow. Puzzle pieces of snow-white and tree-grey alternated outside of the town. A bluish-grey chill was manifest over all. I walked through slushy icy streets whose nested curves were like the ridges of some colossal fingerprint, and reached rue Sainte-Catherine. The whores were smiling and shivering; the department stores glittered with Christmas. Snow thickened on everyone's shoulders.

The light was on. When I rang the bell, Pierre buzzed me in. I could see him waiting for me at the top of the stairs, smiling. He shook my hand; Marie-Claude kissed me *salut!* —smack, smack! Pierre was saying: Do you want some juice? Do you want some coffee? Treat this house as yours; open everything! —and I gave Marie-Claude a vase and she kissed me again, saying delightedly: yes, we don't have!

Pierre and Marie-Claude were Québecois. They were the Old Canadians now, like Champlain, like Amantacha, like Born Underwater.

The Cross

The most difficult part of our identity right now is to understand exactly what we are and what we were before, when the Canadian spirit came to reality. (Thus Pierre.) For me, the problem is this: we never governed ourselves—never! Champlain was the Governor. It was always Paris or London. We were always the colony. It's hard in that situation. You create a national identity, but you don't have the political power to assure this identity. And so it's always a failure. We were New France. After, we were French-Canadian, when the British won the war, and now we're Canadian because the British decide that. That's the only way we're Canadian.*

So, do you think Canada would have been better if Wolfe had been defeated?

*"I'm sure this is what M[arie-Claude] and P[ierre] would say." (Thus Trigger.) "But they have had great political power to regulate the life of everyone in Québec since a provincial parliament was established in 1867, & great economic power since the Quiet Revolution of the 1960s. This sense of powerlessness is a manifestation of false consciousness that powerfully reinforces cultural identity at the expense of individual fulfillment (& justifies individual failures such as we all have)."

No, I don't say that. The English people, they're like United States: they don't like Inuit or Indians. And the French had a lot of *mépris,* a lot of suspicion and bad feeling about the Indians. Some people don't bother about that. They just say: oh well, it's another Country, a great space, a beautiful Country, bizarre people . . . I have no bad feeling; I'm happy to know who I was. But many Québecois don't want to admit they were a part of an Indian kind of life before. How can you analyze our people today with such progress, with white people, television, comfort economically, and so and so, and say: well, not long time ago we were in the bush; we were like those Indians? You look at Indians now and it is hard to say: oh, we were similar. Do you understand? It's hard to figure that we were like them. Now the ideology try to tell us: you are white, and you are pure white. And the Indians have the same ideology for them: we are Indian, we are red, and we are pure red.

Do you think that started with the Catholics?

Oh yes. The Jesuits did it. And then Marguerite Bourgeoys, she opened the first school here in Montréal, and she tried to educate the young Canadian girls and the young Indian girls. She had a very big problem with the young Canadian girls, because they want to become *Indian!* (The Indians, they were okay; they listened quite well.) Marguerite Bourgeoys, she said: those young Canadian girls are so wild! And many, many Jesuits said the same. What was the purpose of the Jesuits? To penetrate the Country, firstly, to penetrate the hearts of those first Indian people. Secondly, to help French grab the Country. The best way to do that is by the religion. We know that the Indians are a very spiritual People. I don't know exactly why they played that game with the Jesuits and the Recollects and every kind of priest that came here. But they did. They played the game, and they lost the game.*

You know, Pierre, when I first started reading about Tekakwitha, I said: What a sad victim she was! She ended up being someone who thought she was so bad that she literally had to torture herself to death. Because she killed herself, she became a Sainte. That doesn't seem right.

But the Catholics at that time always had that kind of ideology, of

*"A profound observation," returns Trigger. "My suspicion is that they played the religious game even more seriously as a consequence of knowing they had lost."

education. We learned, ever since we came into the life, that we are guilty for something.

For Adam?

Maybe, he laughed. And we have to live with that. The educational system here, family system, work system, political system, all work with the same idea.

When you were a boy, and went to church, what did they say to you about the Indians then? Did they say anything?

No. Only in school. And there we had the old books, the old ideas. The Indians were the hypocrites, they were Savage, wild . . .

When was the first time you saw an Indian?

I was young. My parents lived near from Oka. I saw there poverty. I saw criminals. I said: oh, all that the books have told me is true. It took a long time before I analyzed and said to myself it's not so simple like that. And I'm afraid that the majority of people here don't make the same distance. It's the same for black and white, for everything. You know, the government here never recognize that Métis can exist here. No half-breeds in Québec.

So a person is either Indian or white?

Yes.

Do the Indians in Québec consider themselves Québecois?

No.

Do they consider themselves Canadian?

Oh, it's hard for them. It's a failure. I remember ten years ago they said: we are Canadian; we are proud of it. And we are Indian. —Five years ago they began to say: we are the first Canadians. We were here before you. —And now they say: We are Indian. We are not Canadian.

When you used to go to Caughnawagwa, did you feel that the Indians there felt any kinship toward you as a human being?

Not really. The last time that I go there, I play before at a sport called lacrosse. And we played against Caughnawagwa. The RCMP* had to come after the game, to escort us out of the reserve.

For your safety?

Exactly. It was tough. Very tough. They looked for fight.

*Royal Canadian Mounted Police.

What would they have thought if you'd worn relics of Tekakwitha around your neck? Would they have thought about you any differently?

I hope not, because I'm not agreeing with Kateri Tekakwitha. I don't understand why many Indians respect that kind of symbol. For me it means colonialism, alienation. I feel a little painful. For myself, if I were an Indian, I would put fire to those things on my reserve.

The Doll

In Montréal at the dawn of a hot August day surrounded by the sounds of cats and birds, your prayer sits aching, unsleeping, rubbing eyes with wingtips. The grey cat is also awake, and she comes to your prayer's bed with raised ears, turning her head to follow the car-sounds with such regularity that it makes your prayer weary to hear it. Sweat breaks out on your prayer's shoulders. Today at last your prayer will kiss Catherine's relics.*

The shrine dedicated to her is indeed, as Pierre has implied, at Kahnawaké, which place—although it has moved several times since 1668, it is true—may now be reached by taking the number ten autobus to the Pont Mercier, disembarking, and *walking* that bridge's shuddering length (having no other option due to the Voyageur bus strike, now in its second year—well, your prayer could fly, it is true, but the distance is now so negligible!) Upon making this portion of the Exercises it is customary for the pilgrim to *gaze* down into the Fleuve Saint-Laurent with its dull whitecaps of toilet paper from the sewage outflow. Now in the humid haze of the day your prayer sees the greenness of the far side, from which a gilded steeple rises, and your prayer keeps walking, inhaling perforce the exhaust of the big trucks or camions that shake the bridge and make your prayer wobble in their air-wash; and then there is a gap in the walkway through which workmen's curses ascend, and then your prayer arrives at the Caughnawagwa side. Your prayer descends the embankment and passes through the ditch of sumacs and thistles (that is the First Prelude) into the aforementioned Kahnawaké, where brown moths follow

*For the true sense we must have in the Church Militant we should observe the following rules," begins Ignatius. "The sixth: to praise the relics of the Saints by venerating them and praying to these Saints."

your prayer, clinging to sweaty trousers and sweaty wings. The Mohawk, who are not unfriendly, direct your prayer past the cemetery and up the hill to the shrine, just before which your prayer buys itself a Canada Dry. The lady at the cash register says that the temperature will reach 30° Celsius. *C'est bien dommage.*

Now here is the Church with its many ribboned bouquets, its marriage bouquets posted on the door. This is a living Church. Above the altar, high above, is JESUS, arms in Jansenist position. Ignatius is on His left, holding aloft a monstrance. François Xavier with the crucifix is on His right. Just over the flickering candles, an arrow-sign says **RELICS OF KATERI TEKAKWITHA.**

Your prayer's heart beats painfully.

There is her tomb, a block of white marble delectably candied with a golden turtle to represent her clan, and the words

KAIATANORONKATERI TEKAKWITHA1656–1680

behind which stands her wooden statue with its tall elongated shadow. She stands staring ahead of her, clasping her arm over her breast, her robe pulled tight as a shroud. A Crucifix sprouts from her left hand; rosary-roots descend from her right. A pink blossom rests between her crossed palms. Her eyes stare so far away . . . Before her, like another offering, is the text of a prayer to GOD, Who is called in the Mohawk language SEWENNIJO.

A Mohawk woman approaches the tomb. With her is a girl of six or seven years. They kneel. —Ask her to bless everybody, the mother says.

Is she in there? asks the child.

No, but her bones are.

There are two portraits, one on each side of the altar. On the right she is in profile praying. On the left she stands spreading her arms to release a corona of stars. Her hair is jet-black. Her lips are as pink as the flowers of the raspberry called *ronce odorante.* She stands upon a crescent. Above her are two Faces. She is beautiful.

A Hiroquoise genuflects at the altar-rail, hiding herself in jet-black hair.

(Saint Kateri is part of the altar also. Angels hold an immense Crown over her. She is a little unadorned doll in her buckskins, her head on her shoulder, her arms crossed.)

On the wall of the old fortress abutting the Church it says **SMOKE WEED, DRINK BEER, GET LAID.**

The Martyr

At the country house, it was snowing again, and one of the cats was curled up on the sofa by the bearskin which clings to the wall with outstretched claws as if it were flying. Marie-Claude's father had shot it. Pierre mixed me up a Clamato just right, with lemon and Worcestershire, and I sat thinking about how Tekakwitha's fingers were reddish-brown but she wanted them to become as white as snowy alder-twigs transfixed by darkness.

Marie-Claude was always singing and kissing Pierre. (He said to me confidentially: She is an Angel!)

Pierre sat beside me, and I toasted him, saying: Here's to the Roy de Clamato! Here's to the Roy de Sentier! —and Pierre laughed, and Marie-Claude shouted at a woman on television, calling her tart and pig, and the other cat scratched at the window from outside, waiting and licking its snowy paw, and Pierre let him in while Marie-Claude sang a song as beautiful as anything out of the Mohawk hymnal or gradual which the Black-Gowns had composed at Kahnawaké, with its square notes of praise-music rising and falling, and Pierre said:

Here in Québec, you know, many people call Québec *Réserve du Québec.* Because our history is like Indian in a way. And we even have accommodators like Tekakwitha! When French Canadians become Prime Minister of the Canada, they come to speak English and only English. They become proud of the Crown, the British Queen. For me it's exactly the same. And also we have our Saints and Martyrs, killed by the Indians. They tortured them. They too were Tekakwithas. And this is what they tell us: Our good Saint-Father were killed by the bad ugly Savage Indians!

Statement at the Beatification Mass 1980

The last months of her life, said Pope John Paul II, *are an even clearer manifestation of her solid faith, straightforward humility, calm resignation and radiant joy, even in the midst of terrible sufferings.*

Canadians

Since three hundred years, with Jesuit, with intellectual people, they try to tell us we are not Indian, said Pierre. Since three hundred years! And this still continue today, more than ever. Because we don't want to be an Indian. I know for myself I'm not an Indian: little, blond, blue eyes . . . But somatically I think I was. I am, and historically I was. I believe that we half-breed with Indian; we take part in their point of view of the world. We approach the whole continent that way.

I think the best thing for our strength now, said Marie-Claude, is for the Indian, to not search for purity, and the same for us. We should say with the Indian: come on, let's get together and act for our land! It's not the English one way, the French one way, and the Indian another way. It's the same fight. So we should work together. And the Indian must lose this damn search for the *red—red, red, red!* "You're a Métis; you're not an Indian." Like us, we say: "If you don't have grandparents that come from Normandie, you're not a real one." That's one of the things that makes me angry, that bothers me! And one mistake is, we always look what was before. The Indians say: We were here before! Stop fighting like that. In each Canadien Français there is a little bit of Savage. There's no solution as long as the Canadien Français say: We don't want the Indian inside us! And the Indian the same. —What is a Canadian? It's a European that came here, that went Métis, and stayed here. If you admit that, there's no problem.

I said nothing.

We are angry about our dominator, said Marie-Claude. Either France, then England. Of course we are near French, because we speak French. But a French that stay here and doesn't métis, who doesn't breed with the Indian, for me he is as bad as the English that did the same thing. Our identity is here.

So would you say that Tekakwitha was one of the first Canadians in a way? Because she represented that movement, that mixing between Indians and French.

No! cried Pierre. For me, she tried to become a beautiful white, and because of that failure, she kill herself.

She didn't try to become a Canadian! said Marie-Claude. She try to be a French. She did not want to admit that she was Indian.

(But at this I could not but think of Sainte Catherine her namesake being stretched between two spiked wheels, throwing out her hands and screaming with anguish while a light like radioactivity had already begun to glow around her face and JESUS leaned down from the clouds with His arms outstretched for her and a little cherub came flying down with a garland and a river of light and blood flowed upward from her soul-spring.)

What if there were Indians who didn't want to be Canadians? I said. The French and the English who came here had a choice. If they didn't want to become Canadians, as you say, they could go back to France. But the Indians had nowhere else to go.

But, Bill, said Marie-Claude, in 1989 you don't have the choice. You must be Canadian here or you die. You don't have the choice to be Métis, to be free; you don't have a chance.

What about the reserves like Kahnawaké? Are they useless?

It's like a zoo! When you have extinctious animal, you put them there, so you can make experiments, and maybe breed them there . . . But when the last tiger come in the zoo, it will be the last. Maybe if you keep the tiger out, and he try to breed, maybe he have more chance like that! If their soul want to live, they must extend their people!

But, Marie, said her husband, if the Indians go outside the reserve, if you abolish the reserve, in ten years there will be no Indians.

To the Right Honourable Reader

From *Argall*

Due to Vollmann's decision to undertake the arduous task of composing *Argall* entirely in Elizabethan English, this installment of the *Seven Dreams* series is perhaps his most difficult novel to read. We can imagine the sales and marketing people at Viking sighing, shaking their collective heads, and asking themselves: "How are we suppose to sell this?" Still, we can't help but admire the dedication and sheer audacity of such a literary mission. Sometimes these experiments work, and sometimes they don't. In this excerpt, Vollmann the author addresses the reader much in the spirit of the literature of the times. Such author-to-reader asides appear throughout Vollmann's other novels. —MH

RIGHT HONOURABLE,

My duetie remembered, & c:

I FEAR TO COMPOUND my first offense, in penning such slender and tuneless lines as these, by presuming to direct them to yourself, particularly when their subject is a mere Wilderness of insignificant Salvages. For what could bulk more worthy of our puzzlings (save THE ALMIGHTIE Himself), than the hives of GODliness we call *Cities*? And what less so, than Fens & frog-pools? (O darling fat frogs! If witches denied to take you in marriage to be their familiars, we wouldn't need to burn witches!) I incline toward the best, Right Honourable; I'd fain kiss your hand—yet this Book of mine doth drag me down toward the worst. Truth to tell, my own self mires me now. My mind descends and condescends to foulness; the tale I must tell's putrescent with sin—dangerous not to you, Right Honourable, for by virtue of your celestial blood you're proof against infamy's infections, but I own no such liquid armor, being chinked betwixt my platelets with Adam's taint. Therefore, did you give me leave I'd take my leave of *Captaine Argall, John Smith & Princesse Pokahuntas* before e'er their simulacra broach'd your stage! But already I see inferior persons applauding Pocahontas (no matter that some snicker in their sleeves, her dark squatness proving her risibility). She curtseys to a well-trained perfection, tossing to her admirers **.1.** glove of white doeskin embroider'd with green silk. And what else may be won of her? —To this Argall's Sailors shout obscene reply e'en as they troll their ale-bowl lip to lip, moustaches rank and dripping. —Argall laughs: No doubt, villains! But my golden goose is not for sale to such as you. Spit other chickens on your Welsh hooks! —O misbegotten Argall, I love thee not; thy doings disgust me. —But hale him away (no matter that this Dream's call'd after him), and the story-hole remains no less fetid with dishonor, contrivance, cruelty, butchery, stooping sneakiness—why not spade our tale entire into a mucky grave? And belike I might long howl in this strain, like some dog that fears to obey his Master's call, yet must, therefore slinks and whirls in cunning crazy circles, approaching his own fear only because he dreads that his fear might approach him. Howbeit, such eccentric navigations will scarce win us belly-timber—not when there's a whole Globe of fears to be crossed! Let's cross it, then.

* * *

Should it please you, Reader, we'll embark at wise-named *Gravesend*, to put period to our English doom. Life at home being death, why not steal resurrection from Salvages? (No matter that those so named remain diabolically unsalvaged, for they know not OUR REDEEMER. No matter that they likewise in His Book have been en-*graved.* And why not? Even our Queen must die—at least 'till the day call'd *Tombsend,* when CHRIST cometh.) Gravesend, end of all graves! If we could but get beyond that Towne, what colorfully immortal careers we'd make! And by God's wounds, that's easy! For Gravesend leads everywhere. Just as Swineshead's a reliable locale for flax, and *Virginia's* a most likely place to kidnap Salvages, so Gravesend enjoys her own fame, being dubbed *the Station of Limbo:* terminus for London-Towne (which lieth but a **.4.** hours' sail away—tuppence by open barge) —O, throughway she is, birth canal bristling with ships, expedient river-huddle stinking of slops and gudgeons,[*] tavernway for Sailors, tipplers and trulls, merchantway where Astrologers offer lodestones for sale to lost Captaines whose hearts crave piracy and whose sea-boys run a-chasing after scandaled, diseased and lickerish hacksters who do uplift their petticoats for pay. —Why don't the boys sit patient on their penny-purses? After all, in *Virginia,* where they're bound, Salvage wenches fresh-painted with oil and puccoons will be their bedfellows. —Well, you see, Virginia's virgin to their ears, just as Gravesend's GOD send to all of us whirligig-men and layabouts, us jesting time-servers, unqualitied Adventurers, dilettantes, sharp actors, vendors, ferrymen, Watermen, shipwrights, innkeepers, pickpockets, blind historians and upstart yeomen who swim in *Between-Times,* watching half-shut opportunities wag their jaws. Shall we rush in, to percase be devoured, or rather tread water at a safer distance, slowly drowning? Thus in Gravesend we wait, dear comets, rocking 'twixt land and sea.[**]

* * *

In fine, time becalms itself; aspirations swither and swelter. The curtain's not yet up; Virginia's unstoried, and I sit in my swivel chair, not troubling to consult my reference works. (How *did* the Salvages make their arrows?) They call for Pocahontas to make Salvage curtseys anew; they demand to taste her submission to Argall and our Sovereign. They thirst for tales to flow down their gullets. But stay a space, Right Honourable. Look on Gravesend while you may. She's but vestibule to this Dream of mine. When we exit, 'tis for good—ha! at least 'till we come back again: There's Gravesend for you! None can be divided forever from earth's oozy bosom. Burn'd alive on a stage, like convicted highwaymen, or drown'd in shroud and cannonball like Cabin-boys perished of the pest, yet translated flesh must revert: Bone-smoke comes

[*] Certain freshwater fishes (in this case dead ones).

[**] "If bound up-river," advises a yachtsman's manual from 1993, "it is not very useful to arrive at the lock of Gravesend just before high water so it will sometimes be preferable to lie at anchor in the river throughout an ebb tide. This can be done by choosing a quiet spot about a mile downriver from the lock and just below the Ship and Lobster."

down at last to besoot the ground, and the waterlogged youths fall not for all time, but find the *Octopus's* kelpy bed. And we ourselves, briefly resurrected from our womb-grave, paddle down the Thames, lay plots at Gravesend, then fall clay-claimed. *That's* for good, now, isn't it?

Still and all, no voyager returns to his grave unchanged. As for those Adventurers who sail for Virginia, why, still deeper in them bites the strange mordant. 'Tis law that something dies within them before they perish. Like felon at rope's end, crewman at Gravesend, they're divorced from earth. When they beach their aspirations in Virginia's clasp, divorce itself darkens into specious uncertainty; the heart meets nothing to which it can give itself; memory falls away from itself. And if haply they return to Gravesend, for an eye-blink e'en pickpockets stand clear, fearing with a long-clawed snatch to gain not gold, but death. For the Adventurers' faces are as salt-etched mirrors, which do betray the onlooker's own vacancy. *Cain, Methusaleh* and *Lazarus,* who pretended to cheat death in Virginia, all wore leather-green faces at homecoming, & their eyeballs rolled fierce and ghostly like the silver-bluish sea. What did they gain? Ask 'em how many fathoms falls the sea-drop off Ryppe Rappe Bank, or who stands duty today on the .2.nd Dog Watch, and they can answer you; but inquire about Virginia, and Cain will keep silent, Methuselah will mutter only that he's never seen anything like her in his entire longish life, and Lazarus huskily whispers: Virginia's another world, she is. Dangers and suchlike, you know . . . the Great Beyond . . . —And his eyes are wet and blank like mussel-shells. What slew those men? Which fate did they choose from the ships at Gravesend that tremble all in a row? Why, I told you—they wed Virginia so as to taste her .5.-foot codfishes, her cherry-trees & hurtleberries, her turpentine sweet as angelic ichor. They read from the Book of Kings: *I dug wells and drank foreign waters, and I dried up with the sole of my foot all the streams in Egypt.* Thus the story of Virginia—and, indeed, of all these .7. Dreams. The theme: *Success.* But when they returned to bed down at Gravesend, barnacles preyed upon their beards. What faded them? They speak no more. Ask their brethren who yet haunt this place—the new Venturers, I mean. They've been cured ere now in departure's breezes; their Fishwife-lemans swear they've sped to Hell and back, like the Lincolnshire tides. See that salt-stained old jewel? He and his brother sail'd *beyond* Hell to enter Virginia's quim. Quick! Follow them to the Cheer-house! What hath their travels taught them? They drink wisdom in their rum, then piss it out. They go to Church-yards, or to sea, whichever proves their doom. Sailors, why cast yourselves as lots, when you know you must lose the game? What good's gold in the tomb? Aren't all rewards as this crooked Dream of mine, which hath Virginia's virtues, and therefore twinkles like pyrites, but cannot raise the dead?

A drunkard raises his head, turns upon me his sensitive, red-rimmed gaze, and replies: Not true! Death dwells only here. If I can but find a Captaine, he'll save me, for that's his business; he'll take me far away . . .

Very well, dream-sponge, await your Captaine's pleasure for another dozen ale-draughts here at Gravesend! Why *won't* he guide you to immortality? No matter that his nobility's greenish like decayed brass armor-links, his sealed commission speaks but rumors, and your wages prove but promises paid in the currency of desire. In all these many-masted ships crowded together so that they resemble a dead forest trembling on the tide—argosies, shallops, barges, double-masted barks with scarce a pair of stained sails, pinnaces, carracks & caravels, cock-boats & ketches, admirals, swift flyboats whose many taut canvases drink in the wind as if they long to be gone—there blooms perhaps but **.1.** leafy tree in whose bower your good Captaine readies everything. He's rarer than an alligator with a conscience. His name is *Captaine Fortune.* (Drink a round to him!) Nay, his nobility's not verdigris'd at all. But how can one know him, who hasn't served him first? Hurry! Life waits not! Quickly choose him and go! For here comes Death! — There—that's the man to bestow yourself on, for he pities you, and the whores his men haunt say he gives good wages. (*They* know; they've picked pockets, nay, plumbed 'em down to the last shilling. When they robbed the Gunner's Mate they found a gold noble hid behind his balls—that means **.6.** shillings **.8.** pence. So tell me they don't cheerily praise Captaine Fortune! His lads will finance their victory!) —But alas, that Captaine's not yet ready; he commands us all to dacker down, and bide yet more at Gravesend . . .

(Death flies o'er, with whirring wings. He's off to London-Towne, to make a plague. Full **.15,000.** dead, as I did hear.)

Here comes Captaine Not-Death—to wit, Captaine Martin Frobisher in the flagship *Gabriel,* fresh in from misnamed *Greenland,* which is a cold dependency of Cathay. He's fraughted with a dying Esquimau and a lump of fool's gold.* The Queen's alight; he's saved her weeping Treasury! She sends a gold chain, which must forever embrace his neck . . . Tell me he's not Captaine Fortune! He craves to sail back to Greenland again, to clear Her Majestie's last debts. Calling all hands! Sailors, can't you handle a mainsail? He'll pay in jewels of fabulous ice, and for belly-timber you'll have all the Esquimau wenches you can slupper up between your teeth. Make haste! He's provisioning the *Aid* this time; he's signed on Mate and Gunner this very morn; make haste! But, strange Sailors, odd beings, I see that you rub your beards and grin, lurking clear. Damnme if you're not a gaggle of scared pullets! Frobisher entreats, literally impresses, calls you *dainty;* he craves to master you, the better to engraft himself upon the sea. And you disbelieve in his Adventure yet? (Wise-burned souls!) Why duck you down in your nests of tarred ropes wrapped around beams? You prefer to huddle over a pegholed board and play Tick-Tack? Stand clear then! I see his Crewmen crossing yards, reeling in cable about the capstan, weighing anchor. And off sails worthy Captaine Frobisher! He'll never perish. 'Tis said that from a little window of her Greenwyche Palace the Queen herself waves as he sails by . . .

(Death whirs down and stings a Tavern-keeper. Well, Gravesend reeks of taverns, so what's **.1.** the less?)

Here comes Captaine Amadas, who serves Sir Walter Ralegh. We'll tell his biography later, in our "Grammar of Navigators" some hundred pages on. For now, let's just name him the safest, wisest Captaine in the world, excepting Ralegh himself. (Frobisher? A nobody! You fancy that he kens the true meridian? Why, he's not worth **.1.** of our Captaine Amadas's toenails!) Something about his salted face and his strangely menacing mildness, his neck as graceful as the snaking hilt-guard of a fine German rapier, his—but how can I define what Fortune is? His patent, like Frobisher, licenses him to impress any likely men in this haven—to *commaund* you, Sailors, and if need be to clap you in bilboes of bitter iron, so you'll serve him in Virginia. He'll catch you more rapidly than the Slaughterman doth seize upon his prey. Why flee

*As told in the *First Dream.*

your red-latticed Tavern-houses to hide? Isn't he Captaine Fortune? He *smiles* on you. He murmurs that Salvages be passing mild, that *Sassafrass* and *Cinnamon* trees will cure your every whore-pox; why hang back from him? —Sign on, bend the knee! All hands to their proper gear! —O, but now he's gone. What pity!

(Death follows him to Virginia, serving sharks all the way.)

A sly Waterman rows in next. He whispers that should you spy any ship fraught with Spanish plunder (which is to say, *illegal* burthen, by our dear Queen's command), pray send to him at first blink! You'd think his narrow bosom could scarce hold any secret, and yet he knows where all the graves lie. He tattles on Captaine Amadas, who's but Ralegh's dull drudge, as he proves by **.1,000.** syllogisms. Why (sneers the Waterman), Amadas doesn't even ken where Virginia is! Thank God you didn't chance yourself to *him!* For pure affection's sake, the Waterman next whispers that his Agent (nam'd *Maister Fortune*) will do good offices to buyers and sellers of all commodities. The selfsame Agent dwells under the Sign of the **.3.** Doves at Newgate Market. (And, by the bye, Sir, would you lie a-niggling with a sweet doxy? She's called *Fortuna*. 'Tis but a penny for the narrowest quim this side of Heaven! Her Bawdy-house lies but a musket-shot from here . . .) Why wait? Isn't this Waterman your truest chance?

No! —Ralegh's fitting out the *Tiger*. I'd lay my coppers on *him!* The smell of money blows across her weather bow. Why not indenture yourself to *his* glamor-salted men? Ship on! But mayhap Argall will come and . . . —O, o, o! —Too late! The *Tiger's* gone on the tide . . .

Captaine Fortune's never going to come now. Doom reeks in Gravesend's sickly fogs. We wait.

* * *

Chew cloves, quaff water of cinnamon—again the plague springs out. In London-Towne, thrice **.10,000.** more crawl groaning down to death. Charnel accumulates, then drips like candle-wax. Just as laboring beasts do turn tread-wheels for their Master's profit, so life revolves for death, swirling and stopping, sailing in and out, until the pest comes whirring down. May sea-breath keep away that devil's-breath! They say that in *Virginia* (e'en though not all's perfect—for instance, you can buy neither butter nor cream in that Countrey*) there grows an herb which can magick mortality into perfect ease, and I myself once glimpsed there an Alp of fool's gold ripe for the digging. So muster your crew, good Undertakers and Adventurers, rig out your fleets and your winding-sheets; get you safe beyond graves' very endings; farewell, GOD speed; may you escape skeletons' applause . . .

* * *

And so you shall—for now I offer cheerier tidings: This is the tale not only of lonely oceans and barbarous Nations, but also (as hinted) of good *John Smith and the Lincolnshire boys,* who wanted but some honest cheese. They'll keep us company this whole Dream through. —*Flood oh!* cries Captaine Smith. Weigh anchor; up spritsail! Ride the swells of eternity!

Our Almanacke lays out the proper tide, to wit, *The moone South south west, at Graues end full sea.* From high-water time at Harwich, add an hour for Gravesend. From high-water time at Dover, add an hour and .3.-quarters for Gravesend. —But why spend tuppence on any Almanacke? John Smith stands on deck, and kens sea-science as well as any book! Proof: John Smith *is* but a book nowadays, his bones long since laid down in the muck after every charitable preparation. Squat, rectangular Sailor that he is, he speaks in a rustle and flutter of paper wings which cannot fly.

Reader, skim bravely o'er his pages now, like a petrel speeding o'er pale-foamed seas, avoiding sharks and Spaniards, 'till looms *Virginia*—she likewise but a paper continent now, inhabited by mere paper tigers—or mayhap I should say paper wasps and hornets, for don't Salvages carry their own stings? Aren't they all born into poisonous cunning? Hideous rigorous reigns their Emperor, Pokahuntas's own father *Powhatan,* who broils Englishmen (so 'tis said), or pricks 'em full of arrows . . . Yea, he knots up dried human hands in his hair! But be comforted; of him likewise naught remains but old paper and nightmare honor. He'd rise up from John Smith's pages to slay us if he

*Milk our Salvages call Hickory, because they beat hickory kernels in water to make a white liquor.

could, but from all designs hath GOD excused him forever, his paper flesh tamed, time-tanned, tattooed and o'erwritten by letters of the English alphabet, alien epitaphs which he cannot read. He's a ghost cobwebbed with John Smith's words.

And Smith, he utters nothing new, being but the husk of his own monument. His pages whisper like the myriad soft lost voices at Gravesend.

* * *

Ten years ago and more I purchased his writings all complete in a triple-volumed set slipcased in burgundy. How long before they too find themselves fettered in cobwebs, haled back as trophies to death's dingy prison? Not until I die, I swear! So let them take heart; for the present they've been saved. (The middle volume gratefully whispers: *Your Grace's faithful and devoted servant, John Smith.*) On my shelf they stand gloomily elegant amidst many other tomes about Salvages. Nicely busked up in their box, acid-free (at least for now, until I breathe on them), they lord it over Virginia Watson's *Legend of Pocahontas,* Elaine Raphael and Don Bolognese's *Pocahontas, Princess of the River Tribes,* Grace Steele Woodward's *Pocahontas,* and William S. Rasmussen and Robert S. Tilton's *Pocahontas, Her Life & Legend*—howbeit, try as I might, I can scarce unchain my gaze from this last, for the cover's a pageant of Englishmen round a campfire while, in unlikely relief against the darkness, like the subject of a Weegee photograph caught in the glare of powerful flashbulbs, *POCAHONTAS* herself stands half-draped in a tawny blanket out of some Plains Indians fantasy, showing off .1. perfect, hard-nippled breast as she gestures upward into the night. No matter that she actually looked nothing like this. I suppose she reminds me of a Thai prostitute with whom I once had sexual relations.

Yet I fear that while making eyes at the piquant Virginian wench we've mislaid our lodestone of mercantile confidence, good *Captaine Smith* himself, whom GOD fashion'd not to whirligig, but to point sweet and true toward Virginian summers, straight across seas and centuries to reach blue clouds in a brown pool. Some say the grass-heads rushed into his brain, baffling him with rays and reflections, but he faithfully and accurately explor'd many a pudgy blue river-tendril thrusting between alder-lips; his maps prove it so. See how well he aims! Come magnetic storms he may *equivocate,* but lie never (except to Salvages). He's Captaine Fortune. With him we'll win to winegrapes and sassafrass. Another warranty yet: His **.20.**th century editor (himself but lately returned to ooze) loved him, subscribing for stained glass windows in Willoughby Church where John Smith was christened. Which of those translucent monuments can I remember? (For it's been half a decade since I was there.) I remember—*ooze*. The folk of Lincolnshire are half-Salvage themselves, or, as we say here in London, *helobius hoblobs*—namely, *marsh-dwelling Rustics.* Granted, Willoughby's not as squishy as some Fen-ridden Townes, but come a good rain, a sea-tide, a dyke-burst, why wouldn't that Church sink into ooze as doth a fool's foot when he steps in cowshit? —O, but the *windows!* Yes, I seem to see all sprightly and multicolored from his Adventuring our *Sweet John* as he's call'd, with the fog of Lincolnshire glowing right through him; and we've already met Pocahontas, whose Church-glass eyes are as black as Indian plums—and could e'erworthy *Captaine Argall* also be englassed? No, I don't spy him out. (Mayhap he belongs not in this Dream; he's not Man, but Mechanism; nobody knows him.) Well, *all* of them lie lost underground now like old Roman coins. To proclaim them in my Dream is to win them back, salvaging them as GOD did *Israel's remnant,* namely the Salvages. But only Argall requires proclamation. Pokahuntiss craves nothing (altho' Sweet John engraves her into his *Generall Historie* nonetheless); and as for afore-mentioned Sweet John, his words, scorning other proclaimers, proclaim themselves. They trumpet self-belief. They truculently clamor: *Idlenesse and carelessnesse brought all I did in* **.3.** *yeeres in* **.6.** *moneths to nothing.* They promise to teach how to plant Colonies and destroy Salvages at a moderate price. They wheedle and complain themselves into eternal life.

So here's to his mortal remains! Most skeletons rule but a single backbone, while his owns **.3.** spines of burgundy. On each gleams the gilded emblem of the Institute of Early American History and Culture, guaranteeing the *ancientness* of the dead words inside, like the Baker's mark which gets pricked on each loaf of bread in Lincoln Towne, to guard the buyer from sawdust-fraud. —Thus the warranty; now, how about the bread?

Hasten; eat up his words. Ship with him, and may he be Captaine Fortune! For I hear Death whirring down, half-closing his wings to fall on us the faster; his stinger's ready; he's near as inevitable as Argall. Well, well, he's here. On the Virginia Turnpike a car gets front-ended by a truck. The whole front of the car is gone, with small pieces of metal, glass and rubber scattered down the road for **.500.** feet. An ambulance and **.2.** police cars block the intersection, blinking their lights mournfully. The stretcher-bearers unhurriedly carry a litter draped with a white sheet which is already turning crimson in **.3.** places.

* * *

That was why I coveted those burgundied volumes from the very first—for Death assailed me. On **.1.** of his blank charters (my birth certificate) he'd already penned my name. He'd come a-soldiering and a-sailing to find me. He'd come a-riding to smell me out with his hounds of time. How long could I hide? Someday I'd reach my *December,* which is the heel of the year. If only Captaine Fortune would haven me within his slipcased works! Let Death hound me then! I'd be Virginia'd safe into words—not myself anymore, true, but signature of myself, as the empty sepulcher doth signify CHRIST. The Book's the thing. Words live beyond life. Word to word I sought comfort from sweet John Smith; I issued counter-charters and licenses of my own; I called upon Vendors of the Word. Just as in a convoy the **.1.**st ship to descry land must shoot off her ordnance and raise the gladsome flag, so, I commanded, ought every Bookseller to telephone me as soon as those *.3.* books came to light—but since I was no Captaine, they stayed out of patience, or else (afraid to attract Death's notice) they ducked my commission like foolish fretting creepers: *Out of print,* they said. (Tush! Don't we all go out of print? Even this very Dream must someday get waterlogged, and give over voyaging. And you, Right Honourable, **.4.** centuries hence where will *you* be? Down, deep down! 'Twixt Gravesend and Virginia swirls many a watery grave.) But **.3.** harquebus shots away, in **.1.** of those tiny cellar-bookstores in the chitterlings of Manhattan's Upper East Side, the pipe-smoking owner, lifting his arm as if to ward off the gazes of Tax-men, engaged himself to try; and **.2.** months and **.200.**

dollars later (for I had neither gold nobles, nor French louys, nor Spanish ducatoons), I happed to be a-writing a Dream about the Salvages and CROW-SPIRITS of New York when the telephone sang: *I'm Captaine Fortune, and your ship's in harbor!* —That voice! It did most strangely remind me of a Waterman's whisper; and when I look'd around me with proper sincerity, I saw that I was back in Gravesend. After donning my accustomed funereal spirit, I shouldered a pickaxe, in case any of the cobwebs I was likely to meet had fossilized; then I recited the Anglican burial service and descended into that subterranean bed of typeset virtue off Eighty-First Street, where the Bookseller (himself now buried, as I hear—or did he but go bankrupt?) stood ready with the spoils: —my *Complete Works of Captain John Smith,* duly shrouded in brown paper in a cardboard sarcophagus which OUR REDEEMER had postmarked from North Carolina, bastard latecomer of a State, which was but lately (1662) Virginian territory.

* * *

About Virginia herself I scarce ken anything. To find her you'd best know the declination of the Sunne and of the Moone. Watermen and great Captaines keep such arcana at hand; but I, mere half-blind scribbler, scarce know my own compass dial. Yet even had I means, how *could* I find her, after the persecutions of Time? She's broken into vertebrae, like the sickle found in Roanoke Fort. She's decayed into penurious divisions, translated into Counties, States, freeways and naval bases. From her flesh they've lopp'd off *New England, New Scotland, New York, Maryland, Pennsylvania* and *Carolina* (whose wheat yields **.30.**-fold). Poor Virginia! Dig patiently in her, and you may find a tiny white glass bead, a deer's foot, a pouch of deerskin. —Is there value in those? Ask John Smith, who can pen a key to any discovered hoard. He conspires to extend himself a few centuries more, busily remembrance-toiling for hire. He maps her and flatters her with newborn Colonies of English souls. She needs him. Dig, dig! She would not so be mortified, but owns neither remedy, nor miracle now, save him. Archaeologists rape her in her dotage; romanciers misuse her; and at Jamestowne, where her **.1.**st Capitol lies, many a squirrel noses between those stone doorways call'd *Tombs.* (Governor Yeardley might be buried in **.1.** of these, but the records won't tell—they got burned in our recent Civil War.)

So what's left of old Virginia? She lies conquered, her sloughs become but the blank spaces between the chapters of Sweet John's *Generall Historie,* her pickerel-weeds, thalias and lance-leaved arrowheads now but marginal decorations, printer's weeds.

O, but in her day she had fight in her! In her day she shook her bristling tail! Reader, remember this: From 1606 'till 1625, out of **.7,000.** Colonists sent to pickaxe away her maidenhead, **.6,000.** perished! I swear it—**.6.** out of every **.7.** souls! (Where are their bones? They lie rotted under river-slime. An archaeologist writes: *No traces have been found.*) But Captaine Fortune did save us. Virginia, spraddle-legged and weeping, for our sustenance gave up her maidenly ghost! Then the Colonists swore her full affection, calling her Ole Virginny. Her oysters lay upon the ground *as thicke as stones* (runs .1. document), so that any gambler or eater could play the husking-game, hoping to discover pearls. Time further restrained her, assaulted her, then interr'd her beneath her own ooze. Only John Smith remembers (because he drafted it) the *Map of Virginia,* which, however imperfectly, presents her bygone naked charms of Salvage Townes now o'erwritten by bulldozers & steel beams.

I know not what to say, when I scan his pages or tread the grass of Jamestowne—both of those my patrimony, from which I've inherited electric ease and genocidal shame. See a line of a dozen ducks slowly gliding in the still river, as if the heads of ruined pilings have begun to move backwards. John Smith's statue, benevolent and green, turns its back upon the Church tower, which is the **.1.** remaining **.17.**th century structure still standing at this **.20.**th-century national park call'd after our Soveraigne. The doorway of the Church-tower, green-rimmed with age, seems to lead not up into Heaven, but *down* into muck and ooze. Virginia lies lost and silent.

The Stench of Corpses

From
Los Angeles Times (Oct 30, 2001)

This self-review of *Argall* shows that Vollmann is not without a dark sense of humor—a characteristic that runs throughout much of his work, but is often obscured by more "serious matters." For this is a self-defense of his less-appreciated, most difficult-to-read novel, and Vollmann is not beyond poking fun at what may have been the failures of the novel, or the successes that critics of yesteryear failed to notice. The prophet is never appreciated in his homeland, as the old story goes. Appearing on the day the U.S. launched its attack on Afghanistan, the published version omitted a key passage near the end of the review that we have restored here, in bold; it should also be noted that this review appeared eighteen months before the U.S.-led invasion of Iraq. —MH

A HUNDRED YEARS AFTER William T. Vollmann was killed in a gun cleaning accident, I, William the Blind, got commissioned to review the long novel *Argall,* which marks the midpoint of his uncompleted *Seven Dreams* series. According to Dombey's *Easily Digested Biographies of Minor Authors,* which I just happen to have right here inside my reading pod, it was always Vollmann's hope that the "Seven Dreams," which were second in ambition only to his still unpublished essay on violence *Rising Up and Rising Down,* would "somehow, uh, mean something to people a hundred years from now." This desire is best understood as a form of wish compensation. Vollmann lived what can only be called a pathetic life. Isolated within and stubbornly estranged from millennial American society, he consoled himself with a sophomorically romantic belief that art, if protected in time capsules, can outlast Dark Ages. Let's temporarily ignore the fact that Vollmann's so-called "art" was never worth preserving, being infested by individualism, moral relativism and sexual depravity. More to the point, since stars, elephants and gods all suffer death, how could even the greatest art be "immortal?" As we all know, the Liu-Mallinger Act of 2027, which made cranial stimulation devices compulsory for all inhabitants of the Global Trans-Industrial Zone, reduced the printed word to irrelevancy at last. The wearisome wordiness of Shakespeare, the absurdly ambiguous parables of Hawthorne and the poison of the French Decadents were all replaced by pictures whose content could be guaranteed. And so the *Seven Dreams* molder unread in their vanity-plated time capsule. In Senator Mallinger's deservedly famous words, "When I say, 'ball,' I want to know that everybody's seeing the same red, white and blue ball."

Argall, whose story emblematizes a personified and of course feminine Virginia, is no better or worse than any of the other *Seven Dreams.* That is why nobody reads *Argall.* No one looks for *Argall.* No one can find *Argall.* Good riddance, say I. To quote from *Argall* itself (the reference is to a fellow who's searching for Pocahontas's skeleton), "had the critic found her, what would he have done? Coffined her, borne her back seaward to some brown Virginian marsh crowned by grey and yellow weeds? Locked her into his cabinet of curiosities? All he discovered was a menagerie of human and animal remnants. What power could have swallowed her so thoroughly, but ooze?"

Enough. Holding our noses, let's try to take this menagerie of remnants on its own terms.

This book's first sin, as you might have already gathered from the foregoing, consists in its so-called Elizabethan language, whose archaicisms, variant spellings, and preposterous figures of speech substantially impede the reader in any attempt to envision the ball in any uniform fashion. Here is a sentence plucked at random from the mess: "He search'd for an issue of fair water, there to make another well, for he misdoubted him not that the river they drunk from was somehow tainted with disease, yet could discover no convenient place to make his diggings." Much time and trouble would have been saved, had this so-called novelist written what he meant: "In order to get more healthful water, he intended to dig a well, but couldn't." The arch apostrophe, the ignorant substitution of "drunk" for "drank," the ink-wasting double negation, well, really all this makes me crave to spew.

Secondly and worse, Vollmann insists on retelling the revered legend of Pocahontas in the ignoblest possible terms. The majestic Indian princess gets reduced to a childish victim, the resourceful Captain John Smith to a doublehearted, ultimately impotent adventurer, and everybody else comes off much worse. Vollmann conceived *Seven Dreams* as what he called a "symbolic history of our continent over the last thousand years"—a hubristic enough project, to be sure, in which the various benefits which European civilization brought are systematically ignored, and the atrocities highlighted. This perversity becomes wearisome. From the very first volume, in which the iron weapons of the Norsemen get depicted as the reification of evil, it's clear that this idiot literally has axes to grind. You may be sure when you read *Argall* that hardheadedness, military necessity, just retaliation, taxation in kind, free trade and collective survival will never be given their due. For instance, we continually have to see Captain Smith "extorting" corn from Pocahontas's people, the Powhatan Indians, who'd already refused to barter even for English hatchets of the highest possible quality. Measured responses by the English to murders committed by Indians are constantly misrepresented as atrocities. (One can only be glad that Vollmann disappeared from the national scene before having any chance to dribble his venom over our eminently just nuclear retaliation against Afghanistan in March 2002.) In the end, we begin almost to feel that this author believes that this America of which we're so proud was never worth hacking out of the wilderness, let alone preserving and fighting for. In a tone of bored bemusement he tells us that "from 1606 'till 1625, out of **.7,000.** Colonists sent to pickaxe away [Virginia's] maidenhead, **.6,000.** perished!" And yet he seems less sorry for them than for Pocahontas, who by his own admission died married and within hailing distance of an exotic foreign capital (London). Apparently (if Vollmann can be trusted here), she even got to see King James!

This subversion of any utilitarian calculus (the greatest good for the greatest number) is worth investigating, for it helps the astute reader to understand precisely what's wrong with sentimental books such as Argall. In one typical passage, the last I'll afflict you with, Pocahontas, now christened Rebecca, visits the wholesome new metropolis of Hampton, which lies on the site of a former Indian town:

"English children are building Forts & Towers in the floury sand. A sea-otter swims close, raising his head to goggle with huge, sad eyes. The children commence hooting at him, & presently throw stones. But he will not depart. Rebecca wonders if he might be the Spirit of .1. of her dead kinsmen. Is he looking at her, or . . . ? After a time they give o'er their cruelty & ignore him. They're dragging monstrous kelp-weeds out of the sea, with which they would enchain in each other in their play. And always that sea-otter lurks sadly there."

This use (I should say misuse) of the pathetic fallacy taints the scene with spurious mournfulness, when actually there is nothing to mourn about this innocent children's game (note that the otter hasn't even been hurt). Vollmann wants us to regret the inevitable, to privilege the melancholy of the few over the honest subsistence of the many, to slur just conquest—and he goes about it insidiously, never coming right out to say that it was wrong for the English to dispossess the indigenous inhabitants of that spot in retaliation for their terrorism against Jamestown—good God! **If that was wrong, what would Vollmann have said about our obliteration of Iraq in 2003, or the absolutely essential police measures taken in Palestine in 2004?** Not to put too fine a point on it, Vollmann's book doesn't just stink (I think it's the stench of corpses), it's positively un-American.

Melville's Magic Mountain

From
Civilization (Vol. 5, No. 1, 1998)

This published version is (in Vollmann's words) "an extremely cut and extensively rearranged version of my original essay."

SHALL MOUNTAIN BECOME CHASM, and land become sea? Herman Melville gazed upon Mount Greylock and made it so in *Moby-Dick*. The Book of Job: "Canst thou draw out leviathan with an hook? or his tongue with a cord which thou lettest down?" Melville did. He caught a whale between sheets of manuscript and clothes leviathan with life.

No one cared. Who ever took the time?

Too easy to say that the quick, shrill shallowness of our America, whose discourse alternates between self-sensing anger and commercial manipulation, offered its counterpart in Melville's day, in smug rural idiocy. Our whale skinner's contemporary, Thoreau (another extremist), set up house at Walden Pond to free himself from just that, likening his neighbors to blind, greedy prairie dogs. But what if ordinary people, not idiots at all, simply have better things to do than lay hands on imaginary whales? Closer to "reality" than Melville, less blind than he (his eyes had been damaged by scarlet fever), they're equally free to look upon Mount Greylock.

Looking down from Mount Greylock, in the general direction of our whale skinner's house, Arrowhead, one mercifully fails to see the Polymer Processing Technology center or the tombstones yellow and grey sprouting up like mushrooms from new snow. Instead, behold a lovely slate-blue bowl of subordinate mountains that streak the grey horizon with soft and snowy stains. All around, deer hoofs engrave themselves in the snow, under which a stream runs busily. Pine and hemlock branches sprout from tall trunks, backlighted by the glowing grey sky. A tender evergreen sapling bows its head, as if to rest. Trees creak in the cool wind, and the dead leaves, death-tanned and ragged, rustle together with a thin frosty sound.

Isn't this enough? Why turn good land into whales? "Canst thou fill his skin with barbed iron? or his head with fish spears? Lay thine hand upon him, remember the battle, do no more." Melville did it—again and again.

MANHATTAN'S VICTORY (1863-1891)

Of course nineteenth-century America did own cities, too—Albany, for one, with her sea-bound ships and cholera. During the great epidemic of 1832, thirteen-year-old Melville clerked there for a pittance, at the New York State Bank, helping other people's money change hands. Meanwhile, his mother, brothers, and sisters, like characters out of Boccaccio's tales, hid away from disease in the Berkshires, with Mount Greylock ever before them. And remember great Manhattan, site of his father's business failure. At age eleven, Herman Melville ran away from there by night, at the side of that father, literally ducking creditors until they were safely on a night steamer called the *Swiftsure;* swift and sure to Albany, to his father's insanity and death. In 1850, half-orphaned, ocean-seasoned, and married, he fled Manhattan again, like a lead-weighted corpse leaving its funeral ship, gone to the Berkshires at last to write *Moby-Dick.* His paradise: rural idiocy without the idiots! In winter, his thoughts would be attended by delicate, defoliated trees, like arterial maps laid out upon some celestial dissecting-school's felt of most oxygenated lavender. He'd build a tower to rival Mount Greylock once he got money! But he never did. Back to Manhattan, where, mostly poor and anxious, he lived out his last three decades of life.

PROMISE AND BREACH OF PROMISE (1846-1849)

Self-serving anger and commercial manipulation? For Melville's century, such delineations serve equally well as in our own. The literary clique in New York and Boston first patronized, then warned him, then dismissed and ignored him. He'd allowed the reprinting of his first book, *Typee,* to be ideologically and sexually bowdlerized, but the mighty captains and bloodsuckers never forgot his hints of escapades with naked cannibal girls. When he married Lizzie Shaw, the wedding was small and private, on account of the scandal. One reviewer wrote that Melville's cannibal mistress must surely want to sue him now for breach of promise! (In his Bible we find the words: "What man is like Job, who drinketh up scorning like water?") Of his next four books, three—*Omoo, Redburn,* and *White-Jacket*—were well-written "formula" contraptions that harped on his old sea-life (and on source books written by others) to give what he thought his publishers and readers wanted. Between *Omoo* and *Redburn,* his long metaphysical satire *Mardi* had hinted of strangeness like the subtle darknesses within footprints on white snow. Critics and editors cordially warned him then to stick to his entertaining sea stories; if he did that and worked hard, then maybe someday he'd be as good as James Fenimore Cooper . . . In 1849, he wrote his wife's father (who can hardly have been reassured) that "it is my earnest desire to write those sort of books which are said to 'fail.'" *Mardi* failed. In his review of Hawthorne's tales, he wrote, probably both defiantly and defensively: "He who has never failed somewhere, that man can not be great." Melville would have been an outcast in either his time or ours.

THE DIVER (1849)

On the eve of beginning *Moby-Dick,* Melville wrote his uncomprehending publisher: "I love all men who dive. Any fish can swim near the surface, but it takes a great whale to go down stairs five miles or more." And what does our anxious, soon to be embittered diver find? Word-schools and word-krakens, long-suckered octopi of words pulling him into oracular caverns of never before consummated thought! "Sheol beneath is stirred up to meet you when you come . . ."

WINTER AT ARROWHEAD (1997)

Driving out of Albany nearly 150 winters after he hooked his white whale of words, I sank through sleet rushing and foaming in stinging tunnels that trapped the headlights, rattling against the windshield in speckled lances while other headlights approached like bestial eyes.

Sleet exploded like fireworks, enlarging now into winter's grapeshot, winter's bullets whirling at me. In the dark fields, sad snow lay in already dirty patches, cast off, shredded skin of purity, and all the locked churches might as well have been white whales. The car sank horizontally down tunnels of snow. Suddenly, long white lines of snow had conquered the road itself, frosting its blackness greyer and greyer into whiteness. The snow came down so thick that the air was almost green.

He wrote most of *Moby-Dick* in Pittsfield, Massachusetts, Sheol-in-the-Berkshires, or Paradise, in that farmhouse called Arrowhead, after the Indian artifacts he plowed up. Gentleman-farmer, weak-eyed athlete, landlocked sailor (if we exclude his snowy-margined purple brooks of sadness), father-impoverished descendant of the American Revolutionary antiaristocratic aristocracy, he had no business borrowing the money to buy Arrowhead, but he still hoped and believed that his genius would recompense him, finally, for everything. Moreover, he wanted to dwell near Hawthorne, whom he loved and who rarely visited him.

GREYLOCK AS WHALE (1850–1851)

Hawthorne attracted him. But he knew Pittsfield and loved it already. (As a youth, he'd helped his uncle on the farm there. He'd come back and back.) And at Arrowhead, the view of Mount Greylock from his study presented him every day with a whale. His biographers invariably remark on that, because he did.

Indeed, that long, fusiform eminence, highest in the state of Massachusetts, offers two protuberances: first the dorsal fin and then, after dipping down (which is why Melville and Thoreau sometimes called that eminence Saddleback Mountain), the raised blowhole before the falling curve of the white forehead. Moreover, Greylock in winter is so white! In his famous chapter on the "whiteness of the whale," Melville confessed: "What the white whale was to Ahab, has been hinted; what, at times, he was to me, as yet remains unsaid." And: "It was the whiteness of the whale that above all things appalled me."

And he asserted Arrowhead to be his paradise! (Where could paradise be, for him?) Simultaneously, he admitted that the White Mountains of

New Hampshire infected him with a "gigantic ghastliness over the soul." Outside, snow fell down from trees in icy lumps whose sound imitated rain. The blankness of that hue "stabs us from behind with the thought of annihilation," being both God and "a colorless, all-color of atheism from which we shrink." (No wonder that the missionaries did not like him.)

And with these feelings he gazed at Mount Greylock day after day! Or were they a wordsmith's posturings?

SUMMER AT ARROWHEAD (1850-1851)

In Herschel Parker's long biography we read about a happy August picnic on Greylock, Melville hallooing from atop a tall tree, his friends picking yellow raspberries, wild strawberries, the women sleeping in old buffalo robes in the vandalized observatory, with champagne all around. Thoreau, wandering alone one summer, had once slept in the same spot, awaking to find himself "in cloudland . . . such a country as we might see in dreams, with all the delights of paradise." Hawthorne wrote in his *Wonder Book* that "on the hither side of Pittsfield sits Herman Melville, shaping out the gigantic conception of his 'White Whale,' while the gigantic shape of Greylock looms upon him from his study-window."

Greylock, our whale skinner tells us over and over, is Moby Dick. How verdant or moss-backed can that death-dealing personage be? Better (one would think) to pay but a passing nod to summer at Arrowhead; let's picture Melville in his study in winter, half dreaming that he's looking out of a ship's porthole, as he writes his publisher. Sometimes the nightly gales made him feel there to be "too much sail on the house"; he'd "better go on the roof & rig in the chimney."

"NOTHING PARTICULAR TO INTEREST ME ON SHORE" (1847-1851)

Probably he was happy—happier than his womenfolk, who for the longest time weren't allowed to take the horses out alone—and they were so often alone, with Herman locked in his study. In *Moby-Dick* he took (and gave) pleasure in beautiful language, sea-dreamed, wind-dreamed, mountain-dreamed, Shakespeare- and Bible-dreamed. No matter that the tale was one of doom! His work must have given him joy as rich and ineffable as the mysteries of spermaceti. His spade-bearded face seems tranquil in photographs from this time. (He looks more anxious in A.W. Twitchell's oil portrait of 1847.) Whenever his sickly vision and finances, his crops and family (eleven persons lived at Arrowhead) allowed him to work, he did—if not, he might just work anyway. Maybe Arrowhead was paradise. He loved the Chimney Room with its grand hearth. (Later he wrote a tale about it.) His walking sticks and moccasins presided over the mantelpiece. Fire and warm darkness fought against the white glare of the snowdrifts behind the windows. Did his weak eyes ever get dazzled by that brightness, snow and sky bleeding and blending into ineffable whiteness?

His study is now much neater and bleaker than I would have expected from such a magnificently mind-cluttered man. Across the squarish writing table with its quill pens. through a twelve-paned old window, hunches Mount Greylock beneath a cloud. Susan Eisley, the executive director at Arrowhead, told me that her museum couldn't really afford to fill the study with all the old books that Melville would have kept there. As for the tangle that would have done the man justice, had they left anything out unchained, somebody might steal it—his tiny round eyeglasses, for instance, with the folding metal bows that almost resembled dental tools or the multitudinous claws of a Swiss army knife. I'd seen those eyeglasses in a photograph lying out on his desk, with Greylock behind them; now they were chained inside a glass case. But some essence, some feeling, still hooks us, not merely from the blubbery back of Greylock itself but also from the antique relics themselves. In one comer, to the left of our good table, Susan shows me Melville's own trunk, which is now greenish, darkened with age, his name in torn and faded characters on the diamond-reliefed lid. Beneath the window lies Lizzie's trunk, also diamond reliefed, but of a clean, pale, almost translucent tan shade. Hawthorne could have made a tale of this, allegorizing about pretty soul-locks and magical bosoms, about the innermost hearts of husband and wife. Melville wrote alone in there, the door locked, until 2:30 or so every afternoon. Perhaps his sister Augusta would be copying manuscript for him in another room. When his wife or his mother or one of the other members of his household tapped at his door, he'd hook himself back on leash for the day. They'd eat. Then maybe he'd ride down to the post office to check for letters and money, perhaps with Helen or Augusta or Lizzie, sunbeams glancing and skittering warmly from their necks and shoulders.

It was in the *Moby-Dick* season, when he worked so hard and long, that he and Lizzie began to fall out. In her photograph she looks pale and grim. Still, he had their newborn son, Malcolm, to comfort him. (No matter that the boy would grow up to shoot himself, and his other son would die of tuberculosis.) In *Moby-Dick* his China Sailor cries: "Rattle thy teeth, then, and pound away; make a pagoda of thyself." And so he did. In spite of the gloom he dived down to in the writing (like white birch-tree joints on Greylock, knee-skinned to blackness), he preserved a tone almost of bonhomie. In the very beginning, immediately after that famous sentence, "Call me Ishmael," he brightly pens: "Some years ago—never mind how long precisely—having little or no money in my purse, and nothing particular to interest me on shore, I thought I would sail about a little and see the watery part of the world." A little sailing, ladies and gentlemen! A little fishing! A string and a two-penny hook! A cruise! A cure for melancholy! Sail fair on—to Sheol.

GREYLOCK AS ATLANTIS (1884-1891)

I see him looking down into a circle of purple-grey, blue shadowed hills rolling all around like sea waves. Stand on the whale's pure white back and discover those grey mountain-billows and cloud-billows about to engulf you, held back only by the geological hand of God, who permits you not in your mayfly-instant of life to witness the millennial collapse, except through the gloomy premonitions of art. "Fixed by infatuation," he wrote at the end of *Moby-Dick*, "or fidelity, or fate, to their once lofty perches, the pagan harpooners still maintained their sinking lookouts on the sea." We others, infatuated and faithful, admire snow ovals, pools and foaming snow shallows in the Sunday world below us, believing that safe eternities preserve us from the last page of our last chapter. Fate lies innocuous beneath a platinum-colored cloud, like the malignant Moby Dick himself, a fantasy as the protagonist half believes, until he rears up white and terrible from the deep.

Melville knew his Bible very well. I'm sure he knew the psalm that runs: "The LORD is nigh unto them that are of a broken heart; and saveth such as be of a contrite spirit." Inspired when he wrote, he might have temporarily felt himself to be God's servant, hence vindicated against poverty and care; he'd harpooned the whale and actually stood on leviathan's white back, proud, infatuated, faithful, and fated. Those waves around him lay low, gray, and far, with white snow-flesh buried in their hair roots and swatches of lonely evergreen in them; they rose and fell without any reason—how could they not be harmless? Mere heaps of moss made of trees they were, swollen winter hills that intimidated their rare and lonely narrow-roofed houses. We know that in this world nothing ever changes, that treasures never rust, and love always finds requital. Up shield—victory is won forever! (But here comes the whale. Here looms the rushing baleful whale.) "And now, concentric circles seized the lone boat itself, and all its crew. . . ."

Everything has its metonym. On Mount Greylock itself I found a white nodule of quartz, sunk in a bowl of melted snow, with fresh snow towering all around that pebble, ready to reoverwhelm it.

FATALITY OF THE WHITE WHALE (1850–1891)

Surrounded by snow continents of his best fancy that floated on afternoon's indigo water, Melville, defying all bigots, missionaries, and worldly-wise publishers, not to mention his own wife, wrote: "Hail, holy nakedness of our dancing girls! —the Heeva-Heeva!" He wrote exactly what he wanted to write; he paid for the printing. plates himself. Bad reviews rewarded him. Hawthorne, to whom he dedicated *Moby-Dick,* was lukewarm about it and never reviewed it. (This was the time that the Hawthorne family moved out of the Berkshires, leaving him crushed.) Melville would make only $1,260 from *Moby-Dick* throughout his entire life. His next book, *Pierre,* which he dedicated not to Hawthorne but to Mount Greylock's "Most Excellent Majesty," would be not just ignored but execrated.

Steinbeck: Most American of Us All

From
Imperial

In many ways, Steinbeck remains the closest of all to Vollmann as a literary figure, in terms of his willingness to be nonjudgmental, his empathy for the dispossessed, and his use of writing to open doors or windows onto the lives of people who remained invisible for most ordinary Americans. Steinbeck offered a model of commitment that combined fierce literary independence, idealism, the desire to use literature to make a difference, and a willingness to risk sincerity (a "risk," because to be sincere about anything is to make oneself vulnerable to others). How much safer artists are who are able to cloak themselves in the irony, jadedness, and condescension associated with postmodernism. This version was abridged from a chapter in Vollmann's *Imperial*. —LM

I FEEL PROTECTIVE TOWARD this dead writer, who doesn't need my protection at all. A friend of mine has been teaching American literature for a long time in a certain California university. Year after year, she assigns *The Grapes of Wrath*, and they love it. Very likely on account of that selfsame popularity, the critics say that Steinbeck writes, if I remember correctly, "novels with training wheels."

When a scientist embarks on a series of experiments to test a new hypothesis, it is likely that most of his experiments will "fail," reality being more complicated than even the most torturous hypothesis. Science corrects, revises, goes on. In this respect writing is more like science than the other arts (except, of course, for musical composition), because we can replace one word by another as many times as we like, even resurrecting deleted choices; whereas I have only so many chances to paint over my bad oil painting before it turns into a sticky brick. Nonetheless, once any work of art is sent out into the world, revision ends. Writers such as James Branch Cabell, who corrected their novels after publication, are decidedly not the rule. So what would the prudent thing be to do, if *The Grapes of Wrath* didn't come out quite perfect? We find one of Steinbeck's would-be mentors advising him to do the next *Grapes of Wrath,* set this time among the Puerto Rican population of New York City. Had Steinbeck accepted this counsel, he might have created something quite powerful. Who knows? Maybe he could have been another Zola, constructing an entire series of novels about dispossessed or underpossessing Americans. Instead, he chose to devote himself to loopy failures such as *The Winter of Our Discontent* and the never-to-be-finished translation from ancient English to archaic English of Malory's tale of King Arthur, and I love him for it.

People simplify Steinbeck into a populist, a pseudo-common man who idealized the common man, a socialist like Jack London. For an instant corrective to that notion, read his short story "The Vigilante," about a fellow who helps to lynch a "nigger fiend." "Somebody said he even confessed." With genius' restraint, Steinbeck sets this tale in the hours after the murder, chronicling the changes in the vigilante's heart from emptiness to cocky pride. At the end he comes home to his bitter, shut-down wife, who gazes into his face in astonishment and decides that he must have been with another woman. "By God, she was right," thinks the vigilante, admiring himself in the mirror. "That's just exactly how I do feel."* And the story ends. One quasi-socialist thread does spin itself through "The Vigilante" as it does through all of Steinbeck's work: the receptivity of human beings to each other, and specifically of the one to the many. It is the bloodthirstiness of the lynch mob, and later on the admiration of the bartender, and the look in his wife's eyes, which in turn tell the vigilante how to feel. Thus we are to one another, for good and for evil.

Steinbeck's astonishing novel *In Dubious Battle,* which narrates the course of a fruitpickers' strike in California's Central Valley, and which like all his best writing is unbelievably *real* down to the last detail (the

*John Steinbeck, *The Long Valley* (New York: Penguin, 1986, orig. ed. 1938), pp. 134, 139.

mud between the tents, the look and smell of dinner-mush, the ugly dialogues between the apple-pickers and the checkers who dock their pay, the practicalities of sanitation), magnifies the vigilante's susceptibility into something larger, less evil, if still problematic, and more longlasting: the way in which workers can be manipulated for political ends. Just as he did with the vigilante, Steinbeck dares to show the human nastiness of the strikers. "When we get down to business," says one "sullen boy," "I'm gonna get me a nice big rock and I'm gonna sock that bastard." But while he is doing this, Steinbeck does two more things: He makes it powerfully clear to us why the strikers strike, putting much of himself into their cause; and he savages the vanguardist puppeteers who so often infest political movements. Their motto: "The worse it is, the more effect it'll have."*

In fact, were Steinbeck's writing to be simplified into anything at all, the motif would be *distrust of authority.* In 1947 he visited the Soviet Union, and in his account of that journey he says that while Russians, or at least the Russian spokespeople whom he was allowed to meet, tend to support their government and believe that what it does is good, Americans prefer to begin with the profoundest suspicion of government and its coercive powers. Of course this is not true at all. Steinbeck is one of the most un-American Americans of his time.

We might say that Faulkner and Hemingway were not exactly mainstream either, the former spinning out honeysuckled tales of incest, miscegenation and doom, the latter getting involved with Spanish Loyalists (Communists to you, bub); but in both of those writers, the lonely narcissism which characterizes us Americans ultimately obscures social statement. Steinbeck, on the other hand, had things to say. He wanted all of us to be angry and sorry about the plight of the Okies, and his own outrage is what makes *The Grapes of Wrath* a great book. He wanted to tell us that the people in the Soviet Union were not the monsters that our Cold Warriors insisted they were; and because the apparatchiks distorted and limited what he could see, his *Russian Journal* is dated and slight, but true enough to annoy both the Russians and Americans. (Let's call it a failure.) When he wrote *The Winter of Our*

*John Steinbeck, *In Dubious Battle* (New York: Penguin, 1986, orig. ed. 1936), pp. 261, 89.

Discontent, he was worried about American materialism and hypocrisy. The defects of this novel remind me of socialist realism. This is a book with a message, and because that message is sometimes too stark, and other times camouflaged to the point of eccentric mysticism, it makes the story itself waver and warp. Well, fine; so he did have messages; he didn't necessarily want to build for the ages; maybe he hoped to actually accomplish something in his own time, in which case I love him for that, too.

The book of his which I admire the most is *East of Eden.* For a decade now the character of Kate, whom some critics find unconvincing, has haunted my head; she's horrific, she's pathetic, she's steady and successful and lonely; she is perfectly what she is. The retelling of the Cain and Abel story is brilliant, the landscape descriptions lovely and lush, the plotting as careful and convincing as the best of George Eliot. And of course there's a message, a flaw, personified by a Chinese servant who tells us, sometimes at great length, what to think. But Lee has never annoyed me. He speechifies intelligently, at times wittily, and sometimes compassionately. Do I care that nobody I've ever met talks like that? He is sincere because Steinbeck is sincere. And this is what I love about Steinbeck most of all, his sincerity.

He once wrote about his friend Ed Ricketts that the man loved what was true and hated what wasn't. If Steinbeck sometimes mistook sentimentality for truth (which "The Vigilante" shows that he didn't always do), and if in this anti-sentimental era (political rhetoric excluded as usual) we happen to see him as even more sentimental than he was—the way we see, for instance, the Victorians—well, there are worse vices than sentimentality, for example its opposite. He was worried and at times bitter, but he was never cynical. One aspect of his credo which is considered sentimental nowadays is his glorification of individual choice. If I don't like, say, what America "stands for," and if I express that dislike, I may find that certain other Americans dislike *me.* It happened to Steinbeck, too. The many bannings of *The Grapes of Wrath* comprise its badge of honor. This book upset people. It actually had something to say. It was angry, it was unashamedly sexual, and it was un-American. Being un-American, Steinbeck was the most American of us all.

Postface

What I kept coming back to, while Larry McCaffery and I worked on this book (and when I think of Vollmann in general) is the subtitle to *An Afghanistan Picture Show:* "How I Saved the World." Vollmann, as that young man in the eighties, probably believed he *could* save the world, that one man can actually make a difference; he had the opportunity to be the hero he fancied, whether that "hero" was someone he was willing to admit to or not.

I believe he accomplished his goal; maybe not the way he expected, but on microcosmic levels he has saved the world many times over with his writings, his travels, and his deeds—virtuous or debauched, it's up to interpretation. I felt the same way when, in the mid-nineties, I took off to other countries in the name of journalism, the "important" assignment, and the desire to make decent "hazard" money and get my byline from adventures in strange foreign lands. I went to Brazil to find out about the gangs of street kids, abandoned or left to fend for themselves through a life of crime and prostitution; I went to Rwanda and Zaire during the civil war, and acts of genocide, deep in the Congo; I went to Senegal to investigate a screw-up by the World Health Organization and came away disillusioned about the notions of good versus evil, having witnessed corporate greed and waylaid politics. I joked with people, saying, "I'm off to do my Vollmann thing" because I felt like an imposter. This kind of work was not my territory, it was Vollmann's—for I, too, in my twenties and being a tad too idealistic, wanted to save the world, in my own skewed way; but all I saw were a lot of lost, sad, and quite often broken and dead (figuratively and literally) people whom I could not possibly help . . . each and all expelled from Eden . . . and I came home to America far more empty than when I departed. That's not to say the world can't still be saved, because it can—it's that hope that keeps us all going. And as long as we have writers like William T. Vollmann in the world, the world will live on to fight another day.

—Michael Hemmingson
Ocean Beach, California, 2004

In the spirit of much of Vollmann's books (most notably the *Seven Dreams* series) we've added a miscellany of material the astute Vollmann reader, scholar, fan, and fanatic may find interesting. Of course, the reader should know this is but a mere sampling of the quantity of material that we could have used in either these appendices or within the entirety of this book—but practicality, budget concerns, paper, and THE DEVIL have dictated otherwise; and should all the bright and risen angels shine upon us, the material that had to be left out may one day be found bound and printed in an expanded edition or Volume Two.

Appendix A

A William T. Vollmann Chronology

Compiled by Larry McCaffery

THE FOLLOWING CHRONOLOGY HAS been compiled as a means of offering readers a kind of atlas they can use to identify some of the most significant features of the world Vollmann has inhabited, literally and imaginatively. Although the majority of citations relate directly to Vollmann's life and career—important events in his personal life, influences, education and travel experiences, book publications, and the like—I have also included references to historical and political events that Vollmann has written about in his fiction and journals. These include citations concerning the early Norse explorations of Iceland, Greenland, and North America (the subject of *The Ice-Shirt*); the doomed John Franklin Arctic Expedition of 1845–48 and the evolution of the Inuit (Eskimo) culture, including the havoc wreaked by the introduction of repeating rifles on this culture (all treated in *The Rifles*); the seventeenth-century confrontation between the Jesuits and the Iroquois (the focus of *Fathers and Crows*); the events surrounding the famous John Smith–Pocahontas incident (*Argall*); the life and times of L. L. Nunn, the electrical genius and founder of Deep Springs College, where Vollmann attended school from 1977–78 (references to Nunn and Deep Springs abound in *You Bright and Risen Angels*); Hitler's rise to power and the titanic battles between the Nazis and the Russians that turned the tide for the Allies in World War II (discussed at some length in *Rising Up and Rising Down* and also integral to Vollmann's forthcoming collection, *Europe Central;* the ongoing struggles of Afghanistan for independence (the subject of Vollmann's first novel, *An Afghanistan Picture Show,* and of his extended *New Yorker* essay, "Across the Divide"); and the history of Imperial Valley (the subject of a non-fiction work that he has been working on since 1996).

I have also included citations for writers, philosophers, painters, photographers, and other artists whom I judge to have been especially influential in the development and evolution of Vollmann's literary sensibility. These references are hardly exhaustive, but should be sufficient to keep interested readers and future Vollmann scholars busy for years to come.

In compiling this Chronology I have borrowed freely from the chronologies included in each of Vollmann's *Seven Dream* novels and in *An Afghanistan Picture Show.* I have also consulted the following for selected references: Neil Barron's *Anatomy of Wonder* and Brian Aldiss's *Billion Year Spree* (for science fiction); Martin Seymour-Smith's *Who's Who in Twentieth-Century Literature;* William L. Shirer's *The Rise and Fall of the Third Reich: A History of Nazi Germany;* and Robert Kellogg's introduction to *The Sagas of Icelanders* (Norse arrivals in Greenland and Vinland).

Just as the Mercator projection's method of making maps produces increasing distortions of areas towards the Poles, so too have my own personal biases and interpretations resulted in analogous distortions in this chronological map of Vollmann's life and work. I have made every effort to verify the accuracy of these dates and the events they refer to, but there are no doubt errors: "for its many failures I ask forgiveness from all."

Primordial era	Atlas, a defeated warrior, is forced to bear the weight of the world upon his shoulders; in his 1996 book of journalism, *The Atlas,* William T. Vollmann temporarily relieves him of this burden.
??	Having tasted the bittersweet fruit of knowledge, Adam and Eve are expelled from Eden.
??	Cain slays Abel, an event that later resonates throughout Steinbeck's *East of Eden* and Vollmann's *The Royal Family.*
??	Elder Brother and Younger Brother begin the Inuit race.
??	The Sun and the Moon go into the sky.
30,000 B.C.	Siberian hunters cross the Bering Strait land-bridge to the Northern Yukon.

10,000? B.C.	Bering Strait land-bridge submerged.
ca. 8,000 B.C.	End of the last Ice Age.
	Paleo-Indians arrive in Virginia.
2,000? B.C.	"Independence I" (the historical and archeological name for early Greenland society) culture present in northern Greenland, Ellesmere Island, Devon Island, and Cornwallis Island.
500? B.C.-A.D. 1000	Dorset culture dominates the Arctic.
463?-483? B.C.	The Buddha preaches a philosophical doctrine based upon the principle that life is chiefly characterized by sorrow and suffering, that a way of salvation must be found, and that this way can be achieved only by universal sympathy (in the sense of being made unhappy by the suffering of others) and love. Vollmann will the explore some of these implications in *Rising Up and Rising Down* and in several of his novels, most notably in his presentation of Tyler in *The Royal Family.*
49-44 B.C..	Having successfully conducted a series of conquests that brought much of Central and Western Europe under Roman control, Julius Caesar attempts to seize complete political control over this vast empire by commencing a civil war that results in the deaths of tens of thousands, and the enslavement of many others. Vollmann will develop a detailed examination of Caesar's methods and justifications in *Rising Up and Rising Down.*
43 B.C.-A.D. 17?	Life span of Ovid, the Roman poet whose *Metamorphoses* will later inspire Vollmann's *Seven Dreams* cycle.
A.D. 33?	Christ preaches parables that nearly equal the Golden Rule: *Do unto others as you would others do unto you.* In *Rising Up and Rising Down,* Vollmann will examine this maxim (and variations devised by Gandhi, Cortez, Lenin, and others) and conclude

	that it can indeed supply the basis of a truly universal human creed of moral conduct (though he adds the caveat: "The Golden Rule is justified only when applied in acts which all parties affected agree will contribute to their conception of goodness, or when the dissenting party is a bona fide dependent of the moral actor" Vol. 4, 462).
900?-1200?	Thule Inuit migrate east from Alaska, eventually reaching Greenland.
910?	Norse king Harald's favorite son, Eric Bloody-Axe, comes of age at twelve and marries the Lappish witch Gunhild.
930?	Harald dies and is succeeded by Eric Bloody-Axe.
934?	Hakon the Good expels Eric and Gunhild from Norway. They migrate to England to rule under King Athelstan.
945?	Eric the Red born in Jaederen, Norway.
954?	Eric slain in Northumberland. Gunhild escapes to Denmark with her sons.
963?	Eric the Red is outlawed and sails to Iceland.
975-80	Eric the Red's son, Leif Erickson, born on the west coast of Iceland.
980?	Eric's bastard daughter Freydis born.
985?	Eric the Red establishes a Norse settlement in Greenland, where he brings his young son Leif to live; Christianity adopted by law in Iceland.
1000	Leif Eirikson discovers Vinland.
1007?	Gundrid and Freydis sail to Vinland with their husbands and followers. Accompanying Freydis are the Icelandic brothers, Helgi and Finnbogi.
	Japanese author Lady Murasaki Shikibu finishes *The Tale of Genji*.
1008?	Battle between the Vinland settlers and Micmac Indians.

1010?	Afraid of Indians, the Vinland settlers return to Greenland.
1190?	*Graenlendinga Saga* written; this will be one of the major sources Vollmann draws on in developing *The Ice-Shirt.*
1200?	Commencement of Little Ice Age. Climate in Greenland begins to deteriorate.
1284	Roger Bacon describes gunpowder.
1333	Birth of great Japanese Noh playwright and theoretician Kanami Kiyotsugu.
1345	In Greenland, Inuit destroy the West Bygd.
ca. 1400	First known use of rifled gun barrels.
1410	Last ship from Greenland to Iceland.
1500?	The Norsemen are now extinct in Greenland.
1491	Ignatius of Loyola born.
1492	Christopher Columbus discovers the Bahamas, Cuba, and Haiti. His sailors bring syphilis back to Europe.
1513	Machiavelli writes *The Prince,* which soon becomes one of the most influential political tracts of its era; it will later figure prominently in the thinking of several of the major characters in Vollmann's novel *Argall.*
1522	Ignatius begins work on the *Spiritual Exercises;* after a year of meditation, he then makes a pilgrimage to Jerusalem. Vollmann later includes an extended depiction of Ignatius's life in *Fathers and Crows,* whose chapters are loosely "keyed" to the *Spiritual Exercises;* he also chooses an epigraph from the *Exercises* for *Whores for Gloria:* ". . . love consists in a mutual interchange by the two parties. . . ."
1524	Verazzano probably sails past the Virginian coast—an incident mentioned in *Fathers and Crows.*
1535	Jacques Cartier ascends the St. Lawrence, discovers the sites of Quebec and Montreal; Ignatius completes the *Spiritual Exercises.*

15??	Using the maxim "In order to secure and defend my ground, I have every right to conquer you" to justify his actions, Spanish conquistador Cortez commences a bloody campaign against the Aztec inhabitants of Central Mexico; while the Aztecs respond to this threat with a brief period of fierce, violent resistance, they are quickly and mercilessly subdued in a brutal assault that results in the sacking of the magnificent Aztec capital, Tenochtitlan, the execution of the king Montezuma, wholesale slaughter of thousands of innocent civilians, and the enslavement of the survivors. Within twenty years, the population of Central Mexico is reduced from some twenty million to less than one-half million—one of the first great genocides of the modern era. Cortez's actions determine the nature of European and Native Americans for centuries to come. In Vol. 3 of *Rising Up and Rising Down,* Vollmann examines this confrontation between Montezuma and Cortez to illustrate the conflicting claims of justifying violence on the basis of defense of homeland (Montezuma) versus defense of ground (Cortez).
1554	First guns cast in England.
1550s	Wahunsenacawh becomes the chieftain known as Powhatan.
1574	First voyage of Martin Frobisher to the Arctic.
1580	Samuel Argall born. But another source says: "Was probably born about 1580–85." And another: "Born ca. 1572."
	John Smith born (baptized January 19, 1580, or January 9, 1579 Old Style). Local tradition has him born in 1579.
1584	Sir Walter Raleigh gets a patent to Virginia. He sends an expedition to reconnoiter. The explorers decide upon Roanoke as a good location for their colony.

1585	First bomb invented. Shakespeare moves to London.
1586	Sir Francis Drake attacks the Spanish in the West Indies and Florida. On his way home, he finds the Roanoke colonists very hungry; they return to England with Drake.
1587	Sir Walter Raleigh sends out the second Roanoke colony under Governor John White. John Davis sails to the Arctic in the hopes of finding a Northwest Passage.
1595	Pocahontas born; John Smith apprenticed to a merchant in Linne.
1600?	First modern Inuit culture present in the Arctic.
1602	John Smith, a mercenary in Central Europe, is captured by the Turks and delivered to the girl "Tragabigzanda."
1606	(December 19) Jamestown colonists set sail from England. Included: Smith, Gosnold, Ratcliffe, Wingfield. Archer Newport is "Admirall."
1607	(February 21) Smith held as a prisoner for mutiny. (April 26) Land sighted. First permanent white settlement in Virginia, at Jamestown. (Late December) Smith captured, and several of his men slain, during an attempt to explore the Chickahominy River. Smith taken to see Powhatan. The famous Pocahontas episode occurs—and later becomes one of the inspirations for *Argall*.
1608	Captain John Smith's account of the Virginia colony is printed in London. This is considered the "first American book." The English crown Powhatan. Starving for corn, the English (led by Smith) extort it from various towns and "kings," including Powhatan and Opechancanough. Native resistance ends the Anglo-Indian "friendship."

1609 Church of England made the official church in Virginia.

Samuel Argall—whose last name will later supply the title of Vol. 3 of Vollmann's *Seven Dreams* series—sails to Jamestown for the first time, pioneering a shorter route from England.

Wounded by a gunpowder accident, John Smith returns to England.

Powhatan massacres Ratcliffe and most of his starving trading party. During the "Starving Time" that winter, the majority of the colonists die.

Henry Hudson explores Chesapeake Bay, Delaware Bay, and the Hudson River as far as Albany.

Champlain aids the Hurons and Algonkin against the Iroquois; soon, the Jesuits join the fight against the Iroquois, and a century of war is begun.

Galileo sees Mars through his telescope.

1609-14 First Anglo-Powhatan War.

1610 John Rolfe reaches Virginia, already once widowed.

Argall and a Captain Brewster burn two Indian towns because a Werowance "acted falsely." Argall explores the coast from Virginia up to Cape Cod, and later extends Smith's survey of Chesapeake Bay.

Pocahontas married by her father to Kocoum.

1611 Argall sails home to England, ferrying the sick Lord De La Warr.

The King James Bible is printed in England.

Père Biard and Père Ennemond Masse arrive at Port Royal and begin the work of the Society of Jesus (aka the Black Gowns or the Jesuits) in the New World.

1612 Rolfe begins to experiment with tobacco.

Smith's map of Virginia published.

Argall sails from England on the *Treasurer* with a commission to expel foreigners from Virginia.

	Argall concludes a peace with the Patawomekes, who had been hostile since 1609 (q.v.).
	Heretics (who happen to be Unitarians) are burned at the stake for the last time in England.
1613	Argall kidnaps Pocahontas from a Patawomeke town and delivers her to Dale at Jamestown. Dale sends her on to Reverend Whittaker at Henrico, who guards and eventually converts her.
	Argall and Virginia colonists destroy a French colony at Mount Desert Island, later returning to destroy the houses and fortifications of that settlement.
1614	John Smith explores the northern coast of New England. Frenchmen kidnap him in retaliation for Argall's raid on Port Royal.
	Pocahontas marries John Rolfe.
1615	William Baffin searches for a Northwest Passage.
1617	Pocahontas attends a masque given for King James.
	Before or after this, John Smith visits Pocahontas for the first time since 1609. Soon afterward, he attempts a colonizing mission to New England, but gets defeated by ill winds.
	Pocahontas dies in Gravesend, England, aged twenty or twenty-two.
	Argall appointed Deputy Governor of Virginia.
1618	Powhatan dies and is succeeded by Opechancanough.
	Charges of speculation, extortion, oppression, and piracy brought against Argall, who remains Deputy Governor just the same.
	Sir Walter Raleigh executed.
1620	Argall sails on an expedition against Algerian pirates.
1622	John Rolfe dies. Possibly (but not very probably) he is one of the 347 colonists massacred in the Indian uprising led by Opechancanough that year.
	Samuel Argall is knighted.

1622-32	Second Anglo-Powhatan War.
1625-26	Argall commands a fleet of twenty-eight ships in an expedition to Spain. He captures seven ships.
1626	Argall dies (conjectural date).
	John Smith publishes his *Accidence.*
1630	John Smith publishes his *True Travels*
1631	John Smith publishes his *Advertisements* and dies.
1633	Argall dies (alternate conjectural date).
1646	Opechancanough (aged almost one hundred) is captured. An English soldier kills him in prison. Treaty of peace between English and Powhatans.
18th century	The flowering of Japanese *Ukiyo* (wood-block prints), one of the earliest (and most sophisticated) forms of mass culture; when prints by such masters as Hiroshige were introduced into Europe in the late nineteenth century, they had a major impact on early European modernists; they later influenced Vollmann's sketches and ink drawings.
1705	Virginian Indians lose most of their civil rights. Many reservations suffer reductions in acreage.
	Appamattucks now comprise only seven families (one hundred bowmen in John Smith's time). Rappahannocks said to be nearly extinct.
1734	Russian conquests in Kazakhstan lead to their presence in the Afghanistan region.
1741	The Russians discover the Aleutian Islands. They enslave, pillage, rape, and murder the native people.
	An Act of Parliament offers twenty thousand pounds to any British subject discovering the Northwest Passage by means of the Hudson Strait.
	The Chipewyan begin to become dependent on firearms.
	John Franklin, who will one day narrate parts of *The Rifles,* is born.

1775 (December) Leading the first expedition of settlers into the Colorado Desert region, Juan Bautista de Anza crosses the Colorado River at Yuma and enters the vast desolation of what is now Imperial Valley.

1787 Edward Gibbon's *The Rise and Fall of the Roman Empire* is published in two volumes.

1789 The fall of the French monarchy during the French Revolution signals the end of the political and social structure that has dominated Europe for more than one thousand years.

Having begun his first experiments with illuminated printing during the previous two years, William Blake applies some of his new skills in the publication of *Songs of Innocence.*

(July 14) The outbreak of the French Revolution. Blake, Wordsworth, Coleridge, and other British poets, along with most of England's population, greet the events in France with enthusiasm.

1789–1815 The rise and fall of Napoleon, whom Nietzsche would later claim was responsible for all Europe's higher hopes during the nineteenth century.

1792 Former democrat and pacifist Robespierre becomes a warmonger, regicide, and judicial mass murderer when he initiates his own reign of terror in which thousands of French citizens are executed, culminating in the public beheading of King Louis XVI and Marie-Antoinette. Vollmann will examine the various tactics and rationalizations used by Robespierre to justify his reliance on terrorism in Vol. 3 of *Rising Up and Rising Down.*

1794 William Blake develops color-printing methods that he employs in the publication of *Songs of Experience, Europe,* and *The First Book of Urizen.* Blake's seamless integration of visual and textual elements will have a major impact on Vollmann's experiments in book-art, and to a lesser degree, on the importance of visual elements in his print-bound publications.

1798 Wordsworth and Coleridge publish *Lyrical Ballads.*

1799 (November 9–11) Napoleon's *coup d'état.*

1800 Wordsworth expands the brief "Advertisement" which prefixed *Lyrical Ballads* into a "Preface" whose controversial insistence that poetry should be written in "a selection of language really used by men"—and that hence there can be no "*essential* difference between the language of prose and metrical composition"—almost immediately establishes it as one of the most discussed and influential of all critical essays.

1805 Napoleon's first Campaign.

1807 Napoleon's second Campaign; slave-trading made illegal in England.

Franklin helps survey the coast of Australia.

1810 High point of Napoleon's power, with the annexation of Holland and much of Northern Germany.

1812 Napoleon's disastrous defeat at Moscow. Franklin wounded in the Battle of New Orleans.

1818 Franklin sails with the Buchan Expedition to Spitzbergen as second in command.

1819–22 Franklin commands a second expedition from Hudson Bay to the Polar Sea. Ten men die of starvation and exposure. One of them is Hood, Greenstockings's lover.

1825–27 Franklin's third expedition to the Arctic.

1836 Poe publishes his first (and only) novel, the dark, fabulous adventure story, *The Narrative of Arthur Gordon Pym.* Poe's depiction of an alienated hero heading toward some terrible knowledge (and death) at the South Pole—a journey that also allegorizes a longing for finding some means to return to the womb and death—would later resonate with Vollmann.

1837 The British and the Russians send envoys to Kabul as they begin vying for hegemony in the Afghan region.

1838 British efforts to forcibly restore Shah Shuja to the Afghan throne help launch the First Afghan War (1838–42).

1842 Their campaign in Afghanistan having proved disastrous, the British withdraw and are ingloriously forced to pay compensation and leave behind hostages.

1845 Franklin commands a fourth expedition to complete the Northwest Passage.

Poe, doomed poet of the inward, writes his tales of horror, whose romantic urgency, garish intensity, sense of doom, and dark undercurrents of guilt, sin, and incest would all have their counterparts in Vollmann's own work (see "The Grave of Lost Stories"). As with Poe, Vollmann would later produce works that grow out of a volatile mixture of irrationality and scientific rationalism; the resulting clash of these irreconcilable aspects of his sensibility becomes one of the most fascinating features of his writing.

1846 The death of Poe's thirteen-year-old wife and half cousin, Virginia Clemm, an event that haunts Poe until his own death and figures obsessively in his later tales.

Franklin dies of unknown causes. The last Franklin Expedition survivors die of scurvy and starvation en route to Back's Great Fish River. The British government offers a twenty-thousand-pound reward to anyone who can relieve the Franklin Expedition. The first three graves are found on Beechy Island. Robert McClure's expedition completes the search for the Northwest Passage. Franklin's men are officially

	declared dead. Inuit on the south shore of the Hudson begin to give up the use of the bow and arrow. Amundsen becomes the first to sail the Northwest Passage. The musk-oxen population is so depleted around Hudson Bay that the superintendent bans the export of their hides. Drastic drop in the fur market. Mass starvation in the central Arctic.
1847	Marx and Engels publish *Das Kapital.*
1849	Visiting the Imperial Valley area, Oliver Wozencraft becomes the first (but not the last) person to have a vision of transporting water from the Colorado River across the desert.
1853	(March 16) L.L. (Lucius Lucien) Nunn born on a rented farm near Medina, Ohio. The second-born of twins (his twin Lucien Lucius died at age three) and the ninth of eleven children, Nunn would eventually move west in 1880 at age twenty-seven in search of his fortune; he would find it in the mining district near Telluride, Colorado, where he develops a means for his plant to transmit alternating electric current across long distances.
1856–59	Basing his action on the premise that since slavery itself is an act of violence then counter-violence is justified, terrorist John Brown leads bloody insurrections in Kansas and at Harpers Ferry; Brown becomes one of the subjects of Vol. 2 in Vollmann's *Rising Up and Rising Down.*
1860–65	American Civil War leads to the freeing of the slaves.
1864	The publication and subsequent popularity of Jules Verne's *Journey to the Center of the Earth* establishes him as the first commercially successful writer in a lineage that would lead to science fiction—and eventually to Vollmann.
1866–69	Leo Tolstoy publishes his epic study of war, *War and Peace,* in six volumes.

1867 Dostoyevsky publishes *Crime and Punishment* and begins work on *The Idiot.* The central themes explored in these and other studies of demonically tormented figures—the destruction of people by poverty, the revolt against traditional standards of ethics and morality, the value of suffering, the need for universal love and universal forgiveness—will be taken up by Vollmann, perhaps most memorably in *The Royal Family.*

1868 (August) Isidore Ducasse, the twenty-two-year-old son of a French counsel, publishes the first book of *The Chants of Maldoror* in Paris under the pseudonym "Comte de Lautréamont." *Maldoror* will be one of the major influences on the later Surrealists (who first recognized Lautréamont's genius) and on Vollmann's early literary sensibility.

1873 Russia arranges an exchange with Britain, giving up Badakhshan and Wakhan to Afghanistan in exchange for the British recognition of the new frontier they have established in the region. Afghanistan is now the only neutral area in the entire region between the British and the Russians.

1877 The "red planet" Mars, in the first of a series of oppositions with Earth, is observed by Italian astronomer G. V. Schiaparelli, who makes charts of its surface and labels the straight lines running across its surface as "canali"—a word meaning channels which, when translated into the English "canals" starts a whole new train of thought that eventually leads to Percival Lowell's astronomical studies, *Mars* (1895) and *Mars and Its Canals* (1906), Wells's *The War of the Worlds* (1898), the early pulp novels of E. R. Burroughs, and the missing Mars subplot in Vollmann's *You Bright and Risen Angels.*

Birth of the great Russian activist, thinker, and writer Leon Trotsky, whose views about the uses of violence in revolutionary activism figure prominently in Vollmann's *Rising Up and Rising Down.*

The Southern Pacific Railroad penetrates the low hot lands of the Colorado Desert.

1878 Following the rejection of their ultimatum demanding the establishment of a British resident in Kabul, the British invade Afghanistan, precipitating the Second Afghan War (1878–81).

1879 Publication of Dostoevsky's *The Brothers Karamazov.* Vollmann will repeatedly explore the key moral, political, and theological issues raised here, especially "the magnificently crazed notion" that "our only hope of rescuing humankind from its own evil is through acknowledging our kinship with one another to such a degree that we experience guilt and repentance for violence committed by others" (see afterword to Kiš's *A Tomb for Boris Davidovich*).

The British encounter fierce guerrilla-style clashes over the next two years, with the Afghans inflicting significant casualties.

After finally establishing a pro-British government, the British evacuate Afghanistan.

1883 Robert Louis Stevenson's romantic adventure novel, *Treasure Island,* is published. Along with his next novel—*Kidnapped* (1893)—Stevenson's books had an immediate impact on contemporary figures such as H. R. Haggard, Anthony Hope *(Prisoner of Zenda)*, and others interested in developing mythic alternatives to the urban blight sweeping across Europe and America. These works would, in turn, be devoured by Vollmann as a young man.

1885 H(enry). R(ider). Haggard publishes *King Solomon's Mines,* an enormously popular, panoramic romance about the "Dark Continent" that drew heavily on Haggard's personal knowledge of Africa. *Mines,* along with Haggard's next two novels (*She* and *Allan Quatermain* [both 1887]), gave the "lost race novel" its lasting, most popular form—and would later stir the imagination of young Vollmann to dream of traveling to similarly exotic, far-off lands.

1891 With the support of the Western Electric Company, Nunn becomes the first to demonstrate that wires could transmit alternating current over great distances. Electricity becomes the basis of the personal fortune Nunn accumulates—and for the "blue globes" that operate as the central metaphor of Vollmann's first novel, *You Bright and Risen Angels.*

1892 Norwegian novelist and playwright, Knut Hamsun publishes his masterpiece, *Mysteries.* Vollmann would read *Mysteries* and Hamsun's other best-known work, *Hunger* (1888), while at Deep Springs College.

1893 Charles Robinson Rockwood (b. 1860)—later portrayed as "The Seer" in Harold Lloyd Bell's hugely popular *The Winning of Barbara Worth*—presents to the Arizona Land and Irrigation Company his survey of the lands lying west of Yuma, on both sides of the international border. Soon he begins developing plans for irrigating the Imperial Valley by means of a canal that would divert waters from the Colorado River into the usually dry overflow channel of the Alamo River. This will be approximately the same route the Colorado follows during the great diversion of 1905.

1894 Rev. Silas T. Rand's compilation of Micmac legends is published.

Rudyard Kipling's first *Jungle Book* is published. Along with his later children's books *(Puck of Pook's Hill* [1906] and *Rewards and Fairies* [1910]) and later novel *Kim,* Kipling's work displays a gift for significant anthropomorphism and a capacity to make the supernatural seem natural. These qualities, and Kipling's presentation of exotic territories, quests for kingdoms, remote countries contested by doubles, hard riding, and talking animals, would soon become incorporated within the happy hunting grounds of the works of Edgar Rice Burroughs and other early twentieth-century science fiction authors. Collectively, they would later have an enormous impact on young Vollmann when he first read them as a child.

By now a millionaire several times over, Nunn begins creating an educational legacy that will provide young men with a foundation that encourages them to devote themselves to a life of service. He soon opens several other schools for the Telluride Power Company, each offering practical instruction supplemented by studies in liberal arts.

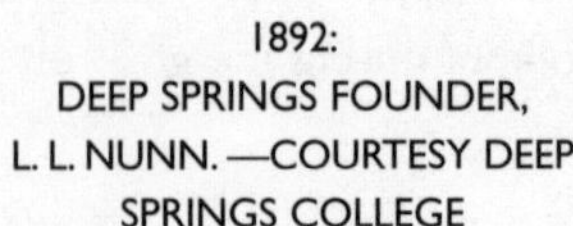

1892:
DEEP SPRINGS FOUNDER,
L. L. NUNN. —COURTESY DEEP SPRINGS COLLEGE

1895 H. G. Wells's first (and finest) novel, the pessimistic, entropic, Darwinian look at Earth's future, *The Time Machine,* is published. Moving away from the romantic implausibilities of the science fantasy writers of his day, Wells establishes a template for serious science fiction that is still in use today.

1896 Stephen Crane publishes *Maggie: A Girl of the Streets* and *George's Mother,* two grim tales of slum life. Crane's meticulously accurate, non-judgmental treatment of this material scandalized American readers at the time, but it also helped inspire authors ranging from his fellow naturalists, like Frank Norris, to the Muckrakers a generation later, as well as Vollmann, to apply journalistic accuracy to their fiction. Like several other authors associated with the rise of naturalism in the United States (London, Norris, etc.), Crane used the travels he made as a journalist as material for later use in his novels.

1899 Frank Norris's early naturalist masterpiece, *McTeague,* is published. Vollmann has obviously been fascinated with the tenets of naturalism, particularly its belief that fiction should serve as a diagnostic science, a probing of life and under-life, psychological and social. He also has developed his own version of the naturalists' belief in the novel as a kind of "experiment" capable of modeling actual conditions in the real world; as a corollary of this view, it becomes essential for the author to research the facts as carefully as possible and then to chronicle, often through the ironic juxtaposition of events, the destruction of all hopes, the smashing of lives.

1901 Under the directorship of Rockwood's newly-formed Colorado Development Company (CDC), the 500,000-square-acre Imperial Valley begins to receive irrigation water diverted from the Colorado River, thus starting the Imperial "Boom."

1905	(February/March) Two major floods create the "Great Diversion" of the Colorado River, which carves across newly developed farmland and forms the Salton Sea.
	(June) As the Colorado continues to pour into the Imperial Valley, the CDC has by now built 800 miles of canals, sold water rights on 210,000 acres, and attracted 15,000 settlers to a desert where five years earlier no whites had claimed permanent residence.
1906	(July) The floods of the previous nine months have dug out and washed down to Salton Sea a volume of earth almost four times as great as that excavated for the Panama Canal; they scour out channels with an aggregate length of forty-three miles, the average width of these channels is one thousand feet, with a depth of fifty feet.
1907	Imperial Valley secedes from San Diego County.
	Jack London publishes the first of his scientific romances, *Before Adam.*
1909	Nunn establishes the Telluride House on the Cornell Campus.
1911	Frustrated by the unappreciative response of Telluride stockholders, Nunn founds the Telluride Association; branches are created at Beaver, Utah, and Bliss, Idaho.
	The California legislature forms the Imperial Irrigation District to oversee the watering of its southwest desert; the IID immediately has to contend with Mexican farmers angry that American farmers were not only stealing their Colorado River water, but also transporting it through Mexican land.
	John Muir publishes *First Summer in the Sierras,* his classic, ecstatic meditation about the beauty and freedom to be found in the same region Vollmann grew to love while attending Deep Springs College.

1912 Arthur Conan Doyle's scientific romance, *The Lost World,* is published. Describing the fabulous adventures of Prof. George Challenger as he leads a party of explorers to the remnant of a prehistoric world on a plateau in South America, *The Lost World* remains the most famous of its type. This same year E. R. Burroughs publishes a six-part serial that is today known as *A Princess of Mars,* which brought the novel with an interplanetary setting into science fiction to stay. Doyle and Burroughs were both early influences on Vollmann, as is evident not only in several of his early stories (see "The Conquest of Kianazor") but in *You Bright and Risen Angels* and *The Rifles.*

1913 Nunn temporarily discontinues his educational work after being bought out by the Beaver River Power Company—only the Telluride House remains.

1914–18 First World War. Afghanistan is neutral.

1916 Rededicating himself to his vision of establishing a new kind of educational institution, Nunn buys a farm near Claremont, Virginia, where he establishes a two-year men's college. It quickly fails, in part due to the allure of social attractions nearby.

1917 Nunn purchases the Swinging T. Ranch at Deep Springs, California, an otherwise deserted valley located between the Inyo and White Mountains just northeast of Death Valley, and founds Deep Springs College as a combination work-study program for young men. The college gives full expression to Nunn's belief that developing a sense of the value of manual labor and responsibility to others must be the first foundation for influencing young men to lives of service.

1917: A VIEW OF DEEP SPRINGS VALLEY. —COURTESY DEEP SPRINGS COLLEGE

1918 Ludwig Wittgenstein completes *Tractatus Logico Philosophicus,* whose propositional method of arriving at logical truths would impress Vollmann when he first encounters Wittgenstein at Deep Springs College; allusions to Wittgenstein recur throughout Vollmann's work, most notably in *An Afghanistan Picture Show* and *Rising Up and Rising Down.*

1919 A constitutional monarchy is adopted in Afghanistan, with Amanullah Khan succeeding to the throne; declaring his country's complete autonomy from foreign power, Amanullah strikes at British holdings along the frontier, thus precipitating the Third Afghan War. A lengthy period of inconclusive violence eventually results in Britain's acknowledging the independence of Afghanistan. Meanwhile, the Russians, who have pleased the Afghanistan monarchy by their earlier recognition of Afghanistan's independence, send their first envoy to Afghanistan—and their first subsidy, as well.

1920 (Summer) San Francisco photographer Ansel Adams spends the first of four consecutive summers working as a custodian in Yosemite, where he first achieves a blend of form and content that has influenced, positively or negatively, virtually every nature photographer (including Vollmann) ever since.

1923 Pulp superstar Edgar Rice Burroughs publishes *Pellucidar,* which depicts a world at the hollow center of the Earth, Inner World, where one day David Innes searches for his lady love, with whom he is reunited after many strange adventures, traveling through savage regions populated by monsters and primitive creatures.

1924 (November 8, 8:45 P.M.) Adolph Hitler jumps on a table in a Munich beer hall, fires a revolver at the ceiling to get attention, and announces, "The National Revolution has begun!" Hitler is arrested the next day, along with everyone else involved in this Beer Hall Putsch, and sent to jail, where he writes *Mein Kampf* during the next two years.

1925 (April 2) Having done what he could to ensure the survival of Deep Springs and the Telluride House, Nunn dies.

1927 Death of the great French photographer, Eugène Atget, whose documentary-style approach to his craft ran counter to the lofty aesthetics of the Stieglitz circle. Making pictures that were documents, not "art," according to the dictates of his own imagination, Atget's method of taking apparently straightforward images of ordinary people and objects that unveiled their cultural value had a decisive impact on the young Walker Evans, who would in turn be a major influence on Vollmann's photo-journalism.

Early 1930s	After spending time living among the farmers and fishermen in California, John Steinbeck begins writing the first of a series of socially conscious novels culminating in *The Grapes of Wrath* (1939). For an account of some of the features of Steinbeck's work that have influenced Vollmann's own writing, see his appreciative essay, "Steinbeck: Most American of Us All."
1931	The Soviet Union and Afghanistan sign a treaty on neutrality and non-aggression that significantly strengthens Afghanistan's claims for independence.
1932	Hitler and the Nazis ascend to power in Germany. World War II has, in effect, already begun.
1933	Arthur Waley's pioneering translation of *The Tale of Genji* is published.
Late 1930s	Hemingway is in Spain as a journalist, gathering material that would be included in *For Whom the Bell Tolls.* Hemingway's willingness to put himself at personal risk in order to provide reports from the front, the fact that he wrote so memorably about war in a number of his books, and his use of precise physical details to describe physical settings that conveyed a great deal about the inner lives of the characters, without too heavy-handedly explaining things to the readers: all these make him another key influence on Vollmann.
1938	Publication of George Orwell's *Homage to Catalonia,* the work Vollmann has said most influenced *An Afghanistan Picture Show.* As with Vollmann, the journalism Orwell did throughout the world often fueled his fiction. *Homage* is an exquisitely well-written novel that is sympathetic to the anti-Franco spirit then still very much alive in Spain, and notable as well for its accurate and fair treatment of the "villains." This again angered Britain's left-wing intellectuals, who had been earlier outraged at

Orwell's *The Road to Wigan Pier* (1937), where Orwell had attacked the left for its near complete ignorance about the atrocious conditions they claimed to want to redress. As with Vollmann, Orwell repeatedly challenged the easy assumptions of left-wingers, especially those based not on first-hand experience but on abstractions.

(October 10) The Glazunov Quartet gives the premiere of Dmitri Shostakovich's *String Quartet, No. 1* in Moscow. Fashioned out of pain, black humor, and violent mockery, and drawing their emotional and artistic strength from the anguish and patience of Shostakovich's Russian countrymen, the fifteen quartets composed by him over the next twenty-six years are profound musical confessions in which he gives expression to his most intimate personal concerns. No other twentieth-century composer has achieved greater notoriety, and no other composer of any era is more greatly admired by Vollmann, whose collection of World War II fictions, *Europe Central,* was in part inspired by Shostakovich.

1938 The publication of Wittgenstein's *Philosophical Investigations,* a work Vollmann will study at Deep Springs College and whose influence is especially notable in *An Afghanistan Picture Show.*

1939 The "Golden Age" of American science fiction is launched with the publication of important works by Theodore Sturgeon, A. E. van Vogt, Robert Heinlein, and Ray Bradbury—four young authors who would be greatly admired by Vollmann and would loom large over the science fiction community for the next thirty years.

(September 1) Hitler invades Poland. Within a shockingly brief period, much of Western Europe falls to the Nazi *blitzkrieg.* Like many American youths, Vollmann will be fascinated by the Nazis' rise to power, by Hitler (the twentieth century's most memorable monster), and by the vastness of the destruction wrought by both sides during World War II. His most sustained attempt, imaginatively, to deal with World War II is *Europe Central,* a collection of stories that focuses on the personal crises experienced by figures engaged in the Russian-Nazi front—where some of warfare's most memorable acts of heroism and courage were seen.

1940 Hemingway's Spanish Civil War novel, *For Whom the Bell Tolls,* and Arthur Koestler's anti-Stalinist novel, *Darkness at Noon,* are published.

1941 Publication of Walker Evans (photography) and James Agee's (text), *Let Us Now Praise Famous Men,* a brilliant and compassionate look at ordinary Americans struggling to sustain themselves during the darkest days of the Depression; its unique and highly effective conjoining of text and image would be a model for some of Vollmann's own non-fiction work (see Vollmann's "*Whores for Gloria:* A Note to Publishers").

Danish report published of a woman's skeleton found beneath the ruins of a cathedral in Gardar, Greenland.

(November 29) Eighteen-year-old Zoya Kosmodemyanskaya (*nom de guerre:* Tanya), a suspected Russian collaborator, limps through the snow toward her execution by the Nazis; the defiant remarks she makes from the scaffold—"You can't hang all hundred and ninety million of us"—establish her as a martyr who will inspire Soviet troops throughout the rest of the war (see Vollmann's fictionalized version of this incident, "Zoya").

(December 7) The United States enters World War II following Japan's attack on Pearl Harbor.

1942 (Early summer) Hitler sends the German Sixth Army

and Fourth Panzer Army deep into Russia in the last great German offensive of the war.

(July 23) Hitler decides his army can simultaneously capture *both* Stalingrad and the rich oil fields in the Caucasus—a gamble that ultimately seals the fate of the Axis.

(August 23) The German Sixth Army reaches the Volga just north of Stalingrad; believing the Russians are finished, Hitler plans to push part of his forces through Iran to the Persian Gulf and then eventually link up with the Japanese in the Indian Ocean.

1943 (January 10) The Russian Army opens the final phase of the Battle of Stalingrad, by launching an artillery bombardment. For the next several weeks, both sides fight with incredible bravery and recklessness over the frozen wasteland of the city's rubble.

(January 31) The commander of the German Sixth Army, General Paulus, radios Hitler that the final collapse of Stalingrad cannot be delayed more than twenty-four hours. In a macabre gesture, Hitler confers on Paulus the coveted Field Marshall's baton and promotes one hundred and seventeen of the other doomed German officers. Paulus will be the central character in Vollmann's novella, "The Last Field Marshall," (included in *Europe Central*). When the Germans surrender the next day, millions of soldiers on both sides have died in the most horrific single battle in human history.

1944 (Spring) Nine hundred days after it began, the Nazis' horrific blockade of Leningrad—which forms the backdrop of Vollmann's "White Nights in Leningrad" (in *Europe Central*)—is finally lifted.

1945 (April 30) Hitler takes his own life in Berlin.

(May 8, midnight) The guns of Europe cease firing and the bombs cease dropping and silence descends there for the first time since 1939. After twelve years, four months, and eight days, the Nazis' Thousand-Year Reich has passed into history.

1947 Yasunari Kawabata completes his masterpiece, *Snow Country.* The chief mentor of Yukio Mishima during this period, Kawabata later becomes one of Vollmann's favorite authors.

1949 Mishima's *Confessions of a Mask* is published. Vollmann will later be fascinated with the odd mixture of idealism, psychotic exhibitionism, and masochism that pervades nearly all of Mishima's work.

Mark Rothko (1903–1970) establishes a formula in his paintings that he will repeat with minor variations up until his death (by suicide): a series of soft-edged rectangles, stacked vertically up on the canvas that remove everything from his work except the emotive power of his color and the breathing intensity of the surfaces. In a chapter of his Imperial Valley book, Vollmann will use Rothko's work from this period as the basis for his description of the interplay of light and color in the Colorado Desert.

1950s Explosion of post-war American science fiction, including many major works by authors like Sturgeon, Dick, Blish, Heinlein, and Bester, whose works would all be later devoured by Vollmann during his adolescence.

The Ihalmiut (Caribou Inuit) suffer mass starvation, possibly because the abuse of repeating rifles had disturbed the caribou migration. First Inuit relocated from Inukjuak (Port Harrison), Quebec, to Resolute Bay, Cornwallis Island and to Craig Harbor (near Grise Fiord), Ellesmere Island.

1953 Wittgenstein relies on "thought experiments" in developing *Philosophical Investigations,* a method that Vollmann applies in creating the theoretical portions of *Rising Up and Rising Down.*

1959 (July 28) William Tanner Vollmann born to Thomas

E. Vollmann (Professor) and Tanis Vollmann (a homemaker) in Santa Monica, California, where his father is completing a Ph.D. in business at UCLA.

1960 Publication of William L. Shirer's *The Rise and Fall of the Third Reich: A History of Nazi Germany.*

(Fall) Vollmann's father accepts his first position as an assistant professor at Dartmouth College.

Early 1960s Helge and Anne Ingstad find remains of buildings in Newfoundland that are of the same character as Viking Age buildings in Iceland and Greenland. The find eliminates any remaining skepticism about descriptions in *The Vinland Sagas* of a camp referred to as Leif's Camp's being built on the northern tip of Newfoundland—at a site now known as L'Anse aux Meadows—as a stopping place for voyages farther south in Vinland.

1962 Philip K. Dick publishes his early masterpiece, the alternative-world novel, *The Man in the High Castle.* With this novel and his next, *Martian Time Slip,* Dick was consciously attempting to create "crossover" works that would allow him to escape from the science fiction ghetto. As a teenager about a decade later, Vollmann would read virtually everything Dick ever published.

Vollmann's sister Julie is born.

Mid-1960s Vollmann grows up a sickly, book-loving child (see "The Land of Counterpane"). Diagnosed with vision problems, the youngster who will later refer to himself as "William the Blind" begins to wear glasses; his vision problems will later make it impossible for him to get a driver's license.

Vollmann is still only midway through elementary school when he writes his first novel, a science fiction adventure novel about astronauts who are picked off one by one while trying to explore another solar system.

In the aftermath of the disastrous results of his Great Leap Forward of 1958, Mao initiates the Cultural Revolution. In the next few chaotic years, as Chinese intellectuals are sent to farms and roving bands of Red Guard youths are allowed to wreak cultural and social havoc on urban centers, tens of millions of Chinese die.

1964 Isaac Asimov's *The Foundation Trilogy* is published. This work, together with Blish's *Cities in Flight* (1970), would have a significant impact on Vollmann's grandly ambitious *Seven Dreams* project that likewise consisted of a series of linked novels.

First national elections are held in Afghanistan; the Soviet-Afghanistan Treaty of Neutrality and Non-Aggression is renewed; United States assistance to Afghanistan continues to average $22,000,000 a year.

1965 Vollmann's sister Ann is born.

1966 In *Butterfly Stories* Vollmann notes that when his alter ego, the Butterfly Boy, is in the second grade he "was not popular . . . because he knew how to spell 'bacteria' in the spelling bee, and so the other boys beat him up. Also, he liked girls. Boys are supposed to hate girls in the second grade, but he never did, so the other boys despised him."

Michael Hemmingson is born to his sixteen-year-old hippie mother, Phyllis.

1967 The publication of Kurt Vonnegut's *Slaughterhouse Five* and Harlan Ellison's anthology, *Dangerous Visions,* demonstrate that the edgy, innovative, deeply pessimistic kind of science fiction associated with England's "New Wave" has arrived in the United States. The next several years will see the publication of major experimental science fiction works by Dick, Ursula K. Le Guin, Gene Wolfe, Joanna Russ, Samuel R. Delany, Thomas Disch, and Roger Zelazny. Not coincidentally, this is exactly the same period when Vollmann begins widely reading science fiction.

1968 Vollmann's six-year-old sister, Julie, accidentally drowns in a pond the two of them are swimming in. His self-lacerating sense of guilt manifests itself in horrifying nightmares about his sister, which he has almost every night up until he leaves home for college, nine years later.

Kawabata is awarded the Nobel Prize.

WTV: When I was nine years old and my sister was six, she drowned. I was supposed to be watching her and I didn't. I always felt guilty about it and my parents kind of blamed me for it a little bit, too, I think. It was a pond in New Hampshire; it had a shallow bottom, which dropped off abruptly and . . . she couldn't swim. I knew she couldn't swim, and I was supposed to be keeping an eye on her. My father and my uncle were out swimming. I just stopped paying attention at one point. I was lost in some sort of daydream.

MSB: Did you talk about it to them much?

WTV: Never. I felt shy and uncomfortable about it. I had nightmares practically every night—of her skeleton chasing me and punishing me and stuff like this—pretty much through high school, and then things got a lot better for me.

—From Madison Smartt Bell's *Paris Review* interview (2000).

1969 Vollmann's youngest sister, Sarah, is born.

English translation of Kawabata's *House of the Sleeping Beauties* is published; *Beauties* collects three of Kawabata's most grotesque stories, each of them reducing sexual desire as a helpless perversity, an incurable sickness in the male, or (if he rejects that), an involuntary evasion.

(Fall) Vollmann's father takes a sabbatical leave in

	Italy. En route, the family stops for several days in Iceland, which enthralls Vollmann.
1969–73	Seeking to disrupt the Vietnamese Army's use of Cambodia as a staging area, the U.S. military drops "twenty-five Hiroshima's" worth of bombs on Cambodia, killing one hundred and fifty thousand civilians (*Rising Up and Rising Down,* Vol. 4, 62).
Late 1960s–Early 1970s	Vollmann devours just about every science fiction book he can lay his hands on, along with other tales of exotic adventures by such figures as Kipling, H. Rider Haggard, Robert Louis Stevenson, Jack London, and Stephen Crane.
1970	Mishima commits suicide.
	James Blish's ambitious quartet of Okies-in-space novels, gathered together in the publication of *Cities in Flight,* is one of many science fiction novels that had a major impact on Vollmann's early literary sensibility.
	Publication of Michael Lesy's assemblage of photography, journalism, and commentary, *Wisconsin Death Trip;* like *Let Us Now Praise Famous Men, Death Trip* is greatly admired by Vollmann.
	(Fall) Vollmann moves once again, this time to Kingston, Rhode Island, where his father has accepted a position at Rhode Island University. Vollmann attends Kingston Junior High.
Early-to-mid-1970s	Vollmann is a bookish, high school kid forever falling in love with girls who he feels probably aren't aware of his existence.
1972	(April) Just three months before he commits suicide, Kawabata writes one of his last works, "Gleanings from Snow Country" (later included in his collection, *Palm-of-the-Hand Stories*), a distillation of Kawabata's *Snow Country;* "Gleanings" anticipates the way Vollmann will later publish similarly miniaturized

	versions of his novels, such as "Fathers and Crows" and "The Rifles" in *The Atlas.*
1974	The Vollmann family moves to Bloomington, Indiana, when Vollmann's father accepts a position at the University of Indiana.
	(Summer) Vollmann has his first experience working with a group for a social purpose when he works as a volunteer for the Indiana Youth Service Bureau. He takes the chairmanship of a group that organizes street dances and sells lottery tickets door-to-door to raise money to help the Bureau bail juvenile delinquents out of jail.
1974–77	Vollmann attends Bloomington High School South. He joins the staff of his high school newspaper and becomes reporter, literary editor, and most prolific contributor. An excellent student, he is an SAT National Merit Finalist and is the recipient of his high school's Founder's Day Award for academic excellence (this despite receiving a D in shop and an F in math).
Mid–1970s	Rise to power in Cambodia of Pol Pot and the Khmer Rouge; using the slogan "When there is rice, there is everything" as the basis of its establishment of a revolutionary new order, they become engaged in a bloody, protracted war against Vietnam that results in the death of millions of Cambodians.
1975–77	While still in high school, Vollmann takes several courses at Indiana University at Bloomington.
1975	(Summer) Vollmann works as a print-framer for what he later refers to (in his scholarship application to the Telluride House) as "a capitalist imperialistic exploitationist outfit." Although he holds down this job for only four days before he is fired for incompetence, he will later become considerably more competent in this area while doing work as a photographer, illustrator, painter, and creator of book objects.

1977 (February) A new constitution is passed, which officially establishes Afghanistan as a republic.

(June) Vollmann graduates from high school.

(Fall) Vollmann enrolls at Deep Springs College; in a letter to the Deep Springs student body dated 1925 (just before his death), L. L. Nunn had written:

Gentlemen, For what came ye to the desert? Not for conventional scholastic training; not for ranch life; not to become proficient in commercial or professional pursuits for personal gain. You came to prepare for a life of service, with the understanding that superior ability and generous purpose would be expected of you, and this expectation must be justified. Even in scholastic work, average results obtained in ordinary schools will not be satisfactory. The desert speaks. Those who listen will hear the purpose, philosophy, and ethics of Deep Springs, for it will need no prodding from teachers . . . to produce superior results in all departments.

One of the teachers who encourages Vollmann at Deep Springs is Alan Paskow, who meets regularly with the students informally; under his guidance, this group begins doing gestalt therapy on one another, and attempts to construct a rigorously developed philosophy of life. Vollmann studies Wittgenstein in a philosophy class taught by Paskow; in *An Afghanistan Picture Show,* Vollmann cites Wittgenstein more than any other writer. Another is Dr. John Mawby, a well-known geologist who authored the "Death Valley" entry for the *Encyclopedia Britannica;* Vollmann will later thank Mawby for having given him "some helpful suggestions that enabled me to better prepare for sketching Arctic plants" (*The Ice-Shirt,* 403).

Vollmann begins an autobiographical novel entitled *Introduction to the Memoires* which he later completes at the Telluride House at Cornell; loosely autobiographical, the novel includes science fiction and Deep Springs materials; at the novel's climax, its protagonist commits suicide by walking into the chamber of a nuclear reactor—in short, *Introduction* is a kind of warm up for *You Bright and Risen Angels.*

1978 (April) Just ten days after telling his confidants that he will soon announce sweeping political reforms, Afghanistan President Daoud and his family are efficiently liquidated and Nur Mohammed Taraki becomes Afghanistan's President and Prime Minster. Pleased by what has occurred, the Soviets sign a treaty of friendship with Afghanistan.

(June 28) Returning home to Bloomington for his summer vacation, Vollmann writes a letter to Freeman Dyson (a physicist at Princeton) volunteering to participate in one of Dyson's outer space projects. "You see, Mr. Dyson, I'd really like to come along," Vollmann notes, adding, "What sort of preparation would you suggest; how can we help make the whole thing happen?" (see "The Advantages of Space [1978]").

(Fall) One of the two courses Vollmann takes in the first term of his second year at Deep Springs College is Fred Bauman's History of Germany, 1870-1945, which allows him to pursue his early fascination with Hitler and World War II (the other course: Poetry of G. M. Hopkins). Vollmann serves as student body president and as chairman of the Deep Springs Committee to Institute Coeducation by Whatever Devious Means May Be Necessary (the committee fails to achieve its goal—and despite measures introduced by the students on an almost yearly basis to allow female students admission, Deep Springs has remained an all-male institution to the present). He also becomes founder and editor of a literary journal, *The.*

I'd like to go on record now as saying that Bill Vollmann will be famous one day, and deservedly so. . . . While at first he was one of the quieter students in calls, during the last year he has gained confidence and become a frequent contributor to class discussions-and one whose contributions are always welcomed. He's now Student Body President and doing a fine job. I understand that even in his labor assignments, where he used to have the reputation of being earnest but clumsy, he has developed into a competent and useful worker. . . . The fame I alluded to in the first sentence will come, I believe, from his writing. Bill is extremely talented, has a unique vision and voice, and, most important, is disciplined and prolific.

—From David Schuman's reference letter in support of Vollmann's application to the Telluride House at Cornell, dated December 7, 1978.

1979 (Spring) The Term XI issue of *The* features Vollmann's story, "The Conquest of Kianazor" (included in this *Reader*), which describes the discovery of the exotic, imaginary Kianazor—"a city of gold in the mountains of Africa"—by Portuguese explorer Juan-Paolo Fransisco García de Paolo.

Vollmann writes a letter to the Saudi Arabian Embassy, proposing that the Saudis consider sending him and his fellow Deep Springer, Jake Dickinson, on a mining operation to the asteroids. "We hope you will consider this seriously," he says—but they never received a reply (see "A Bizarre Proposition (1979)").

(March) With tensions mounting in the area, Radio Kabul claims that Iran has sent four thousand troops in disguise to its border who, along with seven thousand Afghan dissidents, are attempting to unseat Taraki. The Afghanistan government also accused

Pakistan of harboring and supporting the Mujahideen (which they are in fact doing).

(May) In his application to Cornell's Nunnian Telluride House, Vollmann mentions plans to "set up a colony in space or in Antarctica."

While home, he discovers a copy of the Penguin Writers from the Other Europe edition of Danilo Kiš's *A Tomb for Boris Davidovich*, which becomes an important influence on his approach to form/content issues, his presentation of characters, his political views, and much more (see his afterword to the Dalkey edition of *A Tomb*).

(June) Vollmann graduates from Deep Springs College.

(July 1) Vollmann makes his first trip to Alaska accompanied by a woman friend named Erica Bright (he describes this trip in Chapter 9 of *An Afghanistan Picture Show*, "Alaska [1979]"); despite the confidence he has gained as a self-reliant outdoorsman at Deep Springs, Vollmann mostly feels like a bumbling fool on this trip.

(August) Vollmann enrolls at Cornell University as a literature major; he begins living at the Telluride House, which Nunn hoped would serve as a sort of finishing school for the young college students who by now had absorbed the lessons of work and listened to the desert; but two years listening to the desert and picking cow dung from his boots create culture shock for Vollmann, who feels ill at ease among most other Telluride House members. He visits the pools and gorges of Robert Treman State Park near Ithaca, whose descriptions will later be used in *Fathers and Crows*.

(October) Amin launches a major offensive against the Mujahideen in Pakistan and Badakhshan.

(Fall) Vollmann presents a speech to the Telluride House entitled "Deep Springs: An Anti-Nunnian

View," which summarizes his ambivalent feelings about his experiences in Deep Springs. He later incorporates some of the controversial points raised in this speech into the final paper he turns in for his Marxism class taught by Michael Ryan, entitled "Class Opposition and Structural Mediation in Telluride House." This material becomes some of the starting points for *You Bright and Risen Angels.*

(Christmas Day) Soviets airlift troops and tanks into Kabul. Afghanistan's Prime Minister Amin is killed and replaced by Soviet sympathizer, Babrak Karmal.

1980 (May) Vollmann takes part in an anti-nuclear affinity-group protest at Seabrook, New Hampshire, an experience he draws upon in his first novel, *You Bright and Risen Angels.*

Summers of 1980–1981 Inspired by George Konrad's *The Case Worker,* Vollmann works with blind and retarded students during his summer vacation at an Ithaca City Day Camp—an experience that later influences his treatment of mentally retarted people in *The Royal Family.*

(Spring) Vollmann presents a speech, "Mainstreaming the Retarded," at the Telluride House dealing with the conditions he witnessed the previous summer while working with the mentally retarded. He revises the speech and tries to get it published, but it is rejected.

For his *summa cum laude* thesis project, Vollmann develops a comparison between the Seabrook nuclear protests and Canto 19, "The Song of Heaven," from Dante's *Purgatorio.*

Vollmann accepts a fellowship from the Graduate Program in Literature at UC/Berkeley.

(June) Vollmann graduates from Cornell University *summa cum laude,* majoring in literature.

(Summer) After college, Vollmann moves to San Francisco. Determined to join the Mujahideen rebel resistance to the Soviet invasion of Afghanistan, Vollmann defers his fellowship to Berkeley and gets a job as a secretary in a reinsurance company; the job is dismal, but he keeps it until he has saved up enough money to go to Afghanistan.

1982 (Spring) Vollmann begins writing sections of a long essay he will work on for the next twenty-three years dealing with violence—in 2003, it is published as *Rising Up and Rising Down.*

(May 31) Vollmann departs for Afghanistan, where he plans to aid the Mujahideen rebels in their struggle against Soviet domination; his initial lofty hopes of are dashed even before arrival and, after six weeks and weakened by dysentery, he departs.

(August) Vollmann returns from Afghanistan; with the assistance of a $990 award from the Ella Lyman Cabot Trust grant-in-aid, he develops a presentation about Afghanistan using interviews, slides, and audiotapes in an effort to raise money for Afghan refugees. He begins a draft of a work that will later evolve into *You Bright and Risen Angels,* but not knowing what to do with it, he puts it aside and begins working on a manuscript based upon his experiences in Afghanistan. He gives it the same title he has been using for his Afghanistan presentation: *An Afghanistan Picture Show.*

(Fall) Vollmann begins graduate work in comparative literature as a Regents' Fellow at UC/Berkeley. He begins writing a book about his experiences in Afghanistan in which he consciously strives to achieve the sort of combination of narrative description and political analysis found in George Orwell's *Homage to Catalonia.* After four months of work, he completes a draft that he submits to a political science competition at Berkeley—but it fails to be awarded anything by the judge, who writes Vollmann a note indicating that while he liked the book, it wasn't really a work about politics.

Vollmann completes work on his Afghanistan novel and submits the non-agented manuscript for publication at Houghton Mifflin.

"LKG" ends her engagement with Vollmann, whose distraught reaction is memorably depicted in "A Thumbnail Sketch" (*You Bright and Risen Angels,* 387–96).

1983–84 The surviving Powhatan tribes gain state recognition.

1983 (Summer) Vollmann and Seth Pilsk hitchhike from San Francisco to Fairbanks, Alaska, taking many rolls of film; this trip inspires some of the Alaska scenes in *You Bright and Risen Angels.*

(Fall) Dissatisfied with graduate work, Vollmann drops out of Berkeley and takes a job as a door-to-door canvasser, which lasts about six months.

Vollmann passes his Afghanistan manuscript to a literary agent, who declines to represent it because, while it is interesting from a political standpoint, it isn't really a work of literature.

Vollmann receives a $150 grant from Aid For Afghan Refugees for assistance in distributing a slide show about Afghanistan.

1984 Vollmann begins working on "Wordcraft," a writing manual that gradually expands as he jots down whatever insights he has made about the craft, both in relation to his own work and that of others. Although Vollmann has not yet made any serious effort to ready this work-in-progress for publication, he does occasionally consult it when he feels stumped.

Vollmann's friend, Seth Pilsk the Thin, explores Baffin Island.

Partly due to his awareness of the uselessness of his attempts to help the Afghan resistance against the Soviet Union, Vollmann buys his first gun—a

Browning Berretta, BDA .380—and begins to learn to shoot it.

Vollmann meets photographer Ken Miller ("the most dangerous man I know"), who introduces him to San Francisco's Mission District, a stark parallel world inhabited by pimps, prostitutes, street alcoholics, and other lost souls. Sharing Miller's attraction for the ugly and his desire to document the lives of these street people, Vollmann begins hanging out in the Mission District for extended periods to ensure that his depictions will be as accurate and honest as he can make them; gradually, he creates an entire multi-hued collection of interrelated stories that is published as *The Rainbow Stories* (1989). Vollmann later writes a preface and supplies text for a collection of Miller's photographs entitled *Open All Night* (1995).

(Fall) Despite having no experience working with computers, Vollmann accepts a $19,000 per year job as a programmer for NCA Corporation. He is hired by Mike Levinthal, an ex-Deep Springer; NCA (now defunct) operated out of Sunnyvale, located in Silicon Valley, which was then booming. Vollmann lived with Levinthal for a brief period in San Francisco while commuting to Sunnyvale, but when this arrangement ended, Vollmann—who can't pass the DMV vision test—begins sleeping in his office. There, late at night after everyone else has gone home, he begins furiously typing out the manuscript of *You Bright and Risen Angels,* whose treatment of computers, the mainframe, etc., originated here.

(December 19) Houghton Mifflin rejects Vollmann's Afghanistan novel.

Mid–1980s Vollmann begins formulating plans to write a symbolic history of the United States, which he initially conceives to be a single novel.

1985	(November 14) Esther Witby of British publisher Andre Deutsch writes Vollmann that Deutsch has agreed to publish *You Bright and Risen Angels.*
Nov. 1985– Jan. 1987	Vollmann writes the text that will appear as "Ladies and Red Nights" in *The Rainbow Stories.*
Aug. 1985– Feb. 1986	Vollmann writes the text that will appear as "The White Knights" section of *The Rainbow Stories.*
Sept. 1986– Jan. 1987	Vollmann writes the text that will appear as "Scintillant Orange" in *The Rainbow Stories.*
1986–87	At a Women's Craft Fair in San Francisco, Vollmann sees some postcards by prison inmate Veronica Compton being sold by ROSI (Remember Our Sisters Inside). Vollmann's later poem and book object, "The Convict Bird," was inspired by this encounter.
Feb. 1986– Jan. 1987	Vollmann writes the text that will appear in *The Rainbow Stories* as "The Blue Yonder."
1986	(June–September) Vollmann writes the texts that will appear in *The Rainbow Stories* as "Violet Hair" and "The Visible Spectrum."
July 1986– Feb. 1987	Vollmann writes the text that will appear in *The Rainbow Stories* as "The Indigo Engineers."
July– October 1987	Vollmann writes the text that will appear in *The Rainbow Stories* as "X-Ray."
1987	Vollmann visits Iceland, Greenland, and Baffin Island, where he gathers impressions and information that he will later use extensively in *The Ice-Shirt.* For instance, *The Rifles*'s descriptions of the killing of a caribou with a shotgun (pp. 330–31) and the butchering of whales (p. 139) were scenes witnessed by Vollmann on this trip to Greenland, as were his descriptions of the Ameralik Fjord (p. 329 and 391). Vollmann receives the Ludwig Vogelstein Award (for assistance in travel to the Arctic to do research for *The Ice-Shirt*), and (with Ken Miller) a Maine Photographic Workshops grant (for assistance in documenting the

lives of street prostitutes in San Francisco's Tenderloin district).

Vollmann's first book, *You Bright and Risen Angels,* is published by Andre Deutsch, a British publisher who agrees to give him considerable input on the book's visual design, including the use of Miller's photograph of Vollmann holding a handgun to his forehead as the jacket photo (his American publisher, Atheneum, runs a different photo).

Vollmann leaves San Francisco and moves to Manhattan. He soon discovers that his familiarity with the street scene of San Francisco does him little good here; although he grows to dislike Manhattan intensely, he works steadily on several major projects and completes work on *The Ice-Shirt* and *Fathers and Crows* during this period.

1988 (January 1) Vollmann receives a note from his editor at Deutsch telling him the title of his new collection has been changed from *The Rainbow Stories* to *Under the Rainbow.*

(February) Visits Joshua Tree National Monument whose landscape will be transformed into the description of the mount called Olive during the time of Christ in *Fathers and Crows.*

(August 16–25) Vollmann's first visit to Resolute, one of the most northern settlements in Canada, located on Cornwallis Island, where he encounters a landscape of magnificent, utterly unforgiving desolation that he will later describe in the opening section of *The Rifles;* he also relies on this landscape as the basis of *The Rifles*'s depictions of King William Island—which Vollmann was never able to visit—where most of the members of the Franklin expedition perished in the summer of 1848.

Vollmann receives a $20,000 Whiting Writers Award (to work on *Fathers and Crows*).

(September 15–21) Vollmann returns to Resolute, where—assisted by Elizabeth Allakariallak, an Inuk who served as his interpreter—he interviews Levi Nungaq, an Inuit whose recollections of being relocated from Inukjuak (in lower Canada) during the fifties is used in Vollmann's development of *The Rifles.* While in Resolute he also meets an Inuk woman, Reepah, whose fictional version will figure prominently in *The Rifles.* He also visits Eureka (on Ellesmere Island); his recordings of what he observed on a trek just east of Eureka serve as the basis of his descriptions of the landscape surrounding Peel Sound (*The Rifles,* 216, 389).

Native people make up six percent of the general population in Canada and forty-six percent of the prison population.

1989 Soviet troops leave Afghanistan.

Benazir Bhutto comes to power in Pakistan.

Andre Deutsch in England and Atheneum in the United States publish Vollmann's collection about San Francisco under its original title, *The Rainbow Stories.* Vollmann had originally hoped to have *The Rainbow Stories* published with Ken Miller photos, but this idea was rejected as being too expensive.

Vollmann's hands begin to go bad from the exertion of a daily sixteen-hour work schedule (the largest chunk of daily writing time he has ever put in on a book) typing a draft of *Fathers and Crows.* He receives the Shiva Naipaul Memorial Prize for an excerpt from *Seven Dreams: A Book of North America.*

Vollmann visits Kateri Tekakwitha's relics at Kahnawake

(July–August) Accompanied by Seth Pilsk, Vollmann departs for a month-long visit to Pond Island Inlet on Baffin Island; several incidents from this trip will be incorporated into *The Rifles,* including the opening section, and the description of fishing (pp. 199, 388) and of King William Island (pp. 311—which is actually that of Cornwallis Island and Ellesmere Island, which Vollmann visits on this trip); the ballpoint drawings (pp. 158, 241) were given to Vollmann by Inuit children on this trip.

A resolution to apologize to and compensate the Inuit who were relocated to Resolute and Grise Fiord is rejected.

1989 Conclusion of the war between Cambodia and Vietnam.

(December 6) Atlantic Monthly Press rejects *Whores for Gloria;* on this same date, Vollmann receives a note from Pan Books (London) accepting *Whores for Gloria* for publication and rejecting *An Afghanistan Picture Show.*

(December 7) W.W. Norton & Company rejects *Whores for Gloria.*

1990 (February 14) Poseidon Press rejects *Whores for Gloria.*

(May) Larry McCaffery meets Vollmann for the first time in Manhattan to conduct an interview for his *Some Other Frequency* collection; different versions of this interview also appear in the *Review of Contemporary Fiction* "Younger Authors" issue and *Mondo 2000.*

1990: LARRY MCCAFFERY AND VOLLMANN OUTSIDE VOLLMANN'S MANHATTAN APARTMENT AT THEIR FIRST MEETING. —COURTESY OF LARRY MCCAFFERY

(Summer) Reepah visits Vollmann in Manhattan, an episode recounted in *The Rifles.* At a party in San Diego, Mike Hemmingson first hears of Vollmann's work from Larry McCaffery, who announces unhyperbolically, "I have seen the future of American fiction—and its name is William T. Vollmann."

(July 7) Simon and Schuster rejects *Whores for Gloria.*

(August) Conducting research for *The Rifles,* Vollmann visits Inukjuak, an isolated village located on the east side of Labrador.

(Fall) *The Ice-Shirt*—the first volume in Vollmann's projected *Seven Dreams* series, which will eventually depict a symbolic history of North America—is published by Andre Deutsch and Viking.

(October) Henry Holt and Company rejects several submissions, including *Whores for Gloria.*

1991 (March) Wishing to be able to report first-hand the brutal winter conditions endured by the Franklin Expedition, Vollmann is dropped off alone near the magnetic North Pole on a trip partially financed by *Esquire.* To get there, he is flown to a position near the current magnetic North Pole by Dennis Stossel, of the Atmospheric Environment Services (AES), who assists him in getting transportation, first to Eureka, Ellesmere Island, where AES operates a weather station; from there he is flown to Isachsen, Ellef Ringnes Island, located near the current magnetic North Pole. Marv Lassi, inspector of auto stations, gives him a key to a shed he built at Isachsen, and an explanation of the layout of the station and of how to use the station's propane heater—gifts which ultimately save Vollmann from suffering the same fate as most of the Franklin Expedition. *Esquire* supplies $5,000 of the $12,000 he requires to visit Isachsen. Most of the descriptions of Cornwallis Island appearing in *The Rifles* are from this trip as well.

Vollmann returns from the Arctic with frostbitten fingers that, combined with the discomfort he had already been experiencing due to carpal tunnel syndrome, make it difficult for him to spend the long hours at the computer he needs to write his books. To help alleviate this problem, his parents send him one of the first generations of the new voice-recognition systems just then capable of translating spoken words into text on a computer screen. For his first test run of the system, Vollmann slowly speaks the words, "THANKS, MOM AND DAD!"; this message is translated into the following, somewhat ominous pronouncement, "THIS MAN IS DEAD!" Vollmann soon abandons this system, and during the next several years, his symptoms relent enough for him to resume writing on the computer, although somewhat less strenuously.

Vollmann's *Whores for Gloria* is published as a paperback original by Pan-Picador (U.K.) and in hardback by Pantheon (U.S.).

Thirteen Stories and Thirteen Epitaphs is published by Deutsch and Pantheon.

During this period Vollmann also completes work on several book objects: *Whores for Gloria, The Happy Girls,* and *Epitaph for Mien.*

1991: VOLLMANN AND GLORIA.
—PHOTO BY KEN MILLER

(October) Vollmann returns to Resolute and conducts a BBC interview with several of the local Inuits; the Inuit anecdotes provide new insights into their plight, which Vollmann incorporates into *The Rifles* in various ways—although, as he notes in *The Rifles,* "Listening to these stories was almost unbearably painful" (378).

(Fall) Larry McCaffery writes an introduction for a "Post-Pynchon American Fiction Issue" of Tokyo's *Positive* magazine, which announces that Vollmann is unquestionably the brightest star on America's literary horizon since Pynchon, adding that he is also "the only writer I can say with complete confidence who is destined for greatness." The issue also includes translations of Vollmann's fiction and McCaffery's interview with Vollmann.

Vollmann visits Cambodian battlefields for *Esquire* with Ken Miller. He will return to Southeast Asia on several occasions, gathering impressions for *Butterfly Stories.*

(September 9) *Whores for Gloria* is rejected by German publisher Suhrkamp Verlag. At about this same time, Paul Cremo of Spring Creek Productions contacts Vollmann about a possible film project for *Whores for Gloria.*

Joseph Hooper's "The Strange Case of William Vollmann" appears in *Esquire.*

1992 *Fathers and Crows,* the second book of the *Seven Dreams* series, is published by Deutsch and Viking.

(Summer) Vollmann visits Mexico City, a trip described in *The Atlas*'s "Spare Wife."

(Fall) Vollmann visits Sarajevo, Prague, and Berlin.

Despite having just published *Fathers and Crows,* as well as five other books, all released by major houses to strong reviews, Vollmann says in a *Publishers Weekly* interview that "I'm at a tough time in my career: I'll either make it or I'll be out of it fairly soon."

In the "William T. Vollmann" entry appearing in *Contemporary Authors,* Vollmann lists his politics as "Environmentalist egalitarian," his religion as "Agnostic plus," and his avocations as "bookmaking, sketching, wilderness travel, ladies, exotic weapons." He adds that, "The kind of reading and writing that I value is a dying art. While it lasts, and while I last, I intend to write sentences that are beautiful in their own right, to write paragraphs that respect those sentences while conveying thought, and to arrange those paragraphs in works that promote love and understanding for people whom others with my background may despise or fail to know."

Larry McCaffery's "Running on the Blade's Edge: William Vollmann" appears in *Mondo 2000.*

Publication by Farrar, Straus and Giroux of *An Afghanistan Picture Show,* a revised version of the manuscript Vollmann wrote soon after he returned from Afghanistan in 1982.

1993 (January–February) Vollmann visits Somalia to report for *Esquire* on the civil war and the American presence. He travels to several locations in Africa, including Nairobi, Kenya; Mogadishu, Somalia; and Madagascar (en route home, he also stops in Hong Kong and Maui).

Publication of *Butterfly Stories* by Deutsch and Grove.

(Summer) Vollmann is one of the featured authors (along with David Foster Wallace and Susan Daitch) in a special "Younger Authors" issue of *Review of Contemporary Literature* guest-edited by McCaffery. The issue includes McCaffery's interview with Vollmann and the first extended critical examinations of Vollmann's work.

(August–September) Vollmann travels to Thailand and Burma with Ken Miller for *Spin;* during this trip he buys and sets free a child sex slave.

1992: VOLLMANN AND HIS INTERPRETER IN THAILAND. —PHOTO BY KEN MILLER

Sections of Vollmann's *Rising Up and Rising Down* are published in *Esquire.*

Vollmann moves to Sacramento.

Vollmann receives a U.S. Information Agency grant to lecture in Italy, where he reads "The Best Way To Smoke Crack." No reports about the response.

Vollmann visits Sarajevo for BBC Radio 4 and the *Los Angeles Times Magazine.* The four radio broadcasts based on this journey "The Yugoslavian Notes," are later nominated for a Sony Award in News and Current Affairs. Versions of these stories will also be collected and published as parts of *The Atlas.*

"Incarnations of the Murderer" appears in a special issue of *Postmodern Culture* (the first on-line literary journal) guest-edited by Larry McCaffery.

Vollmann visits Arctic Canada for BBC Radio 4 to describe Inuit life in the High Arctic.

Publication in England of *The Rifles,* the sixth book in the *Seven Dreams* series; the American edition is published the following year by Viking.

Vollmann's book object, *The Grave of Lost Stories* is completed.

Vollmann visits Burma on assignment for *Spin,* where he meets with the eerie and charismatic figure, Khun Sa, the self-styled "Opium King," who justifies the use of his enormously profitable heroin trade to maintain a private army in his zone of occupation on the basis of defense of race, homeland, and culture. This interview—later described by Vollmann in Vol. 4 of *Rising Up and Rising Down* as "one of my greatest experiences as a journalist"—becomes part of Vollmann's larger examination of the rise of Pol Pot to power in Cambodia.

1992: VOLLMANN IN PRESS FLAK JACKET. —PHOTO BY KEN MILLER

1994 (May 1) Vollmann visits Serbia, Croatia, and Bosnia to report on the continuing war there for *Spin.* While riding in the back seat of a jeep en route to Sarajevo with his friend Brian Brinton and Francis William Tomasic (a photographer and interpreter accompanying him on the assignment), Vollmann narrowly escapes death when their vehicle hits a mine. Vollmann is spared serious injury by the protective bulletproof vest he is wearing, but up front, the blast kills the driver instantly and mortally wounds Brinton, whom Vollmann has known since high school. Confused about what has happened (he thinks they have come under mortar attack) and in shock, Vollmann tries to comfort his friend, but within a minute or two, Brinton dies.

(June) Following Vollmann's lead, Michael Hemmingson travels to Rio de Janeiro, Brazil, to write an article on homeless children.

(July) Michael Hemmingson goes to Rwanda and witnesses the death of thousands of Hutu at the border of Goma, Zaire. He travels to Senegal later in the year to cover the World Health Organization's failed dam, which killed more people than it saved. He becomes sickened with this type of work and vows never to set foot on the African continent again.

Madison Smartt Bell's profile, "William T. Vollmann's Risky Business," is published in the *New York Times Magazine.*

Vollmann visits the U.S. Deep South to report on voodoo and santeria for *Spin*.

1995 Michael Hemmingson dedicates his novella, *Crack Hotel* (Permeable Press), to Vollmann.

Vollmann visits American "militia" types for *Spin.*

Vollmann visits Japan's Untouchable caste for *Spin*. Publication of Ken Miller's book of Tenderloin District photographs, *Open All Night,* with accompanying texts and a forward by Vollmann.

Larry McCaffery publishes a second major interview with Vollmann in *Some Other Frequency: Interviews with Innovative American Fiction Writers.*

Vollmann visits Malaysia for *Esquire* where he becomes the first journalist to interview the head of the PULO Muslim terrorist group.

1996 Vollmann's *The Atlas* is published by Viking. Blending fiction and journalism, *The Atlas*—which is later selected as winner of an award from PEN Center USA West—is based on Vollmann's experiences while visiting Sarajevo (and other cities in Bosnia), Mogadishu (during the Somalia disturbances), Madagascar, Cambodia, Israel, and many of the world's other "hot spots" during the previous decade. Inspired by Yasunari Kawabata's *Palm-of-the-Hand Stories,* Vollmann organizes the fifty-three sections of *The Atlas* into a kind of palindrome in which motifs, characters, and themes recur and reflect one another.

Vollmann makes two visits to the Cambodian Khmer Rouge for *Spin.*

Vollmann visits Jamaica to seek out the roots of political violence, for *Gear*.

(May 25) Vollmann weds Janice Kong-Ja Ryu; the wedding and reception are held at the White Sulfur Springs Resort in St. Helena, California; guests include Vollmann's mother, father, and sisters, Bob Guccione, Ken Miller, and a number of women who inspired the female characters in his novels.

(July) Larry McCaffery drives Vollmann on a tour of several days through the Anza-Borrego Desert, Salton Sea, and Imperial Valley. On one side trip they discover Salvation Mountain (an enormous work of folk art that Leonard Knight has painted onto a hillside east of the Salton Sea) and the nearby squatters camp known as Slab City—sites that will figure prominently in the latter sections of *The Royal Family;* they also drive several miles into Santa Rosa Badlands, where Larry McCaffery introduces Vollmann to his autistic friend, Patrick Miller, who is living alone (quite happily) in an abandoned truck and who is later transformed into "Waldo," the crazy (but wise) mystic encountered by Tyler near the end of his journey to nowhere in *The Royal Family* . En route to the thriving border town of Mexicali, Vollmann gets his first glimpse of the vast desolation of the Imperial Valley, a region he will return to repeatedly over the next several years, conducting research for a nonfiction study of the area. During their stay in Mexicali's rundown Malibu Hotel, Vollmann photographs a prostitute named Elvira, whose sad stories about the circumstances that led her from an impoverished Mexican village to the hot streets of this urban border town later provide some of the basis of Vollmann's treatment of the Mexican prostitute Beatrice in *The Royal Family.*

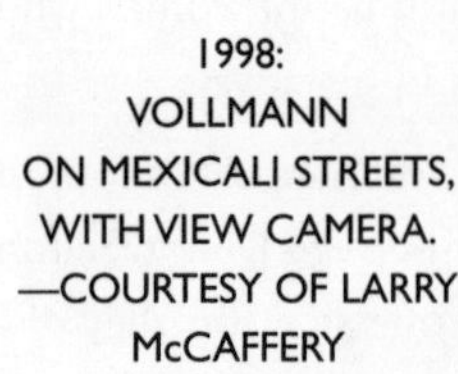

1998:
VOLLMANN
ON MEXICALI STREETS,
WITH VIEW CAMERA.
—COURTESY OF LARRY
McCAFFERY

1997 As part of his research for *The Royal Family,* Vollmann—occasionally joined by his friends Lizzy Gray and Mike Pulley—hops onto several freight cars leaving Sacramento.

Vollmann interviews rock star Ted Nugent for *Esquire.*

1998 (February). Vollmann completes work on his twenty-three-year project, a study of violence entitled *Rising Up and Rising Down.*

Vollmann visits Iraq on Saddam Hussein's birthday for *Gear.*

Vollmann visits Kosovo for *Gear.*

(October 4) Birth of Vollmann's daughter, Lisa Kirsten Vollmann.

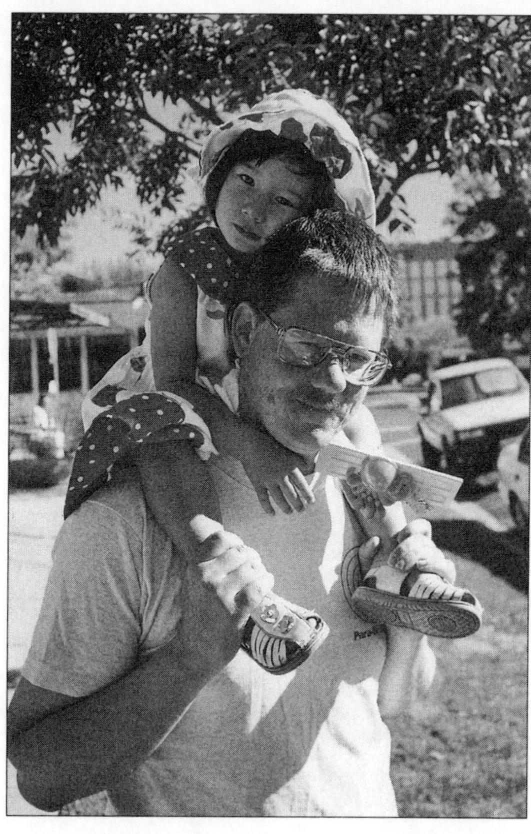

1998: VOLLMANN WITH HIS DAUGHTER LISA AT THEIR HOME IN SACRAMENTO. —COURTESY OF LARRY McCAFFERY

Sensing that fatherhood will necessarily require him to make some changes in his modus operandi—and hence that he will likely have to remove himself from the Tenderloin scene that he has been so immersed in since the eighties—Vollmann completes work on *The Royal Family,* whose elaborate, meticulously accurate descriptions of San Francisco's Mission District comprises what is, in effect, an extended lovingly rendered farewell (see also "The Ghost of Magnetism").

(May-June) Larry McCaffery teaches Term VII at Deep Springs College.

(September) Vollmann is in Tokyo researching an article about the Japanese Yakuza for *Gear;* Larry McCaffery, who is teaching in Tokyo that fall, joins Vollmann one evening to interview a former Yakuza member (see "Regrets of a Schoolteacher").

1999 Vollmann visits Nevada call girls for Gear.

Vollmann visits the new Arctic territory of Nunavut for *Outside.*

Vollmann visits Columbine High School in Littleton, Colorado, for *Gear.*

Vollmann visits Imperial Valley's California-Mexico border to write an article about the trafficking of Mexican "illegals" for *Gear*.

Vollmann visits Colombia for *Gear.*

2000 Vollmann's massive (seven hundred and eighty pages—his longest book to date) *The Royal Family* is published by Viking.

After a fiercely contested civil war, the Taliban rise to power in Afghanistan; when the forces of the Northern Alliance—who would later become America's key allies in its struggle to unseat the Taliban—withdraw from Kabul, raping and pillaging as they leave. The toll on the citizens is enormous.

(Fall) Madison Smartt Bell's interview with Vollmann

appears in the *Paris Review*'s "Art of the Fiction" series.

2001 (January) Twenty years after his first entry into Afghanistan, Vollmann returns to write an article published in the May 15 issue of *The New Yorker* (see "Across the Divide").

(June) Vollmann and Larry McCaffery are taken by motorboat along the last twenty miles of the notoriously polluted New River before it enters the Salton Sea (see "The Water of Life"). On the United States side of the border, Vollmann photographs Mt. Signal (in Mexico), which has long been used by "coyotes" to transport illegals into the United States.

(September 11) The World Trade Center terrorist attack.

(Fall) The United States-led coalition enters Afghanistan with the intention of eliminating Al Qaeda and the Taliban. Dave Eggers agrees to publish Vollmann's four-thousand-page-manuscript about violence, *Rising Up and Rising Down* in seven volumes. An abridged version (of approximately eight hundred pages) is accepted for publication by Ecco Press.

Vollmann visits Hokkaido, the northernmost major Japanese island, to do an article commissioned by *The New Yorker* dealing with the Ainu—the remnants of the culture that was overrun by successive waves of Mongol tribes arriving on the Japanese Archipelago from 10,000–2,000 B.C.

Argall, the third volume in the *Seven Dreams* series, is published by Viking.

2002 (Spring) During a visit to Japan, Vollmann meets the great Japanese Noh master, Umewaka Rokuro.

(December) Vollmann attends the highly charged public meeting in which the Imperial Valley Water District rejects the proposal for sending two hundred thousand acre-feet of water to San Diego via an (as yet unbuilt) aqueduct.

2003 (January 1) Following a route used by "coyotes" to transport illegals into the United States, Vollmann, his friend Meagan Atiyeh, and Larry McCaffery hike to the summit of Mt. Signal located some twenty miles west of Mexicali just south of the U.S.-Mexico border.

2003: VOLLMANN IN IMPERIAL VALLEY NEAR MT. SIGNAL; HIS FRIEND, PHOTOGRAPHER WILLIAM LINNE, IS THE DISTANT FIGURE (UPPER LEFT). —COURTESY OF LARRY McCAFFERY

(January 2) En route to the Parker Dam, located a few miles north of Yuma, Larry McCaffery and Vollmann discover the Cloud Museum; created and maintained by Johnny Cloud, this museum contains rows of ancient automobiles, tractors, and other farming vehicles, and several buildings overflowing with Imperial Valley detritus. Near sunset, they drive north through a maze of arroyos until they arrive at the Colorado River.

(March) While exploring the Mexican border in the mountains along the eastern edge of Imperial Valley, Vollmann and Larry McCaffery stop at the Tower (a local landmark), where Vollmann photographs the sweeping views of the Colorado Desert; they drive up along the upper rim of the Yuha Desert, amidst whose moonscapes de Anza once stopped for water in his 1775 crossing of the Sonoran Desert, and where Vollmann photographs several mysterious intaglios or geoglyphs created by Native Americans perhaps one thousand years ago.

(April) United States is at war with Iraq.

(June) While examining the Imperial Valley's system of canals, Larry McCaffery and Vollmann locate the Hanlon Gate, through which water first entered Imperial Valley in the early nineties.

Vollmann's long search for the Chinese tunnels allegedly existing beneath the streets of Mexicali since at least the Prohibition era is rewarded when he is shown three different tunnels. In one tunnel, he discovers a stash of documents written in Chinese characters, which he photocopies and then presents to the director of the Mexicali Archive Museum.

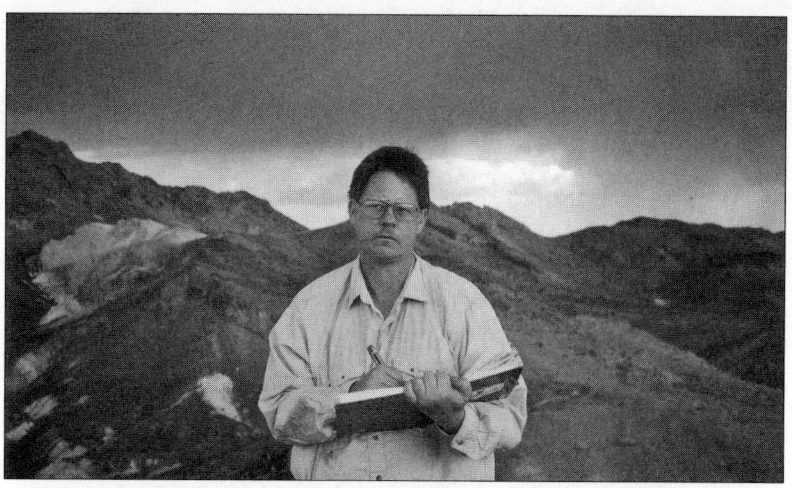

2003: VOLLMANN ALONG THE COLORADO RIVER GORGE IN IMPERIAL VALLEY. —COURTESY OF LARRY McCAFFERY

McCaffery and Vollmann also drive into the rugged mountains along Imperial's western edge, where they take photos of the heavily patrolled U.S.-Mexico border.

(July) Having narrowly escaped being wounded or even dying during his many trips to wild and dangerous places, Vollmann suffers his first serious injury: a car sideswipes him while he is riding his bicycle near his house in Sacramento, breaking his pelvis.

(September). Vollmann spends a month in Berlin, where he does occasional readings and conducts research for *Europe Central.*

(Fall) Publication of the hard-cover edition of Vollmann's *Rising Up and Rising Down,* in seven volumes, by McSweeney's Books.

2004 (January) *Rising Up and Rising Down* is nominated for the National Book Circle Critics Award.

At the California Book Awards, the Commonwealth Club awards McSweeney's Books and Vollmann the Silver Medal for publishing and writing for *Rising Up and Rising Down.*

(Fall) Abridged edition of *Rising Up and Rising Down* is published by Ecco Press.

2005 (Spring) Scheduled publication date by Viking of Vollmann's collection of World War II stories, *Europe Central.*

2010 Vollmann dies of a self-inflicted gun wound; although there are rumors that he killed himself, the coroner reports the cause of death as an accident that occurred while Vollmann was cleaning his gun (see "The Stench of Corpses").

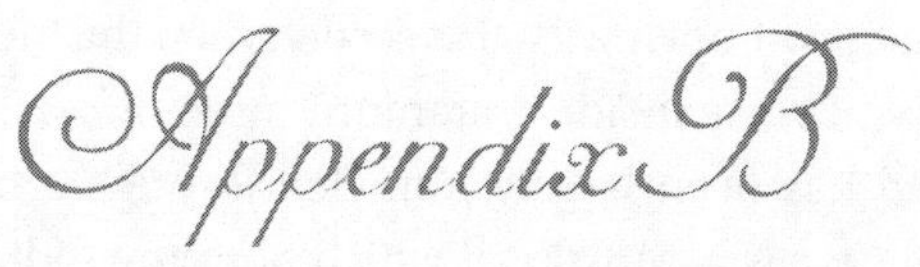

Seven Dreams: Description of Project

Seven Dreams is a work that lies in the grey zone between fiction and history. I call it a "symbolic history." Each of its seven volumes is a self-contained work meant to beguile and entertain, but also to instruct by presenting a poetically true interpretation of real events.

—WTV

1. Summary of Aims

WHEN NORSEMEN FIRST DISCOVERED America in the tenth century, they called it "Vinland" because there were wild grapes everywhere. They rushed from their ship to drink the sweet dew. Vinland would have been paradise were it not for the fact that other people already lived there: —the Indians, whom the Norse called "Skrælings," or "savage wretches." The Skrælings were clad in animal skins. Their food was deer-marrow mixed with blood. Despising them as outlaws, the would-be settlers cheated them at trade or killed them as they slept. Not surprisingly, the Indians fought back, to such good effect that in the end the colonists gave up. Vinland was left more or less alone for six hundred years. But there is a haunting moment in the medieval *Grænlendinga* Saga when

> The fighting began, and many of the Skrælings were killed. There was one tall and handsome man among the Skrælings, and Karlsefni [head of the Greenlanders] reckoned that he must be their leader. One of the Skrælings had picked up an axe, and after examining it for a moment he swung it at the man standing beside him, who fell dead at once. The tall man then took hold of the axe, looked at it for a moment, and then threw it as far as he could out into the water. Then the Skrælings fled into the forest as fast as they could, and that was the end of that encounter. (VII.67)

Seven Dreams will open with this scene, when the Indian leader rejects the axe, and will close inside a uranium mine on a Navajo reservation, when Vinland has been largely tunneled through and concreted over. Implicit in the axe is a reified evil which both the Indian leader and the Icelandic saga-writer recognize. *Seven Dreams* will structure its story upon such reifications: the standard trope in sagas of the weapon that is cursed and turns upon its owner; the Plains Indian trickster-figure Coyote (who in my novel will continue to survive in the metropolis); and the various spirits of the land itself, who shrink and die with its failing possibilities.

In no way will *Seven Dreams* be a factual history of the dispossession of American Indians. It will, however, be erected upon a foundation of fact. As the note on sources at the end of *Seven Dreams* puts it:

> My aim in *Seven Dreams* has been to create a "Symbolic History" —that is to say, an account of origins and metamorphoses which is often untrue based on the literal facts as we know them, but whose untruths further a deeper sense of truth. —Did the Norsemen, for instance, really come to the New World bearing ice in their hearts? —Well, of course they did not. But if we look upon the Vinland episode as a precursor of the infamies there, of course they did. Here one walks the proverbial tightrope, on one side of which lies slavish literalism; on the other, self-indulgence.

In the years which I plan to devote to this project, I will travel from Arctic Canada to New Mexico to New Hampshire in an effort to understand our landscape as it is and was. (In 1986 I went to Mexico, Arizona, Vancouver and eastern California for the book. In 1987, with the kind assistance of the Ludwig Vogelstein Foundation, I visited the Viking site in L'Anse-aux-Meadows, Newfoundland, the remains of Eirik the Red's farm in Iceland, the Norse ruins in Greenland and the icy wilderness of Baffin Island, all of which have found their places in *Seven Dreams*. In 1988 I visited Montréal, upper New York state, Cornwallis Island and Ellesmere Island. In 1989 I went to Québec City, Algonkin Park, Mission Sainte-Marie, and the shrine in Auriesville, New York. In 1990 I went to Inukjuak; in 1991 I made a solo winter trip to the North Magnetic Pole.)

Library research is equally important. I'm studying the French-Canadian Jesuits' *Relations* of the Souriquois and Iroquois, the newspaper narratives of Little Big Horn, the familiar old tales of Pocahontas and Squanto and King Philip's War. At the same time I will still be talking with people and looking at landscapes.

I am happy to say that the theme of *Seven Dreams* is not an entirely grim one, that there are many dreamy moments and wild moments in it. It is a story not only of loss but also of transformation.

2. Technical Specifications

Number of Dreams: 7.
Dreams per Volume: 1.

Average Manuscript Length per Volume: 400 pages, illustrated.*

DREAM	TITLE	SUBJECT
1	*The Ice-Shirt*	The discovery and attempted colonization of Vinland by Norse Greenlanders (9th–10th cent.). [COMPLETED.]
2	*Fathers and Crows*	The wars of belief between French Jesuits and Iroquois in Canada (16th–18th cent.). [COMPLETED.]
3	*Argall*	Captain John Smith and Pocahontas in Jamestown, Virginia (17th cent.). [COMPLETED.]

*Note: Since each *Dream* is self-contained, a commitment on your part to publish any one volume need not become a commitment to publish other volumes in the series. The choice is yours. If you do think you may want to do the entire series, I suggest that we clear all seven titles before publishing the first.

Dreams Chart Continued

4	*The Poison-Shirt*	The Puritans vs. King Philip in Rhode Island (17th cent.).
5	*The Dying Grass*	The destruction of the Plains Indian tribes, especially the Nez Percés (18th–19th cent.).
6	*The Rifles*	The starvation occasioned by the introduction of repeating rifles into the Arctic (19th–20th cent.). [COMPLETED.]
7	*The Cloud-Shirt*	Navajo vs. Hopi (or possibly Navajo vs. oil company) in Arizona (20th cent.). [PARTLY COMPLETED.]

Appendix C

Lists

List of Budget Requirements and Rules for the *Queen of Whores* Film Documentary

These two lists were included in the letter Vollmann sent to Janice Biggs responding to her inquiry about filming a documentary about his interactions with prostitutes. Since, as he notes, these rules "are equivalent to the constraints that I put upon myself when I document an event," these lists provide an insight into Vollmann's own approach to photojournalism and documentation. Equally revealing is their insistence on treating the prostitutes and pimps who are to be the subject of the documentary with dignity and respect. —LM

Please read this rule sheet carefully. I want you to cheerfully accept the following conditions for your presence. These are equivalent to the constraints that I put upon myself when I document an event, and I expect you to follow them also. Please sign, date and return this sheet by 1 June if you wish to film this event.

1. You will arrange your lighting and other equipment on your own time. You will be responsible for positioning your equipment in such a manner that it does not interfere with the event or make people unduly self-conscious or uncomfortable. You will understand that our actors and actresses may be unstable and violent. You will assume responsibility for any and all risks to yourself and your equipment. Ken and I will help you carry equipment if we have the time and inclination, but if we are busy rounding up actresses, etc., then this job must devolve on you.

2. You will keep yourself as unobtrusive as possible. Unless specifically given permission, you will stay somewhere along the back wall or the side walls. You will not come into the action, request retakes, shine bright lights upon these people's faces, or do anything else of the kind. During the event you will not speak to any actor or actress unless spoken to; you will not disturb me unnecessarily. This is not your party, but mine. You are not directing these people; you are making a documentary about my interaction with these people. I will, however, come check on you as often as I can and see if I can help you.
3. If some emergency occurs, you will either take my advice or else not blame me later for whatever consequences ensue.
4. You may film and tape the audition sections, but only after each subject and I jointly give permission.
5. You may film and tape interviews with me, if you wish, for twenty minutes a day.
6. You will be honest and aboveboard with me and all of the actors and actresses. You will be pleasant, respectful and retiring to everyone. You will not ask them questions about me without my knowledge. It is important to make them feel paid attention to, to make them feel that they are the stars, not me.
7. You will graciously tolerate any surliness, nastiness, anger, verbal humiliation, insult, etc. on the actors' and actresses' part. If Ken is difficult you must take it in good part. You will not react in any angry, fearful or defensive way unless you believe that you are in imminent danger of physical attack, in which case you should alert Ken or me immediately. You will not bring excessive personal cash or valuables to this event.
8. You may have one companion if you wish, provided that this person follows all of the above rules.

9. Ken and I will be entitled to bring any companions that we choose. See Rule 2. This is not meant to be discriminatory. Remember that any unnecessary spectators may make these nonprofessionals self-conscious. If Ken or I bring anybody else (which we may or may not do), that will be to gain the benefit of their perceptions for the benefit of this writing project. You may interview these people, but only if they wish it.
10. You will pay expenses in cash. You will have exact change ready in separate marked but unsealed envelopes for each actor for each event (the label will read, for instance, QUEEN 1—NIGHT 1 or SQUATTER # 4, but the amount inside should not appear on the envelope) when you meet Ken and me before the first session. We will check the contents of each envelope together and then seal it. Payments will be made as directed by us in the interests of your and our safety. Please remember that some payees may be dangerous. You have no guarantee of getting receipts.

AGREED: ________________________ DATE: ____________

QUEEN OF THE WHORES BUDGET

Abandoned building	$0.0
Setting up of same with props	$150.00
7 Capp Street prostitutes @ ($30/hr x 3 hrs + $10/tip) x 3 sessions	$2,100.00
Afternoon auditions for same @ $20/15 min.	$140.00
3 enforcers @ same rate for same time	$900.00
Auditions for same	$60.00
3 alcoholics to be kicked out one time @ $30	$90.00
5 squatters to be expelled one time @ $30	$150.00
1 organizer & procurer of whores (Ken Miller) @ $150/day	$450.00

3 Queens @ $400/night + $100/tip for one night each (1 stripper, 2 hard old whores)	$1,500.00
Auditions for same @ $50/30 min.	$150.00
Food, etc. for characters @ $150/night x 3 nights	$450.00
Misc. at $100/night x 3	$300.00
Hotel for Vollmann @ $30/night for 3 nights	$90.00
Hotel for J.B.	$90.00
	TOTAL $6,620.00

List of Accomplishments in Cambodia (1991)

This list has been extracted from a letter Vollmann wrote, dated September 1, 1991, to Will Blythe, editor of *Esquire.* Blythe had sent Vollmann (joined by his friend, Ken Miller) on assignment to write about his impressions of Cambodia, and, as usual, the article Vollmann had submitted was far longer than the four-thousand-word limit he'd been given. After noting that he'd already eliminated most of the descriptive passages to shorten the article, Vollmann then offered this list of accomplishments to help justify its publication. This was one of the trips to Southeast Asia that Vollmann used in developing *Butterfly Stories.*

Dear Will,

1. First U.S. journalist to interview Pol Pot's brother.
2. First U.S. journalist to interview captured Khmer Rouge in Phnom Penh's T-3 prison. (Ken's portraits of them are especially strong.)
3. The first or among the first journalists anywhere to see the reopening of the Thai-Cambodian border at Aranyaprathet.
4. The first or among the first journalists since the liberation to witness an operation at Phnom Penh's 17 April Hospital, complete with power failure during the operation. I didn't want to ask the surgeons questions in the middle of their business, but some of the nurses said they'd never seen journalists before.
5. Got special clearance to visit the battlefield at Battambang. The only other foreigners within many, many miles were relief workers—no journalists.

6. Thoroughly investigated prostitution in Cambodia (I know of no one else who's done this). This will be a separate piece, considerably longer than the first, so I'll send it only on request. Maybe I'll call it: "They Don't Use Rubbers." Do you think that title would have good family appeal?
7. In addition, we did some things that probably everyone else does: visited the Tuol Sleng genocide museum and the killing fields near Phnom Penh, and saw day-to-day life near Phnom Penh. But I believe that I've written about this better than most.

   I failed to cross the border with the Khmer Rouge because since the cease-fire the Khmer Rouge are not very active. This was especially unfortunate since as a result I could not verify Cambodian claims that the Khmer Rouge are violating the cease-fire. I am sorry about that, but given the lull there is nothing else we could have done. At least there is an account of that failure in the article.

If I don't talk to you beforehand, have a great trip to Katahdin. Wish I were going there, too, but the Arctic will do just fine. Thanks again for everything.

Your friend,

Bill

List of Social Changes that Would Assist the Flourishing of Literary Beauty

This list was extracted from his essay, "Something to Die For," which appeared in the *Review of Contemporary Fiction* "Younger Authors" issue in which Vollmann was featured.

1. Abolish television, because it has no reverence for time.
2. Abolish the automobile, because it has no reverence for space.
3. Make citizenship contingent upon literacy in every sense. Thus, politicians who do not write every word of their own speeches should be thrown out of office in disgrace. Writers who require editors to make their books "good" should be depublished.
4. Teach reverence for all beauty, including that of the word.

Appendix D

CoTangent Press Book Objects

Beginning in the late eighties, Vollmann began creating a number of limited-edition "book art works" that were distributed by his own CoTangent Press. Growing out of his interests in the design aspects of his own books and in the visual arts, and inspired specifically by William Blake's experiments in illuminated printing, these book objects combine text with visual and other tactile elements that typically reinforce the central metaphor of the text.

Note that each of Vollmann's book objects is different; the photographs that follow are of my own personal copies. —LM

CoTangent Press: Catalog 1987-88

The Convict Bird: A Children's Poem.
By William T. Vollmann.

"Oh, let us fall on bended knee together,
and worship the Barred Furnaces of Darkness!"

****

1. Limited edition (ten copies available).

   Bound in quarter-inch steel plate by Matthew Heckert, with padlock and hand-forged hasp. (Weight: twenty pounds.) Hinges are drilled bar stock. The steel is black-oxidized, lacquered, and studded with antiqued brass rivets. Just below the title, which is hand-milled into the metal, a hatch cover swings open to reveal a convict's face peering from the darkness of a cell window. (Each face is unique, being hand-etched with gun blueing.) Text is offset printed on acid-free 100% rag stock. Bound with a ragged sheet of black lace paper. To mark the place, a ribbon of barbed wire, brass and light-gauge chain is provided, tasselled with hair bought from a street prostitute. Illustrated with twelve line drawings. Twenty pages. Hand-sewn with Bible thread in a bird's-claw pattern. Numbered; signed by the author and the binder.

2. Mass edition (ninety copies available).

   The same, without the steel case, lace paper or place-marker ribbon. Numbered; signed by the author.

A portion of the proceeds from the sale of this book will benefit a woman in prison.

Our policy: "All books archival; all sales final."

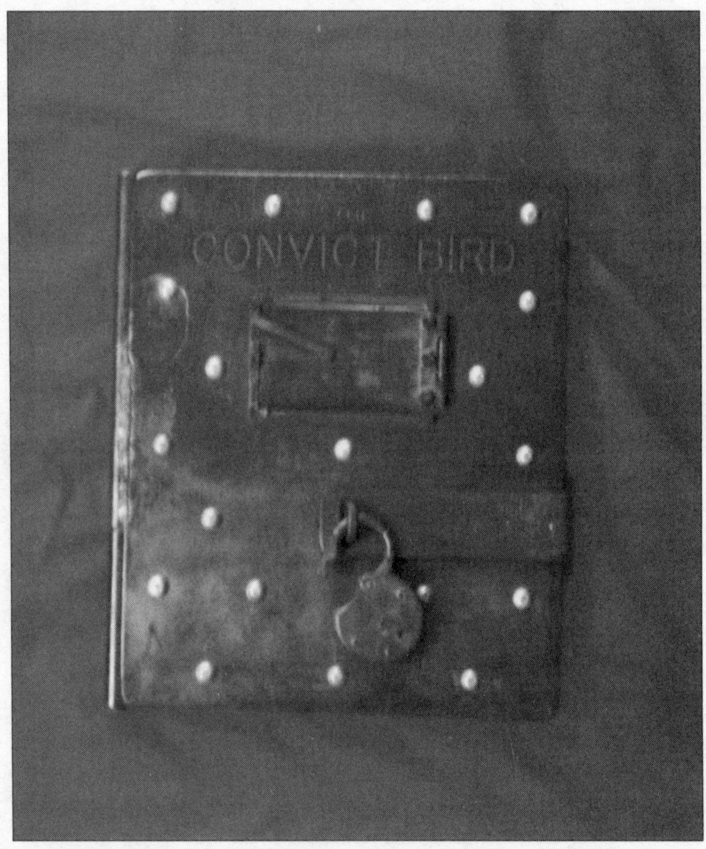

STEEL BOX BY MATT HECKERT.

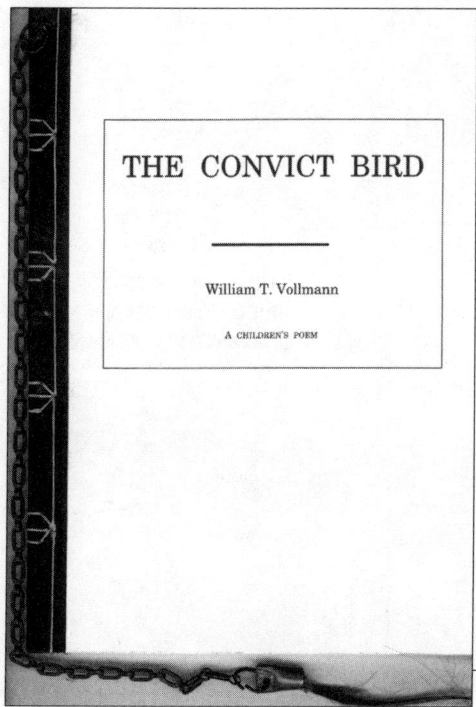

THE CONVICT BIRD
William T. Vollmann
A CHILDREN'S POEM

COVER OF BOUND POEM, WITH ENCASED PROSTITUTE-HAIR BOOKMARK.

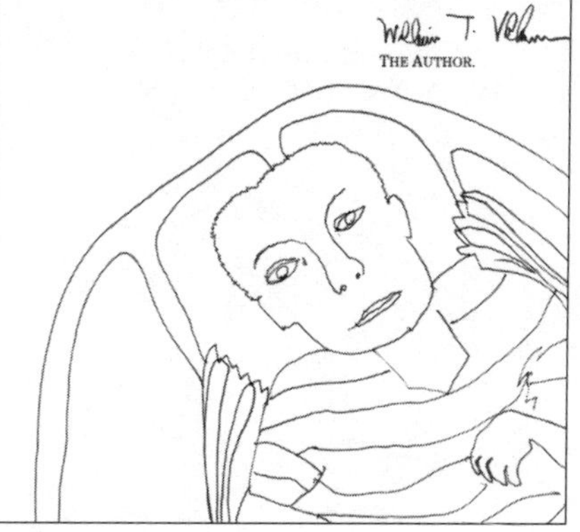

Note To Parents

Because so many children go about their play in ignorance of the True Nature Of The World, I have designed this little book for them, in sincere hopes that it will remedy this deficiency, and fit them for happy subjection to the proper authorities. — Oh, let us fall on bended knee together, and worship the *Barred Furnaces of Darkness!*

William T. Vollmann
THE AUTHOR.

NOTE TO PARENTS; LINE DRAWING BY VOLLMANN.

THE CONVICT BIRD

Sing a
Song of the
CONVICT BIRD
that never
was allowed to
say a word.

Poor Convict Bird!

Poor little
word
that never could
come out.

"THE CONVICT BIRD"
(P. I OF THE POEM);
LINE DRAWING BY VOLLMANN.

JUSTICE

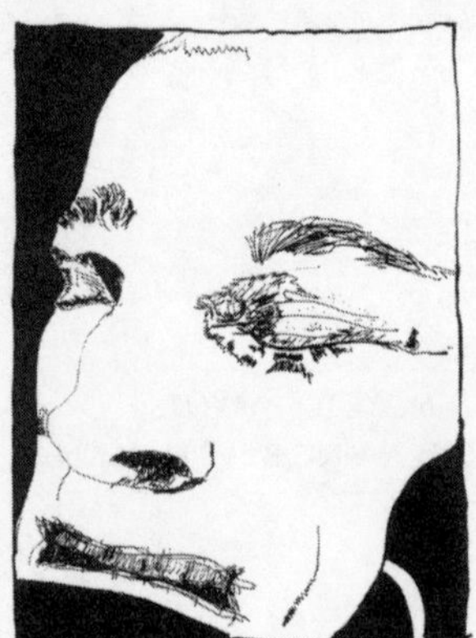

He did another Bird to death,
and so they took his life
by leaving him with his trembling breath
to face the Judge's Knife.
They took his life and sold it to the first who
cared to buy;
by minutes and degrees they kindly let him die.

"JUSTICE" (P. 2 OF THE POEM);
LINE DRAWING BY VOLLMANN.

"TWO BIRDS"
(CONCLUSION OF THE POEM);
LINE DRAWING BY
VOLLMANN.

Two Birds

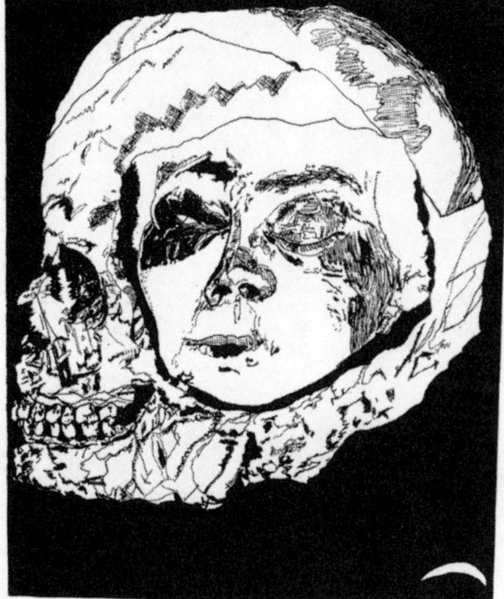

Death dies a thousand ways,
but it always takes wing
to the Place of Skulls, where Wind is King.
So the Convict Bird flew in the haze,
his joy-wings rising, bowing,
as he passed the Dead Bird, all unknowing.

"This last Thursday I went out in a car into town for a mammogram. It was almost cause for hysteria. They put chains and cuffs on both my ankles (which hurt) and a waist chain with cuffs on my upper body. The drive was eerie. They locked me in the back seat of a car that was very cramped with an inner glass partition between me and 'them.' The windows couldn't open and the door handle was taken off. The door automatically locks. I could barely walk; I literally had a step value of about 4 inches! I had to appear chained and cuffed and walk about two blocks in front of children and parents. It was a most humiliating experience . . . Mostly I'm fine."

VERONICA COMPTON, # 276077

VERONICA COMPTON TEXT
(EXCERPT FROM A LETTER TO
VOLLMANN).

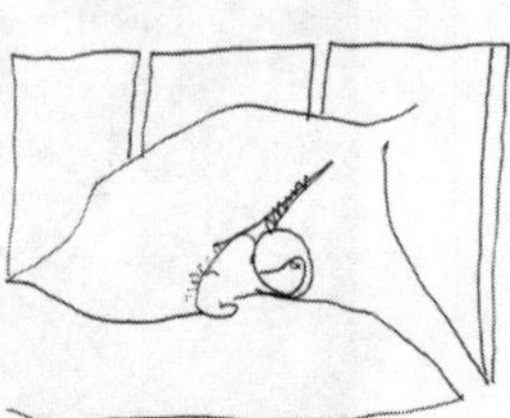

This book was printed in an edition of a hundred copies, of which ten were bound in steel by Matthew Heckert. For each of those ten, a street prostitute sold her hair to make the place-marker ribbon.

A portion of the proceeds from the sale of this book will benefit Veronica Compton # 276077.

Copy number 8 of 100.

BACK COVER OF THE POEM; LINE DRAWING BY VOLLMANN.

CoTangent Press: Catalog 1990

The Happy Girls.
By William T. Vollmann.

"It was Thanksgiving behind the mirror."

****

A similar (not identical) version of the text appeared in the commercially published *Thirteen Stories and Thirteen Epitaphs* (first edition: Andre Deutsch, London, 1991).

1. Limited edition (three copies available).

   Bound in birch wood and mirror-glass by James M. Lombino, with magnetic clasp. (Weight: eighteen to twenty-five pounds, depending on copy.) Each box unique. A peephole slides on tracks (or is hinged in other copies), activating a buzzer and a red lamp which shines upon a photograph of a Thai prostitute's face. When the glass door is lifted, the full photograph (an 8″ x 10″ frontal nude) is revealed. She is scarred with self-inflicted razor-slashes. This image is the front cover of the book proper. Inset into the back panel of the box is a window giving upon a portion of the back cover, which shows a nude from the rear of the same woman. Her tattoo reads: "HURT IN LOVE." Both images are window-matted. The inside of the box is wallpapered with whorish fabric. The book itself is 16″ x 20″. It is lashed securely inside the box by a harness constructed from bra straps. Text is hand-press printed by the author on smooth triple-ply acid-free 100% rag stock, each page in a different color. (Title page palm-printed.) Printing plates are photo-engraved magnesium from dummies typeset, illustrated and composed by the author. The lettering has a slightly broken effect on the acrylic-sized paper, whose texture was chosen to match that of the accompanying photographs. Each page is printed in a different color, using Daniel Smith etching inks. In addition, each page is hand colored by the author, using the most brilliant transparent watercolors available. All versions unique. Bound with three 16″ x 20″ silver prints of Thai prostitutes. These, like the two 8″ x 10″s on the covers, were taken and printed by Ken Miller. Each is signed by him. Including the photographs, the book is twelve pages. Hand-guarded and sewn. The spine is adorned with a fringe of lingerie. Numbered; signed by the author and the binder. Four D-Cell batteries and a spare bulb included.

2. Limited edition (ten copies available).

   The same, with the box made by Kevin Liepfer. Numbered; signed by the author.

OPEN BOX WITH BOUND TEXT.

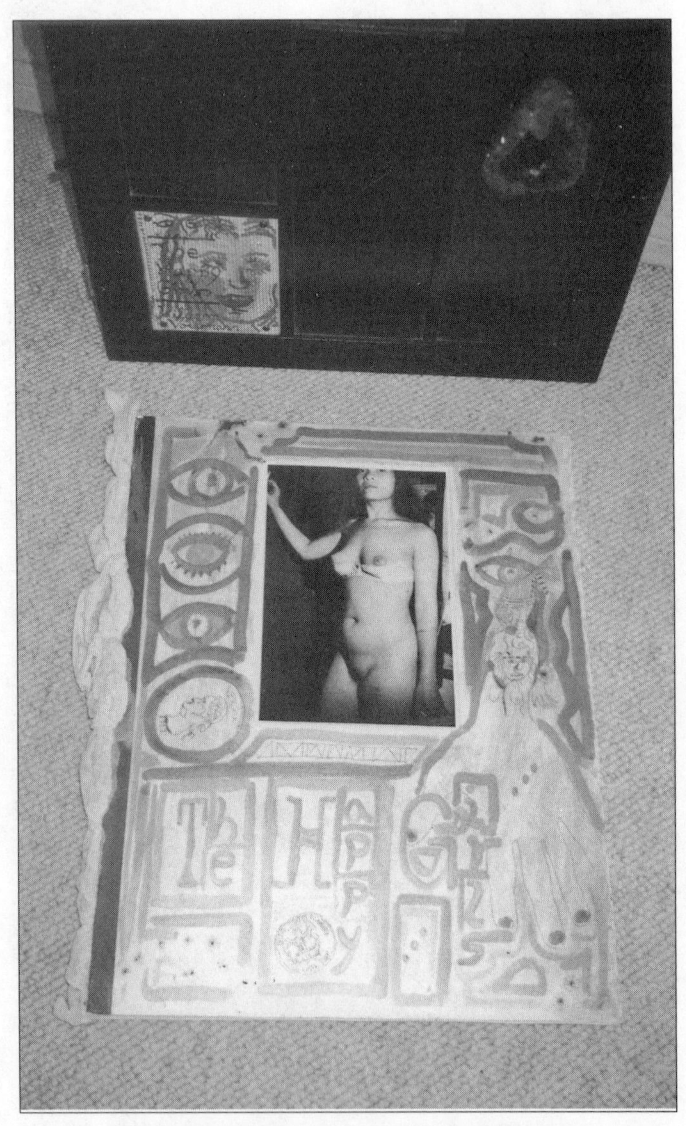

FRONT OF BOX WITH BOUND TEXT REMOVED.

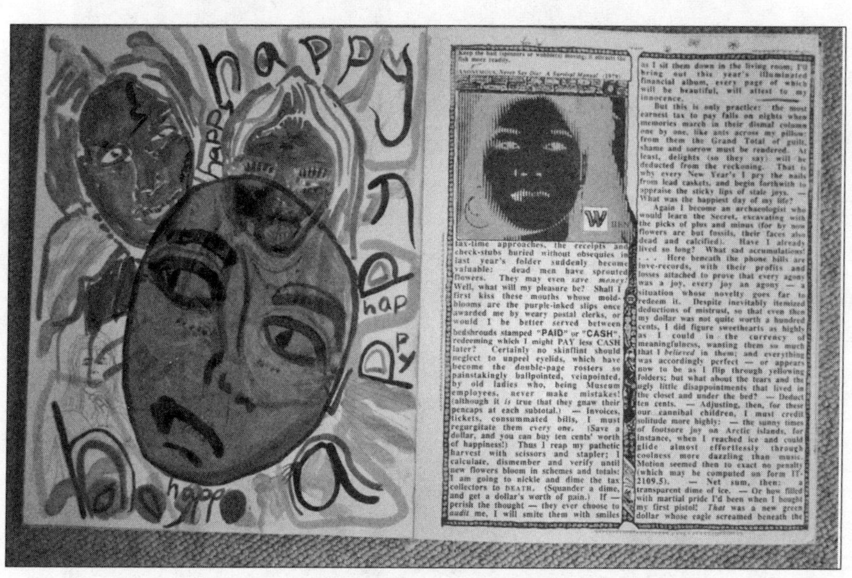

Keep the bait spinners or wobblers moving; it attracts the fish more readily.

— ANONYMOUS, *Never Say Die: A Survival Manual* (1979)

WHEN tax-time approaches, the receipts and check-stubs buried without obsequies in last year's folder suddenly become valuable: dead men have sprouted flowers. They may even *save money!* Well, what will my pleasure be? Shall I first kiss these mouths whose mold-blooms are the purple-inked slips once awarded me by weary postal clerks, or would I be better served between bedshrouds stamped "**PAID**" or "**CASH**", redeeming which I might PAY less CASH later? Certainly no skinflint should neglect to unpeel eyelids, which have become the double-page rosters so painstakingly ballpointed, veinpointed, by old ladies who, being Museum employees, never make mistakes! (although it *is* true that they gnaw their pencaps at each subtotal.) — Invoices, tickets, consummated bills, I must regurgitate them every one. (Save a dollar, and you can buy ten cents' worth of happiness!) Thus I reap my pathetic harvest with scissors and stapler; I calculate, dismember and verify until new flowers bloom in schemes and totals: I am going to nickle and dime the tax collectors to DEATH. (Squander a dime, and get a dollar's worth of pain.) If — perish the thought — they ever choose to *audit* me, I will smite them with smiles as I sit them down in the living room; I'll bring out this year's illuminated financial album, every page of which will be beautiful, will attest to my innocence.

But this is only practice: the most earnest tax to pay falls on nights when memories march in their dismal columns one by one, like ants across my pillow; from them the Grand Total of guilt, shame and sorrow must be rendered. At least, delights (so they say) will be deducted from the reckoning. That is why every New Year's I pry the nails from lead caskets, and begin forthwith to appraise the sticky lips of stale joys. — What was the happiest day of my life?

Again I become an archaeologist who would learn the Secret, excavating with the picks of plus and minus (for by now flowers are but fossils, their faces also dead and calcified). Have I already lived so long? What sad accumulations! . . . Here beneath the phone bills are love-records, with their profits and losses attached to prove that every agony was a joy, every joy an agony — a situation whose novelty goes far to redeem it. Despite inevitably itemized deductions of mistrust, so that even then my dollar was not quite worth a hundred cents, I did figure sweethearts as highly as I could in the currency of meaningfulness, wanting them so much that I *believed* in them; and everything was accordingly perfect — or appears now to be as I flip through yellowing folders; but what about the tears and the ugly little disappointments that lived in the closet and under the bed? — Deduct ten cents. — Adjusting, then, for these our cannibal children, I must credit solitude more highly: — the sunny times of footsore joy on Arctic islands, for instance, when I reached ice and could glide almost effortlessly through coolness more dazzling than music. Motion seemed then to exact no penalty (which may be computed on form IT-2109.5). — Net sum, then: a transparent dime of ice. — Or how filled with martial pride I'd been when I bought my first pistol! *That* was a new green dollar whose eagle screamed beneath the

EXAMPLE OF PAGES IN THE BOUND TEXT;
WATERCOLOR BY VOLLMANN.

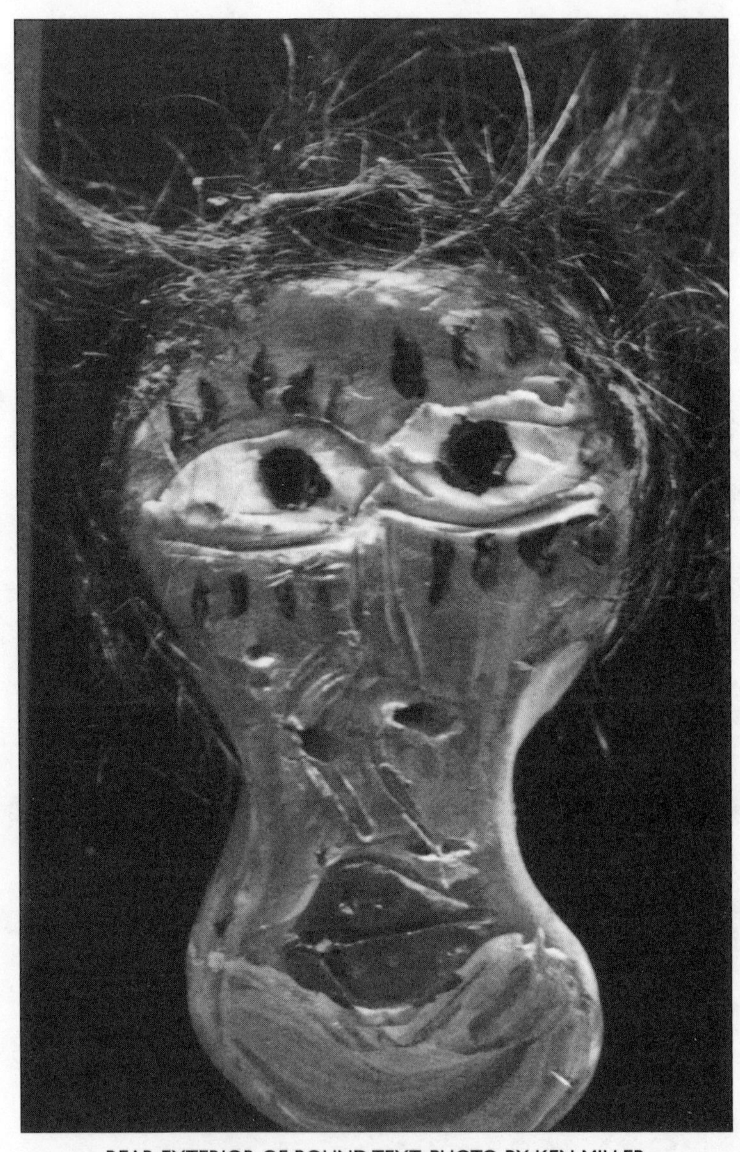

REAR EXTERIOR OF BOUND TEXT; PHOTO BY KEN MILLER.

Acknowledgments

The editors would like to thank the following for their support, encouragement, advice, help, and so on:

William T. Vollmann, first and foremost, for graciously agreeing to come on board this project; although he insisted that the final selection was entirely up to us, his input, encouragement, and patience throughout the complex process of assembling this *Reader* have been invaluable. In particular, we are grateful to him for his willingness to give us access to his personal archive of previously unpublished work, correspondence, photographs, illustrations, and miscellaneous other rare documents that we would never have been able to include here otherwise. Dan O'Connor and Michael O'Connor have been patient and kind in seeing this book through its various stages. John Oakes—what a beast you inherited, and we thank you for your grace, kindness and understanding. The first co-editor who shows up in Manhattan owes Johnny Saunders a round of drinks for the superb job he did copyediting the manuscript. José Jacincto and Terrie Petree for research material and running various errands. And finally (of course), Sinda Gregory and Tara Raines for being who they are, as well as being "faithful" at all times to Vollmann.

Permissions

We gratefully acknowledge everyone who gave permission for material to appear in this book. We have made every effort to contact copyright holders. If an error or omission is brought to our attention, we will be pleased to correct the situation in future editions of this book. For further information, please contact the publisher.

"The Land of Counterpane" from *An Afghanistan Picture Show* by William T. Vollmann, copyright © 1992 by William T. Vollmann. Used by permission of William T. Vollmann.

"The Butterfly Boy" from *Butterfly Stories* by William T. Vollmann, copyright © 1993 by William T. Vollmann. Used by permission of Grove/Atlantic, Inc.

"Under the Grass" and "The Best Way to Smoke Crack" from *The Atlas* by William T. Vollmann, copyright © 1996 by William T. Vollmann. Used by permission of Viking Penguin, a division of Penguin Group (USA), Inc.

"Some Thoughts on Neglected Water Taps" from *The Students of Deep Springs College* by Michael A. Smith, copyright © 2000 by William T. Vollmann. Used by permission of William T. Vollmann.

"The Ghost of Magnetism" and "The Grave of Lost Stories" from *Thirteen Stories and Thirteen Epitaphs* by William T. Vollmann, copyright © 1991 by William T. Vollmann. Used by permission of Pantheon Books, a division of Random House, Inc.

Open All Night by Ken Miller, copyright © 1995 by Ken Miller, text copyright © 1993 by William T. Vollmann. Reprinted with permission of The Overlook Press.

"Zoya" from *Europe Central* (to be published by Viking Penguin in 2005) by William T. Vollmann, copyright © 2005 by William T. Vollmann. Used by permission of William T. Vollmann.

"The Agony of Parker" from *You Bright and Risen Angels* by William T. Vollmann, copyright © 1987 by William T. Vollmann. Reprinted with permission of Scribner, a division of Simon & Schuster Adult Publishing Group.

"Nicole" from *Whores for Gloria* by William T. Vollmann, copyright © 1991 by William T. Vollmann. Used by permission of Pantheon Books, a division of Random House, Inc.

"The Hermophrodite" from *The Ice-Shirt* by William T. Vollmann, copyright © 1990 by William T. Vollmann. Used by permission of Viking Penguin, a division of Penguin Group (USA), Inc.

"Sunflower" from *The Royal Family* by William T. Vollmann, copyright © 2000 by William T. Vollmann. Used by permission of Viking Penguin, a division of Penguin Group (USA), Inc.

"Prayer Against Angels" by William T. Vollmann, copyright © 2005 by William T. Vollmann. Used by permission of William T. Vollmann.

"Subzero's Debt, 1991" from *The Rifles* by William T. Vollmann, copyright © 1993 by William T. Vollmann. Used by permission of Viking Penguin, a division of Penguin Group (USA), Inc.

"Debts and Debtors" from *Fathers and Crows* by William T. Vollmann, copyright © 1992 by William T. Vollmann. Used by permission of Viking Penguin, a division of Penguin Group (USA), Inc.

"To the Right Honourable Reader" from *Argall* by William T. Vo

"To the Right Honourable Reader" from *Argall* by William T. Vollmann, copyright © 2001 by William T. Vollmann. Used by permission of Viking Penguin, a division of Penguin Group (USA), Inc.

About the Editors

LARRY McCAFFERY has published numerous books and essays about postmodern fiction and culture, including *The Metafictional Muse* (1983), *Postmodern Fiction: A Bio-Bibliographical Guide* (1985), and four volumes of interviews: *Anything Can Happen: Interviews with Contemporary American Writers* (1983), *Alive and Writing: Interviews with American Authors of the 1980s* (with Sinda Gregory, 1987), *Across the Wounded Galaxies: Interviews with Contemporary American Science Fiction Authors* (1990), and *Some Other Frequency: Interviews with Innovative American Authors* (1995). Since the early eighties, he has served as co-editor of *Fiction International, American Book Review,* and *Critique: Studies in Contemporary Fiction.* In 1991, he and Ronald Sukenick established FC2's Black Ice Books series, which they co-edited until 1996. He has also edited such groundbreaking anthologies of innovative writing as *Storming the Reality Studio: A Casebook of Cyberpunk and Postmodern Science Fiction* (1991), *After Yesterday's Crash: The Avant-Pop Anthology* (1995), *Avant-Pop: Fiction for a Daydream Nation* (1993), and *Federman, A to X-X-X-X—A Recyclopedic Narrative* (1996). He and his wife Sinda Gregory currently reside in the magnificent desolation of the Anza-Borrego's desert of the real.

MICHAEL HEMMINGSON has been, by the bye, the associate editor of *The Fessenden Review,* a pizza maker and bartender, a musician and band producer, a retail sales person and repo-man; also: the literary manager of the Fritz Theater in San Diego and artistic director of the Alien Stage Project, writing and directing plays and sometimes even acting in them. He's done short stints as a foreign correspondent, a cameraman for porn movies, a scriptwriter for bad TV shows, and a rock journalist. He has not, however, traveled to Tibet to meditate with Buddhist monks upon high mountaintops. He edited *What the Fuck: The Avant-Porn Anthology* and co-edited *The Mammoth Book of Short Erotic Novels.* His other books include *The Naughty Yard, Wild Turkey,*

The Rose of Heaven, The Rooms, House of Dreams, My Fling with Betty Page, and *The Garden of Love,* among many others. He plays the upright bass (about as well as Sherlock Holmes does the violin) and lives in San Diego.

A Traveler's Epitaph

I CAN'T SAY I know much, but I've loved, maybe too much; maybe from love I'll get my death. I've seen Madagascar and walked the frozen sea. I have no trade, make nothing but pretty things which fail against the seriousness of rice. I'm not well or wise; I fear death; but I've never failed any woman I loved. I never refused gold bracelets to any wife who asked them of me. When they did me evil, I received it gracefully; when they were good to me, I gave them thanks. I denied none esteem, never heeded shaming words. I can't say I've done much or been much, but I'm not ashamed of who I've been. I don't ask your forgiveness or remembrance. I'm in the flowers on my grave, unknowing and content.

—WILLIAM T. VOLLMANN